Blood Brothers

The Forgotten Children
of the Mound Builders

Enjoy your journey Susan!

Sherry Cottle Graham

9,23,13

Sherry Cottle Graham
Illustrations by Justin W. Niles

Library of Congress Control Number:		2013908792
ISBN:	Hardcover	978-1-4836-4082-2
	Softcover	978-1-4836-4081-5
	Ebook	978-1-4836-4083-9

This book was printed in the United States of America.

Rev. date: 05/21/2013

To order additional copies of this book, contact:
Xlibris Corporation
1-888-795-4274
www.Xlibris.com
Orders@Xlibris.com
134705

CONTENTS

DEDICATION

I dedicate this book to my family.

This book was inspired by Frank Joseph's book, *Advanced Civilizations of Prehistoric America: The Lost Kingdoms of the Adena, Hopewell, Mississippians, and Anasazi.*

ACKNOWLEDGMENTS

I want to extend my appreciation to my sister, Terry Hobbs, for her enthusiasm that she consistently exhibited to me while I was working on it. I am grateful that she would drop everything to read my next chapter and to respond her feelings about it to me.

I wrote this book for my grandchildren: Aryanna, Brayden, and Isabella Graham; and Victoria, Vincent, and Brooklyn Bonafede. They wanted me to put their names into this book, so I hope that this will make them happy. It's all about the grandchildren and these incredible people who lived here in the Ohio River Valley a couple of thousand years ago.

I also want to thank the local schools for allowing me to share my time with their students while working as a substitute teacher for them. I want to thank Kameron Moline, one of my students, for being so curious about what I was doing and eager for me to get this book to press when he listened to various sections of my story. His enthusiasm was so refreshing to me. The schools that I want to recognize are Allen East, Bath, Beaverdam, Bluffton, Delphos, Elida, Perry, Shawnee, and Spencerville.

My journey into writing was sparked by a friend, Sharon O'Neil. Many times I stop to recall her words, "Now that girl can write." To Sharon, I want to say, "Thank you," as I doubt that you realize the impact that these few words really had on me.

I hope that this book revives the interest in the early settlers that visited the Ohio River Valley and who built hundreds of mounds across our land. Whether they were the Kelts (Celts), Japanese, or from some other race, they deserve to be recognized and given credit for their contributions into our history.

I want to thank Justin Niles for illustrating this book. The long hours that he spent working on my drawings is greatly appreciated. I believe that his illustrations reflected my vision of my characters. I also want to express my delight with his vision for the front and back cover for this book. With a small discussion of my ideas, he came up with a wonderful drawing for me. I think that his drawing captured my vision of Coahoma as he spied on Ethane' as he traveled in the form of a black panther. I hope that everyone who reads this book will enjoy his artwork.

I also want to extend my gratitude to Gene W. Creighton, my electronics professor and friend. He spent many hours proofreading my drafts and highlighting my grammar and punctuation mistakes for me to correct. And with his encouragement, it gave me the confidence to finish this book.

I want to thank my parents, Ruby and Dennie Cottle, for allowing me to live with them while I wrote this book. I know that it took over two years to write it, and I am grateful to them for their patience. I also thank them for taking the time to visit these ancient mounds with me. I enjoyed our time together, walking through the various parks and seeing these ancient sites. I especially enjoyed our time exploring the amazing ancient Adena and Hopewell mounds that are in Marietta, Ohio, and our side trip to see Flint Ridge State Park that is located near Newark, Ohio. I hope that they will enjoy our upcoming adventures to explore these ancient places that will be included in the next book.

SHERRY COTTLE GRAHAM

ANCIENT NORTH AMERICAN MAP

This map shows the location of the Allewegi village that is located in central Ohio and the Choctaw village that is located in southern Louisiana.

Ohi:Yo' River Valley

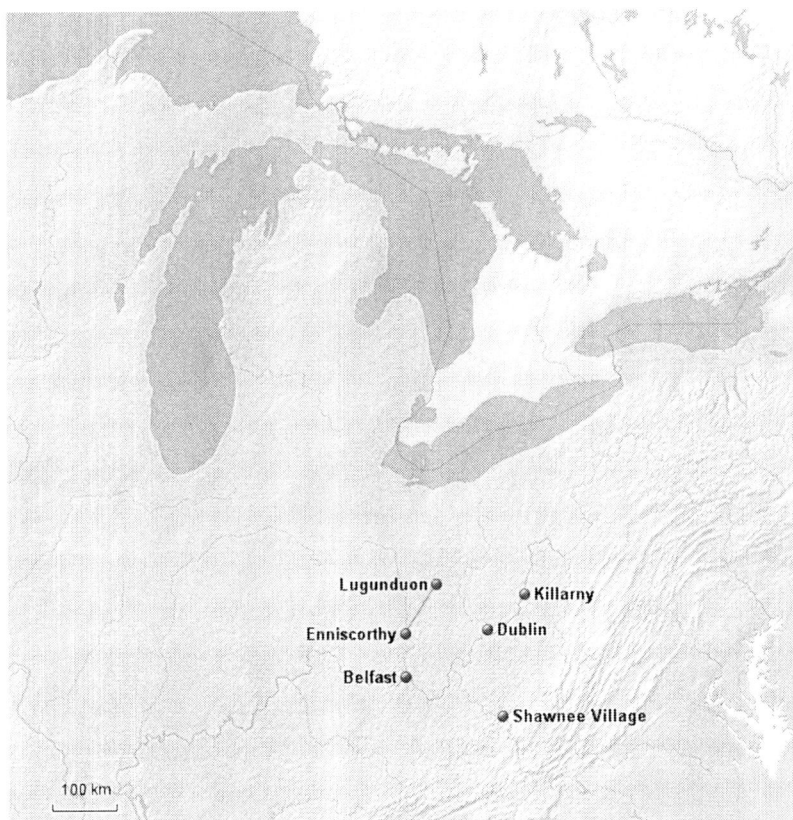

Lugudunon is located near a large underground vein of flint. This area is called the Land of Flint. This vein is presently located southeast of Newark, Ohio, and can be visited at the Flint Ridge State Memorial.

CHOCTAW CHARACTERS AND TRIBAL NAMES

Akando—Choctaw warrior

Akule—(White feathers) A brave assigned to be Moki's decoy

Alawa—Wife of Nashoba and Tiponi's mother; she is expecting her second child

Awock—Laurel's pet, a great horned owl

Chief Ituha—Chief of the Choctaw's and the father of Dakota, Etu, and Coahoma; mated to Sonoma

Chitto—Choctaw warrior

Choctaw—North American Indian Tribe

Coahoma—Chief Ituha and Sonoma's youngest son; training to become a shaman/healer; his double is Etu (Black feathers)

Dakota—Chief Ituha and Sonoma's eldest son and in line to become the next chief; he is Coahoma's eldest brother

Dyani—Wife of Lanto and mother of Fala and Kinta

Erie—North America Indian Tribe

Elsu—Chief Ituha's middle son and Coahoma's brother who was killed at a young age by an alligator

Etu—(Black feathers) A brave assigned to be Coahoma's decoy

Fala—Eldest son of Lanto and eldest brother to Kinta; he is training with Coahoma to become a shaman/healer; his double is Koi (Brown feathers)

Grandfather—The spirit of Laurel's grandfather

Kachina—Name given to the guardian spirit of the bees

Karuk—Choctaw warrior

Koi—(Brown feathers) A brave assigned to be Fala's decoy

Lagundo—Laurel's old brown bear that has endured her life tragedies after along with her

Lanto—Fala's father and a gifted craftsman

Laurel—Old Shawnee woman who was adopted by the Choctaw's; she is a master shaman and is training Pontiac, Coahoma, Moki, and Fala to become the tribes next great healers

Mahkah—Moki's gifted father; his passion is to find new seeds and grow new plants for the tribe to eat

Moki—Coahoma's blood brother and he is also training with Coahoma to become a shaman/healer; his double is Akule (White feathers)

Nahunta—A master carver that lived among the Shawnee that carved Laurel's wolf knife

Nana—Moki's grandmother

Nashoba—Husband to Alawa and father of Tiponi

Nita—Moki's elder sister who is in love with Coahoma

Ohanzee—The spirit of a dead healer

Ojibwa—North America Indian Tribe

One Who Walks with the Bear—The title given to Laurel, the old Choctaw medicine woman

Pallaton—Choctaw warrior

Pontiac—A Choctaw shaman who has been studying under Laurel for many years; he performs a ritual and traps Lugh's soul inside him

Ron-Nong-Weto-Wanca—This Indian title means the fair-skinned giant sorcerers

Sonoma—Wife of Chief Ituha and mother of Dakota, Etu, and Coahoma

Tecumseh—Laurel's deceased husband who comes to her in the form of a spirit; he is the son of a Shawnee Chief whose tribe migrated throughout the Kuhnoie and Kanawha River Valleys

Tiponi—A five-year-old Choctaw girl who is possessed by Morrigan and cared for by Pontiac

Tunghak—Laurel's pet hawk

Wenonah—Name given to the guardian spirit of the rivers

Aylwen and Wakie Wisag Reference

Allewegi or Alli—The name that the Indians called the white giant mound builders who live in the Ohio River Valley; these ancient mound builders are now called Adena

Aylwen—The name that the Kelts (mound builders) may have called themselves

Balor—An elite Allewegi warrior who is in love with Ethane'

Birlinn—Keltic ships that were propelled by leather sails and large oars

Bradan—Son of Lugh and Morrigan; he is an elite eight-foot tall warrior; he is Tomas's twin

Conan—The baby son of Lugh and Morrigan

Creighton—Leader of the Alli that live in the Land of Flint, now called Newark

Cu Chulainn—An elite ten-foot Allewegi warrior

Dahey—Son of Lugh and Morrigan; he is an elite eight-foot tall warrior

Dragon Lady—A birlinn that carried Prince Sangann and Cu Chulainn to battle

Ethane'—The youngest daughter of Lugh and Morrigan; she is engaged to Prince Sangann, but she loves Balor

Gaim—Eldest son of Lugh and Morrigan and is studying to be a Nahullo (shaman); he is crippled and smaller than his siblings

Iron Lady—A Keltic battleship that carried Dahey, Tomas, and Bradan to battle

Kenji—A dwarf shaman of the Wakie Wisag clan; he is friends with Gaim and his family

Kerri—Ethane's friend who lives in the Land of Flint

King Gann—He is an eight-foot warrior who rules over the Allewegi

Kumi-Daiko—Elite drummers of the Wakie Wisag clan that live in Marietta

Lugh—Fierce Allewegi warrior who learns the secrets of the Spirit World; his life dream is to become a wolf; his soul becomes trapped in a Choctaw shaman named Pontiac

Morrigan—A gifted Allewegi shaman and wife of Lugh; she has six children: Gaim, Dahey, twins Tomas and Bradan, Ethane', and Conan.

Murdock—An Allewegi ship captain who sails the *Iron Lady* to the mouth of the Atchafalaya River

Prince Sangann—He is an eight-foot prince and the warrior son of King Gann; he wants to marry Ethane'

Tomas—Son of Lugh and Morrigan; he is an elite eight-foot tall warrior; he is Bradan's twin

Wakie Wisag—The clan of Japanese that lived among the Allewegi; they are now called the Hopewell

Cities and Rivers

Atchafalaya River—A tributary that splits from the Mississippi and runs into the Gulf of Mexico

Atchafalaya Swamp—A swamp that is located in the bayou of Mississippi

Aurora Borealis—The proper name for the northern lights

Belfast—A name given to the city now called Portsmouth, Ohio

Cork—A name given to the city now called Newark, Ohio

Dublin—A name given to Moundsville, West Virginia

Enniscorthy—A name given to the city now called Chillicothe, Ohio

Kanawha River—This river attaches the Kanawha River to the Ohio River; its mouth is located in Point Pleasant, Ohio

Killarney—A name given to the city now called Marietta, Ohio

Kuhnoie—This river is now called "The New River"; it is located in West Virginia and is one of the oldest rivers in North America

Land of Flint—This is a rich vein of flint that lies under the ground near Newark, Ohio (see Lugudunon)

Land of Giants—This land lies in the Ohio River Valley; it is where the Allewegi settled and began to prosper

Lugudunon—The fortress where Lugh and Morrigan lived; it was near the flint quarries in Newark, Ohio

Misi-ziibi—The Mississippi River; a major river that runs north and south through the United States

Muskingum River—A river that is located near Marietta that runs south into the Ohio River

Ohi:Yo'—The Ohio River; it runs west and empties into the Mississippi River (Misi-ziibi)

Siothai River—The river is now known as the Scioto River; it is a major river than runs through Ohio

Spirit Names

Belenus—Keltic sun and fire god

Brigid—Keltic goddess of fire and water

Cernunnos—Keltic god of virility, fertility, life, animals, forests, and the underworld

Cerridwen—Keltic goddess of the moon, grain, and nature

Happy World—This is the Indians' version of heaven.

Hashi Ninak Anya—Choctaw moon goddess

Hashtahli—Choctaw sun god

Impashilup—Choctaw demon spirit that was called: the Soul Robber

Isis—Egyptian supreme goddess of seafaring

Mars—Roman war god

Mercury—The swiftest Roman god; he was also god of abundance, messages, trade, and eloquence

Other World—The sun travels into the Other World at night

Shadow World or World of Shadows—This is another name for the Spirit World; a place where earth-bound spirits roam

Spirit World or World of Spirits—This is the realm where astro travelers intermingle with the earth-bound spirits

Under World—This is the underground location where the demons reside. It is presently called hell.

Zeus—The Greek king of the gods

INTRODUCTION

Approximately 1000 BC, an exotic tribe of people migrated to the shores of Northern America. These people, known as the Kelts (Celts), traveled across the Atlantic Ocean in large oared ships called *birlinn*. Over the next few hundred years, they were able to establish large colonies in the territories surrounding the Ohio River Valley. Now hidden from the bloody European wars and Roman armies, they viciously fought for control over this new land using the large rivers to traverse across it.

These men, who (potentially) called themselves Aylwen, were tall. A few of their elite warriors reached heights of ten feet or more. Many of their women reached heights of seven feet. They had thick rounded skulls, lantern-shaped jaws, beetling eyebrows, white skin, blond hair, and blue eyes. Also, many had strange birows of teeth and six-fingered hands and toes. They practiced head elongation, were gifted artists, wove beautiful cloth, buried their dead in mounds, and worshipped their gods as they pleased.

Their elite warriors were fierce headhunters and cannibalistic. They believed that a man's soul was located inside his skull, whereas the Indians believed that it was located inside his heart. The Aylwen sacrificed their enemies in the name of their gods, beheaded them, and drank from their skulls to enhance the bond between them and their gods: Belenus, Cernunnos, Bridget, and others. They built roads, foundries, mined copper from the Great Lakes, traded goods, collected iron ore from bogs, and crafted many wares with their metal working and smithing skills.

Around 300 BC, a group of Japanese found their way to the Ohio River Valley. These were shorter, more gentile people, spiritual and artistic. They sought an alliance with the Aylwen to be able to survive in this hostile land. They were accepted by the Aylwen which the Indians called Alli, Allewegi, Azgen, etc. One particular name that the Choctaw gave to the Aylwen was Ron-Nong-Weto-Wanca which means "fair-skinned giant sorcerers." Another popular name was Yam-Ko-Desh which means "people of the prairie." Eventually, the Allegheny Mountains were named after them.

As these two races evolved over the next few hundred years, they carved their initials into the face of North America. As they intermixed with the natives, they left genetic markers, customs, language, artifacts, mounds, and legends among them; creating a story that is so magnificent yet the memory of their blood, sweat, and tears has been lost in antiquity and forgotten by our mainstream historians.

This story was derived by pulling a few of the skulls that were recorded in Frank Joseph's book, giving them a name and creating a story about their lives. It is a story that is filled with spirits, demons, beasts, gods, and their love of life. Hopefully, this story will encourage our historians to rethink their theories on these mound builders and revise their books to reflect a more intelligent and civilized story of these people who time has forgotten.

PRELUDE

Legend speaks of a time long ago when our people were happy and we lived as one with our Great Mother. But this changed on one cold winter morning as Hashtahli painted the sky in his prismatic shades of blue. It is said that, on this day, a great sadness swept over our land when he heard the cries of his children drifting on the wind. They say that tears filled our skies, and our Great Mother shook when he looked down and saw their arms stretching up. He stopped and listened to their prayers that came in the form of songs and poems. He heard their voices asking him for protection against the evil witches and black demons that were terrorizing the hearts and souls of their loved ones.

Hashtahli took pity upon these kindred souls as he summoned the Four Directions and the spirits of the forest. He said, "Go among the humans and bring to me the names of those who are capable of mastering my knowledge. I will share my deepest and darkest secrets with these chosen ones. I will carry them to the edge of insanity where I will bind their souls to mine. They will become my disciples, and I will become their greatest ally. And let it be known that they will walk with one foot in our world and the other one in theirs. And from this day forward, you shall call these chosen ones *shaman*."

Ituha,
Chief of the Choctaws

CHAPTER 1

First Light

Coahoma
*Youngest son of Chief Ituha, Coahoma is training
with his elders to become a healer.*

"Coahoma, wake up," a soft voice whispered.

Startled awake, Coahoma pushed his covers aside and sat up as he looked for the face that belonged to this strange voice. When he felt the tingly sensations of a spiderweb on the back of his arms and neck and an eerie cold that chilled his bones, he knew that a spirit was nearby. Searching through the lavender haze that filled his hut, he spotted its silhouette hovering quietly beside him. He slowly pulled his knees into his chest as he recalled his teacher's words, "Calm yourself, Coahoma. Allow your mind to drift down until you find the voice that wishes to speak to you." But before he could find it, the shadow drifted into the tiny streams of luminescent light that pierced through his doorway and faded from sight.

Just then, he heard a timber wolf singing in the distance. Its long lonely cry announced his existence to this remote Choctaw village that was carved inside this hostile land of moss-covered swamps. As its high-pitched songs echoed through the sea of pine, Coahoma noticed that his brother and his parents were watching him.

"I saw a shadow person," he said as he glanced over to his father, "but she is gone now."

Coahoma didn't know why she had come to him on this chilly winter morning, but he knew that her presence worried his mother. He could see by the way that she stiffened her shoulders and the expression that reflected in her almond eyes. He didn't want to hurt her, especially with things that she couldn't control.

In a soothing voice, he said, "Mother, the shadow meant us no harm. She was only warning me about that wolf that is howling in the distance." He lied, but to soothe her fears, he continued, "Don't worry about that old wolf. If it gets too close to us, Father will kill it. Won't he, Dakota?"

Dakota pushed his covers aside and stood up. He brushed his long black locks away from the side of his face. He said, "You seem to know more about this wolf than I do. Is he running with a pack?"

"I don't know," Coahoma responded. "But be careful when you go into the woods," Coahoma warned. "I have a bad feeling about this one."

He looked at his mother as she handed him his clothes. He watched the way that she arched her back, and he knew that something was troubling her.

"Coahoma," she said, "I am worried about you. Last night, I dreamed that you were trapped inside the Spirit World. You were calling for help, but I couldn't find you." She looked at Coahoma, folding her arms, drawing her mouth into a strange bent position, eyes glaring. She continued, "The things that you see and do scare me. Son, it isn't too late to change your mind."

Coahoma reached out and gently tugged on a lock of her hair. "Mother, please don't worry about me. Someday you will be proud to call me your son, 'the medicine man,' and I promise, I will grow old, and

SHERRY COTTLE GRAHAM

my children will watch my skin wrinkle up and my hair turn white," he teased.

Coahoma didn't say a word as he pulled on his shirt and felt the smooth soft suede pressing against his skin. This outfit was fitting for the son of a chief. It was handsomely adorned with hundreds of handmade beads, and the skin was warm. He knew that it had taken her a long time to make it for him. However, it was a bit too large, but this didn't matter to him. He knew that it would fit next winter.

"Take your long spear with you when you leave," she said. She reached over and lightly tugged on the bottom of his fringed tunic. Satisfied with the way that it fit, she said, "Coahoma, try to keep these clean. I want you to look your best when we sing and dance in honor of your brother and grandfather during our upcoming planting ceremony."

Coahoma saw the pain in her eyes and heard it spill over into her words. The spirits of the animals were always among them, warning of impending danger. But on that foggy morning in early spring, Elsu's guardians escorted him into the Spirit World when an alligator pulled him from sight.

It was said that Elsu's spirit grew into a massive force on that day. His spirit rose up and plucked his friends from the murky water. He tossed them onto the shore as if they were twigs that had fallen from a mighty oak. His story became a legend among the Choctaw. On that day, Elsu saved Dakota, his father, and Moki from a feeding frenzy of mean-spirited alligators.

Life in this land of moss-covered oaks and black-surfaced swamps was cruel. Every creature that slithered or walked within this magnificent sea of evergreen held the power of life. Respectful of their venomous gifts, the Choctaw built their homes into these canopied swamplands onto sturdy poles that lifted their lodges into the air. They laced their thatch and leather-covered winter lodges with insect-repelling herbs and encouraged the smoke from their fires to sweep underneath.

"Are you going hunting with us today, or are you going to play with the spirits?" Dakota asked as they headed outside.

Coahoma walked over to the smoldering fire and threw a heavy log on to its embers. He picked up a long stick and poked the embers until a small fire erupted.

"I am flying with the spirits," he said, but he didn't tell his brother that he was going to spy on a demon. He thought about the grief that they felt when his brother had died. *Perhaps someday I will tell them my stories, but not today.* He didn't want to disturb them with his whereabouts. Facing demons was a small part of becoming a great healer, but he knew that Dakota didn't understand this. *Perhaps someday he will know that I am not a coward*, he thought as he kicked a log back into the flames.

Coahoma's mind flashed back to a foggy morning in early spring when he was ten. He recalled the face of a beautiful spirit that appeared to him beside the river. He recalled her long blue cloak and shimmering white dress. He thought about her rounded pale blue eyes that were highlighted by her contrasting white skin and long jet-black hair. His first reaction was to run, but he was charmed by her smile.

"You have been chosen to become a shaman," she sang. "Go and study with the One Who Walks with the Bear, and take your two friends with you. Her days are fading, so you must not delay," she said as she disappeared like a wispy fog during the heat of the day.

Interrupting his vision, Sonoma said, "Coahoma, please be careful. I don't want to lose another son," as she placed her arms around him and pulled him close.

"Ah, Mother, I'll be fine. Pontiac is always with me. But sometimes I think that he treats me like I am a child. I am a man," Coahoma said as he pulled away. Wanting to distract her, he stretched his arms out and swung around. "Look how well this fits," he said. "I like your beadwork," he continued as he ran his right hand down over his left sleeve, feeling the smooth rippling texture of her beadwork. "And I like these new leggings and moccasins too," he said as he bent over and touched the ground.

She placed her hands on her hips and searched deep into his elusive brown eyes, sensing the secrets that he hid from her. She whispered, "Son, I know that you are determined to become a great medicine man, but look how thin that you are getting." She reached over and gently squeezed his right arm, but before she could press her fingers on his chest, she heard a familiar whistle blast across the clearing. She didn't have to ask. She knew that Moki and Fala had arrived. As she turned to greet the two boys who were walking toward them, she asked, "What are you boys going to do today?"

"Pontiac is going to teach us about Impashilup," Fala answered before Coahoma could stop him.

"What? Impashilup . . . the soul eater? Son, he is a dangerous demon! Do you know that if he catches you that he will steal your soul? "

"Ah, Mother, you worry too much. He will not see me," Coahoma said as he squatted down and swooped up a large armful of dry sticks and tossed them into the fire.

"Are you ready to go?" Fala asked as he shifted his weight on to his right leg. He knew that he had spoken too quickly when Coahoma squinted and nodded a finger, signaling him to be quiet.

Coahoma was eager to get to the lodge of the old woman who walks with a bear. He grabbed a long spear and his bow and quiver that his father had filled with arrows. As he hooked the quiver over his right shoulder, he signaled his mother that he was leaving. The pain in her eyes haunted him as he jogged with his friends through their village and raced toward their elder's lodge. As he climbed the small hill, seeing the faint outline of her lodge through the trees, smelling the scent of pine, and hearing the sound of their footsteps as they walked along this narrow path, feeling empowered by the secrets that he was learning, Coahoma was eager to begin today's lesson.

From the time that a Choctaw infant breathed in its first breath, he was taught to remain silent. Making small talk was considered rude, but Fala didn't care. Holding his spear in his right hand, poking it on to the ground as he walked, he said, "It's getting easier for me to cross over into the Spirit World. How about you . . . ?"

"Yea, it is getting easier for me too," Moki said as he skipped ahead and kicked a small pebble with his right toe. He was delighted to see it fly into the air and land a short distance away.

"You two are lucky," Fala said.

"What do you mean?" Coahoma asked.

"It's not fair. Coahoma, you change into a panther. And, Moki, you are a buck. And me, I change into a little black crow," Fala spat. "I want to be a cougar or bear or anything that has teeth and claws . . . Anything but not a crow!"

"The gods are strange. Who knows why they decide these things?" Coahoma said as he stepped across the stones that marked a large earthen medicine wheel around her lodge. She was different. Her lodge was different—not built on stilts like theirs, but on top of a hill, away from the river, and on solid ground. Since he was a small child, he felt her dominance whenever he stepped inside her magical world.

"Ah, look who's here. Boys, come—join me," Pontiac said. They saw him sitting on the ground, facing a warm fire that was burning near the center of her musty old smoke—and herb-scented home. They saw Pontiac bend forward and toss a small bundle into the fire. He leaned back and inhaled a long deep breath from his favorite pipe. As he exhaled the intoxicating fumes of his sacred blend, he said, "Put your weapons down and prepare to travel."

Stifling his excitement, Coahoma tossed his weapons on the ground beside the entrance and walked over and sat down beside the fire. It was difficult for him to remain calm. This was so exciting, moving into the World of Shadows, learning forbidden knowledge, and shifting into the totems of powerful animal spirits; and today, he was going to spy on a well-known demon.

He won't see me, he thought. *If he does, Pontiac will protect me from him.*

Yet he was keenly aware that if this demon or any other demon would latch on to him while he was inside their world, he would be completely helpless against it. But he was the son of a chief, and he knew that Pontiac would willingly sacrifice his life to save his. But life was a mystery, and this was the game that he had chosen to play.

Coahoma looked across the fire and watched Moki and Fala as they sat cross-legged down on an old blanket on the ground. He knew, by the way that they shifted their bodies and straightened their backs, that they were excited too. However, when he saw Fala lean forward and suck in a long deep breath, he knew that he was going to complain.

Exhaling as he spoke, Fala's asked, "Pontiac, can I be a mountain lion today?"

"Fala, you must be patient," Pontiac said. "And stop complaining about your totem."

Fala's chin dropped, and the edges of his mouth twisted slightly when he heard Pontiac's response. *Perhaps someday Fala will understand why he is a crow*, Coahoma thought as he stared into the fire. Not wanting to upset his friend, he thought, *I am glad that I am a panther*, as he stretched his hands out over the flames to feel its warmth.

Wanting to get started, the boys watched Laurel from the corner of their eyes as she gathered something from her sleeping area. They loved her, her old bear, and her lodge. But most of all, they were grateful that she had taken them under her wing. Even though she walked with a slight limp, her dark red skin was covered in wrinkles, and her long white hair was thinning on top, she was beautiful to them. On many occasions, when they walked with her inside the Spirit World, they knew that she possessed powerful knowledge about life, death, medicines, and their gods. Sometimes they grew impatient with the timing of her disclosures, but they knew that she would reveal another secret only when she knew that they were ready to receive it.

While he waited, Coahoma distracted himself by silently naming the plants that she was drying on her wooden racks. He breathed in the thick pungent aroma of cedar, sage, and tobacco that hung on her racks. He reveled in the mystical melodies of the buzzing insects and chirping birds that enchanted the surrounding forest with their sweet songs. All of these things were so intoxicating to Coahoma that he fought the temptation to drift into the Spirit World without her.

"Ah, here it is," Laurel said, interrupting his thoughts as she entered the room, carrying two leather fringed bags. She asked, "Are you ready to learn your fate?" She sat down and removed her mask from the large sack. Without saying another word, she pulled it over her face. She bent forward and dumped the smaller bag of bones on to the ground. Using her right hand, she rubbed the bones against the ground with one swift swoop. She studied the bones and saw a message. "It has started," she said as she scooped up the bones and placed them into their bag. She removed the mask and gently placed it back into its sack.

What is started? Coahoma thought as he glanced at Moki and Fala. He wanted to ask her what the bones said, but he knew that she would scold him for asking. He looked over at Pontiac and watched the muscles in his jaw tighten as he drew in a long deep breath and held it. His eyes reflected a knowing. *What does Pontiac know? What is Laurel talking about?* Coahoma wondered. *Does it have to do with that wolf that I heard this morning?*

"Boys, get ready to travel," Pontiac said as he picked up his rattles. "We are going to teach you the way of the bees."

"Bees?" Fala asked. "What about Impashilup? I thought that we were going to spy on him?"

"No, Fala," Laurel whispered. "We have something more important to show you." When she saw the disappoint that flashed through them, she continued, "Boys, believe me, we will spy on this demon but not today."

Immediately, Coahoma sensed that something was wrong. *One day I will learn what those bones said*, he thought as he closed his eyes and prepared to travel. As he sped through his secret tunnel and landed inside the Spirit World on all fours, *I am a panther*, he thought as he lifted his paw and flexed his claws. *Where is the little crow?* Coahoma wondered as he cocked his head and saw his friends standing behind him. He immediately recognized this young white-tailed buck and the little crow that was perched on top of an antler.

"Hurry up," Pontiac said. He motioned the boys to follow him as he turned and headed into the singing forest.

Are they going to share this secret? Coahoma wondered as he followed him. He studied Pontiac and Laurel's brilliant auras as they led the group down a magical path, leading them to an unknown destination. As he looked for clues to their odd behavior, he heard a loud buzzing noise a short distance ahead. He didn't have to look. He knew that they were approaching a massive beehive.

"Change back into your human forms," Pontiac said. "The guardian of the bees is coming to greet you," he said. Coahoma watched as Laurel and Pontiac raised their arms and welcomed the approaching stranger. "We come as friends," Pontiac said. Coahoma listened to Pontiac as he spoke. "Kachina, we are honored that you have agreed to teach our young shaman about the way of the bees." He turned toward Coahoma and said, "Kachina, I want to introduce you to Coahoma. He is the eldest by one summer, and he is the youngest son of Chief Ituha."

When she turned to greet him, Coahoma felt a strange spark ignite deep inside him. Until this precise moment, girls were boring, and he wasn't interested in them. But this changed when he lifted his eyes and met hers. He wanted to know everything about this translucent beauty.

She said, "So you are Ituha's son. Coahoma, I am pleased to meet you." He stared into her twinkling brown eyes as she cooed, "I have watched you gather the honey from our hives." She stretched back and smiled. "I can tell that you are a good son," she said. "Your father must be very proud of you."

Coahoma couldn't find the words to respond to her praises. He quietly stood before her, grinning at her with his boyish charm. *She isn't like any of the other spirits or guardians that I've met*, he thought. *What is it about her that is so intoxicating?* he wondered. He wanted to reach out and touch her, but he knew that this would be rude, so he withheld his temptations to lay his hands upon her. When she twisted to greet Moki and Fala, he tried to smell her sweet scent. *I can't show my feelings for her, or she might get angry*, he thought as he inhaled a long breath and held it for a short time.

"Boys, follow me," she whispered as she headed back toward her hive.

Coahoma was right behind her, causing Moki and Fala to fall in line behind him as they followed her back to her home. Coahoma watched her white robe as it fluttered in the breeze. He noticed the long silver cord that she had draped around her waist and her mysterious headband of little pastel flowers and seashells that she wore around her head and a matching one on her wrist. *The bees are lucky to have someone so beautiful to watch over them*, he thought as he watched her purse her rose-tinted lips into a smile.

As he followed her, he thought, *Kachina—her name means, "sacred dancer." What is it that I must learn from her?*

The boys followed Kachina over to the entrance of her hive. This particular hive was found inside the trunk of an old pecan tree. *If Dakota could see me now, he would surely choose to be on this path and not the warrior one*, Coahoma thought as he waited for her lesson to begin.

As he stood in front of the hive, Coahoma noticed that a few bees were shimmering in small circles as they returned from their journey. "What are they doing?" he asked.

Kachina giggled as she said, "Silly boy, can't you see that we live a simple life?" She turned toward her hive as she continued, "In the beginning, when the bees and flowers were struggling to survive, our Great Mother heard their prayers. 'We are starving,' the bees cried because we cannot find food. The flowers cried, 'We cannot make our seeds because we don't have any pollen.'"

Coahoma listened to her story, but he knew that this wasn't what his masters wanted him to learn. *What does Pontiac want me to learn?* he wondered as he watched the graceful movements of this alluring spirit. As he wondered about their stingers and how they assembled into wild swarms, he asked, "Kachina, what can you tell us about how you protect your hives?

Kachina looked at Coahoma and smiled as she explained, "My bees are friendly, and they will go about their business gathering the sweet nectar. However, if something threatens their hive, the bees will merge into a unified force. They will sting an intruder until it either runs away or dies," she said.

"Kachina, how do we treat a person who has been stung by a swarm?" Coahoma asked. When Pontiac stiffened and listened to his words, he knew that this was the reason for their visit.

"This depends on the severity of the stings. In extreme cases, you want to use the Sacred Seven and apply them as a poultice to the body as you sing your most powerful songs to Hashtahli, asking for his help with this healing."

"What are the Sacred Seven?" Coahoma asked.

"They are chamomile, comfrey, crowfoot, dock, evening primrose, goldenseal, and burdock. Blend these sacred plants together and apply them to the stings. Next, you will need to call on the spirits of these plants to help you. The body knows what it needs, and it will heal itself if it is its will."

When Coahoma heard these words, he was pulled through his mystical tunnel and back into his sleeping body. When he opened his eyes, he found himself back in the old woman's lodge sitting on the ground in front of her crackling fire. He looked across the fire and watched Moki and Fala. He saw their breathing increase as they opened their eyes. They had returned too. And they knew the ingredients of the Sacred Seven.

"Why couldn't you tell us this?" Coahoma asked Pontiac.

"Coahoma, everything happens for a purpose. Our lesson is over for the day. It is early, so you are free to go hunting or fishing or go practice your chants. We will see you tomorrow morning. Same time . . . ," Pontiac said as he swung the door open and disappeared.

"Do you want for me to stay and help you?" Coahoma asked Laurel.

"No, Coahoma. I am going to walk into the forest and stay with Lagundo. He's been sleeping on the moss beside the little creek. It's time for him to come home. But if he is still asleep, then I want to put a few more braids and feathers into his hair," she said. "You can walk with me if you want to."

"Coahoma, let's go gather some honey from the tree and take it home to our mothers," Fala said as he headed toward the door.

"That's a good idea," Coahoma said as he picked up his weapons and prepared to leave. As he pushed the door open, he noticed that Laurel was heading toward her stockpile of weapons. *Maybe we should go with her. No, she will be all right. She's a master in the forest*, he thought.

Before he exited she warned, "Coahoma, there is a strange pack of wolves nearby, so keep your eyes open if you go into the forest."

When the boys were gone and her lodge was quiet, Laurel sat down and gazed into her fire. She drifted back to a time when she lived with the Shawnee. She was inside her father's long house, leaning on her knees across a smooth piece of black slate and gripping a sharp rock that was shaped to fit her hand. She was cutting thin strips of venison and carefully stacking each slice on to a hand-carved wooden tray. She was safe and happy.

She was the daughter of the well-known healer of the Eastern Woodlands, wife of the chief's son, and cherished princess of her tribe. She was wearing her favorite knee-high deerskin boots, a soft suede dress, and bone and shell talisman that her father had given to her. She was helping her family prepare for the upcoming long winter as she enjoyed her time with them. She felt her long black hair wisp across her shoulders as she stretched and turned, working on her task.

She saw the door of their long house open, and Tecumseh entered, balancing a small package in his arms. Studying the odd expression on his face, she realized that he was toting a precious cargo as he placed the bundle on the ground in front of her. She studied the delicate movements. She wondered what he had hidden inside.

"What is this?" she asked as she unwrapped the bundle and revealed a brown bear cub. Only a few days old, the baby whimpered as she reached over and picked him up. Then he became silent as his eyes met hers. "Can I keep him?" Laurel asked.

Tecumseh said, "His mother attacked us while we were hunting on the far side of Rattlesnake Ridge. When we saw that she was nursing a cub, we followed her tracks back to her den and found him. He was alone in her den."

She gently grasped the squirming infant and hoisted him into the air for everyone to see. "Oh, great spirits of the forest," she whispered. "Please watch over this little one and help him to grow into a strong bear." It was truly a magical time in her life when she clutched this tiny cub to her breast and announced, "We will call him Lagundo."

CHAPTER 2

Whispering Spirits

Timber Wolves
The timber wolves that roamed the land were
revered by the shaman who lived during this time.

Exiting her lodge, the old medicine woman entered a shimmering pool of sunlight that was streaming down through the cool dark shadows of the surrounding pines. She arched her face upward and welcomed its warmth as it saturated her.

Pausing for a moment, she thanked Hashtahli for giving her the gift of seeing another sunrise as he illuminated the eastern horizon. Whimsical and majestic, Laurel watched the clouds as they drifted overhead, forming into whimsical figurines as they passed by. It wasn't long before she spotted the image of a wolf. Its mouth was open as it launched a silent attack against its unsuspecting prey. *Another warning*, she thought as she gazed into the surrounding forest. *I must keep a close watch over my students until I know what is headed our way*, she thought.

She walked into her lodge and inspected the large selection of spears, knives, bows, and arrows that she had collected over the years. She decided to take the deadliest ones with her today. She picked up a quiver and filled it with many fine-tipped arrows. She placed her arm through the long leather strap and pulled the quiver over her shoulder *Lagundo must come home with me today*, she thought as she strapped a long blade around her waist and twisted it until it fell comfortably into the small of her back.

She hiked the bottom of her dress up and pulled her obsidian knife that she kept strapped to her thigh from its sheath. As she held it in her hand, she recalled her father's sparkling eyes and the tone of his voice. He said, "Laurel this is for you," as he handed it to her. It rekindled a happier time in her life when life was simple as she felt its smooth handle against her skin. Then she looked at the delicate carving of a she-wolf that Nahunta, her tribe's master carver, had carved into the bone. The sight of the wolf's piercing eyes and the way that he had pulled the edges of her mouth up into a smile and tucked her tail around her always remind her of the danger that lurked nearby.

As she placed it back into her holster and dropped her dress, she recalled her father's words, "Laurel, beware of those who will take this from you. It has many secrets that you will discover when the time is right." Since that moment, she never left it out of her sight.

During her long journey, when she was banished from her tribe, and each day was a struggle to survive, she learned its secrets. When life seemed hopeless, it was there for her like a beacon in the night. Now it possessed the uncanny ability to rekindle fond memories of her childhood, her heritage, her ties to the children of the Eastern Woodlands. Just by touching it, her recollections of her past came flooding back. It was her secret weapon. Only she knew how to wield its power. Now with her knife firmly strapped to her thigh, she felt complete.

She picked up her bow and her favorite lance and headed toward the path that ran down her hill and toward a small creek. As she gazed at the surrounding timberline, listening to the frogs' rhythmic croaking, she heard a small voice that was whispering on the wind.

It asked, "Laurel, is something troubling you?"

"I am worried about Pontiac and the boys," she said.

"Why do you worry about Pontiac? He is well, and he knows the ways of the spirit," it asked.

"The gods have spoken. They have warned me that death is on its way," she said as she headed toward her sleeping bear. "And Pontiac believes that it is coming for him because of the nightmares that he has been having about witches and giants. I just hope that they aren't coming for Coahoma," she said as she walked past a clump of poison ivy. "I do not have the heart to tell his parents that they have lost another son," she whispered.

As she walked down the knoll, she reached into her medicine bag and extracted a small obsidian necklace that Lanto carved for her and pulled its long leather strap over her head. *This is a wonderful weapon*, she thought as she allowed it to fall and settle near her waist. *It's not heavy or bulky, not like these other weapons*—as she juggled her bow—*but it certainly has frightened many animals away*, she thought as she felt the smooth central hole with her index finger and thumb. She loved this whimsical weapon. By grasping the leather strap and wailing the stone around in a rapid circular motion over her head, the sound, along with a well-pitched shriek, was usually enough to deter a predator from attacking but not always.

Standing utterly silent for a second, she listened to the faint breath of the westerly wind as it gently blew across her meadow, carrying with it the musty aroma of the vast swamp and the smell of pine. She smelled the pleasant aroma of hundreds of morning meals that were cooking over the fires in her village that stretched along the long smooth-flowing Atchafalaya River at the bottom of her hill.

As the sounds of the insects and migrating birds faded, a tiny voice appeared. It whispered, "Good morning, Laurel. It's going to rain later today, so be prepared for a long cold shower, but I'll wait for you to take Lagundo home before I deliver it to you, so hurry."

"Good morning, wind," she responded, stretching her bow and lance toward the sky. Slowly turning east, she enjoyed the sensation of the sun upon her face. She continued, "I'll hurry, but can you send me a warning before you arrive? Can you do this for me, or should I ask the rain god to remind me?"

"No," the wind responded. "I'll take your message to the rain god for you. He's terribly busy creating the storm, so hurry because he's going to soak the soil to press the flowers out of their hibernation."

"Thank you. I'll be watching for it," she said.

Then she turned her attention to spindly pines that stretched around her like a nonending wave of entangled evergreen branches that were covered in thick layers of green—and amber-colored needles. Looking through their cascading arms, she knew that these trees loved the creatures that lived among them, especially the humans. They were always standing guard over their friends. They were always willing to sacrifice themselves to ensure the survival of their woodland friends.

To talk to these ancient pines, Laurel calmed herself. When the noise of insects and chatter of the migrating birds merged into a hum, within a few moments, the songs of these creatures ceased to exist. The sounds and colors of the forest evolved into something extra ordinary. She plunged into a fourth dimension—one that only a shaman can reach. It was a magical deep spiritual realm—one that bonds a shaman to the mysteries and powers of the universe, one that is always there for the taking once a person learns how to tap into it.

She loved this beautiful place. She loved the hues of the rainbow that glowed around her: reds, blues, yellows, lavenders, pinks, and greens. She loved to feel the vibrations and watch the spectacular prismatic colors of the grasses, trees, earth, insects, and rocks that lived on the Great Mother.

Then she heard the eloquent chorus of the trees that were singing their unique songs, singing to one and another, saturating the air with their harmonic music. Finally, she found the telltale beat of the Great Mother as she announced her presence into the universe. As this Great Mother breathed in and out, she brought with her the promise of unconditional love and the continuation of life.

Altogether, they blended together, forming a symphony, loving and beautiful, communicating on a grand scale, transferring knowledge, and displaying their kindness and love for one another. Then all of a sudden, a whisper rose above the rest.

"Laurel," a voice cried out from among the pines. "Laurel, your bear is in trouble—you must go! A large pack of wolves is surrounding him."

"Where is he?" she asked.

"He's down past the bathing pool, near the eastern edge of the Black Swamp where you planted that cluster of raspberry bushes last spring," it said.

Laurel knew exactly where he was and quickly turned north, gripping her spear. She started running. Before she completed three steps into her stride, she looked up and saw her hawk, Tunghak, screaming past her and flying straight toward the impending battle.

Remaining in her lowered state of consciousness, Laurel commanded, "Tunghak, I command you to allow me to see through your eyes."

Her legs knew every inch of this old trampled path. She felt a surge of terror ripple through her as she ran. *What if I can't get to him in time?* she worried as she ran. She ignored her aching joints and the sound of her heart as she raced down the hill and into the forest. When she entered the woods, she reached a small stream that trickled across her path. As she plunged into its shallow water, she reached down and hiked the bottom of her dress up. As she splashed across it, she knew that the fight had started. She saw through her mind's eye that the wolves had surrounded her old friend.

When she approached the battle ground, she glanced up at the tree line. She counted five buzzards that were circling in the sky directly above her. She heard Awock, her pet, hooting as he flew over her head and past the buzzards. Having raised him from a hatchling, he was always with her, warning her of danger. Today, he was screaming, "Danger! Danger!" as she spotted the pack of wolves.

I must get into that old oak tree, she thought. She crafted a plan as she raced toward it. *It's just the two of us again. We will not lose this fight*, she thought as she trampled through the brambles, moving toward the tree. As she approached the wolves, she knew that, win or lose, she wouldn't leave without her bear.

As she reached the low-lying branches, she heard her friend's roar ricochet through the cypress-lined canopy. It was one that she hadn't heard in many years. It echoed in through the pines but was quickly dampened by the timber. But it wasn't long before the air was pulsating with another volley of violent screams, warning the wolves to stay away! Laurel shifted the spear into her left hand, and with her right, she pulled the gemstone pendulum from her neck, drew it back, and twirled it in the air. As it built up speed, she knew that she would have to react quickly if she wanted to make it to a nearby tree. When the stone emitted a low undulating tone, she used her upper muscles to swirl it even faster and faster as she ran forward. When she approached two young wolves, she let out a deafening scream as raced past them. Now that she was inside their circle, she knew that she would have to react quickly, or the pack would overpower her.

She dropped her pendulum and lance. She positioned the bow into her left hand and drew an arrow from her quill with her right. She positioned an arrow into its sweet spot, and with a single motion, she aimed and fired a single shot at a young wolf that was approaching her bear's left flank. With a whoosh and thud, the arrow found its mark. Then a high-pitched yelp echoed through the air as the animal fell into a quiet heap on to the ground. Laurel knew that her fight to save her bear and herself was now in full throttle. She also knew that her kill wasn't enough to drive these wolves away.

Recognizing that this was an old woman, the alpha male knew that she wasn't a threat to the ultimate outcome of this fight. Sensing her vulnerability, they knew that she wasn't strong enough to overcome their finely honed skills. They immediately addressed this target by splitting into two teams. Six wolves turned toward the bear as the remaining eight lowered their heads and headed toward Laurel. Exposing their deadly canines, snarling deep-throated growls, they quickly relayed their intentions that she would be their next meal.

The knife that was securely strapped to her leg began to tremble. She knew that it was warning her of impending danger. Not allowing herself to become distracted, she noticed that an older female was running straight toward her. The wolf launched her massive body into the air, hoping for a fast kill as she focused on Laurel's juggler. However, Laurel swiftly dropped on to one knee and hoisted her lance into the air to receive the unsuspecting wolf. The female hit the end of the spear and fell on to the ground with it protruding through her.

Laurel pulled another arrow from her quiver and prepared for another attack. She knew that they would rush her as the pack grew into a frenzy. Without thinking, she primed an arrow, pulled the bowstring back, and released a shot at another female, probably the daughter of the one that was lying at her feet. And soon, she too yelped and crumpled into a heap not far from her mother.

Laurel turned toward her bear. She watched two wolves running toward Lagundo, attacking him on his blind side.

"Lagundo, turn!" she yelled as she threw him a signal to turn around.

Understanding her command, he quickly drew upright onto his hind legs. Standing nearly eight feet tall and weighing more than a half ton, he dug his back claws into the ground, bracing himself for the incoming ambush. Massive and powerful, he towered over his enemy, flashing his razor-sharp incisors as he swung his head from side to side, spewing saliva as he roared. He wasn't a stranger to fights as he had the scars to prove it, and he wasn't about to let a pack of wolves end his life nor hers today.

A deafening roar reverberated through the forest as he greeted the wolves with experience. As he had anticipated, two wolves sprang into the air and sailed straight toward his throat as their piercing yellow eyes reflected "Kill." But Lagundo reacted with grace and agility. He met them with a double swipe of his powerful claws. He sent both wolves flying about ten feet across the grassy embankment and into opposite directions. They both hit the ground with four long gaping wounds sliced across their torsos. They lay quietly in the grass as a pool of dark blood oozed from their bodies. It ran down over their matted hair and dripped on to the ground beneath them.

Looking around, seeing a few more wolves that were coming directly toward her, Laurel reached for a limb and swung up into the oak tree, holding on to her bow as she climbed into its branches. Once she reached a safe distance, she positioned herself so that she could see Lagundo. When she found him, she saw that he was surrounded by wolves.

I have to hurry, she thought as she reached back with her left hand and pulled an arrow from her quiver. *Where did all of these wolves come from?* she wondered as she placed her fingers in her mouth and whistled. *I need some help*, she thought. She circled her hand high above her head and yelled, "Tunghak, attack!" as she pointed toward Lagundo. As Laurel positioned an arrow in the sweet spot of her string, she watched Tunghak launch from a nearby tree and dive toward an unsuspecting wolf. She saw him drop his talons and rip the tops of the wolf's ears off. Frightened and in pain, she watched the wolf flee into the woods, yelping as he ran.

I've fought wolves before but not this many, she thought as she watched the wolf disappear into the forest. She knew that she had to find their leader if she wanted to end this battle. *Where is he?* she wondered as she pulled her sacred knife from its holster. Show me their leader! she commanded as she pointed it toward the wolves.

When she pointed it toward a large male, her knife began to vibrate against her palm. *So that's him*, she thought as she looked at this haggard-looking wolf. She saw a large scar that ran along the entire side of his face. She noticed that he was missing part of one ear, and he had a long crooked tail. *Prepare to die*, she thought as she pulled back her arrow. She knew that her arrow had found its mark when he fell into the grass.

Just as he fell, the oak whispered, "Laurel, help has arrived."

She looked around and saw three wolves fall and then a fourth. Each of these wolves had an arrow firmly embedded in them.

She was relieved when she glanced up and saw Coahoma, Moki, and Fala running toward her. They were screaming, "Go away! Get away from her!" as they raced ahead. Then she was grateful when she watched them prime their bows and release another volley of arrows at the wolves.

Realizing that they were outnumbered and their leader was dead, the remaining wolves swiftly retreated into the forest

Following in rapid pursuit, the three young shamans were intent on banishing these varmints from their land as they vanished into the bowels of the forest, swinging their tomahawks as they ran. They were reinforcing a stinging lesson to these wolves to STAY AWAY!

But Laurel knew that many more long dark days lie ahead.

CHAPTER 3

Possession

Tecumseh
Shawnee Prince and Laurel's husband who walks in the Spirit World

Laurel watched Lagundo as she slithered across the branches and dropped down on to the marshy ground. *I hope that he isn't hurt,* she thought as she raced through the tall grass to him. She heard his deep-throated grunts reverberate through the eerie stillness as he shifted his massive body from side to side in quick procession, mashing through the heavy grass as he sauntered forward to greet her. "Lagundo, come here," she called. She happily watched his tiny white feathers that she had woven into his chestnut coat twirling in the wind.

I must see that wolf, she thought. "Is he the one that the gods were warning me about?" she whispered out loud as she carefully approached the suspicious animal.

Wanting Lagundo to stay back, she raised her right arm and threw her hand up in such a way that her palm faced the bear, signaling him to stop. He recognized this gesture and stood motionless in the tall grass as he watched her.

She cautiously dropped on to a knee beside the eerie wolf. She reached down and grabbed the hair on his neck and yanked his head up so that she could look into his eyes. She drew her knife when she saw that his eyes were blue. *This is a blue-eyed witch*, she thought. He is a shape-shifter from the mound builders clan. She knew the powerful black magic that he possessed. *Why is he here?* she wondered as a shiver ran down the center of her spine. *It's been a long time since I have seen their magic.*

Laurel reached down and grabbed the wolf's leg. Before his eyes shifted to black, she flipped him over, aligning her blade with his sweet spot. Just as she prepared to plunge her knife inside his chest, she heard Pontiac ask, "Can I help?"

Pontiac loved this old woman, and he made it his duty to watch over her. He was in the prime of his life. She needed him, and he knew it. She was his mentor, his guide post, feeding him powerful information and sharing her most intimate secrets with him. She taught him many ancient rituals and powerful chants. She introduced him to a menagerie of plant medicines, as well as how to love, to laugh; and she always encouraged him to respect all of their gods' creatures. He walks freely in her world of spirits and shadows. He knew her enemies and recognized the dangers that lurked in her reality. Mystical and many times terrifying, he has never backed down from a fight. Thriving on the knowledge that was turning him into a powerful man, he wanted to become his tribe's next spiritual master.

Then in his mind's eye, when he saw the wolf approaching her, his heart missed a beat as a cold shiver ran down his spine. He sensed the evil radiating from within this beast, and instinctively, he knew that she was in danger. Recognizing the place, dropping the wood that he was fetching for his hearth, he raced toward the lake. He was barefoot, carrying only a knife. Heart pumping, muscles pulsating, leaping across obstacles, plowing through thickets, and splashing through the water, Pontiac saw her flip the dead wolf on to his back. When he reached her, he heard her yell, "Rip his heart out!"

Hot and sweaty, out of breath, he leaned forward and hovered slightly over the wolf. Then with a sudden forceful thrust of his knife, Pontiac broke through the animal's rib cage. He could hear his bones cracking as he cut through them. He pulled the beast's ribs apart and ripped his heart away from its body.

"Hold it high in the air and claim the power that it holds to be relinquished to you," Laurel commanded.

This was a powerful ritual, demanding the Mighty Spirit to transfer the knowledge and memories from the beating heart to the one who recognizes its magic and knows the song to make this shift happen.

Over the past few years, Pontiac was perfecting it, burning its words and movements into his memory. He never missed an opportunity to expand his superiority. He wanted to be more powerful than any witch, shape-shifters, demonic shadow, or a blue-eyed sorcerer that roamed the land.

Lifting the heart into his palms, he held it slightly above his head and pointed it toward the north as he chanted, "Oh, great spirit, transfer the power held in this wolf's heart into mine." Then he turned slowly toward the south, still holding the heart above his head. He continued, "Let it bind with my soul and in my control."

He slowly lowered the wolf's heart and took one large bite out of it. He chewed and swallowed it. He said, "Now we are one." Then he carried it over to the closest pine, kneeled down on to one knee, took his knife, and dug a small shallow hole into the dirt. He placed this heart into the small earthen grave and covered it up. His deed was done.

When Pontiac turned toward Laurel, she saw this energy shift. He looked stronger, wiser, and more dangerous than ever before. She recognized that the change was perfect as she watched it, flowing through him. The ritual was complete, and she was pleased with it.

"Laurel," the pines interrupted, "your people are coming."

Then a voice broke through the silence and asked, "Laurel, are you all right? What happened?"

Looking around, she saw Pallaton, the tribe's fastest runner and wittiest hunter, standing right behind her. He was slightly bent over, and his coal black hair was draping down along both sides of his face. It was held in place by his favorite alligator strap. His large almond eyes were gleaming with passion. He was hoping that she would allow him take control of the wolf.

"Do you want me to prepare him for you? Do you want to dance with his hide in the upcoming ceremony?" he said as he reached around her and grabbed on to the wolf's front leg, pulling it up at an angle so he could examine his belly. "What an ugly beast! Do you think he's a witch?"

"Yes, he's a shape-shifter, and I want his hide. I want it with his head and tail," she said. Holding her hands over him, she said, "I can still feel his power. We must not turn our backs on this one." But she hid her concern that more may be coming.

She was wondering who this shape-shifter was when she looked up and saw her tribe running toward her. Many of them were still in their bed clothes. Their hairs were wild and unkempt as they rushed forward. The younger and stronger runners were the first to arrive. Not far behind them was Coahoma's father, Chief Ituha. He was leading a large group of his tribesmen toward her. The warriors were in front. They were followed by many women and children who wanted to assist. They were armed with bows and arrows, spears, and knives; and they were prepared to fight.

Rushing up to her, they looked at the carcasses that were sprawled across the grass. Realizing that they are too late, they relaxed. They knew that the battle was over, but they didn't care. It was the most excitement that they have had all winter.

Looking up, she watched a few men carting many long poles from the forest. They were heading straight toward the fallen wolves. Within a few minutes, they were secured to the poles, and they were on their way back to the village. These wolves were destined to become a part of their legend. This story will be told over and over, starting at tonight's campfires.

Alawa, a young mother, heavy with her second child, approached Laurel. She was holding the hand of her five-year-old daughter. She was pulling her gently along beside her as she stopped to talk to her medicine woman. Laurel knew that it wouldn't be long before Alawa would give birth to a boy.

"He will look like his parents with high-arching cheek bones, large dark brown eyes, long black hair, and the nose like an eagle's beak. He will be sensitive yet brave, ready to fight the fieriest enemy; a hard worker, working from dawn to dusk, never complaining; and eventually, grow into a loving husband, fathering children of his own," the spirits said.

"What can I do for you, child?" Laurel asked. "How are you feeling?"

Alawa gently rubbed her belly in a wide circular motion and said, "I'll be happy to welcome this one into my lodge. He's a strong one. I can't sleep because he kicks so hard. I think he wants out to hunt with his father." She laughed.

"Of course, he is. He is going to keep you stocked in meat," said Laurel. "Now what's bothering you, child? How is Little Tiponi?" she asked. Squatting down, looking into the child's eyes, she realized that she was feverish. Laurel asked, "Alawa, can I take Tiponi home with me? I want to give her some medicine to stop her fever."

Just then, Chief Ituha strutted in between the two women as he held out his hands and placed his palms on Laurel's shoulders. In his rich baritone voice, he said, "Are you all right?" Waiting for her response, he looked at Alawa who had stepped two paces backward from him. Seeing her swollen belly, he knew that she would soon announce another member into his tribe. He looked forward to these special events. It was a time when everyone would gather around the ceremonial fires. They would sing and dance, tell stories, share food, and barter their wares. They would thank the Almighty Spirit for watching over them during the winter and for ushering in their new planting season.

Before Laurel had time to respond, Chief Ituha continued, forgetting that he had even asked her another question, "How many more days do I have to prepare for our spring ceremony?" as he handed her bloodied lance back to her.

"It will arrive three days after the next full moon," she said.

He asked, "Are you going to become this old wolf during our upcoming ceremony?"

Laurel said, "Ah, you will have to wait and see," just as she heard a rumble in the distance. Remembering her conversation with the wind, she announced, "The rain god is coming. Hurry home before he gets here."

Laurel picked up Tiponi and prepared to leave with her, but Pontiac stopped and took the child away from her. "I'll carry her to your lodge," he said. "And I'll stay with her until you return with Lagundo."

Pontiac didn't want to interrupt the women, but he wasn't certain if Laurel could reach the safety of her home before the rain hit. He knew that she would stay with her bear and that they would be walking in the rain if Lagundo had his way. Pontiac wanted to get Tiponi into Laurel's warm dry lodge so she wouldn't be chilled by the rain.

"Alawa, child, go ahead and walk with Pontiac to my lodge and wait for me there," Laurel said as she gently swooped her hand toward her lodge. "Pontiac will prepare a tea for Tiponi's fever when you get there."

As soon as the crowd dispersed, Laurel placed two fingers in her mouth and exhaled a long breath, releasing a loud whistle. Then she raised her arm and signaled for Lagundo to come to her.

Lagundo slowly pushed himself up from the grass and was soon standing beside her.

The pines said, "Laurel, you must hurry. The rain god is coming, and he is bringing a storm with him."

Reaching down, Laurel wrapped her arms around her bear, hugging him tightly. The two stood alone, enjoying each other's presence. Rubbing her hand through his thick bushy hair, she said, "Tomorrow, let's get you cleaned up. I'll brush you and fix your feathers. I am so happy you are coming home." Leaning forward, burying her face into his neck, the jingle of his shells triggered old memories of their horrendous challenges to survive through the night.

As these memories came flooding back, she felt her muscles stiffen, and then her heart began to swell, beating so fast that the sound echoed through her ears like large drums, blocking out the sounds of insects and birds that were screaming around her. Her heart doubled in size, filling her chest with such pressure, pressing against her lungs, blocking her ability to breathe. Then the tears came. Welling up, they flooded down the side of her cheeks as she buried her face into Lagundo's side and sobbed. The visions started, all at once, unstoppable: the traumatic ones, moments in time, frightening ones, ones when she was alone with her bear and lost. She was wandering under the endless canopy of the ancient woodlands, looking for a new family. Struggling to survive, she evaded the haunting shadows and wild animals that were always nearby. Slithering and snarling, always teasing and testing her, trying to seduce her into their world of madness, not knowing where to go, reliant on her extreme survival skills to live through the night, she was always grateful to wake up to see the light of yet another sunrise. They persevered—she and her bear.

Pushing her fingers deep into Lagundo's thick coat, intimately feeling his warm skin with her fingertips, working to regain her composure, wanting to stop this flow of unpleasant memories, she felt the hairs on the back of her neck begin to tingle. Familiar with this sensation, as she had felt it several times before, she knew that Tecumseh was with her.

Rugged and handsome, appearing as an aura of blue light, young and healthy, he reached out for her. His muscles flexed with perfection as he moved. His lean muscular body rippled as he moved, giving him the appearance of a brawny hunter who was filled with passion. He was a leader by his birthright, ready to challenge the most ferocious enemy to defend his loved ones. He always reassured her of their eternal bond as he surrounded her with the energy of his undiluted love. Today, he brought news of the child, Tiponi, and her friend, Pontiac.

"Laurel," he said, "beware when you go home. Things are not as they seem with the sick child."

Releasing her grip on Lagundo, she turned looking at Tecumseh. The memories stopped. Recovering her composure, she searched deep inside his dark brown eyes, looking for a clue. She asked, "What is wrong with her?"

"She has a tick behind her left ear. It is gorging on her blood. It is infecting her with the spotted fever," he said.

"I've treated spotted fever many times. What else is wrong?" she asked.

Laurel saw his face paled as he continued, "The wolf that you killed was a giant white shape-shifter. You remember them? The ones that live in the Land of Flint?" Tecumseh's voice was filled with sorrow when he said, "His wife is with the child, and she is planning to take revenge on you. Laurel, she has tied her silver cord to the sick child, and now she now sees through Tiponi's eyes. Your problem will be to outwit her. But beware. You must not break her lifeline until you understand her magic. If you do, then her spirit will be severed from her body—like her husband's."

"Will you be able to help?" she asked, noticing that her bones were too aching as she thought about his words.

In a firm soft voice, he said, "No, I will not come this time. Laurel, ask the four winds for help, use your wit, fly with the raven. Remember, the witch is a shrewd sorcerer. She is a blond-haired giant drawing strength from her ancient ancestors who reside deep within their sculpted hills. She is tapping into their dark magic, and she will use it to avenge her husband's death. Use your three young apprentices to help you fight this witch. Take heed. Alawa must stay away from Tiponi during this time. If the blue-eyed witch realizes that you have discovered her, then she might jump into the unborn child. Your battle will be lost if this happens."

"What happens if I lose?" she asked, worried that she might not have the savvy to outmaneuver this witch.

He drew close, looking straight into her eyes. He said, "If you lose, then you must banish yourself away from these people who love you. You must take your bear and disappear into the swamp and never return to this place. The unborn child will grow up to be your mortal enemy—hating, stalking, and stealing your powers. You will be powerless to stop him. Do you understand?"

Hesitating for a couple of moment, "Yes, I understand," she said as she studied the outline of the ominous shoreline.

Then as he faded back into the Spirit World, he said, "Beware of Pontiac. He is changing."

Laurel sensed the presence of her three young students who were staring at this ghost from the edge of the woods. They knew something unusual was happening and that Laurel was receiving information from the World of Spirits. They watched intently—not moving, not breathing, silently observing as information was shared between the ghost and the old lady without a gesture or a word. They knew that she was receiving guidance from this spirit, and they hoped that she would share this information with them.

Without warning, the spirit lifted up and surrounded Laurel with its brilliant blue light. Pausing as it engulfed her, it shielded her like a mother bird does with her child. Then the orb of brilliant blue light moved away from her and surrounded her old bear. Hovering silently for a few moments, it lifted up and blinked out of sight.

Watching this incredible series of events unfold before their eyes, the boys were grateful to be privy to such a rare occurrence. This bond that existed between these two was greater than the laws of death. They were amazed to see how he reached out to her to comfort her. Realizing that they just watched something spectacular, they stood quietly but anxiously, wondering how it was going to affect them.

When the ghost was gone, they watched Laurel. She turned and looked directly at them. She was renewed with the energy that she needed to continue her fight. She pulled her upper limbs tightly up against her body, brought both legs together, and pointed her fingertips toward the ground. Then clutching her right fist into a ball, she pressed it against her heart, giving them the signal to prepare for a fight. They immediately knew that something was wrong, but they didn't know what it was. But they knew that it was going to be bad.

CHAPTER 4

Spirit of the Ohi:Yo'

Gaim
A blond-headed Nahullo who lives in the Land of Flint;
an Allewegi shaman and the brother of Ethane', Dahey,
Tomas, and Bradan; son of Lugh and Morrigan

Gripping their bows at the edge of the woods, the three young shamans impatiently held their positions. When they saw Laurel lift her hand and flip her wrist at them, they lunged forward, racing as fast as their outstretched legs would carry them. They skimmed across the grass and pulled up to a halt only when they were close enough to reach out and touch her.

Unable to hide their excitement, they surrounded her, blocking her way toward the woods. Jousting their weapons between their hands, they showed her that they are willing to receive her orders. Like young bucks, they began to prance, shifting their weight from one leg to the other. They were fearless. Their eyes said it all, "Bring it on!"

Looking at the boys, she said, "Hurry, meet me under the old magnolia that is beside my bathing pool. I will walk with Lagundo and meet you there." Then with a slight flip of her wrist, she signaled them to leave.

Running slightly ahead of Lagundo, Laurel thought that he would lag behind. But to her surprise, he kept up. She could feel his rhythmically stomping feet, inhaling and exhaling with strong deep bronchial breaths that fell as warm rushes of rank air upon her back. Sensing her feelings, Lagundo wasn't going to be left alone. No matter how far or how fast she traveled, he wasn't going to let her out of his sight.

Glancing back, she saw her avian companions fly into the air. They remained behind the group for a short time, and then they soared up against the billowing clouds. She watched as they turned and headed home. Yet she knew that they were still watching her.

Looking up, she saw the ominous clouds that were drifting across the afternoon sky escorting in the predicted storm. As they cast their dismal gloom over the land, they warned the small group of healers that the storm was approaching. The winds began to blow. It increased in intensity as it approached from the west, carrying with it the familiar smell of pine.

All of a sudden, a rumble shook the trees, sending the birds into a panic, squawking as they flew overhead. A bolt of lightning flashed across the darkening sky. It connected with a distant object, sending a loud crack ricocheting through the air, warning everyone to seek shelter.

Listening, she heard a spindly pine yelling, "Hurry, Laurel, hurry, or you are going to get soaked." Trudging closely behind the boys, she heard another pine call out, "Yes, you are going to get wet if you don't hurry."

Laurel didn't respond. She was bewildered by Tecumseh's message. She recalled his words, "Pontiac is changing . . . The girl is possessed . . . You must banish yourself . . ." As she trudged toward the magnolia, she recalled her knowledge of possessions and exorcisms. *But how can I chase this spirit from Tiponi if I don't understand her spells?* However, deep inside, she knew that this fight was going to be fought inside the World of Shadows and with black magic.

SHERRY COTTLE GRAHAM

She thought of these blue-eyed witches and their skills as she stomped through a patch of stinging nettles and jumped over an old rotting stump. When she looked up and saw her old magnolia a short distance ahead, she decided, *First, I must hide Alawa in the forest and far away from her daughter before all hope is lost.*

Laurel ducked under the long waxy evergreen branches and joined the boys who were underneath. Looking up, she spotted Tunghak and Awock as they alighted onto a branch above her. She looked up at the incoming shower and noticed that it had changed from a cold drizzling rain into a sheet of stinging sleet. As these pellets whipped from the sky, she heard a loud drumming sound as they bounced off the surrounding foliage, spreading an eerie chill beneath the old magnolia as the throttling winds ripped past their tops. Thinking of the danger that they were in, she heard the boys who were standing beside her.

"Laurel, what is wrong?" Coahoma asked. "Does this have something to do with your bones or the shadow that visited me this morning?"

"Are we going to war?" Fala asked as he juggled his bow in his hands.

Focusing intently on the way that she moved and the sound of her voice, Moki asked, "Who are we fighting?"

Ignoring their questions, she raised her hand and signaled Lagundo to lie down. Once he was comfortably stretched out on to the ground, she sat down and leaned against his side as she has done a thousand times before. She knew his warm spots. And she used them when she needed his warmth to keep her safe during difficult times.

Turning her attention to her three young students, she said, "Come, sit beside me. We have much to do. Sit down and ready yourselves. Meet me on the other side."

Crossing their ankles, the three boys dropped on to the ground. Sitting upright, backs straight, legs crossed, arms folded, the boys closed their eyes and shifted their consciousness down to meld with hers.

Remembering their shamanic lessons, they relaxed, inhaling and exhaling, confirming their secret place in their mind's eye. They visualized each other, walking together, moving deeper into the shadows of this ancient forest. As they moved deeper into their private world, looking up through the needle-covered canopy, they noticed how the trees seemed to fade overhead into the sky. Listening to the sweet murmur of a nearby stream as it gurgled freely along, they spotted their mysterious cave as it lay waiting for them to enter its cool dark mouth. As the boys climbed up its earthen ramp, they heard the melodic song of a mockingbird, singing its love songs to its mate and the familiar tapping of a redheaded woodpecker, drumming for a meal on a nearby tree. Without hesitating, the boys walked deep down into its mystical core. On their way, they listened to the soothing melodies of dewdrops as they chimed their melodic tunes inside their crystalline chambers. Relaxing and beautiful, it urged them on.

Seeing a faint light shining ahead, recognizing their target, increasing their haste to reach it, the boys rushed through the long dark tunnel and plunged straight into the light. Entering as their animal spirits, they moved without limitations or boundaries. Once inside this world of prismatic lights and symphonic sounds, hearing the trees singing their songs of recognition, warm and inviting, they anxiously joined Laurel in her world.

What seemed like hours only took minutes for the boys to make this crossing. Coahoma was the first to enter into the Spirit World. As he walked around, he recognized his physical body. He was sitting cross-legged on the damp ground, dripping wet and perfectly still. Like all boys, he chose to cross over and assume the image of his totem—the panther.

"Hey, look at me," he said, jumping into the air and landing on the ground behind himself. He planted his deadly paws firmly into the dirt. He stretched out his claws and flicked a small cloud of dust into the air. Looking around, seeing the wind and rain, he was pleased that he could move freely about without limitations and without getting wet.

Curious, Coahoma reached out and sniffed himself, he said, "Strange, I don't smell anything."

"Are you serious? You probably smell like sweaty feet." Moki chuckled. "Hey, look at our wet clothes. I bet we smell like rotten fish." He laughed.

The elegant white-tailed deer stood behind Coahoma. He gracefully swung his antlered head from left to right, looking for something. He asked, "Coahoma, where is Fala?"

Before Coahoma could answer, Fala landed on the ground beside him. Standing in his full glory, Fala was pacing back and forth on his squatty legs. He started again, just as he does every time that he shifts into his avian form. Fala squalled, "I don't want to be a crow. Laurel, I want to be a panther like Coahoma . . . or a bear or lion, or how about a wolf?"

Laurel was standing quietly in the background, waiting patiently for the boys to settle down. She was smiling as she walked out to greet them. She hoped that she could distract Fala. She said, "Boys . . . ," but Fala started complaining before she could say another word.

"Caw, caw, all I can say is caw," he scowled. Turning around, he flicked his long black tail into the air and squirted out a little glob of blackish white poop. Now he was thoroughly annoyed. Bobbling back and forth, shifting his weight from one foot to the next, he cried, "All I can say is caw. No matter how angry I am or what I have to say, it always comes out as caw, caw. And I have to poop all the time . . . eat and poop. Laurel, will you please change me into something else—please."

Fala never ceased to amuse her, but she knew that she didn't have time to deal with his constant complaints about being a crow, at least not today. A valuable life depended on their ability to work together, and she needed all three of their talents to defeat this witch.

"Hush, Fala. We will talk about this another time! I need the crow," she said.

Not wanting to deal with the boys' animal spirits and the issues that it created, Laurel stepped in between them and said, "Boys, switch back now and listen to me. Something tragic has happened today, and we are going to have to work together if we are going to discover this trickster who is hiding among us."

Coahoma asked, "What trickster?"

Laurel said, "I have been warned that Tiponi is possessed by a witch. I do not know who it is, but I will find out."

Moki asked, "Can I help?"

"Tiponi has the spotted fever, but I am not concerned about her fever. My plant helpers will take care of it, but we must find out who possessed the child and what evil does she bring. More importantly, what does she want? Boys, if we are to save this child, then we must learn the answers to these questions," Laurel said.

Coahoma was stunned by her revelation. He asked, "Do you have a plan?"

Laurel stared at her three young apprentices, shifting her body slightly on to her right foot, she said, "One thing I know is that we will fight this witch in our world and in the spirit one. We must be cunning like the fox and surprise her like the snake in the grass. She does not know that I have been warned about her presence. And we will use this to our advantage.

However, we must learn the source of her black magic. Once we know this, then we will be able to fight her."

Fala asked, "How are you going to find her?"

Laurel answered, "If she has attached her silver cord to the child, then I will find it. It will take me straight to her."

"Can we go too?" Fala asked. He knew about the soul's attachment to the body, but he had never seen it or followed one. But now that this mystery deepened, he didn't want to be left behind.

Laurel said, "Maybe . . . But you must wait for me here! Do you understand?"

She lifted up and blinked out of sight. She headed straight up the hill and toward her lodge. Once she arrived, she looked for a single silver thread that drifted down from the heavens and entered into her musty lodge. She was a master, and it didn't take her long to find this delicate thread that was shimmering against the grayish sky.

Returning to the magnolia, seeing the boys under the tree, she signaled for them to join her. She knew that they were about to catch a rare glimpse into the Spirit World. She knew that they were safe as long as they stayed with her.

As the three approached, Laurel said, "Stay close to me and stretch yourselves apart. Don't crisscross over your silver cords. We are going on a long journey, and I don't want you to muddle your lines together."

Eyes wide with excitement, Coahoma asked, "Where are we going?"

"We are going to find the witch's home," said Laurel. "Do you see her silver cord?" she asked as she pointed to the glittering thread that magically hung in the air. She added, "Do not touch or break this cord. If you do, her spirit will be trapped inside Tiponi's body. Do you understand?"

With a nod, the boys responded, "Yes."

Traveling in the astro world, they rose above the trees and followed this exciting tiny little shimmering line. They were racing against time as they flew hundreds of miles over the dense green canopy stretching across the horizon as far as the eye could see. Every once in a while, they would see a gap that was etched through the forest. As they flew across them, they saw many crystal blue lakes and shimmering rivers that lie below.

Not long into their northern journey, the wind and the rain stopped, and they flew into a beautiful blue sky. As the small group flew over the Eastern Woodlands, they noticed that the rolling hills were replaced by towering evergreen mountains that were separated by deep valleys with long winding rivers that carved their paths through their basins.

Occasionally, the team noticed small trails of smoke, drifting up through the dense canopy. They were like pillars of white mist, marking the location of a village that existed below. They heard the cries of timber wolves as they crossed over these breathtaking mountains, calling to their mates or warning their predators to stay away.

As the small party approached the sloping foothills of the Ohi:Yo', recognizing the outer edge of her homeland, Laurel knew that she would fly over her childhood village if she didn't change her course. However, Tiponi's life was more valuable to her than the pain that she was about to suffer.

There it was—her old village and the people who had cast her out of their lives. She recognized their lodges that were built with saplings, grasses, and mud. Visions of her life with these people came flooding back as she flew past. Memories of the forest—hunting, fishing, planting squash, dancing around the ceremonial fires, laughing with her father, feeling the loving arms of her mother draped gently around her, seeing the dark reddish bronze wrinkled face of her grandfather leaning over and smiling, smelling the aroma of their musty lodge—came flooding back as she gazed down at the magnificent Kuhnoie River as it twisted through the white laced foothills.

Ignoring the pain that ripped her heart, she watched the Kuhnoie's gentle current as it swung northward to extend its passage through this splendid gorge. Reflecting the dark silhouettes of the leafless trees, she recognized the healing white willows, the handsome elms, the wide-spreading and shady ash, the giant acorn-producing oaks, and the sweet sappy sugar maples that lined its way. She loved these trees. At one point in her life, she had bonded with each and every one of them, and she knew their unique songs by heart.

As they approached the Good River, she heard a voice calling, "Laurel, is it really you, child?" As this melodic voice sung to her, she flashed the back of her hand to the boys, signaling them to stop. Hovering in midair, the boys inched forward until they were by her side.

Becoming still, Coahoma knew that he was witnessing something extraordinary. Not sure if he should speak, he held his tongue, watching, breathing in slow deep breaths, tuning his senses into every sight, sound, and smell. Watching the area around him, keeping Laurel in his sight, he spied it. In the center of the river where the Kanawha merged into the Ohi:Yo', the surface began to ripple.

He saw an image of a woman's face form on top of the cold water's surface. It was shimmering in shades of blue and white as it rose to greet them. As this mysterious gray-blue-eyed beauty approached, the three boys wondered if she would reach up and pull them down into her watery world.

Without hesitating, Coahoma followed Laurel over to the shoreline. He stood with his friends on the bank of the Kanawha River, watching this shimmering spirit. Mesmerized by this unusual sight, he wanted to reach out and press his fingertips into her aqua form and feel her cold wetness as she approached Laurel, but he restrained his temptations to do so. Just as her silvery face leaned forward and she prepared to speak, Coahoma knew that she was a gentle soul. He also knew, by the way that she puckered her lips and the way that she wrinkled her brow and squinted, that she carried a grim message to them.

"Go back, child," she warned. "Do not take these boys across the river and enter the kingdom of the Ron-Nong-Weto-Wanca. They are growing in numbers and spreading across the land like a disease. Go back! Save yourselves!" she warned.

Pointing her finger toward the delicate silver thread that floated overhead, Laurel said, "I have to find its owner. A small child's life depends on it."

The spirit of the Ohi:Yo' moved closer to them. Her eyes betrayed her love and concern for this elderly shaman. She continued, "Child, I have missed you. I miss your feet upon my banks. I miss your laughter and feeling your bare skin within my waters. I felt your pain and understood why you had to leave. I also respect your desire to help this child, and I am prepared to assist."

"Then who will I find at the end of this cord?" Laurel asked.

Fala couldn't restrain his excitement as he lunged forward and asked, "Who are you?"

"I am Wenonah, the river guardian. I oversee the rivers and streams that zigzag across the land, making sure that they flow in the right directions. And I watch over the plants and animals that live in my world," she answered as she looked over at Fala. Smiling at him as she turned away, her voice changed, becoming deeper and more distressed as she continued, "Laurel, the person that you seek is named Morrigan.

You know her. She is the giant redheaded sorceress who wears a raven on top of her head. Beware, she is angry and seeks to avenge her husband's death."

Laurel's heart skipped a beat as she recalled the mysterious wolf with the haunting blue eyes that she had killed. She remembered yelling to Pontiac, "Rip his heart out!" *Oh, what did I do?* She fretted.

Gathering her thoughts about Pontiac, Laurel thought, *Lugh is no match for Pontiac. Pontiac is a gifted medicine man. He can take care of himself.*

However, before she could come to terms with herself, she heard Moki say, "Do you really know these giant sorcerers?" Ignoring his question, Laurel raised her arm and flashed the back of her palm toward him, giving him a signal to be quiet and listen.

Wenonah continued, "Laurel, we deplore the ways of these yellow-bearded men and their mean-spirited women. They are still the same ruthless people that you once knew. But heed my warning, child. You are heading into a trap. Morrigan is waiting for you. And if she catches you, she will kill you."

Ah, failure, Laurel thought. *What is "failure" but the lack of resourcefulness? And how many times have I looked into this awful reality, only to find that by the grace of my gods that I overcame my nightmares and lived to see another sunrise?* When she glanced over and saw Coahoma, a rush of guilt overwhelmed her. *How can I lead him into this vile land?* she wondered. *What if something terrible were to happen to Coahoma?* As the memories of Elsu's tragic death swept through her, she pondered, *How could I tell Sonoma that she has lost another son?*

Wenonah recognized by the way that Laurel stiffened her back and shifted her head that she was leaving. She was going into the land of the Ron-Nong-Weto-Wanca. Wanting to help her beloved friend, Wenonah said, "The rain god will deliver a blizzard to hide your presence from the giant sorcerers." But Wenonah saw that Laurel was filled with shame as she spoke. She knew by the way Laurel twisted her face and dropped her shoulders that she was grieving. Sensing the reason for Laurel's reaction, Wenonah continued, "Morrigan's village lies inside the Land of Flint. Look for a dwelling that is surrounded by the skulls of her enemies. You will find her there."

Wenonah was still for a few moments as she listened to a tiny voice that was whispering to her on the wind. When it stopped, she looked over at Laurel. The small group of shaman knew that she had received some distressing news by the way she arched her neck and wrinkled her brow. Wenonah said, "The four winds say that Lugh has lost his soul and that he will not survive long without it. They say that it resides in a shaman named Pontiac. They say that this is your reason for journeying into this vile land, but, Laurel, you must know that you are no match for these giant sorcerers and their gods." Wenonah knew the truth. She knew the source of Laurel's pain as she withdrew. *Laurel, your knowledge has created this problem, and now you will have to resolve it by yourself,* she thought as she disappeared from sight.

Moki sensed the emotions that flowed between his elder and the mysterious woman, but Fala didn't. Pride bubbled through him as he slapped his right palm on to his chest and said, "Laurel, you did it. You stole Lugh's spirit."

"Hush, Fala," Laurel scolded. She had made up her mind. She was abandoning these boys and making this journey by herself. Shock flashed through their eyes as she commanded, "Boys, go home and wait for me under the magnolia. "

"No! We want to go with you . . . You need us!" Coahoma argued, but he could see by the scowl that flashed across her face and the glare that shot through her eyes that his words were useless.

Feeling rejected, the boys' hopes of spying on these golden-haired giants were fading as she disappeared from sight.

Hesitating for a moment, Coahoma's love for his elder consumed him. She needed his help, and he knew it. Realizing that it was her love that caused her to abandoned them on this snowy shoreline, he said, "I am going to follow her. You can stay here if you want to, but I am leaving."

Nodding in agreement, they were all going into the land of the Ron-Nong-Weto-Wanca with or without her permission.

CHAPTER 5

Miles to Go Before We Wake

Balor
Red-bearded elite warrior who is in love with Ethane'.

Racing against time, Coahoma and his two friends zipped across the frozen land. Flying faster and faster, watching the gentle rolling hills as he flew, Coahoma knew that the success of his quest depended on his ability to reach the mysterious destination before the storm hit. As he traced the webs across the sky, he wondered, *Would Dakota have made this same decision? Would he have disobeyed his elder and led his friends into this hostile territory?* But he didn't have time to think of the consequences of his decision as he spotted the sparkling threads twisting toward the earth.

He knew that their old medicine woman was hiding somewhere inside this giant village that was quietly nestled inside this lonesome valley.

Coahoma looked down and saw the wind whipping through the leafless branches, bending their fragile tips from side to side. Glancing toward the west, he saw an eerie mist that was moving toward them, engulfing everything in white.

Coahoma wondered what his father would do as he turned around and saw the contorted eyes of his friends staring back. His first gut reaction was to withdraw and return home, but his pride won't let him do this. Seeing the faint outline of the fortress below and the dark silhouette of several gigantic dwellings within, wondering if he should stay, he heard a small voice whispering in his left ear. It said, "Coahoma, hide behind the barricade. It will protect you from the incoming storm."

With the flick of his wrist, Coahoma yelled, "This way!" as he flew straight for the mighty barrier that surrounded this mysterious village. As he approached his target, he noticed the vast sizes of the dwellings that were tucked inside. *Who are these people?* he wondered as he landed on the outskirts of this massive fortress.

Huddling together, scanning the landscape, gathering as much information about their location and the position that they were in, the storm hit. The wind ripped through the village, bending and twisting the surrounding trees, upheaving everything that wasn't strapped down. It quickly turned the land into a frozen world of white.

Bracing against the squalling snow and blistering wind, Fala was disgruntled with this situation. He asked, "Wenonah wasn't kidding when she said that she would send a storm to protect us, but this is a bit much, don't you think?"

"Ah, I've never seen the likes of this," Moki said.

Becoming annoyed at his younger partners, "Stop complaining!" Coahoma said. "Look where we are . . . Wenonah was right. This will hide us from what lies within," he continued as he pressed his hands against the gnarled rough bark. Looking up, he estimated that it was as tall as six men stacked on top of each other. It was built with the sturdy trunks of a thousand trees. Each log was cut into similar lengths and shaved into a sharp point on one end and buried deep into the ground with the other. These knotted posts were bound in a manner that seemed to create an impregnable barrier around these giants.

SHERRY COTTLE GRAHAM

Walking forward and pressing his face up tightly against two poles, attempting to look through a small slit that existed in between them, Fala asked, "Coahoma, do you know where she is?"

"Her cord went down over in that direction," Coahoma said, pointing to the opposite side.

Crooking his head around the nearby corner, Moki was blinded by the stinging wind and snow. However, a slight movement caught his eye as he fought to see what was on this side. He walked straight into the blizzard and discovered that he was standing in front of a large wooden door. In front of this sealed entrance was a smooth large stake. Looking up, Moki tried to determine what was dangling on it, but his vision was obstructed by the pelting snow. Wondering what it might be, he lifted up to see. Quickly, he realized that he was looking at a dead man. This guy was tied to the top of this pole, and his rotting corpse was left there to rot in the wind.

Stifling his desire to flee, Moki screamed, "Eee! Coahoma, come here!"

Coahoma and Fala raced toward Moki. Rising up to see what he had found, they immediately recognized the horrifying remains of a boy who was skewered on top of this pole. Silently, they studied his pasty blood-streaked face and hollow eyes. They saw that his bottom jaw had dropped open, forming an endless scream. They knew that it reflected his suffering as his captors ended his life.

As Coahoma regained his composure, he noticed that the top of this boy's skull was missing, and his eyeballs were gone, leaving two large black cavities inside his skull. His facial features were so distorted by the flaps of loose skin that draped down over his face that it was difficult for Coahoma to learn anything about this boy or his life.

"I think," Fala whispered, "that we should go back home!"

Moki flew down and waited beside the base of this demonic pole. He waited beside it for his friends. When they appeared, regaining his composure, Moki asked, "What will they do to us if they catch us? Coahoma, do you think that they can see us?"

Recovering from this horrifying sight, stilling his nerves, Coahoma said, "Only a witch can see us . . . I think, but I am not sure what kind of powers that these people possess." Coahoma thought about leaving and returning to the river to wait for Laurel, but the mystery of what lies within was more enticing to him. Coahoma whispered, "We are traveling in the Spirit World. Even if, they do see us, they cannot kill us and tie us to a tree like this poor boy. You can go back, but I am staying. This is your decision to make."

Ignoring the terrible omen that he had found, Moki said, "I'm staying." Wanting to evoke a sense of strength, he continued, "I am not afraid of these people. I want to see these giants and get Laurel. I want to help her rescue Tiponi if it is possible." Wanting to leave this awful site, Moki stepped forward and walked away from his friends. However, as he led Coahoma and Fala into the blinding snow, he sensed that something was terribly wrong.

When they reached the opposite corner of the barricade, they spotted another group of poles that were rising up from the frozen ground. Seeing a flutter and hearing a strange musical sound, they slowed their pace. Not knowing what lay ahead, they crept forward. As they moved past these isolated poles, they looked up and saw the skewered bodies that were dangling from them. Sickened by what he saw, Coahoma asked, "What kind of vile people live here?"

"I don't know," said Fala, "but look up there." He pointed toward another set of carcasses that were draped on these poles. Fala whispered, "If we get separated, don't leave me here!"

Coahoma looked up and saw a cluster of mangled and dangling corpses. He watched in horror as the squalling wind and snow ripped against them, making them bend and twist from their perches. Coahoma saw the way that their hair, clothes, and arms moved in the storm, making it appear that they were alive. As he listened to the shrieking wind, Coahoma knew that it was the spirits of these corpses that were filling the air with their terrible cries.

Whispering under his breath, Moki repeated, "I'm not afraid . . . I'm not afraid," trying to convince himself that he was safe, but he knew that his life had changed on this stormy afternoon.

"We need to hurry. Let's find Laurel and get out of here," Fala said as he walked past another set of festering corpses. He maintained his steady pace through the high-pitched wails of the piercing wind, moving toward the rear of this fortress. As he walked along this spiked walk, he asked, "Do you think that Laurel is still here?"

"She's still here. I can feel her," said Coahoma. He pressed against the wall, seeing a massive dwelling on the other side. "Come on . . . Let's go inside and find her!" Coahoma yelled as he turned and disappeared from sight.

The boys immediately fell into formation and followed Coahoma inside. Afraid to lose sight of their blood brother, they flanked Coahoma, keeping as close as possible, forming a single unit as they forged onward. They stopped when they reached the rear of this massive shelter. Now they were trapped between the storm and what lies inside this frightening place. Their only option was to find Laurel and finish what they had started.

Before pushing into its interior, Coahoma looked back at the blackened outline of their jagged barrier. *Living behind this wall is a good thing*, Coahoma thought. *Hum, look, it is strong. It keeps out the carnivores that roam this land and their enemies, but it wasn't strong enough to keep us out*, he mused. He was pleased that he had discovered a weakness in their defenses.

"Are you ready to go inside?" Coahoma asked. Assuming leadership, "Let's split up. Moki, go in over there," Coahoma said as he pointed toward the far end. "Fala, you can go in over there," he continued, pointing to a spot straight ahead. "And I'll go in . . . near the front entrance." Before they split up, he added, "Stay in the shadows. If something happens, bark two times and get out. We will meet back where we landed."

Fala was the first one to reach his position beside the dwelling. Within a few seconds, he disappeared inside, beginning his analysis of these strange people and hoping against hope that he would find Laurel.

Adjusting his eyes to the dim light, scanning the interior, watching for his friends, Coahoma immediately implemented his shamanic skills by slipping into the dark crevices of this massive earthen lodge. Standing perfectly still, blending into his surroundings, he observed the inhabitants without them knowing that he was among them. Watching for his friends, he gazed around their grass, mud, and fur-lined walls. He saw his friends. They were hiding in the shadows—watching, learning, looking for their teacher, but mostly, they were watching the people.

Inside this musty and smoke-filled place, a pungent odor saturated the room, insinuating that these inhabitants hadn't bathed in a long time. They saw three fires that were evenly spaced through the center of this massive shelter, glowing with hot embers, popping and cracking, releasing small streams of smoke that floated effortlessly up and into their vent holes.

People, singing and playing instruments, captured their attention. They had never heard such sweet sounds—different, surely the music of gods, calming, soothing, reducing the children's fears by distracting their attention from the storm that raged outside.

Looking around, they noticed a teenage boy was playing on an unusual instrument made with many small greenish copper metal tubes bundled together in a straight pattern with each tube producing a different melodic sound when he blew into its end.

Then beside him, an older man clothed in dark leather winter clothes was sitting cross-legged on the ground on a black bearskin rug, complete with its head and outstretched paws, near the warmth of the fire. He was bent over, staring into the flickering flames, as he contently beat a slow deep rhythmic tune on his wooden drum. The boys inspected the beautiful images of flowers and birds that were meticulously carved into its surface. The drum was stained in a handsome shade of black. Its flowers were stained with a vibrant hue of yellow, and the birds were stained bright red. The ends of the drum were covered with thin sheets of leather that were held in place with a long red cording. The man contently beat his drum with a long wooden stick that had a rounded tip. As he struck the leather with his stick, he created a lovely beat for the flutist.

Harmonizing with the instruments, many of the people were singing words and humming along with the musicians. Sitting on the ground, they were working on a project. The boys noticed that there were many men, women, boys, girls, and a few babies scattered throughout the lodge. The people were sitting on a thick layer of fur, and they were dressed in their heaviest leather and fur garments.

Listening to their songs and studying their movements as they sat alone or in small groups, working on their projects, the three blood brothers realized that two remarkably different races of people were inside. A few had delicate olive-toned features, straight black hair, black eyebrows, and downward slanting brown eyes. The men appeared to rise nearly five and a half feet tall, while the majority was shorter than five feet.

Three strapping men were sitting side by side on a wooden plank. They were roasting a slab of meat over a smoldering fire. They captured

SHERRY COTTLE GRAHAM

the boys' attention when one of the men stood up. Reaching forward, he turned the wooden handle that held the meat. The boys held their positions, watching in absolute silence, as these sights and sounds unfolded.

Looking at these giant men, the boys estimated that they were as tall as large grizzlies, standing on their hind legs, and weighing about the same. When one of these giants turned around, they saw that he was a white man. He had white ruddy skin with rosy cheeks, and he had blue eyes. His hair was the same color as wheat. It was thick, and it covered his broad lantern-shaped jaws and upper lip. This giant man had wrapped a small piece of sinew around the base of his chin, gathering his long facial hair together, and allowed it to drape down the center of his chest.

Without warning, the man stretched his arms into the air and released a yawn as he bent over to sit back down. He emitted a series of loud moans and grunts as he moved. The boys were mesmerized by this huge man. Wanting to get closer, the boys slithered through the shadows toward him. They watched him, absorbing every detail about his physical appearance and his demeanor. When the man opened his mouth one more time, they realized that he had birows of teeth. His teeth filled his mouth, protruding in different directions, causing his lips to contort as they covered them.

Coahoma decided that it was time to continue his search for Laurel. Moving along the entrance, he noticed a large pile of beautiful waxy multicolored flint boulders. He slid over and looked at this pile of rocks. He noticed that there were a wide variety of sizes and colors of these precious stones. He saw a few sand-colored ones that were striped with veins of crimson and black. And another one was black and striped with silver and red. He noticed a delicate sparkle coming from one of them. He bent down to examine it. He was pleased to see a cluster of tiny crystals that enhanced its beauty. Watching the warm flickering light glowing inside these crystals, he realized that he was in the Land of Flint.

Wishing he could take a bit of it home, Coahoma knew that he had much to learn about astral traveling. *How can I pick things up?* he wondered. *I must ask Laurel to teach me how to do this trick. If I knew, I would take some of it to Father.* Moving on, Coahoma found a pile of spears that were propped beside the door. He could tell that the heads of these spears were made from the flint that he had just seen. Reaching his hand around the wooden shaft, he was awestruck by their size. Their shafts were tailored to fit the massive hands of these giant men. Measuring nearly fifteen feet in length, these spears could only be wielded by one of them.

Stifling his emotions, Coahoma wished that he could walk up and speak to one of these giants. However, he knew that this was impossible, not because they couldn't see him, but because he was an unwelcome intruder. But he wanted to hold one of their twelve-inch knives in his hand and learn how they knapped their blades. He knew that his father would sing praises of his adventure during their upcoming celebration, but his journey wasn't over yet. Becoming anxious, he wondered, *What if Father becomes angry with me for disobeying my elder and leading my friends into this vile Land of Flint?*

At the far end of the building, Moki was watching the giants that were sitting together beside the fire. He saw Coahoma slithering in the shadows, inspecting the weapons and piles of flint. Moki noticed a small group of girls who were sewing a few large pieces of leather together. At first, he thought that it was a large blanket, but as he inspected its size and shape, he realized that they were working on a thick fur coat. *That coat,* he thought, *will fit a giant, like the ones sitting on that log beside the fire.*

As Moki wandered through the shadows, watching the activities of these people, he realized how talented the gentile people were. *Where did they learn their crafts? How can they be so cruel?* he wondered as he spied on a few men who were busy creating many beautiful items. A few men were diligently knapping out blades and spearheads, while a few others were chiseling little pipestone figurines. Then Moki noticed something strange, something that he had never seen before. He slid over and stood behind a man who was pounding on a thin strip of mica. Twisting it in front of him, Moki realized that the man was pleased with this work when he saw his reflection bouncing back.

Without warning, one of the giants turned toward the other two and drew his knife from his sheath, holding it upright, speaking in a strong Keltic accent. He said, "If he so much as looks at her, I'll rip out his heart and feed it to my hounds."

The lodge became quiet. The music and singing stopped. The little girls who were working nearby retreated to the opposite side of the shelter.

"Balor, you're a fool. He's the king's son," grunted one of the giants who remained on the bench.

"I won't allow it. She's mine. She loves me—not him," responded Balor.

The man sitting in the center of the bench swung forward and stood up. He stared at Balor as he walked a step toward him. Bending forward, coming face to face, eyes blazing, he was not happy with his friend's words; and he was preparing to fight. Pulling his monstrous knife from its sheath, holding it in front of him, he pointed its blade toward Balor as he growled, "You utter the words of a fool. Heed this warning, my friend. If you leave this place and take Ethane' with you, we will hunt you down, and you will suffer a long slow death!"

Without warning, the last giant stood up. He towered over the other two men. Standing approximately ten feet tall and weighing close to six hundred pounds, he was covered with red hair. He was agitated by this conversation. He stomped toward the door, picked up a large fifteen-foot spear, and hammered its base down into the dirt. Holding the shaft close to him, he said, "Balor, you are no match for my wrath. Stop speaking these words before I get angry. No one will go against our prince and his woman."

Seeing and hearing enough, deciding that Laurel wasn't in this community shelter, raising his hand Coahoma flashed a signal to Moki and Fala to meet outside. He was ready to leave this place. He wanted to find his teacher and return home. He had seen enough.

As Coahoma turned, he thought that he saw a shadow, moving across the room. He hoped that it was his imagination. As he exited the lodge to rally with his brothers, he prayed, "Please, I don't want a ghost to follow us home!"

Streaming with excitement, moving from side to side, Fala asked, "Did you see those giants? Did you see how tall they were? What did you think about their teeth? They have so many teeth that they can hardly talk. No wonder these lodges are so tall. Those men are monsters!"

The memory of the shadow lingered in Coahoma's mind. Looking around, seeing the thick haze of the blowing and drifting snow, with a nod, Coahoma said, "Let's find Laurel and go home. Didn't Wenonah say that her lodge was surrounded by the skulls of dead men?"

"Yes, she did," Moki said.

"Good, let's find those skulls and get her," Fala said as he turned in a circle, looking for these landmarks.

The boys walked around the side of another large dwelling when Coahoma spotted it. It was Morrigan's lodge. It was humongous. It was covered with grass, bark, and mud, and it was taller and wider than her neighbors. Just as Wenonah had described it, her lodge was surrounded by a menagerie of human and animal skulls.

Huddling together, the boys trudged across the clearing. They pressed through the blinding wind and pelting snow to reach this dreadful lodge. Remaining quiet as they passed beside the row of severed skulls, Coahoma saw the fear rising inside his friends as they passed between them. He didn't know what made him look, but he gazed at a frozen and withering head as he walked past it. It seemed to shout, "Go back or be prepared to accept your fate!" Coahoma was relieved when it faded from sight.

As he rounded the side of Morrigan's lodge, he was happy to see that it blocked the wind and snow. He looked at its odd exterior and wondered if he had made the right decision by allowing his friends to join him there. *If I die tonight, then this is my fate*, he thought. *But by what right do I have to escort my friends to their deaths?*

As a feeling of glum overshadowed his sense of adventure, Coahoma spotted a tiny silver line that lead inside. With the flick of his wrist, "She's here," he signaled to his blood brothers. He was relieved to know that she was inside.

"I'm going in over there," Coahoma whispered, stilling his nerves as he prepared to enter. However, before he could push against the wall and enter, he sensed that something terrible was about to happen.

He saw that his friends were feeling the same way. Wanting to relieve the tension, he hit his fist on to his chest and gently whispered, "I am the leader of the ghosts that haunt this village." Coahoma removed his feather from the back of his headband and stuffed it in front. "I am not afraid of anything."

Moki and Fala restrained their laughter. Smiling as they watched Coahoma's childish antics, they knew that he was attempting to reduce their anxiety. They knew that he was using his shamanic skills to increase their confidence.

Then without warning, a shadow lofted from its hiding place, ripped across the clearing, and plowed straight into Coahoma. It knocked him off his feet, and he fell belly side up into a huge show drift.

CHAPTER 6

The Gatekeeper

King Gann
An elite Allewegi who rules over the mighty Ohi:Yo' River Valley.

Coahoma recalled her words, "Stay focused and listen with your heart, not with your eyes," as he pressed his hands into the snow and stood up. Wishing Pontiac was there to protect him, he knew that he was on his own. *What other choice did I have?* he wondered as he nodded, signaling his brothers to gather beside him. Knees bent, legs apart, hands up, truly the son of a chief, he waited for this demon to show itself.

Worrying about the danger that they were in, Coahoma glanced at his two blood bothers—his two best friends—and saw that they were all right. But after years of training with his old teacher, learning to walk and talk to the spirits, he was irritated with his inability to locate this fleeting phantom. Determined to stay alive, he noticed the subtle way that his brothers moved and the tension that gripped their souls that they too felt the presence of death lingering nearby. "Be still," he recalled her words as he stood motionless, listening to the sounds of the moaning wind.

Coahoma felt sick, wondering if they would survive the next assault, but there was little that he could do now. Ignoring the bleating cries of his heart, watching the wind as it whipped the snow into swirling streams of white, he wondered how his mother and father would react to the untimely news of his death as he felt a tap on his left shoulder. *So it starts*, he thought as he reached up and slowly slid his hand across his shoulder. Just as he felt his braid against the palm of his hand, he felt another tap on his right. "Don't panic," he repeated to himself as he turned around to confront this horrifying black entity.

Just as Coahoma broke rank, Moki and Fala noticed the tension that pulsed through his face. Eyes wide open, not breathing, muscles taut, they instantly knew that something was terribly wrong. Without speaking a word, he screamed, "Something is behind me!" to them. Preparing for the worse, Moki's and Fala's hearts skipped a beat as they slowly turned around to meet their fate.

Floating only a few feet away, they saw the grotesque apparition of a teenage boy who was not much older than themselves. And he was staring back at them through his dead hollow eyes. Standing their ground, the blood brothers noticed an unnatural light that intensified the repulsiveness of his sunken eyes, broken nose, and gapping jaw. Stifling their gut reactions to flee, the boys took a single step backward when they spotted a thick stream of dark gurgling blood that oozed from his mouth and flowed down the front of his heavy leather tunic. They noticed that his hair was much like theirs, but it fell into thick bloody mats over his shoulders and down his chest. And the front of his tunic was ripped away, displaying his bare skin underneath. Glancing down at his heavy fur-lined boots, they saw that they were caked with a thick layer of mud and blood. Worst of all, when he moved, they saw that the top of his skull was missing, causing his skin to sag over his brow, casting a wretched gloom around him.

Her words were "When you see a demon, one so hideous that it clouds your heart with fear, close your eyes and calm yourself. Things aren't always as they seem. You must be brave and find out why it approaches . . ."

Following her lesson, Coahoma shouted, "Who are you? What do you want with us?"

Unscathed by Coahoma's outburst, the ghost raised his broken arm and said, "I am a brother of the Erie tribe. My name is Donehogawa." He placed his hand to the top of his head as he angrily spat, "Those nasty giants held me down and sawed off the top of my skull. I have looked for it, but I can't find it anywhere. Can you help me find it?"

Moki's heart ached for this pitiful boy as he listened to his pleas. Wanting to assist, he glanced over at Coahoma. "Maybe I can find out where his skull is . . . ," Moki said as he saw a startled expression flash across Coahoma's face. He realized that his friend was uncomfortable with his words by the way that he shook his head "No." However, Moki understood that Coahoma was troubled by his lack of training and the absence of his teachers, but this didn't matter to him. He wasn't afraid. As he pushed his boyish fears aside, disregarding Coahoma's warning, he stepped forward and said, "I am an empath. I want to help you find your skull. But to do this, you must let me touch you."

Moki knew, by the way that Donehogawa dropped his head and arched his neck, that he accepted his terms. When Moki saw the hideous boy lift his mangled arm and twist his hideous bent and blackened fingers out toward him, he drew in one last breath, bracing himself for what he was about to see. Stilling his nerves, he closed his eyes as he reached forward and clasped the hideous ghost's ghastly arm. Spinning through a long corrugated tunnel that linked the two, Moki found himself deep inside Donehogawa's mind.

Coahoma impatiently stood beside Moki as he watched the color drain from his friend's face, and he knew, by the way that he struggled for each breath, that he was suffering. Coahoma was worried when he saw a stream of tears flowing down the sides of Moki's face. When he began to tremble and to cry out loud, worrying for his sanity, Coahoma broke the tie that Moki had with this ghost. As he shook his friend, he repeated, "It's all right, Moki . . . Moki, come back!"

Moki stopped shivering, and after a short time, he woke up. He recognized Coahoma and Fala, wide-eyed and nervously standing beside him. Sharing Donehogawa's horrible memory, Moki said, "I left in the middle of the night. It was during the hot days of summer, and I traveled by moonlight. This was so that I could hide my whereabouts from the giant warriors who chased us from our lands. I heard the pleas of my mother and father, calling to me to come back, but I ignored them. I felt pride in my decision to play this game, to sneak back onto our land, and take some of our flint that we once called ours. But I was foolish and entered the forest before the sun set. And I didn't see the giant who approached me from behind. The next thing I remember I was tied to a pole in the center of their village. I saw a raven flying over me, and he screamed, 'Poor boy . . . poor boy . . . You are in the Nahullo's land.' Then he said, 'Poor boy . . . poor boy . . . Say your prayers . . . and prepare to die.' Coahoma, I was bound so tightly that I couldn't move, couldn't think. A bunch of giant men and women surrounded me. They were dressed in the strange clothes, wearing horns on their heads, shaking rattles and beating drums. I was terrified. Then this beast approached, carrying a metal blade. He looked like a wolf, and they called him Lugh. He drew his knife, and without warning, he bent over and sliced his blade across my throat . . . That's when I heard you calling me. Coahoma, I didn't see where they put his skull, but I think that it is still here, somewhere."

Worried about his friend, Fala leaned forward and whispered, "Moki, are you okay?"

Coahoma saw the pain that flowed through Moki's eyes and heard the sadness in his voice as he spoke. He knew that Moki was serious when he said, "Coahoma, we have to find Donehogawa's skull and return it to him, or he will never be able to leave this place."

Seeing Moki's devotion to this pitiful spirit, Coahoma said, "I give you my word. We will help you find your skull." He didn't know how they were going to keep this promise, but he knew that they had to try.

Clinching his mangled fist over his festering heart, signaling his appreciation, Donehogawa said, "My name means '*he who guards the gate at sunset.*' This is where you will find me—beside the front gate." Then he vanished from sight.

Fala was the first to speak. Obviously distressed, he asked, "Coahoma, where is your feather?"

Reaching up, rubbing his hand across the top of this head, "It's gone," he said as he stroked his hair in disbelief. "The wind must have swept it away when I fell." Turning his attention toward the lodge, Coahoma's voice trailed off as he spoke. "I am going in and get Laurel. Both of you, stay out here and stand guard. I won't be long . . ." Moving ever so cautiously, Coahoma disappeared from sight. He was eager to find his old teacher, but more importantly, he wanted to see this nasty red-haired witch that lived inside.

Wanting to see what was inside, Moki said, "Fala, stay here and stand guard for us. I will go inside and help Coahoma find Laurel so we can leave this place." Before Fala could respond, Moki faded from sight, leaving Fala outside to fend for himself.

Fala hoped that the uneasy feeling in the pit of his stomach would fade as he remained outside, isolated and alone. It wasn't long before Fala felt a warm rush of rank air on the back of his neck as the tiny hairs on his arms began to rise. He wasn't alone, and he knew it. Stifling his fears, Fala turned to see what was behind him. He saw the dead eyes of Donehogawa staring back. Angrily, he spat, "Donehogawa, what are you doing here? Why aren't you guarding the gate?"

He knew that something was wrong when Donehogawa stared toward the front gate and said, "King Gann and his son, Prince Sangann, are coming here to see Lugh and Morrigan, but be warned, my friend. The king can see the spirits of our dead who walk among these walls." As he faded from sight, he howled, "Hurry, warn your friends before it's too late!"

Fala knew, by the way that Donehogawa twisted his mangled body and the tone in which he spoke, that he was serious. Wanting to issue this message to his friends, Fala stilled his nerves as he plunged inside to find his friends. As his eyes adjusted to the dank dwelling, he found Laurel standing right in front of him, but before he could say a word, she nodded a finger and flinched her head toward the scene that was quietly unfolding.

Smelling the strong scent of lavender and sage, Fala felt secure as he settled beside Laurel. When he moved backward, away from the heavy aroma, she reached over and latched onto him. She held on to Fala until he adjusted to the intoxicating fumes, causing him to forget Donehogawa's news about the king.

Comforted by the sight of his blood brothers and elderly teacher, Coahoma settled into the shadows of this vast circular-shaped dwelling. *Their homes are so different than ours*, he thought as he looked around. Watching his friend from a distance, he saw Fala arching his neck as he examined the heavy beams that crisscrossed throughout this lodge.

Impressed by their work, Coahoma knew that Fala would relay this information to his father.

Coahoma was amazed by the large roaring fire that burned in the center of this room. Even though, it was much like the fires that they built, it was still different from theirs. They trimmed the edges of their pit with a thick layer of heavy rounded gray rocks, and on the ground around the rocks was an attractive layer of shiny black slate.

Coahoma wondered what his father would think as he watched Morrigan untie a small strap that held her hair in place. Dropping her head, she allowed her long red mane streaked with gray to flow forward. Then with a quick jerk, she flung her head backward, whipping her wild red hair over her head, allowing it to settle down at the center of her back. Standing nearly seven feet tall, she had ruddy wrinkled ivory white skin, dark piercing green eyes, red eyebrows, and a delicately rounded face with a slanted forehead. When she moved her hands, they noticed that she had a nicely shaped thumb, but to their surprise, she had six fingers.

Signaling to Coahoma, capturing his attention, Moki excitedly pointed to his fingers, emphasizing his discovery of her sixth finger.

"Yes." Coahama nodded. He had seen it too.

Looking over toward Fala, seeing his signal, he asked, "Is she a witch?"

"Yes." Coahama nodded with a slight shake of his head. This is the witch that Wenonah called Morrigan and the man, sitting quietly on the ground beside the fire with a blanket draped around him, was clearly Lugh.

Morrigan walked over to a shelf and pulled a heavy shawl from it and threw it around her shoulders. Then she walked over to Lugh, grabbing him by his arm. "Lugh, come with me and lie down," she said as she struggled to lift him.

Spoiled since birth, hotheaded and cunning, the long jagged purple scar that ran down the side of his left cheek was a symbol of Lugh's dedication to his king. Marred by deformities, his thick rounded skull, regal tattoos, six-fingered hands and toes, missing teeth, and eight-foot stature placed him in an elite group of Allewegi. A warrior at heart, wielding a sword and blade was as natural to him as eating or breathing, but his lust for power was elevated one day when he lay wounded in battle and his spirit lifted up. As he looked down, seeing himself bleeding and unconscious, a handsome she-wolf appeared and whispered to him promises of a life filled with bliss. Running side by side through the

SHERRY COTTLE GRAHAM

singing forest, she showed him the wondrous powers that lay hidden within her world. On that day, when Lugh woke from his coma, his obsession to become a "wolf" began.

Now reduced to a shell of a man, Morrigan gently coached him to lie down on his thick fur bed that was padded underneath with a thick layer of dry grass. Looking at her dying husband, Morrigan bowed her head, allowing a thick wave of her disheveled reddish hair to settle as she whispered, "Don't fret, Lugh. I know where your spirit is, and I WILL return it to you! I will bring this man that is called Pontiac and his old medicine woman that he loves so dearly here to our village. We will call upon the mighty Belenus to return your soul, and we will rejoice when you lob off their heads."

Seeing the expressions that flashed across her students' faces, Laurel smiled and spun a finger in a clockwise direction beside her right ear, sending them a message that Morrigan was crazy.

Fala caught Moki's attention, showing his teeth, and then jerking his head toward Morrigan. He asked "What about her teeth?"

Moki hoped that she would speak or yawn or do something so that he could see them. He was pleasantly surprised when Morrigan shouted, "Ethane' . . . Ethane', come here!" He knew, without a doubt, like the other giants that they had seen, she too had birows of teeth.

Soon, a tall slender girl entered the room. She was wearing a heavy hip-length black mink jacket with an attached hood that was softly cradled onto the center of her back. She wore a meticulously handwoven red and white checkered shirt underneath her jacket and a dark suede skirt that draped slightly above her knee-high fur-lined boots.

When she entered the dank dimly lit room, Coahoma noticed that the energy inside the room changed when she pushed the heavy curtain aside and walked inside. As soon as he saw Ethane', something sparked deep inside him. Looking at her, he couldn't understand how someone so beautiful could be the daughter of these two wicked parents. It was difficult for him to confirm her age, but she had to be around his age, maybe fourteen or fifteen. She had a thick long mane of blond hair that fell in long flowing strands below her waist. The Mighty Spirit acknowledged his existence inside her sparkling deep blue eyes that blended in perfect harmony with her stunning blue aura and pale white skin.

When she raised her hand to brush a few of her locks away from the side of her face, he noticed that her six-fingered hands were rough and stained black, reflecting the harsh life that she had to endure. He looked at her flattened forehead, wondering how anyone could do such a harsh procedure to a child. As Coahoma studied the conical shape of her skull, being a healer, he realized that the binding procedure that she suffered had affected her eyes, causing them to cross ever so slightly, adding an extra touch of mystery to her essence.

Love was a feeling that Coahoma knew well. He loved his family, the forest, the Mighty Spirit, the plants, and animals. He loved all of these living things that lived upon the Great Mother's breast. However, a strange feeling kindled deep inside him as he beheld the vision of this stunning six-foot tall blond-haired giant teenage girl. Then he felt an unfamiliar weight crushing his chest, forcing the air from his lungs. Struggling to breathe, his cheeks and neck began to flush with excitement as a tingling sensation pulsated through his heart, ending in the sensitive pit of his loins. He was falling in love, and he couldn't stop it.

Coahoma knew Ethane' was worried about her father by the delicate way that she moved and spoke. Then when he heard her call, "Mum, can I help? Will Papa be okay?" he felt a chime deep inside his heart as he listened to her speak. Her thick accent and the odd way that she formed her words in his eyes only added to her beauty. He wondered, *How did I miss the odd way that her teeth pressed against her lips?* But it didn't matter. He was now entirely under her spell. He knew it was wrong, but he didn't care.

"Morrigan, Lugh, are you here?" a baritone voice called from the front of the lodge.

Recognizing the king's voice, Morrigan swung around, lifted the corner of a blanket and disappeared. When she entered the front room, standing before her were two towering blond-haired men with long snow-covered mustaches and wind-chapped red faces. She recognized both men. Rushing forward, she showered greetings of welcome to King Gann and his son, Prince Sangann. Standing knee high beside these two eight-foot tall leaders was Kenji, the king's favorite spiritual guide and healer. The three leaders stood beside the front door, shaking and stomping a thick layer of snow from their heavy winter clothes. The men pushed their hoods off their heads, pulled off their fur-lined hats, and slid off their gloves.

King Gann said, "Morrigan, we have traveled a long way to meet with you and Lugh. Where is he? We are here to make arrangements for the wedding of Sangann and Ethane'. My son wants to marry her at the upcoming summer solstice if you agree to this union."

Watching Morrigan and her family from the hidden recesses, the young spies moved through the sidewalls. They wanted to learn more about these strangers as she greeted them. They slid into new hiding places, except for Coahoma. Lagging behind, watching Ethane', wanting to reach out and touch her, Coahoma wished that he could appear and tell her that things will be all right; but he knew that this was a foolish fantasy. However, he kept his silent vigil hidden in the background, learning about her way of life as well as enjoying the calming effect that her charisma held on him.

The sound of a wailing baby filled the room. Silently, Ethane' waited for her mother to tell her to help her baby brother.

"Ethane', get Conan and feed him," Morrigan commanded.

Lifting the curtain, Ethane' quickly passed through it, moving toward the crying child. As she moved, Coahoma followed her. Keeping his distance, he crept behind her as she walked into the adjoining room. Looking around, Coahoma realized that this was where she slept. This area was heated by a small central fire, and it had five thick grass mat beds that were covered with a thick layer of colorful blankets. He saw the boy who was standing in the corner of the room, leaning against a wooden barrier, watching his sister as she approached.

As Ethane' lifted him into her arms, she whispered, "Conan, are you hungry? Sangann and his father are here, so you must not cry."

Coahoma loved the way that Ethane' hugged her brother, soothing him to be quiet. He saw her gentle nature as she pressed her fingers around his bindings, trying to relieve a bit of the pressure that it was causing to his skull. Being a healer, Coahoma wondered, *How can these people do such a harsh thing to their children?*

Conan was wearing a thick fur-lined jacket, long pants, and fleece-lined moccasins that laced up around his ankles to protect him from the chill that radiated through his lodge. He had a thick red mane of hair, green eyes, a rounded face, six fingers; and he was nearly three and a half feet tall.

He looks just like his mother, Coahoma thought as he watched them from the shadows. *But his aura looks like his sister's.*

As Ethane' stood near him, bouncing her little brother in her arms, she took the time that she needed to calm herself. She knew that her mother would ask her to join them in the front living quarters. She also knew that her parents were pleased with her betrothal to the king's son. Soon, she would become a duchess and rule over the Eastern Woodlands with her husband. Perhaps in a few years, she would become the queen and rule over this wild and glorious kingdom.

While gently tugging her brother on to her hip, tears welled in the eyes of Ethane'. She bent her head forward and whispered softly into her brother's ear, "Conan, can I tell you a secret?" Ethane' searched for the words that would betray her inner thoughts. She leaned forward and buried her face into his little chest as she recalled her mother's words, "We have given the king our consent for you to marry Sangann."

Ethane' knew that she was alone with her brother and that no one would hear her as she whispered, "I love Balor . . . not Sangann. I do not want to marry the prince nor do I want to rule over this land. I want to marry Balor, have his children and grow old with him—not Sangann. When the leaves return to trees, I am going to leave this place. Balor will take me far away from here, somewhere where no one will find us. When I am gone, I will think of you. Conan, I would rather die a thousand deaths and be staked to the outside gate than marry him. He doesn't love me. He never has and never will. He only wants my dowry . . ."

Stunned, flushed with anger, Coahoma was clearly in an emotional tug-of-war as he watched his first true love weeping. Feeling her pain, seeing her tears streaming down her face, standing beside her, helpless, wanting to comfort her, but he couldn't.

Confused, Coahoma wondered, *Why would her parents promise her to a man who doesn't love her? She doesn't love him. She loves Balor. What kind of man is Balor to hide a girl inside this dangerous forest? Could she ever love me?* Looking up, he continued to watch and listen, thinking, *I will help her! I am not sure how, but I will!*

Pooling tears streamed down her cheeks, streaking her face, dripping down on her fur jacket as she tugged Conan tightly to her breast, rocking back and forth, trying to soothe herself as well as her little brother. She wept. Knowing that she would be summoned into the front room, she stopped, wiping the tears from her swollen face, inhaling a long soothing deep breath, pushing the bitter thoughts from her mind; she was ready to greet her visitors.

SHERRY COTTLE GRAHAM

As Ethane' turned toward the curtain, Conan's aura began to glow in a bright blue, becoming so powerful that it lit up the room, looking directly at Coahoma, reaching out with both arms, signaling that he carry him.

Seeing Conan's motion, Ethane' turned around to see who Conan was signaling.

Realizing that Conan could see him anticipating every move of Ethane', Coahoma quickly slid backward into the dark recesses of her exterior wall. He wondered, *Did she see me?*

Standing quietly, Coahoma smelled the musty grass as he visualized her exotic beauty. He was thinking of her as he agonized over her current situation. He wanted to love her, but he knew that this was utterly hopeless. Then as she exited the room, he heard her ask, "Are those pesky spirits visiting you again? Do you want me to set up another dream catcher and trap them for you?"

When the room was quiet, Coahoma joined his brothers in the front room. He knew that they were still watching and listening to the conversations of these dangerous people. He carefully slid along the interior wall, stopping when he was close enough to reach out and touch her. Wanting to be near her, he grew careless with his movements. While he remained hidden in the shadows watching Ethane', he listened to the conversations that were taking place behind him.

King Gann and Prince Sangann were sitting at a large wooden table on the opposite side of Morrigan on seats that were made from the trunks of trees. They were growing loud and boisterous as they ate and talked about the wedding, gods, and their plans to seize control over the rivers that bordered the great Ohi:Yo' and the Misi-ziibi.

Then without warning, Morrigan stood up and called upon her god. "Oh, mighty Isis," she said, "Behold these powerful leaders who now sit here before you. Come join us, learn how they are defending your vision over this new land, and protect them as they sacrifice their blood to expand this mighty empire in your name."

Turning toward the king, "Your Highness, something tragic has happened to my husband," Morrigan said. "A young shaman who lives near the mouth of the Misi-ziibi has stolen his spirit. Dahey will talk to you about this problem. But on the day before this happened, Lugh told me that he had discovered another powerful section of land for Belenus.

He said that it is located somewhere in the swamplands, and that it is located on top of a small hill near the Atchafalaya River."

When the boys heard Morrigan's words, they knew that she was speaking of their land. The young spies looked over at Laurel. They watched her pull her hands up to her mouth and spread a smile on to her face. Baring her aging teeth, she pointed her wrinkled finger toward the ceiling and twirled it around. She sent them a message that these men were out of their demented minds if they think that they can seize control of their homeland.

Standing on top of a chair, positioned between the prince and the king, leaning against the large rustic table, Kenji raised his arm and firmly banged his clenched fist down on it. The tiny shaman demanded the royals' immediate attention, and he promptly received it. With every eye focused on him, he said in an ominous tone, "We must speak with caution because these walls have eyes."

Before he could say another word, the royals were distracted by Baby Conan. They watched the baby extend his arms toward the wall. They saw him flex his six fingers toward the spirit who stood nearby watching Ethane'. He cooed, "Hallo."

King Gann saw Coahoma. He yelled, "Kenji, get that boy standing beside Ethane'!" as he pointed toward him.

Kenji Jumped down from his lofty perch and disappeared from sight, reappearing as he rounded his obstacle. He ran in a pivoting motion as he bore down upon the startled Coahoma. With his right hand, he reached over his belly and on to his left hip. He drew a bizarre onyx dagger from its sheath under his jacket. As he masterfully aimed his deadly blade, he felt the thrill of death as he closed in on this strange boy who was standing near the wall.

Seeing the danger that Coahoma was in, changing into the crow as he sprung from his hiding place. Fala flew directly into the Kenji's face. He grabbed on to one of Kenji's copper earplugs with his sharp talons as he blinded him with his wings, hoping that Coahoma would run away.

A buck charged across the room, head down, antlers primed, running directly toward this tiny shaman. Moki plunged directly through him, knocking him to the ground. Kenji lost his dagger when he hit the dirt floor. As it spun away, Kenji crawled on his hands and knees in a desperate attempt to retrieve it. King Gann saw that Kenji was in trouble as he swung off his chair and ran forward to help his tiny friend.

Coahoma knew that the king was a well-honed warrior by the way that he moved and wielded his sword. Springing across the room in the form of a panther, Coahoma landed in front of the ivory and onyx weapon. He pressed his paw down on to the blade and snarled, "*Try and you die!*" Baring his teeth, the panther lowered his head and locked his merciless eyes on to Kenji's throat. He felt his ribs widen as he forced the cold moist air down into his powerful lungs. He dropped his incisor-laced jaws and blasted a series of powerful blood-curling roars ricocheting through the shaman's dwelling. He terrified everyone who could see and hear him, and he was ready to fight.

Just as King Gann and Morrigan approached, the boys heard three loud drum beats and Laurel's voice calling. "Come home . . . Your journey is over!"

CHAPTER 7

Twisting Fate

Chief Ituha
A Choctaw chief; Coahoma and Dakota are his sons and Sonoma is his mate.

Coahoma knew that he had changed as he spun through the long corrugated tunnel. As he entered his body, he briefly thought about Laurel's lessons about time and space and how she called them "an illusion," but today, he knew that his feelings weren't an illusion. His heart was filled with many painful memories of a foreign land. When he felt the cold damp ground beneath him and the chilly breeze blowing against his skin, his mind burned with visions of a charming girl named Ethane'. He recalled her haunting blue eyes, her charismatic smile, her secrets, her tears; all of these things created a throbbing feeling so deep inside him that it nearly choked off his ability to think, to breathe. But his anger at her elders was so intense that it sickened him when he thought about what he had seen and heard.

Coahoma listened to the soft patter of the drizzling rain beating on the surrounding foliage around him. As he calmed his mind, he knew his priorities, but this didn't ease his frustration. *She is my enemy. How can I love her?* He fretted. Trying to make sense of his feelings, he recalled Laurel's words, "When you have lost your way, still your mind and open your heart. And remember . . . Time is always your greatest ally."

Torn between love and rage, Coahoma fought to block these memories that came in waves, crushing against his heart. When he opened his eyes, he was relieved to see Laurel standing beside her raggedy old brown bear, holding a drum in her hands. He was home. He knew that he had left as a reckless and immature teenage boy, and he had returned a man.

As he watched his blood brothers awaken from their journey, his thoughts shifted to Donehogawa. *How am I going to help that poor guy?* he wondered as he listened to the sounds of the singing forest. *He will have to wait*, Coahoma thought as his focus returned to Tiponi. *Anyway, what can I do to help him right now?* he wondered.

"Coahoma, are you all right?" Fala asked as he ran up, grabbing his forearms. "Ah, did you see those giant men? Did you hear the things that they were saying?" Fala asked.

Then Moki joined them, asking, "That little guy was fast, wasn't he? But we sure showed him, didn't we?"

Before Laurel could intervene, Fala began to prance, punching his arms up high over his head, hopping and swinging in circles, bending, twisting, swaying, and smiling as he chanted, "Ah, we did it. We did it. We sneaked into the witch's house, and she didn't catch us . . ."

"Fala, stop," Coahoma commanded. Coahoma wasn't surprised by Fala's passionate outburst. In fact, he was waiting for it as this was typical of his bubbly personality, but it wasn't time to be boasting about things that ended on a sour note, at least for him. Coahoma said, "We have much to do. Remember, Morrigan knows where we live, and she has made threats against us and our land."

Fala said, "You've had a long day, huh, Coahoma? You were knocked down, lost your feather, and about killed by a man who was about half your size. I think that the Mighty Spirit was with you tonight," as he punched Coahoma's arm.

Forgetting about being hungry and tired, Coahoma said, "I owe my life to you. I would be walking with Elsu if you hadn't stopped those witches . . ."

"Yea, but when you changed into the panther and roared, it even scared me, and I knew that it was you," Moki said, smiling as he crossed his arms and leaned back on to his right leg. Clinching his fists, "Let them try to chase us from our lands," he said. "Wait till your father hears about this . . ."

The old medicine woman permitted the boys a few moments to talk about their personal experiences that they had, but it was time to move on. *Perhaps,* she thought, *in time, they will realize what this trip has taught them.* As she watched them from the corner of her eye, she thought, *Ahh, they are learning that to be a man is much more than just hunting and fighting, but I hope that Ituha won't be too angry when he learns that his son disobeyed my orders and placed his friends in danger. Ah, but he was young once too. Soon, he will see the good that he will bring to us, but we had better go before it gets dark.* She could see, by the way that they responded when she beat one loud beat on her drum and said, "Boys, we must go," that they were ready to leave. "We have much to do before we can talk about our journey into the Alli's land."

But before she led them out from under the old tree, she walked over to Fala, holding the beautifully carved black, yellow, and red drum in her hands. She gently handed it to him. She said, "Fala, this is yours. Your quick thinking saved Coahoma's life today. When you sit around your fire and tell your stories to your children and your children's children, beat on this drum to remind yourself about your swift thinking and courage that you displayed to us today."

Fala took the drum and slightly rotated it in his hands. As he inspected its meticulous carvings, he asked, "Laurel, where did you get this?"

Twisting her mouth into an odd smile, she said, "I found this drum in a lodge where three giant warriors were arguing. I thought it would make a good reminder of this dangerous game that played with the Alli. What do you think? Do you like it?"

Fala examined the drum. He reached out and stroked its smooth skin. He slapped a single beat on its surface to hear the rich sound that it created. Smiling, Fala said, "I saw the man who was playing this drum when those giant warriors began to argue." Fala looked over at his elder as he asked, "Laurel, when are you going to teach us to move things when we are in the Spirit World?"

"Ah," Coahoma said, "I wanted to bring some flint back to Father."

Smiling, she said, "You have much to learn before I can teach you these things." They saw her mood change when she said, "Pick up your weapons. Coahoma, walk beside me. From now on, you must be alert. Watch the shadows and be aware of everything that is around you. Morrigan will be coming back soon, and she will bring her spies with her."

Signaling the boys to follow her, she led them out and into the rain. Coahoma was walking on her right side, and Lagundo was on her left. As they began their trudge home, Lagundo led the small group through the gloomy forest. When they entered the field and began their trek up the shallow hill, they spotted Tunghak and Awock soaring overhead.

Worried about what she would find inside her lodge, she was silent as they trudged along. Coahoma knew, by the way that she moved her eyes and breathed, that she was walking with one foot in the Spirit World, listening to her grandfather. When they reached the midpoint of the incline, she turned to Coahoma. She said, "Coahoma, listen very carefully to me. Our success depends on our ability to work together. Moki and Fala, this includes you too. Do you understand?"

"What do you want me to do?" Coahoma asked. His cheeks flushed with pride as he looked at her, waiting for his orders, hoping that she was going to send him back into the Land of Giants. *Maybe I'll get to go back and spy on Ethane'*, he wished as he watched Laurel draw in a breath and waited for her instructions. He wanted to see Ethane' again, now more than ever, but his sense of loyalty to Tiponi was stronger than any feelings that he had for this mystical girl.

"I want you to cut a large hole in the back of my lodge. Do not make any noise. Do this when I play my drum and chant to Tiponi. She must not see or hear you," Laurel said.

Laurel noticed the disappointment that rippled through him by the way that the edges of his mouth and his shoulders dropped. She heard his frustration when he asked, "How big do you want me to make this hole?"

It didn't matter how wet, cold, or tired he was. He loved her, and he would do whatever she wanted, and he wouldn't complain; but as he walked beside Laurel, his mind drifted back to the Land of Flint. He smelled the musty odors of the lodge of Ethane', hiding inside the shadows, watching as she rocked her little brother, and listening to her secrets.

"Make it large enough for Pontiac to crawl through," Laurel said, disrupting his dream. "Then go home and wait for Pontiac to meet you there. Do you have any questions?" Laurel asked.

Coahoma asked, "Is Morrigan with Tiponi?"

Pausing for a moment, her eyes glazed as she listened to a message that only she could hear. "No," she said, "but she is on her way."

"Can we stop her?" Coahoma asked.

"Boys, come here," Laurel said.

Coahoma knew, by the way that she squinted and licked her lips, that she was preparing to share some grim news with them. Waiting for her to gather her thoughts, he listened to Lagundo's lumbering footsteps and his deep bronchiolar breaths that came in strong rushes of warm air as Fala and Moki silently moved beside him. When she lifted her head, the rain stopped; and when she began to speak, the clouds parted, leaving only the wind to shield her words from the surrounding forest.

"Boys," she said, "today, you followed a silver cord into the heart of the Allewegi. You looked upon the faces of our enemy, and you saw how their gods made them very different than us. And their magic is very strong, maybe stronger than ours—this, I don't know. But I do know that Morrigan's spirit travels here to spy on Pontiac through the eyes of a sick child, and Lugh—the man that they call the Ol' Wolf—was here this morning, leading that pack of wolves. I knew there was something strange about that animal when I shot my arrow into him, but through my arrogance, I commanded Pontiac to eat that precious piece of the wolf's heart that holds the essence of Lugh's spirit. Now through the power of our Great Mother, Lugh and Pontiac are fighting for control over Pontiac's soul. But I believe Pontiac is strong enough to win this fight with the Ol' Wolf. And if I am right, then the man that we saw in the lodge will not survive much longer without it. Morrigan also knows this, and she will do whatever it takes to retrieve it."

Ignoring her wet clothes and aching body, she continued, "Boys, our first battle is to save Tiponi, and to do this, we must travel in between both worlds." Arching forward so that she could look directly into their eyes, she said, "Today, Morrigan saw your animal spirits. So from now on,

SHERRY COTTLE GRAHAM

you MUST NOT change into them while you are in Tiponi's or Pontiac's presence. Our success now depends on keeping this a secret." She patted the side of Lagundo's head and said, "Moki, here, take my spear. I want you and Fala to go home and stay put. I will send for you when I need you."

"Come on, Lagundo. Let's go home," Laurel said as she continued her trek. Coahoma sprinted up to her side. She continued, "Coahoma, I want you to run ahead and wait in Lagundo's lean-to for my signal. Then after you finish cutting the small opening, go home, eat, rest, and wait for us. Tell your father about our journey and tell him that I will meet with him before the bewitching time is upon us. He must not leave your lodge. Can you do this?"

Yes, of course, I can do this, Coahoma thought as he prepared to race ahead to carry out her orders, but when his foot hit the ground, the bottom of his moccasin slipped out from under him when he stepped forward on it. He fell face down into a small puddle of mud.

Before Laurel could react, Moki and Fala sprinted around her. They grabbed Coahoma's arms and lifted him back onto his feet.

Stepping into the grassy fringes of the muddy path, Laurel and the boys looked at Coahoma as he looked back. Restraining their temptations to laugh lasted only a few moments when Fala broke the silence. He laughed and laughed until tears streamed down the sides of his face.

Standing before them, Coahoma had dirt packed in between his teeth, in his braids, and on his clothes. He was drenched from head to toe in mud. It was caked in his lashes and eyebrows. It was dripping off the end of his nose and running down the sides of his face and into this mouth, leaving only the whites of his eyes showing in the cloudy afternoon haze.

Coahoma's eyes flickered with anger as Fala laughed. Then he realized that Laurel and Moki were standing still, donning strange smiles, not breathing as they gritted their teeth. He realized how silly he must look, thinking it is good to laugh, thinking, *But why me?* as he bent over and spitting out the mud that was grinding in between his teeth. *But Mother is not going to be happy . . .*

Within a few seconds, Laurel was able to regain her composure as she asked, "Are you okay?"

"Yes," he said as he spat out the gritty dirt. He said, "I don't feel as hungry now."

"Good, let's go," said Laurel, turning in the direction, looking toward her lodge. "We have much to do."

Fala looked at Laurel and asked, "Can we run home?" Raising his arm, Fala pointed toward the western border of the grassy meadow toward the dense cedar forest. He said, "We live on the far side of those trees. We can be home before it gets dark." Then he added as Laurel granted them permission to leave, "We will meet you tonight at Coahoma's lodge."

"Here, take this," Laurel said as she handed Moki her lance. "You may need it. Tell the chief that Pontiac will bring Coahoma home."

Laurel watched Moki and Fala run through the tall grass, breaking a trail as they ran. She quietly stood for a few moments, watching them as they plodded through the waist-high thrushes. She knew that they were headed into the scariest part of their forest.

"Coahoma, I hope that they can make it through the forest before it gets dark. It's a scary place to get lost in. They only have a few arrows and my long spear to protect themselves against any wild animals that they might face."

Watching his friends sprinting through the weeds, Coahoma said, "Ah, they'll be all right. They will follow an old animal trail that leads to the other side—close to their lodges."

The wise old woman nodded in the direction of the boys' lodges. Laurel asked, "Coahoma, do you know that a wolf can smell blood from here to where they live?"

Forcing a smile on to his face, Coahoma said, "Don't worry, they are too hungry to stop. I bet you that they will be warming themselves beside their fires before you reach your lodge." Coahoma noticed that the forest was getting darker. "Perhaps, we should leave," he said, but before she could respond, he asked, "How are we going to fight her?"

Laurel flushed with joy when she heard his response. She knew that he was maturing into a powerful shaman, asking specific questions at the perfect time, seeing his leadership coming to life. She said, "We will use magic, trickery, and illusion against her. And it will take all of us working together to defeat this one."

Laurel raised her hand and with a stern tone, she said, "Lagundo, go home!" But her old bear sensed that something was wrong and refused to leave.

Coahoma smiled as he waited for his next set of orders. She said, "Coahoma, run along. Lagundo will walk with me." When Coahoma had taken a few steps, she said, "Bad bear . . . come . . . Let's go home."

Laurel watched Coahoma as he scampered up the path toward her lodge. As he moved, she wondered, *What is different about Coahoma?* She studied his aura against the lavender haze of the evening sky. She saw that it was beaming in bright streaks of yellow and pink. *Oh my*, she thought. *That boy is in love! Who is he in love with? Ah, this could bring big trouble!*

It wasn't long before Laurel reached the outer edge of her home. Looking over at Lagundo's lean-to, she saw Coahoma lying on the ground with his legs bent upright, right leg hoisted over the left, kicking his muddy moccasin up and down into the air, staring into its thatch roof. Pointing her finger toward his shelter as she gazed at the pink highlights that were radiating around him, she said, "Lagundo, go lie down and listen to Coahoma's love songs."

Knowing that food and water were always available near his bed, Lagundo happily strutted toward his lean-to that was positioned behind to the northern corner of her lodge. Anticipating food, he picked up his pace as he trotted toward it.

When Laurel approached the door to her dwelling, she felt her blade vibrating against her leg. She knew that it was warning her of something ominous. Then a strange breeze blew across her, sending an eerie chill down her spine, causing the tiny hairs on the back of her neck to rise. She knew that a trickster was nearby, and it was watching her. She turned and looked across the grassy meadow. She spotted a black vapor streaking across the tops of the high grass, moving toward Moki and Fala. *They will have to fight this by themselves*, she thought as she gently pulled her door open and stepped inside.

As her eyes grew accustomed to the dim lighting, she smelled the sweet aroma of goose, cooking over a hickory fire. She saw the lights of her fire, flickering against the faces of Alawa, Nashoba, and Pontiac as the door closed behind her.

Alawa was shocked by Laurel's appearance as she moved across the room. Alawa picked up a blanket that was folded across a wooden rack and gently draped it around Laurel's shoulders. Alawa asked, "Laurel, are you all right? Do you want me to make you some tea to warm you?"

"No, I am fine," Laurel responded as she looked around her lodge for Tiponi. She found the little girl sleeping on her bed in the far corner of her hut. When she saw the child, she knew that she had to get Alawa and Nashoba away from her. She moved in front of the child, placing herself between the parents and Pontiac. She asked, "Pontiac, how is Tiponi?"

"I pulled a gorging tick off her, and now I think that she is coming down with the spotted fever," Pontiac said as he looked at her thin wet hair. He sensed that something was wrong. He asked, "Where are those boys? Old woman, what took you so long to get here?"

Laurel saw the image of Lugh, surrounding Pontiac. Keeping her secrets, she said, "They are sitting beside the fire with their families. I was tired from my fight with the wolves, and I fell asleep under the magnolia." She knew that her greatest fight had just begun.

Listening carefully to Pontiac's responses and his movements, she realized that Pontiac was quickly losing his battle against Lugh. She knew that she had created a monster when Pontiac said, "Ol' woman, go and change into some dry clothes and get me some food. I am hungry."

What did I do? Laurel wondered. *How am I going to reverse this spell?* She saw and heard the difference in Pontiac. She felt sad as she walked over and stood beside her fire, warming herself against it flames. She wanted to know how strong Lugh's control was over Pontiac. But she couldn't bear to look at him as she asked, "Pontiac, are you going to wear your new Griffin mask tonight?"

Pontiac said, "Yea, ol' woman. Bring it to me and I will wear it."

His response created a surge of repulsion to explode in the pit of her stomach. Chasms of hot and cold clashed in her throat. She knew that this mask did not exist. Even if it did, Pontiac would never use it to treat a child.

Pulling the blanket around her neck, she motioned to Alawa and Nashoba to follow her. She said, "Come and walk with me. The rain has stopped. Tomorrow, I will need a few of Tiponi's favorite things." Then she turned and walked out into the grass and headed toward the path that swung over the western rise, leading down the hill to their village.

"Wait, Laurel," Nashoba called as she fled away, trying to distance herself from Pontiac. She wanted to move far away from him so that Pontiac wouldn't hear what she was about to say. Feelings of guilt were churning inside her as Nashoba grabbed on to her arm, forcing her to stop.

"Wait, what is wrong? This is not like you. Tell me what it is so I can help," he said as his breath rose in evenly spaced heaves. Harnessing her in place, she could feel the power in his hands as he gripped on to her arms and swung her around. She knew that he was the strongest warrior in their village, hearing the strength in his voice; she relaxed as her eyes met his.

Deciding not to disclose the intimate details of her secrets, at least not at this time, she looked at Nashoba and said, "Listen carefully and don't ask why. Take Alawa home. You must stay with her at your lodge, and I will come for you. Tiponi will need her favorite doll and blanket. I will collect these things when I come for you." Then she turned toward Alawa. She saw fear, swelling inside her eyes. She said, "Alawa, Tiponi will be all right. Now go home and rest. I will call you if I need you."

Studying her movements and hearing the tones of her words, Nashoba knew that she was hiding something from him. Flexing his chiseled jawline, he asked, "Do I need to take my daughter away from here?"

"No," she said, holding her position, trying to reassure him that Tiponi was perfectly safe in her lodge. She added, "She will live to an old age and have many children. We just need to keep Alawa away from her so the sickness doesn't jump into your unborn child."

Nashoba knew that she was keeping a secret about his daughter. This was not like her. Perhaps by telling the full truth, it might distress Alawa. He dropped his hands and backed away. Taking Alawa by the shoulders, he guided her toward the path. They walked a short distance down the hill and toward their village. He twisted around toward Laurel and said, "I will have Tiponi's things ready for you tonight."

Laurel knew that Nashoba would keep Alawa away from her lodge. She also knew that Pontiac would protect Tiponi because she housed the spirit of his mate. Even though he was forever trapped in Pontiac's body, she knew that Morrigan would be able to come and go as she pleased, and she would use this to her advantage.

As Laurel headed toward her lodge, she watched the twilight spill over her land. She watched the colors fade into shades of charcoal, and she knew that the blackness of the night will soon engulf her. Looking up, she saw a window open into the night sky. She saw Orion, Ursula, and Venus arrive against the backdrop of the twinkling stars, saturating the heavens like billions of finely polished diamonds. She listened to the sounds of the night creatures calling out reminders to her of their existence, and she heard a solitary ol' timber wolf howling in the distance, singing a song to his mate. This reminded her of her own mortality as she absorbed the awesomeness of her private world.

Standing a moment to gaze upon Orion, a sense of permanence washed over her as she knew that the warm days of spring were on their way. Standing in the darkness feeling the chilly breeze upon her cheeks, listening to Awock hooting in the distance, smelling the scent of fresh rain, knowing that her situation was dire, a personal sense of hope welled up in her. Pulling the blanket tightly around her shoulders, looking toward the tree line in a quiet positive tone, she said, "Yes, there has to be a solution. Why not? For every problem, there is always a solution. I have faced death many times before. This is not the first time, and it will not be the last. I will not stop until I make things right with Pontiac and save Tiponi. This, I promise."

Then she felt something brush up against her right side. Looking around, she saw the mud-streaked face of Coahoma looking back. He had washed his face in Lagundo's water pot, but he still was covered in a thick layer of dried mud.

"Coahoma," Laurel said, "all of our plans have changed."

Coahoma asked, "Why? What happened?"

Just then, the sound of a drum filled the night air as Pontiac began his ritual of chanting and drumming, working to drive the fever away from Tiponi. Singing in his rich tenor voice, his songs echoed through the meadow, filling the lodge with hope, hope that he will stop the fever, leaving Laurel with the problem of removing Morrigan's possession.

As the two stood in the dark shadows looking toward the fading shape of her lodge, Coahoma asked, "He loves her. I can hear it in his strange songs, but he sings words that I do not know."

"Yes, Coahoma. He is chanting the words of the white giants. Tiponi will be comforted by them. They are strong words," Laurel said as she listened to his song.

Coahoma turned, looking at Laurel. He asked, "Who are his gods?"

Smiling at Coahoma's questions, a sense of pride swelled inside her as she responded to his inquisitiveness. "They have many powerful gods. They call them Bridgett, Isis, Zeus, and many that I do not remember. But their gods are not as powerful as ours."

As Laurel stood beside Coahoma, the pines began to whisper in the breeze. Laurel immediately recognized that they were speaking to her.

Stepping over into their world, she heard them say, "Laurel, your young companions are lost and are running toward the swamp."

Laurel said, "Coahoma, we have to hurry! Moki and Fala are in trouble. Go tell your father that they are heading toward the swamp. Now run!"

CHAPTER 8

Missing Boys

Ceremonial Lance
A special lance that Laurel entrusts to Moki.

Moki wasn't surprised when Laurel handed her lance to him and told him to be careful. He knew, through the way that she expressed her words, that she didn't want him to take the shortcut through the forest, but he wasn't afraid. He had frequently traveled along this path, and he knew it well.

When she said, "Moki, here, take my spear. I want you and Fala to go home and stay put . . . ," he was grateful that she had entrusted it to him.

As he wrapped his hands around its smooth polished shaft, he knew how important it was to her. "I'll return it to her tomorrow," he vowed.

Moki gazed at the long shadows that stretched over the meadow as he ran across it with Fala, trailing behind him. He listened to the rustle of the weeds and smelled their rich aroma as he chiseled a thin trail through them for Fala to follow. Moki felt privileged to be part of this elite group, seeing and hearing things that others could only dream of. As he watched for snakes that might be slithering across his path, he recalled a story that Coahoma's father would often tell. Visions of an early morning in late spring filled his head. The chief was sitting beside him, listening to her stories. She was showing them how to quiet your mind and speak to the spirit of a plant, and how to ask for its help to heal a person. Then without warning, the chief stood up, walked over to her lance, and carried it back to them.

"Do you know how she got this lance?" he asked as he propped its shaft against the ground and gently leaned against it. His face softened. Pride flowed through his words as he sucked in a breath and began his story. "Many years ago," he said, "before you boys were born, Laurel's reputation as a great healer spread throughout our land." He smiled as he gazed down at the soft leather strips that were attached to it. He rubbed his hand lightly across the sacred symbols that were burned into its leather. Gathering his thoughts, he continued, "I still remember that chilly morning in early spring when a Natchez messenger came to our village. He said that his chief had heard many stories about the woman who walks with a bear. He wanted Laurel to come back to his village and bring her powerful medicine with her to heal the chief's son if I would allow it."

He recalled how Ituha looked over at Coahoma as he said, "I know the feeling that a father keeps inside his heart for his sons. So I ordered six of my strongest warriors to accompany her on her trip up the Misi-ziibi with the Natchez. I sent her in our best white birch canoes, and we dressed her in her finest beaded fur and feathered outfit. We filled one canoe with many of her plant medicines and amulets. They paddled for four days, taking only a few small breaks. When they reached the Natchez village, she discovered that the boy was verily alive." Ituha glanced over at Laurel. Smiling, he said, "The chief placed his faith in this old woman, but who truly knows the way of the Great Spirit better than her?"

Adjusting the angle of the lance, Moki recalled how Ituha sat down beside Coahoma and continued his story, holding it out to him. As Moki felt the weight and balanced the famous lance in his hands, he listened to the chief. He said, "Laurel said that the Natchez chief had built a large medicine hut for her on their sacred ground. When she entered it, she asked the chief to send in his best craftsmen to her. When they arrived, she ordered an unusual fire ring made with a certain number of rounded rocks, arranged in a certain order, stacked to a specific height, and the base had to be trimmed with a layer of flat rocks. She also ordered them to make a special cooking grate for her to make her teas, broths, and salves—like the one that you see here. She said that she sat beside the boy, beating her drum and singing to him. She wore her favorite mask—the one with a broad smile and funny-looking eyes carved in it. She rubbed salves on to him, took her sucking pipe, and sucked on his lower abdomen, pulling the demons from his weakened bowels. Eventually, she said that she was able to feed him her broth. She fed him with her little wooden spoon that she always carries inside her medicine bag. Eventually, she added quail eggs, mushrooms, and onions into his diet. But mostly, she prayed to the spirits of these plants to heal him. She said after that, the child's fever broke, and it wasn't long before he was walking with his father." Chief Ituha lifted the lance, holding it between his hands. He said, "This was a gift to Laurel from the great Natchez chief for saving his son."

Moki looked up and saw that he was getting closer to the entrance into the forest. He felt the brambles slapping against his leggings as he ran. He ignored the pain that these plants were inflicting on his hands and feet as he scored through them. He slowed down when he reached the timberline. As he broke a pathway through the brambles, looking for the narrow path that lay just on the other side, he stumbled across a small flock of mallards that were nesting nearby. As the ducks launched skyward, they distracted the boys as they frantically hoisted into the lavender sky, whooshing and quacking—they fled from their enemy.

His mother's words, "Demons roam inside the forest at night . . . ," haunted him as he waited for Fala to catch up.

Struggling to catch his breath, inhaling and exhaling in loud deep breaths, searching for a little spit to moisten the back of his parched throat, Fala brushed the stinging drops away from his eyes as he asked, "Are we going to make it home before it gets dark?"

SHERRY COTTLE GRAHAM

"Yes, we can make it," Moki said, "but we have to hurry."

"You lead, and I'll follow, but don't run so fast. I can't keep up with you, carrying this drum," Fala complained.

Moki pushed against a tree branch, opening an access point for them to enter into this untamed world. The boys quickly found the narrow animal trail that ran straight into this dangerous habitat. As they jogged deeper into the musty, dark, and dank woods, they listened to the songs of thousands of nesting birds, screaming warnings to each other as the boys ran past them. Just as the last bit of sunlight was about to blink from sight, Moki saw a break in the trees and recognized that his home was a short distance away. He was relieved that the demons that haunted this forest hadn't scooped them up. "Look, there's the end of the trail. We made it," Moki said. "I can't wait to get home and tell Father what we saw today!"

"Ah, me too," Fala said. "I can't wait to get out of these clothes and get something to eat too. I'm starved."

Then Moki stopped to look at a small wax myrtle that was growing beside the path. He bent down and touched its waxy leaves.

Fala asked, "What are you doing?"

"This is the plant that I have chosen to bond with. I chose it because I want it to keep those blood sucking insects off me," Moki said.

"Good choice . . . Has it spoken to you?" Fala continued as he plucked a small leaf from the myrtle, twirling it in between his fingers.

"Yes," Moki said. "It is speaking to me right now. Do you hear it?"

"What is it saying?" asked Fala.

Moki became very quiet as he listened to it say, "Look behind you!"

Slightly confused, "Look behind me?" Moki asked.

Then Fala leaned forward and tightly gripped Moki's shoulder.

Feeling Fala's energy, Moki knew that something was wrong.

Moki felt the temperature of the air drop. It was growing colder, the hair on the back of his neck started to rise, and he felt spiderwebs spinning across the top of his head. As he turned, remembering his mother's words, "If they catch you, they will eat you," fear swept through him as he prepared to greet the demon that was behind him.

As his eyes adjusted to the dimming light, he recognized Donehogawa's grossly disfigured face. When their eyes met, Donehogawa asked, "Where is my skull?"

Shocked by his presence, Moki answered, "How would I know? I haven't had time to look for it."

Donehogawa responded, "You promised to get it. Why aren't you looking for it? What are you doing here—hiding?"

"No!" Fala said. "How did you find us?"

Donehogawa held out his broken right hand and showed them a beautiful black-and-white-tipped eagle feather.

"That is Coahoma's feather!" yelled Fala. He stepped toward the pitiful ghost and tried to snatch it away from him, but Donehogawa tucked the feather behind him as he drifted backward.

"I know where you live, and I will follow you until I get my skull back. I will haunt you for the rest of your lives and your children's lives if you do not keep your promise."

"We will keep it!" said Moki, stepping forward, stomping the end of the lance's shaft into the ground. "We have a sick little girl who needs our help right now. After we finish our duties to her, we will find your skull and return it to you."

"We just need more time," Fala said.

They were wasting time. Moki and Fala could see that the sun was setting, watching the light dissipate from the forest. They hoped that Donehogawa would accept their words and leave. They saw a look of desperation in his face, and they saw the truth in his eyes—he would haunt them until his demands were met. As he began to drift backward, merging into the darkness, he whispered, "You will find me at the gate. If you do not come, I will find you!" and he disappeared.

Moki saw an odd expression flash across Fala's face. Turning to see what his blood brother was looking at, Moki saw a strange shape that was standing a few feet away from them. Moki whispered, "What is it?"

"I don't know. It's not a bear, but it looks like a man, but look how long its arms are. And it's standing on two legs," Fala whispered.

Huddled together, seeing the blackness of night draping through the canopy, watching the color fade from sight, the boys knew that they were in trouble—serious trouble. The joy of returning safely home was turned into their worst nightmare. A large animal was stalking them, and their weapons were useless against it.

As the boys retreated one giant step backward, the object moved one step forward. Moving in its position, seeing its silhouette against the

SHERRY COTTLE GRAHAM

dimming tree line, both boys knew that this creature was moving toward them.

Reaching out, Moki slapped Fala's arm as he turned back toward the path that lead back into the bowels of the woods. He yelled, "Run!"

Fala dropped his drum and followed Moki back into the forest. Hearing the thuds of the beast's heavy footsteps beating against the earth and its deep bronchial breaths coming in rhythmic waves, they ran.

Lost among the trees, weaving deeper into the venomous forest, trying to stay focused on keeping ahead of this pursuing beast, Moki spotted a large magnolia tree a short distance ahead. "Fala, crawl under these branches. Maybe it won't find us under there."

Diving to the ground, the boys shimmied underneath the large branches. Huddling close to the trunk of this broadleaf tree, feeling the ground around them, and smelling the rich thick aroma of musty earth and rotting vegetation, they looked for venomous spiders and snakes that might be sleeping under it. As they felt their way through the dark underbrush, Fala felt a hole in the ground beside him. As he investigated it, Moki watched for the beast. It wasn't long before they heard its footsteps, stopping directly in front of them. Then they heard a strange roar that sounded like a woman screaming into the blackness of night, causing an eerie silence to follow.

Lying under the branches on the musty ground, Moki said, "Fala, do you remember Laurel's lesson about how to see the world through the eyes of an owl?"

"Yes," said Fala. He asked, "Do you think that we can do this without our rattles?"

"I don't know, but we have to try," Moki said. "Do your breathing, breath in and out. Visualize the ancient forest around you. Now lower your mind and relax. Listen to the chattering frogs and sounds of the night," said Moki. "Continue your journey down . . ."

Calming their emotions, relaxing, moving their center of attention down, moving together, the boys entered into a deep meditative state. Opening their eyes, they saw the forest that was highlighted in shades of red.

They heard the beast's heavy footsteps, stomping around the edge of their hiding place. They heard its basal grunts and rhythmic breaths as it moved. Whatever it was that was after them, it wasn't leaving. Instead, it seemed to grow extremely agitated at them. It dropped on to its knees and began to shove the long waxy branches aside. It reached in with its long hairy arms and tried to grab them.

Moki pulled himself into a small ball and kicked the beast with his foot, trying to deflect its hands from grabbing on to him. As he warded off its attack, Fala began to push him away from the center of the tree. He was pushing him toward the opposite side of the tree and away from the grasping arms.

"What are you doing? Stop pushing me!" Moki commanded.

"Skunks!" cried Fala.

Before Fala could say another word, Moki spotted a skunk. As they scurried away from the skunk unhappy with their presence, it lifted its tail and shot its awful stream of foul-smelling spray at them.

As its nasty odor saturated their clothes, they pulled free and heaved into a running position. They ran as fast as their out stretched legs would carry them, weaving deeper and deeper into the terrifying forest. They did not know where they were going, not caring, moving as far away from the beast as they could get. Listening to the rhythmic thumps of the beast, they did not know where to run as the beast gained on them. All of a sudden, the land disappeared, sending them reeling through the air. They landed into a thick pool of sloppy black muck.

Sinking, Fala realized that he was hopelessly trapped inside clenches of this pool as it sucked him down into its belly. Seeing the branches of a small bush beside him, he reached up and grabbed it. Fala wrenched this body through this merciless death trap, looking for Moki. When he spotted him a short distance away, Fala pulled off his tunic and tossed one end toward Moki while he held on to the other. He yelled, "Moki, grab on to my tunic and hold on!"

Moki reached up and latched on to it. Leaning forward, allowing his body to go limp, Fala pulled Moki toward him. When Moki was close enough, Fala reached out and pulled him to his side.

Muddy, wet, stinking, and frightened, Moki reached up and grabbed on to another branch. Disoriented, he looked up and saw the beast reaching over the embankment, trying to grab on to him. He saw the face of his assailant; it was a young Sasquatch. She wanted to pull him from this deadly pit.

"It's a Sasquatch," Moki said. "A Sasquatch is after us."

Covered in stinking black goop, the boys huddled together, desperately hanging on to the draping vegetation, trying to stay alive, when they heard another set of powerful trotting footsteps approaching from the distance. They saw a second Sasquatch appearing twice as large as the first one. A large male peeked over the edge and stared at the boys. Then it bent forward, sniffing the air above them. When he smelled the skunk odor, he rose. He opened his jaws, displaying his daunting set of sharp canines. He tilted his head backward, filled his lungs with air, and then he exhaled, emitting a mighty low-pitched wail that blasted through the surrounding black veil, sending the birds fleeing from the safety of their nests into the night sky. Then he grabbed on to the smaller one, jerking it upright, grasping on to its forearm. He disappeared into the night, pulling the smaller one along with him.

Struggling to hold on to the plant, hearing the beasts crashing through the brush, Fala turned toward Moki and said, "Wow, I thought that we were going to be joining Donehogawa tonight. I thought that they were going to eat us."

Moki tried to grab on to another branch with his other hand. Wanting to get out of this cold pool of black slime, he began to squirm, making him sink deeper into it.

"Stop moving," Fala said. "The branch is breaking!"

The boys looked around the edge of their pit, looking for a way out of their predicament. Moki noticed that he was about to cry. Concerned about him, Moki said, "Don't cry, Fala. We're going to be all right. I know we are going to get out of here somehow."

"I'm not crying. This skunk odor is stinging my eyes. I hate the smell of skunks!" he said.

Then the boys heard something flying overhead. They looked up and saw Awock, Laurel's famous owl, as it swooped down across the muddy pit and landed on a tree branch.

Joy erupted as Fala yelled, "Laurel is here. I know it. Her owl is here, and he follows her everywhere. She's going to get us out of here."

Moki cried, "Where's her lance? Ah, I lost it!"

Fala didn't know what to say to comfort him. They had been through a terrible ordeal, and he knew that Moki's heart was torn by this loss. Then he said, "Maybe you dropped it. We'll look for it tomorrow."

Recalling his lessons on how to find things that are lost, "I'll call upon the spirits to show me where it is," Moki said.

All of a sudden, a rope spilled over the side of the muddy drop off, landing in the muddy water beside the boys. They grabbed on to it and tried to wrench free from the murky fingers that gripped on to them, but they were unable to pull themselves free from it.

Moki heard a limb snap in the distance. Moki asked, "Fala, did you hear that noise?"

"Yes, I heard it. Someone is coming," responded Fala.

Together, they shouted, "Help! We're over here!"

Seeing the familiar halo of flickering torches that were headed toward them, they knew that their fathers were coming to save them.

"They are over here!" yelled Coahoma as he looked over the side of the drop-off and saw his friends below. When Coahoma turned around and motioned the men to hurry, he tripped over the rope and fell backward into the pit.

He lay motionless for a moment, struggling to catch his breath as he began to sink. Before he had a chance to understand the severity of his situation, Moki and Fala reached out and pulled him to safety.

Chief Ituha looked at them over the shallow ridge and saw his son and his friends below. "Pallaton, get them out of there," he said.

Six of the village's warriors stepped forward, splitting into two groups of three men, latching their arms together, forming two chains, they dropped two men over the side of the steep embankment, inching them into position to be able to reach in and pull the boys from the swamp.

Watching the men, seeing their strong lean muscular faces coming closer, seeing their blackened hardworking hands stretching out for them, Fala said, "Hold on, Coahoma. They are coming to get you."

Dropping over the edge, stretching out on their powerful legs, Pallaton and Akando reached out and grabbed on to Coahoma. Pulling with a slow steady motion, they lifted him up the side of the embankment and into the arms of the other men. The tug-of-war between the men and the mud was won by the men, but the mud kept its prize—Coahoma's leggings and his breechcloth.

Smiling, "He lost his coverings," Fala whispered to Moki. "Hold on to your belt."

They moved over and quickly pulled Fala free and passed him up the embankment. As they passed him up their line, the brawny men smelled the foul odor that radiated from him. But they didn't let this hamper their efforts as they quickly hoisted Moki up their line.

SHERRY COTTLE GRAHAM

Standing together inside this dark forest, stinking and covered in black mud with only the whites of their eyes showing, the boys were happy to be alive.

Fala was bare-chested, and Coahoma was bare-legged as rescuers distanced themselves from their stench. "Are you okay?" Chief Ituha asked. He was concerned about their injuries, but he didn't want to go any closer to them.

"Yes. Can we go home now?" Coahoma asked.

Chief Ituha, Pallaton, and Akando pulled off their heavy buckskin shirts and handed them to the boys. Pallaton winked at Moki as he handed him his shirt. Pallaton said, "Burn it when you get home. I don't want it back."

"Come, let's go home, Coahoma," the chief said. "You and your friends can follow us, and stay about twenty paces behind us. We will deal with you later."

Exiting the forest, the boys saw the flickering fires scattered through their village, welcoming them back into the arms of their loving families and friends.

Moving toward the slow moving Atchafalaya River that flanked the edge of their village, they saw many men and women who were working together to build a large bonfire for them.

Wanting to warm themselves, the boys ran over and stood beside the glowing flames. They reached out with their mud-caked arms to feel the heat of this crackling fire. When they turned around to warm their backsides, they saw their entire tribe quietly standing a clear distance away.

Coahoma spotted his mother. She was standing beside his father, and they were both silently watching him from afar. Sonoma was glaring at her son's bare legs and the thick layer of black mud that was caked on him. Sonoma asked, "Son, what did I tell you when you left this morning?"

Coahoma dropped his head and lightly kicked the ground with his muddy foot. He responded so that his whole tribe could hear, "You said not to get dirty."

First, there was a slight chuckle, and then a muffled snicker broke the silence. Then the whole tribe burst out laughing. The sound of laughter rippled through the masses at the sight of the boys and at Coahoma's answer. Then they started laughing with each other and at each other, bending over, knee jerking, leg slapping, tears streaming down their faces—they laughed. Once they'd start to slow down, they'd start laughing all over again.

When the laughter began to wane, Sonoma knew, by the way he shifted his weight, that Coahoma was all right. Still frustrated by what she saw, she said, "We are building a teepee for you to sleep in. We are building it beside the river. Son, do not leave this place until the smell is gone—then you can come home." Crossing her arms and with a stern look, she said, "Stay put, and we will talk when we return. And be prepared to answer our questions!"

SHERRY COTTLE GRAHAM

CHAPTER 9

Bewitching Hour

Dakota
Eldest son of Chief Ituha and Sonoma and Coahoma's eldest brother.

Sitting safely in front of a warm glowing fire, listening to it as it crackled against the chilly breeze, Coahoma asked, "Did you see the fear inside my mother's eyes when she spoke to us?"

Despite his training, Fala was losing his battle against the demons that were festering inside him, but abiding by his customs, he didn't complain. Perhaps if the skunk odor wasn't so intense, he would have noticed Sonoma's fear, but he didn't. "No," he said as he cradled his head between his hands.

Not speaking, Moki shook his head "No." As he gazed toward his village, he spotted the silhouette of an elderly woman moving through the darkness. He recognized his grandmother. She was walking toward him, carrying a heavy bundle of blankets with her. When she entered the firelight, he saw how it highlighted her deeply wrinkled red skin and her long strands of gray hair that fell in streaks across her shoulders. He watched her sniff the night air as she dropped the blankets on to the ground. She said, "You've had a bad night, huh, Moki? I was worried about you when Ituha gathered many men to go into the swamp to look for you and your friends."

"Nana, guess what I saw today," Moki said.

Pressing her finger to her lips, "Shh . . . The shadow people might hear you," she said as she glanced around. "I thought that I saw one standing over there, watching you." When Moki stood to greet her, she reached out and pulled him close. She smelled the odor, saw the crusted mud—she felt his pain. Her heart ached for her grandson as she reached down and handed him his blanket. When he took it from her, she whispered, "Ah, Moki, you are a horrible mess. Come here, child. Let's get you out of those clothes and burn them. Wrap yourself in this blanket. It will keep you warm until your parents come for you."

"When will they get here?" Coahoma asked, looking toward his lodge that was on the far side of their village. "We want to wash this muck off us," he said, but he dreaded the idea of getting into the dangerous river at this time of night.

"Coahoma, your father is in a powwow with Laurel and many of our men. I don't know what they are doing, but you'd think that we are preparing for war by the way they are acting. I'm not sure what he has in mind, but he has asked us to do many things. You will see." When they settled back down on to their mats, she asked, "Are you hungry?" She opened a small satchel that was filled with strips of dried meat. "Maybe if you eat, you will feel better."

"Nana, I can't eat right now. Maybe later . . . I have to get this smell off me," Moki said.

"Me, either," Coahoma said as he spotted Hashi Ninak Anya rising above the eastern forest. Returning from her daily journey through the Other World, Coahoma was filled with hope as he watched her dominate the sky with her illuminescent light. As he watched her glide past the twinkling stars and shimmering Milky Way, his thoughts turned back to the bones and how Laurel had responded to them. He recalled her words, "It has started," but the reality of her words sunk in as he listened to the helter-skelter that was taking place all around him. His heart ached with another awful truth that loomed over him. He didn't know how to defend himself or his friends from the demons that were coming.

Just as the pain from Fala's head merged with his rancid gurgling stomach, he thought that he was going to vomit. He knew that Moki's grandmother and Coahoma were watching over him, but he was happy to see that his mother, Dyani, and his little sister had arrived. As they moved through the amber firelight, he noticed that his mother was lugging a bladder of water and his little sister, Kinta, was jostling three small red clay bowls in her tiny arms as she tried to keep up with her mother's pace.

Dyani was shocked when she saw Fala. Her son was trembling, and his lips and skin had turned into an odd grayish color. She was afraid that he wouldn't live through the night, but she didn't want him to see her fear. Remaining calm, smiling, she asked, "Fala, are you all right?"

"Is the river going to be cold?" Fala asked.

"Yes, Fala. It will be cold, but we will get you out as soon as we can and bring you back to the fire to dry. Laurel is busy preparing a powerful tea for you to drink. Her medicine will keep you strong through the night and protect you from the demons," Dyani said, trying to prepare her son for this terrifying event.

"Mother, don't worry. I know that the demons will come for us, but I'm not afraid," Fala said.

"Yes, Fala. You will be fine," Dyani lied. "I know that Laurel won't let anything happen to you or your friends."

Breathing in shallow breaths, scanning the naked boys who were quietly sitting with their blankets pulled tightly around them, Dyani was concerned about the condition that they were in. When she saw the torches flickering across the meadow, she said, "Fala, tell Coahoma and Moki that it's time for us to go to the river."

Leaving the warmth behind them and moving into the cold starlit night, they saw the stars twinkling on the Atchafalaya's slow-moving black surface a short distance ahead. This old river had split away from her mighty sister, the Misi-ziibi, far to the north and drifted southward, gently gliding through the swamps and past their homeland. She finished her journey when she emptied her cargo into the Great Father's salty aqua blue water.

This meandering old river was filled with edible tubers, crayfish, crabs, frogs, alligators, and a wide variety of fish. On occasion, she escorted visitors traveling by raft or canoe to the banks of their village. She was a natural place for them to bathe or to just to hang out. Yet there was a darker, more sinister side to her sweet allure, one that Coahoma had learned to respect. When his brother had died, he learned the dangers that she hid in her belly. Creatures such as alligators, giant catfish, toxic cottonmouth water moccasins, nasty bloodsucking leaches, and on occasion, a rogue shark—all looking for their next tasty meal.

In early spring, when the sun grew warmer and the days grew longer, Coahoma had seen this mystical beauty mutate into a raging torrent, sweeping everything away that was in her path. He had watched her grab an innocent victim who challenged her strength and pulled him into her web of twisted roots and hallowed limbs, never to be seen or heard from again.

But tonight, as Dyani led them toward her sinister shoreline, Coahoma was walking on Fala's right side, and Moki was on his left. When Coahoma saw the color drain from his friend's skin, he asked, "Fala, are you all right?"

"It's just this mud and smell," Fala responded, trying to stay alert. "I hope that there aren't any gators around here."

Coahoma heard a heavy flapping sound, passing overhead. "Laurel is coming," he said as he watched her great horned owl disappear inside the willow's long weeping branches that elegantly stretched over the side of the embankment. Then he spotted her, moving through the shadows. She was walking at a very fast pace, lugging a large bag with her.

As they approached the river, Coahoma saw several men and women running through the shadows toward them. His thoughts drifted back to the haunting blue eyes of Ethane' as he watched the tiny flames weaving through the air. He wondered if he would feel her sweet seduction again as he grew weary, wondering where this game was leading him. He felt his strength waning as he heard a voice yelling in the distance, "Wait! Don't enter the water!"

Fala was comforted by the sight of his elders who were coming for him. He hoped that his father was among these glowing amber lights that were weaving through the night air, but as he fought to stay focused on the people around him, he knew that he was in trouble. Suddenly, his

SHERRY COTTLE GRAHAM

vision began to fade, and the sounds of the surrounding forest mutated into a hum. He felt his legs buckle, but he couldn't stop himself. He fell.

From the corner of his eye, Coahoma knew, by the way that Fala was wavering, that something was wrong. Realizing that he was falling, he yelled, "Grab him!" as he dropped his blanket, allowing it to fall into a heap around the bottom of his legs. As the cool night breeze brushed against his bare skin, Coahoma was worried about the demons that were festering inside his friend. He had lost one brother, and he feared that tonight that he might lose another.

When Coahoma turned around, he saw Fala's father, running toward him. With all the years of training, he felt helpless as he struggled to hold Fala upright. *Never again will I be so helpless against these demons,* Coahoma thought as he watched Lanto pitch his torch on to the ground and lift Fala into his arms. He felt Dyani brush against his side and saw the terror on her face when Laurel joined them.

As Coahoma pulled the blanket back around his shoulders, he vowed that he would never be left feeling helpless like this again. As the nauseous odor and festering demons consumed his ability to think, breathing in short gasps, he promised himself that he would learn everything that Laurel and Pontiac would offer him, and he would master it without complaint. Coahoma stood quietly, watching Laurel press her fingers into the side of Fala's neck. He knew that she was searching for the delicate heartbeat that lay beneath. He was relieved when she smiled and said, "Lanto, Fala will be all right. Come on"—she motioned—"let's get him into the water and wash this stench off him."

As Lanto carried Fala toward the river, Pallaton and Akando stepped forward with three burly men donning decorative bone amulets, painted faces, and feather and fur headdresses, wearing their skimpiest loin clothes and high-laced leather boots. They were armed with brightly burning torches and fishing spears. These five men assembled themselves beside the edge of the river bank. They scanned the river for any dangerous animals that might be lurking nearby. At Chief Ituha's signal, they started at a common point, spreading apart. They walked into the river. Moving together, they swept their spears under her creepy surface, pushing themselves further and deeper into her frigid belly, stopping only when they had formed a protective ring for the chief's son and his friends. Pallaton yelled, "It's safe! You can bring your sons in now!"

Lanto, carrying Fala, was the first to enter the bathing pool. Alongside them, Dyani entered the river to help him bathe their son. She carried a large rabbit fur and a blend of fat that was laced with finely ground magnolia bark and witch hazel oil that Laurel had given to her.

Behind them, Coahoma and Moki prepared to enter the shimmering pool with their semiclad fathers. Coahoma looked over at his mother and said, "Mother, do not come in here. I can do this myself."

"You too!" shouted Moki at Mahkah, his mother, as he entered the pool walking beside her. Trying to divert his attention from the cold, Moki studied his father's downward arching eyes, his high cheek bones, his rough sun-dried wrinkled red skin, and his full set of lips that outlined his wide downward drooping mouth as he waded into her protected center. He was surprised to see how long his father's black and silver hair had grown over the winter. He looked at the alligator strap that banded his hair into place, allowing it to drape freely over his shoulders and whisk across his muscular arms as he moved.

Coahoma watched many members of his tribe gather beside the shoreline, toting long blazing torches with them. From the corner of his eye, as he moved beside his father into the river, he saw them form a single line along its bank. Then one by one, they stretched their hissing torches out and over the water, providing a comforting halo of heat and light for them. As Coahoma turned, he saw his father's loving eyes looking back. Just as he began to dunk down into the black murky water, he heard the melodic sounds of flutes and the rhythmic beats of a drummer, echoing across his creaking and croaking river. Then their families began to chant, joining the flutes and drummer, singing their childhood songs to chase the evil ones away from their young heroes. At that moment, Coahoma knew that his life was meaningless without them.

Moki saw his mother standing on shore, holding a blanket and dry clothes for him. He knew that they were preparing to greet him and his friends when they exited the water. He knew that they would escort them back into the warmth of the large roaring fire.

"Ah, Moki, loosen your braids and dunk under the water," Mahkah instructed as he lathered up the rabbit skin with his cleansing agent.

Trying to keep his teeth from chattering, Moki quickly untied his braids. Bending his knees, holding his breath, he plunged under the cold water. The cold instantly consumed him. It shot through his legs, chest, neck, face, and ears. Planting his feet firmly into the rocky bottom, he

SHERRY COTTLE GRAHAM

pushed up with his legs, holding his head backward, allowing his hair to hang down his lean back, placing his hands over his eyes as he rose from the water. "Ah, this is cold. Let's get this over with."

Blue lips, chattering teeth, rubbing, splashing, they scrubbed the muddy stench from their faces, arms, chest, and legs. At the same time, their fathers rubbed the cleanser over their skin. Dunking again, they rinsed the mud from their body and hair.

Taking one last plunge, Moki surfaced and gazed past the flames and singers. He spotted many men and boys a short distance away. They had erected seven teepee frames, arranged in a circle with six on the outside and one inside. Moki knew that they were using these teepees to form a medicine wheel, much like the one that surrounded Laurel's lodge. He spotted another group of men who were pulling heavy bundles of hides toward the frames. He wondered what Laurel was planning for them as he prepared to go ashore.

Chief Ituha was the first to reach her muddy bank. Standing waist deep in her, he lifted each of the boys into their families' arms. As he hoisted them up, he said, "Do not speak to anyone about your journey. Keep it a secret until I call for you."

"No problem," Fala said as his grandfather gently wrapped a blanket around him.

"I won't tell anyone," Moki said as his mother reached out and pulled him ashore.

When the bathers were dressed in their clean outfits and wrapped in their warm fur-lined blankets, they were quickly shuttled over to sit on a thick bed of dry grass and blankets that were draped on the ground close to the bonfire. When Coahoma sat down, he asked, "Father, when can I tell you about our journey?"

"Later, Coahoma," Chief Ituha said as he raised his right arm and pointed toward the teepees. He continued, "We will move you and your friends on to this sacred ground when Hashi Ninak Anya passes over those trees. Tonight, we will fight the demons that will come for you inside our sacred ground."

"I know, Father. I know that Fala is fighting them already," Coahoma said as he looked at his blood brother who was sitting close to the fire, leaning against Laurel, sipping tea. Coahoma asked, "Father, can I go and sit beside Fala?"

"Yes. Go on . . . ," Ituha said. "I'm going to help the men build those teepees. We will come for you later," Ituha said as walked away.

As Coahoma watched the hypnotic flames flickering in front of him, Dakota appeared behind him. When he sat down beside Coahoma, he asked, "Coahoma, what happened today? Where were you? Father has been so secretive . . ."

"Father told me not to say anything to anyone," responded Coahoma.

Dakota retorted, "I am your brother. Father won't care if you tell me."

"No," Coahoma responded.

Dakota pressed on. "It will be our secret. Father won't know . . ."

"No!" Coahoma said as he walked away.

Coahoma knew that Dakota was angry with him, but he didn't care as he pulled his blanket tightly around his shoulders. He strolled over and sat down beside Fala. He watched Kinta as she bounced around the fire, playing with her cups. She tapped on Fala's left shoulder when she saw Coahoma and Moki approaching through the firelight.

"How are you feeling?" Coahoma asked as he sat down beside Fala.

"You certainly took the strongest hit from that ol' skunk, didn't you, Fala?" Moki said. "I am glad to get that smell off me. Aren't you?"

"I can still smell it. It is in my skin," Fala responded, holding out his arms. "It helps when I keep them under this blanket and breathe through my mouth."

"Coahoma, here's your cup. Moki, here is one for you too," said Kinta as she handed them one of her precious little clay bowls. "Laurel, can I pour them some of your tea?" she asked, looking at Laurel with her innocent brown eyes.

"Yes, of course, child. Here, let me help you." Standing up, Laurel picked up her clay flask of hot tea that she had simmering beside the fire. "I was hoping that you boys would join us before we go to our new shelters," she said as she looked toward the teepees that were springing into life in the background. "It is going to be a long night. Fala is already showing signs of battling the Spirit World," she said as she looked down upon him.

"I'll be all right. I can fight them," Fala said, pulling his knees up to his chest, leaning forward against his thighs, keeping his blanket securely in place. He continued, "I am a man. I will not submit to a shadow. I am not afraid of death!"

SHERRY COTTLE GRAHAM

Moki stood up, looking down at Laurel, holding out his cup. He bent over and let Kinta pour him a cup of the special brew as Laurel assisted the child by holding the bottom of the heavy container. Raising the cup to his mouth, Moki took a small drink of the tea. "Argh, this is bitter. Do I have to drink this?" he asked.

"Moki, you will be fighting the spirits tonight too. You might be fighting them for the next few nights, you poor boy," she said in a gentle tone. "This will help you sleep tonight, and it will relieve your headache."

"How do you know that I have a headache?" asked Moki.

"I can tell everything about you. It is written in your eyes," Laurel said.

"I lost your lance. I dropped it in the forest when the beast was chasing us," Moki said.

"Moki, do you remember your lesson about losing things? Son, nothing is ever lost. If the gods want me to have it, then it will find its way back to me."

"I will find it and return it to you, I promise," Moki said, but he could see, by the way she leaned forward and sniffed his clothes, that she wasn't interested in the lance. She was concerned about the demons that she saw inside him.

"I must get those demons out . . . ," Laurel whispered.

She looked at Fala who was quietly sitting beside her. She saw the evil spirits were festering inside him. She rubbed her hands together and placed one hand over Fala's eyes and the other on the back of his head. She gently held her hands in place, shielding his eyes from the heat and light. She whispered, "Hold on, Fala. We will be moving you to your teepee very soon now."

Laurel watched her goddess slide across the jeweled sky. Her presence filled Laurel with hope that her plan would be executed with absolute precision. It was the chief's son and his two blood brothers. She knew that if she lost one that it would hinder the spiritual growth of the other two. When she saw a brilliant white light streaking across the twinkling canopy, she knew how fragile the balance is between life and death. When she felt Fala's warm body press against hers, listening to him struggle for each breath, she grew impatient with the men that were assembling her battleground. As she sat in front of the fire, feeling its warmth against her flesh, she heard the voices of the surrounding trees.

They sang, "The soul robbers are gathering inside the tunnel. They are coming for your young ones who are growing weaker by the moment."

Watching the tense moments tick by, stepping carefully in and out of her Spirit World, Laurel felt the fear that grew around her as the bewitching hour approached. She knew that the portal would open, allowing the hordes of horrifying ghouls to come for the souls of her sick boys, but she waited with confidence that her counterattack would stop them.

Seeing the moon move into its predefined position—straight up, overhead—she knew that the bewitching hour was upon them, the portal was opening, and the demons were coming. Looking through the flickering yellow-tinted flames, seeing the silhouette of the cone-shaped teepees resting among the backdrop of the rippling river and the grassy meadow, seeing a circling of fire, springing forth to life, she said, "It's time."

SHERRY COTTLE GRAHAM

CHAPTER 10

The Soul Robbers

Laurel drew the outer edge of Fala's blanket back and pulled five masks and a torch out from underneath it. She thrust one end of the torch into the fire and set it ablaze. *The demons are coming,* she thought as she heaved it up high into the air, swinging it back and forth. She signaled the youngsters who were hiding behind their lodges to come.

Her heart leaped when she saw their torches springing into life from across the clearing. She said, "Put these on and stay behind me," as she handed a mask to Coahoma and Fala. When she looked down at the third mask, she knew that it belonged to Fala. She could tell, by the way that it was carved and the intricate details that adorned its smooth polished surface, that Fala's father had made it for him. She recalled a time, long ago, when Lanto was a young boy, and she recognized his talent. Now that he had grown into a gifted craftsman, he enjoyed carving toys for his children, and tonight, he had chosen the face of a forest fairy to hide his son's face. How fitting, she thought, that Lanto would choose this trickster. "I hope that you will hide Fala from these soul robbers as well as you hide my things and play tricks on our babies," she said to the mask.

As she ran her finger down his long oval face and along his pursed lips, she thought about Pontiac. *I hope he doesn't get in my way tonight.* She fretted. *But Pallaton has his instructions . . . ,* she thought as she felt the long sprays of white egret feathers tickle the back of her hand, stifling her feelings of guilt.

"Ahh, you silly old woman," the mask said to her. "You are a fool if you think that you can save these boys," it scoffed. "If the demons don't drag them away, then they will surely die by the knife of the giant sorcerer who hides among you. You old fool, you should prepare them to stand tall and die like men and not run into the night like rabbits!"

"Stop!" she said. "Do your job and hide your master! This is the honorable thing for you to do," she said as she quickly passed it to Fala. "Fala, put this on and don't take it off until I tell you to. Your friends are coming for us, and they will guide us to your teepee."

"Can I walk with Coahoma and Moki?" Fala asked.

"Yes, Fala. Can you walk by yourself?" she asked, knowing that he couldn't.

"Don't worry about me," Fala muttered as he pulled the mask over his face. "I'll be fine."

She signaled to Coahoma and Moki to help Fala as she clasped Kinta's small hand into hers and pulled her close. As she slid Kinta's cute little bird mask over her face, seeing the child's innocent little eyes looking at her through its well-placed holes, her heart swelled, nearly choking her as she felt Kinta's tiny hand touching hers. Life here was always a simple one. One that required her to battle the elements and animals, but when she felt the fear that hung in the air like a thick fog, she paused to ask her gods for help. When she opened her eyes and saw the silhouettes of her elderly and their pregnant women on the far side of the towering flames moving into her circle of teepees, stilling her heart, she prepared to move the boys into her circle with them. Just as she lifted Kinta into her arms, she heard a small voice whispering. "The demons are coming," it said.

"Hurry, put your masks on and don't take them off until you are told to do so!" she yelled at Coahoma and Moki. Calming her tone as she bounced Kinta in her arms, she whispered, "Kinta, we are going to play a little game. If you want to play, then you must keep this mask on for Nana."

"Yes." Kinta nodded.

Just as Coahoma and Moki locked their hands around Fala, they saw a stream of torches bobbing toward them through the night air. As they approached, Coahoma recognized his friends. They were wearing their heavy fringed buckskin clothes and their favorite elaborate painted and feathered ceremonial masks. Coahoma recognized that Laurel's plan of deception was well under way when he turned around and saw her hiding behind her mask. He recognized it. It was the same mask that she had worn earlier in the day when she had read her bones. Without speaking a word, he heard her say, "The demons can spell fear so remain calm!" as their friends surrounded them.

Lost inside a group of his peers, Coahoma saw Dakota appear beside Laurel. He could see, by the way that his brother moved, that he was playing a critical role in this game of deception. He was pleased when he saw Dakota reach out and hoist Kinta into his arms. He saw his brother's aura brighten as he moved around this odd-looking group. *He is a born leader*, he thought as he watched his brother control this mixed group of teens and adults. Using the slightest hand signals, accompanied by a whistle or bark, they understood and obeyed him.

Feeling dizzy, Coahoma was relieved when six tall boys walked up beside him. He recognized Koi's voice when he said, "Let go. We're taking Fala with us," as they pulled him away and secured Fala between them.

The remaining four boys split into teams of two. One team tagged Coahoma and said, "Walk between us. We will guard you." As he fell in between them, he watched the other two boys sweep their arms behind Moki, stabilizing him; and all at once, they were hidden inside this masked group and moving toward her battleground.

Looking into the surrounding darkness, seeing demons in the distance, Coahoma left his guards and ran behind his brother. In an alarmed voice, he whispered, "Dakota, the demons are here . . ."

"Shh, keep walking," Dakota warned with the flick of his hand.

Just as Coahoma reached the ring of fire, their drummers began beating on their drums, drowning out the sounds of the creaking forest with them. They filled the night with their loud rhythmic sounds. Then he heard singers singing their tribal song, asking the Mighty Spirit for protection against the soul robbers that surrounded them. *Will I ever be as gifted as her?* Coahoma wondered as he watched the children grab their rattles and whistles and form a line. *It's working*, he thought. *The demons don't see us*, he realized as he watched them flying overhead. Then his mind drifted to Ethane' as he watched the children, shaking their rattles and blowing their whistles, as they danced around the teepees. He wondered what she would think of his old teacher now that her battle was in full swing.

Smelling sickness on the wind, the demons were excited as they charged over the masked ranks. Like a school of sharks frenzied over a bloody meal, they were anxious to add few more souls to their eternal clan. Glancing toward the sky, Coahoma saw them swooping across them.

Cloaked in black, they were invisible to the naked eye, but to the eye of a trained shaman, they were here, and they were deadly.

"Stay close," Dakota signaled as he merged his gang into the dancing ring, hearing the familiar beat, boom-ba-ba-ba, shifting their weight from toe to heel and foot to foot, swinging their bodies in well-orchestrated movements, jumping and swooping as the children shook their rattles and blew their whistles. On the outer perimeter, armed with torches and amulets, their elders stood guard over them as the demons swirled overhead trying to find their sick boys.

With a slight flick of his wrist, Dakota flashed a signal to Coahoma. "Your entrance is straight ahead."

Just as Coahoma passed in between the scorching flames, *How clever is this old woman?* he wondered when he saw his father waiting for him. *Maybe her magic will save us,* he hoped when he saw Pallaton close the gap with a stack of dried stack of branches and logs and set it ablaze. It shouldn't have surprised him, but it did, when Pallaton picked up a large bag of dried sea salt and poured it into a smooth stream on to the ground. As he finished her circle of salt, Coahoma saw yet another boundary that Laurel had placed around him and his blood brothers.

Coahoma followed his brother over to the center teepee. *She placed us into the center of her medicine wheel,* he thought as he watched Kinta lift the protective flap and disappear inside. When he followed her inside, he was quickly greeted by the thick aroma of dried sage and tobacco that were burning inside.

Now we will test the power of her magic, Coahoma thought as he glanced at the smoke that was spiraling upward toward the vent. Feeling disoriented, he felt the little witches spreading in him as he peered through the eyes of his mask. *Stay strong,* he thought as he spotted the stones that outlined her fire. Just as he started to count the rocks, he heard her say, "Lay Fala down over there. Coahoma, Moki, you can take your masks off now and lie down over there," as she pointed to a cushion of blankets.

Even though he wasn't feeling well, Coahoma complained, "I don't need to lie down. I'm not sick."

Laurel saw through Coahoma's lies. He was a son of the chief, and she wouldn't have expected anything any less from him, but she knew that the sickness was growing inside him. She knew that her plant helpers would help him fight his witches. To appease him, she said, "No, you aren't as sick as Fala, but you need to rest. I will wake you when it's my turn to sleep. You will take Pontiac's place for me tonight. That is, if it's all right with you."

But when he heard her words, a sense of doubt flooded through him. He asked, "Do you trust me? I've never attended a sick person all by myself."

"There is always the first time for everything. Now go, lie down and sleep. I will wake you when I need you," she said.

Coahoma knew that their mothers had been there when he saw his childhood blanket neatly folded on his mat. Just as he pulled it around him, he knew how sick Fala was when he saw him crawling over his. When Fala fell over and pulled himself into a fetal position, Coahoma wondered if Fala would join his brother in the Spirit World. *How can she help all of us at the same time?* he wondered, but he saw his father standing beside the doorway and knew that it was hopeless to complain, so he obeyed.

Laurel was relieved when Ituha picked up Kinta and disappeared outside, taking Dakota and the other six boys with him. Now she was free to move about as she pleased. Listening to the hullabaloo that raged all around her, she welcomed its energy that it provided to her. *It's time to get those witches out of my boys*, she thought as she flipped her wolf skin cape over her head, allowing it to fall over her shoulders and down her back. As she positioned its head over hers, she knew that Coahoma was watching her as its legs thumped against her thighs.

She walked over to the edge of her fire and reached into her medicine bag. She pulled out three small turtle shell bowls. Then she reached in and pulled out a few bundles of carefully tied white willow bark, catnip, nettles, wild garlic, thistle, and dandelion root. She placed them on to a flat limestone rock that was on the ground beside the fire.

She picked up a spool of finely twisted sinew, pulling her knife from its holster. She carefully cut a small length of string to wrap around her herbs. "Thank you for promising to help my boys," she said to the plants as she secured them with her string. When she finished making her infusion, she dropped it into a pot of hot water to brew.

She picked up her large leather medicine bag and pulled out a few bundles of leather. She had placed a stack of dried tobacco leaves that were tied together with small lengths of hemp inside each of them. She collected two bundles and walked over and kneeled down beside Fala. She carefully unrolled one on the ground beside Fala. When she finished, she picked up the second one and unrolled it beside Moki. She said, "I love the power that hides inside these tobacco leaves. Its spirit is so enticing to the witches that hide inside our bodies that they can't resist its juice. All you have to do is to unroll these leaves beside a sick person and sit back and let these leaves do their work. Just watch, look at all of those little witches that jump out of your bodies on to these leaves. See," she said as she pointed to a leaf beside Moki, "they can't wait to drink its juice." Leaning forward, she said, "Boys, you must always keep tobacco in your medicine bags!" as she watched the tiny black specks that crawled over them.

Coahoma lifted on one elbow and asked, "Can I help you do that?"

"No, Coahoma. I know you can do this. Go to sleep, child. I will wake you when I need you," Laurel said.

Coahoma reached down, grabbed a fresh blanket, and pulled it up and over him. Then he pulled the bottom blanket back, raking hands full of the underlying dry bundles of grass and sage toward him, fluffing it up to form a rounded mound to rest his head on. Then he turned over, pulling his blanket snuggly up around his neck, and to Moki's surprise, he fell asleep.

Moki watched Laurel as she stood up and headed back toward the fire. Bending over, she picked up the hot pot of tea that she was brewing for them. Pulling the small herbal bundle from the steaming water, she laid it down to the large flat rock that was beside her fire. She poured the brew into their turtle shell bowls and carried them over to them.

She said, "Moki, drink this. It will reduce your headache and upset stomach, and it will also help you to go to sleep."

As Moki lifted it to his lips, he wondered how she knew that his stomach was upset. He hadn't told anyone as he tested its temperature with his tongue. It wasn't hot, so he drew in a long breath and chugged the nasty-tasting brew. As he handed her his bowl, he said, "Ah, that's bitter. That will certainly make my braids grow longer."

"Ahh, it will make many things grow longer," she said, smiling. "Now lie back and go to sleep if you can."

Moki closed his eyes, wincing as the bitter taste of these herbs radiated through his mouth and seeped into his stomach. As the effects of the brew flooded through him, he said, "I hope I don't have to drink any more of

SHERRY COTTLE GRAHAM

that stuff for a long, long time." He turned on to his side, being careful not to roll on to his tobacco leaves, and shut his eyes.

She asked, "Fala, can you sit up?" As she handed him his brew, she said, "I want you to drink a little tea before I start. It will help you relax while I drive those nasty little witches out of you." She reached down and helped him sit up. Once he was sitting upright, she handed him his bowl.

Fala asked, "Ah, why does it have to taste so bad?"

Laurel said, "It's medicine. It is supposed to taste bad, so you won't drink too much of it. Here, give me your bowl and let's get started."

She stood up and walked over to the fire and laid down the empty shells. She reached into her bag and pulled out her favorite rattle and her spitting bowl. This was her favorite rattle because Lanto had given it to her when Fala was born. *How fitting*, she thought as she looked at its old chipped and worn surface. *I'm going to use Lanto's rattle to chant for his son.* When she looked down and saw Fala looking back, she hoped that she would live to see the day when their gods would complete his transformation.

Facing east, holding the spitting bowl in her left hand and the rattle in her right, she shook the rattle. Closing her eyes, shaking the rattle faster, harder, hearing its beaded rhythm blending with the pulsing drums, dropping into a low meditative trance, she began calling to her helpers to join her as she continued to shake her rattles. As she turned toward the east, she said, "Oh, my healing spirits, I am calling, calling, calling to you." Turning to the south, still shaking her rattles, she continued, "Please come and join me, and show me these harmful spirits." Turning to the west, "Who are hiding, hiding, hiding in this precious soul's body?" Turning northward, "Come, let's work together. Help me drive them away," and turning back toward the east, "And set them free, free, free to live another in another place."

She continued to shake her rattle as she dropped into a trance. When she became still and her eyes glazed over Fala and Moki, the spirits of two elderly men appear in front of her. They appeared to be about the same height and weight. They both had waist-length oily black hair, wearing beautifully beaded and fringed buckskin clothes, and glimmering multicolored halo's surrounded them. The boys watched these spirits as they drifted toward Laura. In a soft tone, she said, "Grandfather and Ohanzee, it is good to see you again. I have two boys who need your help," as she nodded toward Fala and Moki.

Laurel's grandfather and Ohanzee knew that the boys were watching them. They smiled, and with a slight nod, they sent a message to the boys that they were going to help as they moved toward Laurel.

Standing still, Laurel held her rattle in her right hand and her sucking bowl in her left. She waited for the two spirits to move inside her. Then with a small jerk, she felt her energy change.

Fala felt the energy around him change when she walked over and stood beside him. He saw the shifting features of these two spirits weaving inside her. Flushed with fever and ill, Fala hoped that they would find the little witches that were hiding inside him. As he waited, he was captivated by the brilliantly colored lights that flowed around her. It reminded him of a star twinkling against the infinite black sky. When she looked up and stared directly into his eyes, he knew that she had found what she was looking for.

In an odd blended voice, they spoke at the same time. They said, "Fala, we see the intruders. Lie still, child. We are going to suck them out of you. You will feel better real soon."

Kneeling down beside Fala, she lifted his tunic, exposing his soft belly underneath. She dropped her rattle on to the ground and shifted her spitting bowl close to him. She leaned forward and placed her mouth directly on his stomach, slightly above his navel. She began to suck on his skin. Drawing in long deep breaths, she sucked these tiny black spirits into her mouth. When she finished, she leaned over and dry vomited them into her spitting bowl. She repeated this two more times, filling her bowl with the tiny black spiders that she drew out of him. When she finished her spitting, she rubbed her hands together and placed them over Fala's belly. Again, speaking in an eerie blended tone, she said, "Come out and drink the juice from these tasty tobacco leaves," as she waved her hand over the leaves.

Fala felt a crawling sensation as these demons passed through his skin. He realized that his headache had stopped, his stomach had stopped gurgling, the tension in his neck and shoulders relented, and he could breathe again. He felt her moving her hands over his skin. He felt the fever fade away, and soon, the stench evaporated, and he felt well again.

"Fala, close your eyes and rest. We are finished with you," the blended voices said.

When the little witches covered her tobacco leaves, she rolled them up into a neat little bundle. She picked the infested bundle of leaves and her spitting bowl. She placed these two items on a flat rock beside her fire. She returned and stood beside Moki. In her odd, blended voice, she said, "Moki, we are ready to treat you. Son, close your eyes and try to sleep. This won't take long," as she kneeled down beside him.

As he closed his eyes, he heard her rattle shaking over him. Then he felt her warm hands whisking over his skin, chest, belly, arms, and legs. When he heard the voices speaking to him, he opened his eyes and looked up. When he saw the hologram of three faces looking back, he knew that their message was important. They said, "Moki, your witches are gone. They moved into the tobacco, but, child, be aware. You will soon notice that your empathic powers are growing stronger. Don't let your visions consume you. If you need help, call to us, and we will come. Now stay here and rest. Do not leave this teepee because the soul robbers are outside looking for you. If they catch you, then we will not be able to alter your destiny."

Laurel rolled up his bundle of tobacco leaves, picked up his spitting bowl and her rattle. She walked over to her fireplace. She dropped her rattle on the ground beside the fire, picked up Fala's bundle of tobacco and his spitting bowl, lifted the flap to their teepee, and disappeared into the night.

Chief Ituha was the first to spot Laurel as she rounded the teepee and headed straight into the burning flames. Ituha yelled to the drummers, "There she is! Look, she is carrying the sickness with her!"

The drumming stopped, the night grew strangely silent as the masked children and their parents gathered behind the drummers. Then the drummers started up again, drumming fast repetitive beats—boom, boom, boom—revving up the pace until they reached the speed needed to guide their gifted warriors into a deep trance. As the painted and feathered warriors swung around, twirling and undulating to the rapid beat, the rest of their tribe watched Laurel stroll directly into the roaring flames, carrying the remnants of her night's work with her. As she passed through the singeing embers, they saw that she was dressed in her beautiful white-beaded leather dress. She was wearing her high-laced leather boots, and her wolf skin cape covered her face and back. When she walked beside them, they realized that she was still in a deep trance as she moved toward the swamp.

"Look," an older man said, pointing his hand toward the surrounding darkness. "The demons are after her!"

As the demons swarmed around her, swatting at her with their cold skeleton claws, moving away from the crowd into the clearing, hearing three loud simultaneous drum beats—boom, boom, boom—recognizing her signal, she stopped, planting her feet firmly on to the ground, leaning back. She released a deafening high-pitched shrill, allowing her grandfather and Ohanzee to fly out of her body.

Her grandfather and Ohanzee began to swirl around her, forming a protective shield between her and the advancing demons. Appearing as flashes of brilliant white light against the night sky, they pushed the soul robbers away from her. Then the sky lit up as the spirits of her tribe's strongest and wittiest warriors came charging in. They had successfully crossed over into the Spirit World, dragging images of their mightiest spears and knives with them. These fierce warriors began stomping through the swarm of specters, swinging and jabbing at them with their spears and knives, grabbing and flinging these nasty little demons out into the darkness; but they kept coming. Like rain drops, they flooded the sky.

The spirits of the forest saw what was happening and joined the fight to protect their human friend. Still, the soul robbers continued their attack, grabbing, biting, and scratching her. Just as the hope of winning this battle seemed impossible, a powerful grizzly bear flew past her warriors and knocked the demons away.

Laurel welcomed the sight of her totem, her guardian spirit—her grizzly. She watched him plow through this massive army of black shadows, knocking them aside as he moved through their mighty forces. He grabbed them with his powerful jaws and tossed into the night. When he felt her touch, he circled around her, roaring as he drew his ears back and dared the demons to come for her; but unrelenting, they came.

Her war against these horrifying soul stealers seemed hopeless. Then out of the dark, the combined voices of all of her friends, all of the spirits of the forest, came together, forming into one unified force. The warriors, who had crossed over at her signal, bent over and covered their ears just as a deafening sonic scream blasted through the void, penetrating through this evil horde, knocking them to the ground. The battle was over as quickly as it had started. The demons left.

The drumming stopped, and the meadow became quiet. Holding her tobacco bundles and spitting bowls firmly in her hands, she said to her people who were standing near her, "Thank you! The battle is over, and the boys are fine. But I must hide these tobacco strands inside the swamp where no one will find them, and I will return when I am finished."

Chief Ituha was relieved that this battle was over and that his son was safe. He commanded, "Pallaton and Akando, get your weapons and go with her." Then he looked over at the people who had gathered around him. He said, "Remove your masks and go home . . . Get some sleep," but in his heart, he knew that there would be many more battles in their future.

The tribe erupted in a loud joyous noise, jumping and swaying as they ripped off their masks. Gathering together, they herded their families back toward their lodges and disappeared into the night.

Exhausted, Laurel walked toward the deep eerie southern swampland. This was going to be a long walk for her, but she didn't care. When she looked overhead, at the sky, she spotted an orange flame flickering across it. Just as Pallaton and Akando ran up beside her, carrying torches, they saw a starship streaking across the night sky. They knew that it was carrying their people back to their village that was hidden on the dark side of the moon. "Someday we will meet the star people," she said, looking at the glittering sky. "They will bring something important to us, and they will call us friends."

Smiling as she turned, she let the two tall muscular men walk ahead of her, holding their lighted torch to lead the way. It was a long refreshing walk, feeling secure as her guardians escorted her into the mossy, stump-filled, and water-saturated forest. Walking along the high ground, she saw a low-growing limb of an old walnut tree. *This place will do*, she thought as she gently hung the witch-infested tobacco leaves over it. When she was satisfied that they were all right, she picked up her two spitting bowls and carried them over to a puddle of water and rinsed them out. "I am finished. Let's go home," she said.

"Good, let's get out of here," Pallaton said as he reached over, grasping on to her arm with his strong muscular hand. "I will be happy to get out of his forest. It is not safe to be in here this late at night."

"Yes, I know. I am anxious to get back to the teepees, but we still have a lot of work to do if we are going to save Tiponi and Pontiac," she said.

It was a long walk back to their village, and she was relieved when Pallaton lifted the protective flap for her.

"Thank you, Pallaton. Thank you, Akando. I will see you tomorrow," she said as she entered through the doorway and disappeared inside.

Once inside, she had one more thing to do before she could sleep. She looked at the three boys were sound asleep. She closed her eyes and said, "Grandfather and Ohanzee, please join me so we can finish what we have started."

When her grandfather and Ohanzee appeared, merging back into one, she stood over the boys. Then one by one, she placed her hands over their hearts and shot a brilliant blue light into them. As quickly as they had arrived, her grandfather and Ohanzee were gone.

Standing alone inside the teepee, listening to the soft sounds of the sleeping boys, she whispered, "Coahoma, Moki, Fala, when you wake up in the morning, you will discover that this night has changed you forever."

SHERRY COTTLE GRAHAM

CHAPTER 11

The Crossing

"Dream well," Laurel whispered as she watched the boys' soft movements as they slept. Then sadness flowed through her words as she continued, "You will need your strength for the long days ahead." Smelling the thick aroma of sage that filled her teepee, she was pleased that her helping spirits had put them into a deep sleep, but before she could relax, her mind spun back to the giant witches that had entered into their world. *How am I going to save Tiponi or Pontiac?* She fretted. *Their black magic is so powerful.*

Laurel knew that she needed to sleep, or she won't have the strength to continue her fight against these cruel witches. *Will I be able to trust these boys to help me fight this battle that I have created?* she wondered as she listened to the night creatures singing in the distance. As she looked around her teepee, she was relieved to see that her tactics had worked and, at least for the time being, that her students were safe.

When are these boys going to stop being so reckless? she wondered as she watched Coahoma shift under his covers. Then her mind drifted back to the real danger that was headed their way. Shrouded with uncertainty, *There are so many things that I need to teach them before they can fight these giant white witches*, she thought as she glanced at them. *But will I have the time to pass my knowledge to them?* She fretted. *At least, their powers will grow faster now, but it will be up to them to master these gifts that we have given to them*, she thought as she walked over to her sleeping mat.

Just as she leaned over and pulled back the corner of her blanket, she heard Awock hooting in a nearby tree. "May the spirits of the forest protect you tonight, my friend," she whispered, but before she undressed, she noticed that her fire was dwindling. *I must keep them warm tonight,* she thought as she walked over and prodded it with a long stick. When she saw the flames spring out from under its ashen logs, she decided to add more wood. She selected a couple of logs that were stacked beside the doorway and carefully laid them over the flames. *This should last us through the night*, she thought as she returned to her bed.

Nearly exhausted, she was pleased to see that someone had taken the time to arrange a comfortable mat for her. They had covered it with a beautiful handwoven blanket, and on the ground beside her bed, they had arranged a few soft rabbit skins, a small bowl of chamomile-scented lotion, and a clay container filled with water. They draped a beautiful hand-beaded and embroidered night gown across her bed. When she rubbed her fingers over the soft suede, she knew that Sonoma had been there.

Laurel lifted the wolf skin headdress off and placed it on the ground near the end of her bed. She pulled the corner of her dress up and untied her holster and slid it under her mat. When she had finished undressing, she picked up the cleanser and a soft fur. As she saturated her bare rough skin with the lotion, she worried about the white spirits that were spying on them. *Will I be able to save these people from these cruel mound builders?*

After she spread the soothing aromatic chamomile over her chapped and aching body, she hoped that she would be able to sleep. For many nights, she found that sleeping didn't come easy for her. Her mind raced with the problems that she continually faced in this harsh life, and many times she would see or hear the spirits of their dead. But tonight, the chamomile's spirit was strong, and it quickly escorted her into her private world of dreams.

Speaking softly as he hovered gently above her, Tecumseh called, "Laurel, Laurel . . . ," smiling as he looked at her. He watched her blink open her eyes. When she recognized him, he said, "Laurel, come with me. I want to show you your new home," as he stretched his hand toward hers. She clasped it and allowed him to pull her into his Happy World. To her, this transition was as easy as a butterfly, spreading her wings and lofting into the wind for the first time, leaving her old torn and tattered cocoon safely behind her.

She was beautiful and young again, alive and in her prime. She felt her thick black hair whisking across the center of her back. When she saw her lover and saw him smiling back, her heart soared like an eagle. A sense of pure joy rippled through her as she glided through the tunnel, moving toward the white light. She felt warm and safe as her body pressed against his. When she landed in his symphonic world that was filled with many new radiant colors, he said, "Laurel, I missed you." She choked back her tears when Tecumseh wrapped his powerful arms around her and said, "Welcome home."

"Tecumseh, you live here?" she asked, seeing a beautiful rainbow stretching overhead and felt a bright white light spilling down on her head and across her cheeks. It seeped into her soul, soothing her worries with its kinetic warmth. She listened to magnificent chiming sounds. It sounded like striking a thousand silver spoons upon a thousand crystal glasses, each crescendo more beautiful than the last. Each sound blended with the next, mesmerizing her with its divine melody. Overwhelmed by her emotions, she buried her face into his chest. Feeling his masculinity, she asked, "Where am I? Am I dead? Did I cross over?"

"You are here with me. This is all that matters," Tecumseh said as he bent over and kissed her.

As they stood embracing each other, feeling the joy of their reunion, she pressed her cheek against his and whispered, "I missed you. I would wake up every morning hoping to find you lying beside me, but it was always the same. My bed was always empty, and I am always alone."

"You were never alone, Laurel. I was always with you. I was there when my father cursed you. I heard him blame you for my death, and I watched him ban you from our tribe. I was with you as you traveled with our bear cub through the forest. I was helpless when I watched you cry yourself to sleep at night. When you thought that you were alone, I was there with you as you struggled to survive those long cold winter nights during your long journey. Laurel, you couldn't see me, but I chased away many wild beasts, shooed away the poisonous snakes, and I sent the hawk to guide you to your new home. Whenever you cried, I cried. But that one frigid night, when you were lost and thought that you were dying, sick, and alone under the black canopy of the never-ending forest, and you made the decision to walk with the spirits, my heart soared because I knew that you would find me."

"I remember. It was terrible, wandering alone in the woods. I lost you . . . my home . . . my family . . . everything. Lagundo was my constant and only companion. If it weren't for him, I wouldn't have survived. Then the hawk found me, he told me to follow, and I did.

He was always there a short distance ahead of us, calling to me, and I followed," Laurel said.

"Remember this," Tecumseh said as he grasped her shoulders and gently pushed her backward so that he could look into her eyes. "I am always with you. It is vital that you remember this!" Then he reached down with his strong rough-skinned hand and firmly grasped on to her left. He pulled her forward, "Come, I have something to show you."

As they walked across the emerald meadow, she was awestruck by a pair of shimmering rainbows that curved across his turquoise sky. "Welcome home," they signaled to her. As she looked around, she saw that the surrounding mountain range was covered in her favorite white pines. In the sky, she heard an eagle screaming, "Hello, Laurel!" She was awestruck by the sights and sounds of this new world as he led her onward.

She spotted an amber-colored lodge a short distance ahead of them. As they walked toward it, she realized that Tecumseh had built his home on a terrace overlooking an emerald valley. As she swung around, looking in all directions, she realized that his mountains were covered with her favorite white, pink, and red flowering rhododendrons, dogwoods, and laced with thousands of white flowering laurels. When they reached his home, Tecumseh said, "Laurel, this is where I live. Do you like it?"

"Yes, I love it," she said. "It is more beautiful than I could have ever imagined." Then she heard the sounds of babbling water and a thundering waterfall. Reading her expression, Tecumseh pointed toward a cluster of laurels that were growing behind his lodge. "Look, I built our lodge on the bank of a cold mountain stream. I remember how you loved the sound of water as it slaps against the rocks and the taste of cold mountain water. Laurel, look at this place. It never rains here, so you never have to worry about floods."

"But where will Lagundo sleep?" she asked.

"Look up there," Tecumseh said as he pointed toward a rocky outcrop overlooking their lodge. "Do you see your totem standing up there watching you? He will decide on Lagundo's fate."

When she looked up, she saw a powerful grizzly standing on the edge of a cliff. When she realized that he was watching her, she recalled his anger as he charged through the soul robbers to protect her. Even now, as she stood safely beside Tecumseh, her totem wasn't ready to abandon his duty.

"I must go and convince him to let Lagundo live with us," Laurel said.

"Later, Laurel. Come over here. You must see this," Tecumseh said. Grasping her hand, he led her to the edge of a cliff. As she looked down, she saw a beautiful green valley that stretched across the land far below. She gazed at a large cluster of long houses that were scattered across the valley. Then she gazed at a long beautiful stream that gently meandered past their homes and disappeared into the evergreen mountains. She felt the waves of pure love ripple through her as she studied the distant bowl-shaped mountains that rose and fell as far as she could see, and woven in between their shades of green were large clusters of white and pink.

It was hard for her to capture her breath as she adjusted to this magnificent canopy of streaming colors and pastel lights. Just as she thought that she had seen it all, she noticed that a group of people were gathering beside one of the faraway lodges. She leaned forward, squinting to see the inhabitants below. She saw that there were many men, women, teens, and children of all sizes and shapes. "Who are they?" she asked.

"Laurel, those are our people. Your mother and father are down there. They have been waiting for you to join us. Laurel, do you want to go down and see them?" Tecumseh asked. Then his voice grew soft, as he said, "Laurel, they suffered too when you left."

As her heart bubbled with excitement, "Yes. Can I? But how do I get down there?" she asked as she searched for a pathway.

"Ah, that's easy," he said as he scooped her up into his arms. "Hold on," he said as he stepped off the edge. They drifted down the side of the mountain and into the valley waiting below.

As she clung to her lover's neck, feeling his heart beating against hers, she spotted a waterfall cascading over the nearby cliff. She listened to its thundering song as it fell alongside the rose-tinted wall and into an aqua-tinted pool below. She was delighted when she saw how the sun lit up its surrounding mist, turning it into a halo of shimmering little diamonds and an occasional tiny rainbow.

"Look, Laurel. Your parents are coming to greet you," Tecumseh said as he nodded toward a group of people who were rushing toward them. When his feet hit the ground, she was surrounded by a large group of people. Instantly, she recognized her mother, father, grandmothers, grandfathers, and her siblings.

"Mother," Laurel whispered as she pressed her face into her mother's neck. "I missed you," she said.

"Laurel, child, I missed you," her mother said as she wrapped her arms around her and pulled her tight.

Laurel was soothed by her mother's warmth. Then she heard her father's voice beside her. When she saw him, she said, "Father, you are so young. You look just like you did when I was a child."

"Yes, Laurel, I have chosen this form. It was my favorite time during my life. I was strong, witty, full of life . . . ," he said as he pumped his arm muscles and grinned.

Like her, he was a well-known healer among the Shawnee, but when she was forced out of their tribe, she never knew what had happened to him. Maybe it was the way that he smiled or blinked his eyes that was magical to her. Whatever it was, she recalled his words, "Laurel, when you make a child laugh, the Great Mother laughs with you."

Then out of the corner of her eye, she noticed that he was carrying his favorite little bird mask with him. She remembered it. He would put it on and chase her around their campfire with it. When he'd catch her, he'd throw her into the air and tell her that she would learn to fly someday. Then he'd squat down and pretend to lay and egg and cackle and laugh, but more importantly, she recalled how he would wear this mask whenever he was healing a sick child. He told her, "This is a gift from our gods. It has magic in it."

Covering his face with his mask, he asked, "Laurel, do you remember this?"

"Yes, Father. I do," Laurel said.

"It was on that stormy night when Spotted Eagle was fighting for his life that I learned its secrets. The witches were so arrogant that they thought that anyone who would wear such a silly mask would be no match against their black magic, but when they got lost in my web of silly tricks, there wasn't a child around that I couldn't help . . . Funny thing about witches and demons, they think that they are so smart, invincible at times, but this makes them so vulnerable, doesn't it?"

"Yes, Father. It does," Laurel said.

Tecumseh said, "Laurel, come with me. I want to show you our bathing pool. We will return after you've seen it."

Laurel asked, "Mother, is it all right if I go with him?"

"Yes, Laurel. Go ahead," her mother waved. "We will be here when you return."

As soon as Tecumseh tugged on her hand, time flicked forward like a blink of an eye. She found herself standing near the bottom of this magnificent waterfall feeling its mist, looking into its clear aqua belly.

"It's strange how life works," Tecumseh said as he turned toward Laurel. "Sometimes when things seem hopeless, you have to stay focused on the things that you understand. Things like the rise and fall of energy, the path that the sun takes across the sky, the love a parent has for their child, the unreasonable fear that grips even the bravest of souls, making them tremble under the right conditions, and how a dream may seem like life, and how life may seem like a dream."

"What are you trying to tell me?" Laurel asked as she looked up him. She was amazed how strong he was as he skipped across a few large boulders that flanked the side of the pool and tossed a small pebbled into it.

Then he waved to her. He said, "Come here, Laurel, and look into this pool. And see what your destiny holds for you."

"My destiny is here with you," she said as she felt the water's cool mist on her skin. "You have created a home more beautiful that I could have ever imagined for us."

"Come, Laurel, before it's too late. You must see this," he said as he perched atop a large rock, gazing into the mysterious depths.

"Fine, let's see what it has to say," she responded as she skipped over the boulders. What was so important that she had to follow him there? When she jumped on the rock beside him, he turned and pulled her close. She felt his warm breath on the back of her neck and saw him point into the center of the rippling pool.

As she gazed into it, she saw an image forming in its center. "It's Tiponi," she said as she dropped on to a knee, trying to see what she was doing. Laurel said, "She was sick, but I couldn't tend to her because Pontiac wouldn't let me. Then the boys got sick. I abandoned her to help them."

"Yes, I know, Laurel. And I also know that your work isn't finished yet. You have to go back. You are the only one who can save her," Tecumseh said.

"But how can I? I don't understand her magic. It's different than ours . . . strange . . . cruel magic . . ."

"Trust in yourself and use what we have told you. And let your students help. They have chosen to travel down this path of witches and black magic, and they understand the risks that come with it.

"Yes, I know. When I sucked the witches out of Fala and Moki, I looked into their futures. I saw that their path led away from us," Laurel said.

"Laurel, you must let go of Coahoma. He is a man now. And you must let him go and let the Great Spirit decide his fate."

"But what about Pontiac? What do you see in his future?" she asked. Her guilt flowed through her words as she said, "It's my fault that he has the spirit of the white witch locked inside him."

"Laurel, with or without you, he would have performed this ritual. You know the risks that you take to make our gods reveal their secrets to you, and he has chosen to play this game. If he wins, then he will become the most powerful healer on the Great Mother, but if he loses, then put him under the knife, and do it quickly . . ."

"Laurel, wake up," Pallaton whispered. When she opened her eyes, he asked, "Where are the boys? The chief wants to see you and them at the high council's lodge," as he looked at their empty beds.

Disoriented, Laurel sat up and looked around. She said, "I don't know where they are. Go find them," she instructed as she watched his lean muscular body lift the corner of the flap and disappear.

Pallaton ran around the teepee and into the one behind it. As he entered, he spotted Akando who was sitting on the ground beside the fire, eating some roasted alligator meat. Akando saw that something was wrong.

"What now?" he asked as Pallaton walked over to his stash of weapons that were carefully stacked beside the doorway. "Get your weapons. We're going hunting again!"

Akando grabbed his weapons and followed Pallaton out of their teepee. Before he exited, he said, "Go tell the chief that we will bring his son back to him when we find him," and then he turned and disappeared.

Strapping their knife and tomahawk holsters to their hips, pulling their quivers filled with arrows across their shoulders, juggling their bows and spears in their hands, the gifted warriors jogged back to the boys' teepee. They looked for their tracks, and it wasn't long before they found them. Pallaton and Akando followed the tracks over the smoldering

ring of fire and confirmed that they were running northward across the meadow and straight back into the swamp.

"What are they doing? Why are they going back to the swamp?" Akando asked, running beside Pallaton.

"Ah, who knows *what* goes through the heads of those young shamans? This makes five winters that we have been chasing these boys around in these forests." Then fear clung to his words as he added, "Last night, I had a bad dream about the boys. I saw them. They were lost inside a very dark place, and a wolf with wicked yellow eyes and walking on two legs was following them."

CHAPTER 12

Voices from the Void

Just as Hashtahli chased his children from the sky, Coahoma woke up. He wondered what had happened to him as he turned over and saw Laurel sleeping on her mat. When he saw her frail movements, he wondered why she did not wake him. As he crawled toward his blood brothers, he stifled his fears as he moved, but when he saw their soft movements and the color of their skin, he knew that the demons had not taken them away from him. *She did it! She beat them*, he thought as he studied the outline of Fala's face.

It was early, and Coahoma knew that Laurel needed her sleep. He hoped that she was resting peacefully as he moved beside his two blood brothers, smelling the heavy blend of tobacco and sage as he gently shook them awake. When they sat up, he saw their eyes and knew, by the way that they moved, that their sickness was gone. *Her medicine is strong*, he thought as he pressed his finger to his lips and motioned for them to follow him. As they fled outside, he recalled the sage, the salt, the music, the dancers, and their masks. He wondered what other magic that she had used that he didn't see. *I'll ask her about her magic when she wakes up*, he decided.

Once they were outside, Coahoma felt the warm rays and knew that it was going to be a sunny day. *Spring is coming*, he thought as he looked over at Fala. "How are you?" he asked.

Fala smelled his arms. Then he sucked in a long cleansing breath and released it. His eyes lit up as he nodded and smiled, signaling to his two friends that he was all right. "I'm good," he said as he looked over at Moki. "Coahoma, what happened last night? I don't remember anything after I lay down," he asked.

"Me, either," Moki said. "I remember running with my mask on and seeing the demons flying over me. And I remember her sucking on Fala's stomach, but that's the last thing that I remember." Then his eyes widened and his mouth dropped as he said, "The lance—it called to me in my dreams. It said that it was waiting for me where I fell into the swamp." He wrinkled his brow and squinted, looking toward the forest. He said, "You can stay here, but I'm going to go back and get it." Without warning, he sprinted forward and jumped over the smoldering ring of fire.

Coahoma looked at Fala. With a slight nod, the boys were in agreement. They jumped over the ring and sprinted over the clearing and stopped when they hit the outer edge of the forest.

"What is wrong?" Coahoma asked as he pulled up beside Moki.

"Can't you feel it?" Moki retorted as he pressed his hands into the cold air. "Donehogawa is here. I can feel him. And he is angry!"

Just as Coahoma stepped forward, he saw Donehogawa. He saw the anger that spewed from his hollow eyes and heard it spill over into his words.

Losing his temper, Donehogawa hissed, "Why are you running into the forest? Are you trying to hide from me? I can see it in your eyes and through your words that your promises are weak. You don't have any intention to keeping them, do you?"

Coahoma remembered her words, "Don't let the spirit of the dead frighten you. If one should threaten you, stand your ground and spit on their feet," as he moved forward. "You don't frighten us," Coahoma said as he pointed his finger toward the ghost. "Return to your gate and leave us alone!" he said, growing impatient with pitiful spirit. "You have a choice, go home or follow us . . . Either way, we don't care," he said as he headed toward the path that led inside the forest. When he felt the tiny hairs on the back of his neck begin to rise, Coahoma turned around and spat, "We will help you, but not until we are finished here. And we will decide when that time comes—not you!"

Donehogawa realized that Coahoma was not afraid of him. He saw the determination in his eyes, and he knew that it was useless to argue. But he wasn't about to give up. In a deep sinister voice, he said, "No use hiding from me because I will find you, and I will follow you wherever you may run," he snorted as he blinked out of sight.

"Then follow us!" Coahoma yelled as he took off running. He shouted, "Come on! Let's go! I want to get back before Father wakes up."

Coahoma lead his blood brothers across the high ground, running deeper into the foreboding forest, charging in as fast as their outstretched legs could carry them. They followed their old tracks, jumping over rotting stumps, zigzagging between the ancient trees, until they reached the edge of the swamp.

Coahoma looked at the broken branches and the rope that still ran over the side of the deadly bank. He said, "The spear must be around here somewhere. Watch out for snakes and crocs . . . I see their tracks," as he pointed toward a few skid marks in the embankment. Then he sniffed the air. "Do you smell that rank smell?" he asked.

Moki tapped him on his shoulder as he pointed toward a large oak that was draped in grayish moss that grew beside the eastern bank. He whispered, "Look! Over there . . . It's the female Sasquatch that we saw last night, and she has Laurel's lance!"

Standing near the shoreline, she stamped the end on to the ground, running her hand along the leather swatches, taunting the boys with it. Her eyes were gleaming as she hoisted the spear out in front of her, encouraging them to take it from her.

"What kind of game is she playing with us?" Coahoma asked as he studied her temperament. "Moki, what do you think she wants?"

"She wants me to take the lance from her," Moki said as he assumed leadership of the group, leading them toward the female.

He watched her eyes and listened to the crazy voices that were inside his head. They said, "When she runs, follow her." Just as Moki was close enough to reach out and grab the lance, she ran into the brush, carrying the spear with her.

"Follow her!" Moki yelled as he chased after her.

As the boys moved through the brush, plunging deeper into the dark recesses of the woods, flanking the outer bank of the swamp, keeping her in their sight as they jogged over and around obstacles, jumping, weaving, sliding down shallow dips, running up the inclines, they were relieved when she slowed down and came to an abrupt halt.

"What is she doing?" asked Coahoma, standing beside his friends, watching her as she bent over a small creature that was lying on a grassy mat on the ground. As Coahoma scanned the surrounding area, he asked, "Do you see the large male? He must be around here somewhere. Look at all of those footprints," he said as he pointed toward the ground.

SHERRY COTTLE GRAHAM

"Look, it's a baby!" Fala said as he stepped forward. He kept an eye on her as he studied the infant that was lying beside her feet. "He's not moving," Fala said. "I think that he's unconscious," as he studied its movements.

"Stay here . . . I'm going to get the lance," Moki said as he slowly moved toward her. For some unknown reason, he knew that she wouldn't hurt him as he reached out and took the lance with one hand and gently touched her thick matted arm with the other. As her memories flashed through him, he knew that she wanted them to help her son, and she knew that they would try.

Moki moved back toward Fala, carrying the lance with him. "Fala, she led us here to help her baby. Do you think that you can help him?"

As Fala moved forward, she retreated. When he stood over the infant, a voice said, "Fala, look into his mouth. He is strangling on a bone." Fala twisted the baby over as he listened to the whispering voices. They said, "Tilt his head back, and when his mouth drops open, gently reach in with three fingers. When you feel the bone, press down on it and lift. You will be able to remove it without any trouble from the mother."

Fala felt Moki's presence beside him as he obeyed his guides. He glanced up at Moki when he pulled a small gnawed rib bone from the baby's throat, allowing him to breathe once more.

Coahoma was amazed at Fala's ability to work with this beast. He watched him turn the baby on its side and rub its back, while his mother stood guard a short distance away. But then, something caught his attention. It told him to turn around and to look into the thick grove of towering pines. Coahoma turned around and saw a brilliant beam of blue light, pulsing up toward the morning sky from the Great Mother. He didn't have to ask. The voice in his head said, "Coahoma, this is the Great Mother's powerful connection to her father above. It reaches into the home of your gods. Tell the ol' woman who walks with a bear where it is. She will know what to do."

Wanting to get a closer look at this energy field, he silently slipped through the overgrowth and walked up a shallow incline and on to this sacred ground. He trusted that Fala and Moki were able to take care of the baby Sasquatch, leaving him the freedom to explore this discovery. He knew that this would be a significant find for Laurel. He wasn't certain how she could use its power, but he knew that she would.

"Moki . . . Fala, move away from the beast!" Pallaton yelled, hoisting his spear as he charged forward. As he placed the female inside his crosshairs, he knew that Akando was attacking too.

"No!" Moki yelled as threw himself in between them. "Stay back! She's friendly!" he screamed as Fala jumped up and stood beside him, blocking their warrior's path to her.

Coahoma heard the men's voices and rushed toward them. As he raced through the brush, he made so much noise that it distracted the warriors. "Stop! Stop! Don't hurt her! She's friendly!" he yelled as he slid down the shallow hill and tripped over a log, sprawling head first into a clump of waist-high weeds.

Pallaton and Akando slowed down and dropped their spears as they watched Coahoma wrestle free from the clinging vines and hop up. They were stunned when he yelled, "I'm fine!" and ran forward to greet them. From the corner of their eyes, they saw the female bolt over and pick up her infant, and they watched her disappear into the creaking shadows with him.

"Boys, what are you doing here?" Pallaton asked. Accessing their situation, a sense of frustration welled up inside him. He leaned forward, balancing his powerful body with his weapon. He groaned, "Um, where are your weapons? After all of these winters, haven't we taught you anything?"

Confirming Pallaton's distress over their recklessness, Akando scolded, "I wouldn't want to be in your lodge tonight when your parents' learn that you traveled into the swamp without a spear. I think your mothers are going to be like angry little hornets tonight."

Fala couldn't hold back his lighthearted reply to redirect Akando's annoyance as he joked, "But we have a spear. We just had to come here to pick it up."

"Hum . . . I think that you will be carrying water for many moons," Pallaton responded.

"Never mind," Coahoma said. "I have to go see Laurel. I have something important to tell her." Then a strange expression flashed over Coahoma's face. He slowly raised his hand and signaled Pallaton with a slight twist of his finger, whispering, "Move slowly toward me."

Before Coahoma could finish his warning, Moki lunged forward, driving his right shoulder straight into Pallaton's side, wrapping his arms around his waist as he flew, knocking him on to the ground. Just

SHERRY COTTLE GRAHAM

as Pallaton hit the ground, Fala hurried into his spot. He stood directly between Pallaton and a large rattle snake that was coiled under a nearby shrub. They heard a loud spit, and then they heard its rattles, warning them to move away!

Akando whispered, "Fala, move back . . . ," as he crept forward. He raised his spear, trying to find a clean shot at the rattler that was curled into a tight ring. Its head was up, mouth open, tail buzzing, and baring its two large protruding fangs as it prepared to launch its venom into Fala.

Akando was shocked when Fala refused to budge. He saw a calmness radiate through Fala as he raised his hand, and with a gentle twist of his wrist, Fala commanded him to "Stay away." Not wanting to frighten the snake, Akando stood perfectly still as he watched Fala playing his game with the deadly serpent.

Fala slowly waved his hand in front of the snake. When he had its full attention, he whispered, "Shh . . . big brother. Ah, my friend. Come to me." Fala repeated his powerful words as he slowly waved his palm in front of it. Then to everyone's surprise, the rattler dropped his head, uncoiled his body, and slithered out from under the bush, heading directly toward Fala. "Come to me, my friend," he said as he stooped over and picked up the snake, holding his head with his right and secured its body with his left. As Fala held it, he saw the stunned look on Pallaton and Akando's faces when he said, "Meet our brother. He wants to be your friend."

Pallaton stood up, standing a clear distance from Fala. He said, "Fala, put the serpent down. We are pleased that he is our friend, but tell him that it's time for us to leave."

Fala gently released the snake, allowing it to slither into the brush. When the serpent disappeared he turned around and caught the wrath of Akando who was standing an arm's length away. "What are you doing? Are you mad?" he choked. His heart was still racing from what he had just seen.

Pallaton moved toward Fala, grasping his arms. He warned, "Don't ever do that again. Yes, your totem is strong, but this is not the time to test the gods! What good would come from your death?"

Regaining his composure, Akando recognized that the boys were different. They looked the same, but as he walked over and stood beside Pallaton, he saw an odd gleam in their eyes. "What is happening to you?" he asked.

"Akando, something happened to us last night. I do not know what it was, but this morning, when I woke up, I knew that I was different. I hear voices and see things I cannot explain."

"Yes," Moki responded. "When I woke up this morning, I heard voices of men and women, and they are telling me things. Sometimes they speak to me about things that are yet to be—secrets that I don't understand."

"What kind of secrets?" asked Pallaton.

"Pallaton, you are going to take us into a new land. There you will fight a giant white warrior to save a stranger. I can see blood all around you, but you will survive. Your deeds will bring honor to our people, but to the strangers, they will seek their revenge on you," Moki said.

"We must go," said Pallaton as he hoisted his spear to his side. "Let's get back to the village before your father gets angry." As they exited the forest and saw their village a short distance ahead, they smelled the cooking fires and saw many of their friends milling around their lodges, waiting for them. It didn't take long for the story to resonate through their village about these escapades, and today was no exception.

"Morrigan is here. I can feel her," Moki whispered as they walked across the clearing.

"Where is Pontiac?" Pallaton asked as he glanced over at Moki. He watched Moki's expression change as his eyes gazed straight ahead. He saw, by the way that he twisted his head, that he was listening to someone or something. A shiver ran through him when he heard Moki say, "Pontiac is heading toward the councilmen's lodge, and he's bringing Tiponi with him."

"Wait," Coahoma said. "Does Pontiac know that we were at Morrigan's lodge the other night?"

Moki watched his elders, moving in the distance toward the high council's lodge. He quietly dropped his head as he said, "No. They believe that we were the angry spirits of the dead men that fester on top of those poles." Just as he took a small step forward, he turned toward Coahoma and said, "Coahoma, my guides are telling me to warn you about Pontiac. They say that he is changing into something that we don't understand . . . something that has never been and that we need to walk with caution when we he is nearby."

"Look! Over there . . . standing beside Ituha. It's Pontiac . . . ," Akando said, pointing toward the circle of teepees. "And he has Tiponi with him."

"Yes, and he's looking this way," warned Pallaton.

"Should we join them?" Akando asked.

"No!" Coahoma whispered as he intercepted the signal to "stay away" that his father sent to him. He knew, by the way that his father tilted his ceremonial lance toward him, that he was not welcome. He had learned many signals from his father. He was their chief, and he was gifted with the ability to see the truth. No matter how hard a man would try to hide it from him, he would see through their lies and make harsh decisions to punish them if necessary; and he knew, by the way that he was standing and the tilt of his spear, that something was wrong. When he saw his father tilt his lance toward his gathering lodge, Coahoma said, "Father is signaling to us to join him at his lodge, and he is signaling danger."

"Yes," Pallaton said. "I see. We must proceed with caution."

As Coahoma and his friends strolled through their village of lofted huts, a group of children who were waiting for their morning meals spotted them. Not wanting to miss the excitement that always followed these distinguished boys, they ran over to greet the group. They shouted, "Hey, Coahoma, Moki, Fala, wait up!" as they ran forward, laughing, smiling, skipping and hopping, wanting to be near their young heroes. They wanted to discover their secrets as they anxiously surrounded around them. "Are you going to the high council's lodge? Can we come with you?" they asked as they trailed along.

Fala was the first to speak. "Come with us if you want, but you cannot come into the lodge. However, you can go fishing with us when our meeting is over. Maybe you can help us catch a few nets of fish for Laurel's bear."

"Yea!" they erupted as they danced in circles, clapping their hands. Their faces reflected small white sets of teeth and twinkling eyes within their vibrant upturned lips. "We'll get the nets from our fathers, and we'll wait for you at the river. Hurry up and meet us there!"

As they stepped across the rocks, Nita, Moki's tall and elegant sister pushed the children aside to speak to her brother. "Moki, how are you? We missed you at our morning meal," she asked, looking at Coahoma through the corner of her eye.

"The chief wants to talk to us. I will come back to eat when he is finished with us . . . I promise," Moki said as he looked over at Coahoma.

"Your friends say that you are going fishing. Can I come too?" Nita asked. She smiled as she waited for Moki to answer.

"Ah, I do not care. Come if you like. But you must wait for me at our lodge, and I will walk with you when I am finished," Moki reassured her.

As they approached the door, Nita turned toward Coahoma and asked, "Are you going to go fishing too?"

"Yes, I will be there," he responded, looking pleased that she had asked him.

"Great, I will bring our nets and something for us to eat. I will see you soon," she reassured him as she turned and retreated from the maze of chatting children.

"She likes you," Moki said to Coahoma, smiling. "She will wait a long time for you, but I see that you are in love with another . . . But time will be her ally."

Coahoma asked, "Who am I in love with?"

Before Moki could answer, the flicker in his eyes exposed his knowledge to Coahoma.

Coahoma whispered so only Moki could hear. "Ah . . . Don't say anything to anyone else about this," Coahoma said with a scowl, looking somewhat miffed at Moki for potentially exposing his intimate secret, but Coahoma knew that things were different now. He knew that it was impossible for him to keep any secrets from his blood brothers and that they wouldn't be able to hide any from him.

Sensing Coahoma's displeasure with his words, Moki said, "It's going to be a wild journey for all of us . . ."

CHAPTER 13

Parting Ways

When Coahoma reached the lodge, his heart ached when he saw his greatest mentor leading Tiponi by the hand. He knew, by the way that he hunched his shoulders and stomped his feet, that Pontiac was losing his battle against this witch, and Lugh was winning. *Will her magic be strong enough to save him?* he wondered. Then in the distance, Coahoma saw his father motion, telling him to go inside. As he entered, he thought, *Now we'll see how well Father can play this game of deception.*

Being the son of a chief had its privileges. He calmed his emotions as he guided his friends to their places. As he walked through the luminous streams of silvery white light that penetrated down through the scantly woven walls, he silently prayed, "Please help us," to his Mighty Spirit.

Coahoma smelled the rich aroma of many custom blends of tobacco, jimson, and hemp-laced smoke. He saw its whimsical streams as it freely floated throughout the room. He felt its effect on him as he walked with his friends. *Why is this smoke so thick?* he wondered as he spotted his blanket stretched out on the ground. As he headed toward it, he heard a small voice inside his head say, "Take shallow breaths . . . The smoke is to calm Pontiac."

Without saying a word, Coahoma slowed his breath. When he signaled to Moki and Fala to sit down on his blanket, he noticed that they were doing the same thing, but before they settled down, he heard a murmur resonate through the room. When he looked up, he saw Pontiac enter into the lodge behind them. His heart froze. He wondered, *How much do these men know?* as he scanned their faces. When he sat down, he spotted Laurel sitting directly across him. He was pleased when he saw her signal, asking him to send Pontiac over to sit beside her.

As Pontiac approached, he saw that his spirit was different. He wasn't the same fun-loving man that he used to know. When he saw his wild eyes and grimacing smile, Coahoma pressed his memories of Pontiac aside as he directed him toward Laurel. "Go sit over there," he commanded. "She wants you to sit beside her."

"Yes," Moki nodded as he held Laurel's lance upright, hoping that she would see it.

As Pontiac walked away, Coahoma wondered, *What has he done to his clothes and his headdress? He doesn't even know how to display his feathers any longer.* Then as he watched him sit beside Laurel, he saw Pontiac raise his eyes and stare at him. When he saw his face contort into a strange smirk, he knew that he was dangerous.

As he waited for his father, Coahoma glanced over at his elders, and he saw them staring back. This was the first time that his father had invited him to join his private world. He was excited as he saw his tribe's prominent men wearing their uniquely adorned costumes, signifying their ranks among his people. He counted three shamans sitting toward the rear of the lodge alongside their wise men and storytellers. The shamans were wearing their customary wolf skin capes, carting their ceremonial masks and rattles, toting large leather bags filled with jimson weed, hemp, and tobacco. They were sitting in small groups, passing around these powerful plants. The men were stuffing their pipes with their sacred blends and smiling as they shared this time with their comrades.

Then Coahoma spotted Dakota sitting in the back among a group of braves. He was pleased to see that his brother and his buddies were wearing their brightly beaded tunics and leggings as well as their fancy breastplates, amulets, and hoisting their meticulously handcrafted and brightly beaded fur and feathered headdresses. They were a brave group of ruthless yet compassionate young men, never killing unless the situation warranted it, always willing to sacrifice their lives to save another, never shedding a tear, screaming, or moaning in pain. They were like the mighty mountain lions strutting their symbolic uniforms that are adorned with their long serrated bone and onyx blades and rounded tomahawks.

The primary rule that their elders honored was to protect their loved ones, and they took this rule seriously. As Coahoma studied them, he was pleased to see these lean and athletic men sitting together yet separated into smaller groups with the older more experienced warriors with their long flowing headdresses in front, whereas the newly inducted ones, donning smaller racks, were sitting toward the back, including his elder brother, Dakota.

When Coahoma glanced over at Dakota, he heard his brother's thoughts spinning through his mind. He said, "Why is my brother and his loco friends here with this council? They aren't warriors. They are just a bunch of little boys trying to pretend that they are powerful shamans. They have never fought in a battle or ever saved a single person. In fact, we are always pulling them from some stinking hole or finding them lost in the forest. I don't understand Father's reasoning for this. He's always been father's favorite, but Coahoma will never become our chief—I will not let him!"

Coahoma was shocked to learn of his brother's contempt of his presence among his elders. *I don't want to become chief*, he thought as he wrestled with his brother's words. *I still don't understand my gifts—why should he?* he thought as he turned his attention to a group of their elite warriors that were sitting in front of him. He listened to their stories about fighting against the demons as they waved their arms in exaggerated motions, smoking their beloved ceremonial pipes. Coahoma knew that they were oblivious to the real danger that they were now facing, and he was glad.

"Ah, everyone is talking about their battle against the evil spirits last night. I am sorry I missed it," Pontiac said, leaning over, addressing Laurel who was wrapped in an old tattered blanket. "I couldn't leave Tiponi, or the demons would have come after her too. Are you angry with me?"

"Nah, we are not angry. How can we be angry? You did what you must do. How is Tiponi?" Laurel asked. "Where is she?"

"She is with Sonoma. Her fever broke, and the spots have faded, so I brought her with me. But Sonoma took her so I could join you."

As Coahoma watched Pontiac speaking with Laurel, he heard another murmur echo through the room. "Father is coming. And look—Tiponi is with him," he said to Moki and Fala. "Father never brings children in here. Something is wrong . . . I can feel it," he said.

Chief Ituha looked at Coahoma as he approached him. He was dressed in his favorite beaded and fringed clothing. He was wearing his new furred and eagle-feathered headdress that covered his forehead and draped over the back of his neck. Just as he reached Coahoma, he said, "Coahoma, take Tiponi and make her sit beside you," as he passed her to him.

Coahoma whispered, "Father, what is happening? Why is Tiponi here?"

"Tiponi, sit down and be quiet, child—stay with Coahoma," Ituha said, ignoring Coahoma's question, but he smiled at Moki and nodded in satisfaction at the lance that he was holding.

Ituha strutted toward the front of the lodge, carrying his speaking lance with him. This lance was trimmed along its entire length with a beautiful pattern of young eagle feathers. On the opposite side of the staff, Fala's father had carved a lovely arrangement of feathers, tip to end, breaking it a little off center where Lanto whittled an obvious notch to match the chief's fingers. And on top, he had inserted a smooth hand-knapped white flint arrowhead.

When Ituha saw his new lance, his eyes lit up. Holding it carefully, he rubbed his hand over the carvings and quietly inspected its intricately carved feathers. Then he wrapped his fingers into the grip and stamped its base on to the earth. He was so proud of his new status symbol, declaring to all that he is chief that he strutted around with it in his hand for the next three days. Now he only uses it when he conducts meetings, sensing that it links him to the infinite wisdom of his gods.

Raising his arms, the chief hoisted the seven-foot lance into the air, capturing his councilmen's attention. When all of their eyes were on him, he positioned its deadly shaft gently on to the hard ground. Then he lifted his head and softly prayed, "I give thanks to our gods from the Father Sky, the sun, the moon, the gods from the four winds, and the gods from the Great Mother. I thank you for protecting our people from the black forces that swept through our village when the darkness blanketed our land. If it were not for your intervention, many of our young men would be walking among the soulless shadows and lost in this land of the dead." Then he dropped his hands, taking his time. He scanned every face that was seated before him, taking a mental note of those in attendance. He continued, "I have called you together to thank you for saving my son and his friends during this great battle with the demon spirits. I am proud to call you my friends, and our gods thank you for your bravery. Like the bear protecting her cubs, you fought hard to protect our young, and the spirits are happy with you."

Then he glanced at the ground and took a breath. Then he continued, "I have talked with the spirits, and we are going to hold a celebration in your honor. We will dance around the fire and sing our songs of praise to our gods. We will honor your bravery at the next full moon when the flowers paint our land. Tell your wives to prepare a feast for us as we dance under the light of the full moon, and we will tell our story of our victory over the soulless demons."

As a muffle of approval hummed through the room, wanting to make his decisions before the sweet aroma affected his mood, he continued, "Laurel, please come forward," as he swept his arm toward the old woman who was sitting beside Pontiac.

When she heard her name, she tossed her blanket aside and stood up. Bending over, she picked up her mask and rattles and joined the chief in front of the gathering.

"Does this concern Tiponi?" she asked as she stared across the room toward the child.

"Yes. I have just learned that her mother is sick with the fever, and you must leave us, take your medicine, and tend to her. We will keep the girl here with us, but before you leave, I think that Moki has something that he wants to return to you. Moki, come forward, son," he said as he looked at Moki. Raising his right hand, he flagged Moki to come to the front of the room and to join them.

Moki knew that the chief was pleased with him as he carried it toward them. He wondered who like it better as he handed it back to Laurel. When she took it from him, he said, "We hope that you are pleased with its return."

Moki saw a sense of pride rush through his chief as Laurel pulled it to her side. He was delighted when she stroked her fingers across its engravings and smiled. After a few moments, she handed the spear to Ituha and said, "Please hold this for me," as she pressed her hand toward Moki. When Moki accepted hers, she delivered a message to him in such a way that no one else knew of this exchange.

"Moki, return to your place," Chief Ituha commanded, signaling him with a twist of his wrist.

Trying to keep his eyes from disclosing his secrets, Moki kept his head down and avoided eye contact with Tiponi as he sat down. Quietly, he leaned sideways and lightly touched Coahoma with his shoulder, stilling the voices inside his head as he warned his friend about Tiponi. "Morrigan's presence is strong inside Tiponi, so keep your thoughts silent," he said.

Coahoma felt a chill run through him as he watched Moki pass his warning on to Fala. Beginning to panic, he heard her speaking to him. "Coahoma, clear your mind and call upon the powers of our Great Mother to steady your emotions. Son, relax and feel her energy flowing from the earth and into your spirit. She is your rock—your constant guardian."

As Coahoma blanked his mind and called up the Great Mother, he heard his father say, "Laurel, Tiponi's mother is sick. You need to take your medicine and go to her. The child will stay with the ol' woman who walks with a limp."

As he expected, Pontiac jumped up and demanded, "The child stays with me!" as he stomped toward the front of the gathering. Disregarding their custom of obedience, Pontiac scowled, "She still has the spots and needs my medicine."

How is Father going to handle him? Coahoma wondered as he saw Lugh's temperament spilling out in front of them. *Now everyone is going to know of his possession*, he thought as Tiponi ran and stood beside Pontiac. When she reached up and grabbed his hand, Coahoma saw the love that existed between the two, but he also saw their cunning—their wickedness.

Coahoma knew that his father had won this first round of wit with his enemy. Pontiac had challenged and won his right to remain with Tiponi in Laurel's lodge, while she would walk away to pray to her gods and to devise her strategy with his father.

As Tiponi stood beside Pontiac, she pressed her tiny frame against his. Coahoma watched his father raise his lance and say, "The decision is made. Tiponi will stay with Pontiac, and Laurel will leave our village to care for Alawa." Then Ituha motioned for Pallaton to come forward. He said, "Pallaton, I am placing you in charge of protecting Laurel. Gather a few of our best men and go with her and DO NOT carry any news back to me of snakebites or wild beasts.

Coahoma knew that his father had one last task to accomplish before the gathering was over. He knew that his father was going to send him and his friends to stay with Pontiac, and he waited for his father to begin down this next path of deceit with this wild man. He heard his father say, "Coahoma, go home, collect your things. You will meet Pontiac and Tiponi at Laurel's lodge. Fala, Moki, I will talk to your parents, but make arrangements to meet Coahoma there."

SHERRY COTTLE GRAHAM

Pontiac spat on the ground and kicked the dirt with his toe. He yelled, "No! Those mangy brats are going to stay with us!"

Was it time to put him under the knife? Coahoma wondered as he watched his rage. Never before had he ever witnessed such blatant disregard for one's superiors. As the tension mounted inside the lodge, and many of their braves jumped up to defend their chief, Laurel stepped forward. She held out her hand and motioned for them to sit back down.

"Pontiac," she said as she placed her mask over her face, beginning her charm. "The boys will take care of Lagundo while I'm away. I'm certain that they will not interfere with you, but if you want to haul his water and gather his fish, then we will not send the boys to help with these daily chores."

Coahoma saw a bewildered expression pass over Pontiac's face. He knew, by the way that he rolled his eyes and took a long breath, that he didn't want to tend to the old bear. As he gathered his thoughts, he said, "They can come, but if they get in my way, then I will send them back to you."

"Ah," Ituha said. "If you send them back to us, then we will take the child, and you will be relieved of your duties to her. Do you understand my conditions?"

Coahoma knew that his father had pushed Pontiac into a trap. He knew the gathering was over when Pontiac picked up Tiponi and said, "They can stay, but they must obey my commands," and stomped out of the lodge carrying her with him.

Coahoma was the first to speak after his father had released them from the gathering. As they followed the men outside, Coahoma said, "Moki, Fala . . . Go home . . . Tell your mothers what has happened. Meet me at the river and bring some food to share. After we eat, we will spear a few fish for Lagundo. He will be hungry so bring your fishing spears with you."

"I'll bring a net," Moki volunteered.

As Coahoma swung around his neighbor's lodge, he spotted his mother standing outside, tending a large pot that was hoisted over a roaring fire. "Mother!" he yelled as he headed toward her. "Guess what, I'm going to be staying with Pontiac and Tiponi at Laurel's lodge."

"I know," she responded. "I have packed a few of your things for you. They are inside the lodge on the rack beside the entrance."

"How did you know?"

"I know many things. I am your mother," she said. "Son, I want you to be careful. I do not know how this is going to work out, but I know that the gods will be watching over you." She stared into her cooking pot as she asked, "Are you hungry?" She hoped that he would stay and eat with her, but she knew that he wouldn't.

"No, Mother. Many of us are meeting beside the shallows. We are gathering food for the old bear, and Nita is bringing some food for us to eat. I will eat whatever she brings."

"She is such a lovely girl. She likes you, you know."

"Mother, I don't have time for her right now. Maybe someday, maybe when I'm older."

"Son, don't let life pass you by. You will always want to make time in your life for those whom you love and the ones who love you," she responded as she reached out and drew him close. As she wrapped her arms around him and nuzzled her cheek against his, she said, "I love you. Your father and I will be here when you return." When she pushed him back a step, she recognized that he was different. He wasn't the young boy who lived in her lodge and ate her food. He was leaving the safety of her nest, and life, as he knew it, would never be the same.

CHAPTER 14

Keeping Secrets

Seeing the sadness in his mother's eyes and the evilness in Pontiac's, he recalled her words, "A man's eyes are the windows into his soul." He felt the heaviness of these words as he shoved his feeling aside and opened his medicine pouch. He smelled its sweet odor as he pulled his favorite stone from it. As he felt its cool smooth surface and saw its calming turquoise color, he spotted his father strutting toward him. As Ituha walked through the white layers of wispy smoke that drifted past him on the western wind from the women's cooking fires, Coahoma saw the fear in his eyes and felt his agony as he approached. He had only seen this expression one other time in his life, and it was when he carried the news of his brother's death to him. When he spoke, Coahoma heard his sorrow flowing through his words.

"Son," Ituha said, "you looked into the eyes of a crazy man today, and you saw the soul of a witch that is locked inside him. Son, I have heard stories about such things from our old medicine woman, and now I see that her stories are true." He stopped and untied the holster that was strapped to the side of his hip. Coahoma felt his fear as he pulled his knife from it and held it up for him to see its smooth polished black blade. "Son, I know that you are a healer, but I need for you to strap this on. It is the right size and shape to slide into the belly of a man," he said as he slid it back into its sheath. "I am sending Pallaton and Akando to watch over you tonight. They will be outside if you need them," he said as his sad eyes contorted with worry. "Son, may the gods be with you," Ituha said as he handed his knife to Coahoma and walked away.

Seeing his traveling bags and tending his weapons, a few villagers raised their clenched fists and signaled, "Be safe, my friend!" as he walked by; and he knew, by the way they stiffened their bodies and watched him through the corner of their eyes, that they were participating in this game of illusion with him.

"May the spirits be with you," he responded by clenching his fist into a firm ball as he passed beside their raised lodges, leaving the smells of the cooking fires behind him.

He jogged toward an old path that meanders alongside the Atchafalaya River. As he moved into a grove of tall pines that shaded the banks with their outstretched arms and smelled their heavy aroma, he spotted a group of his friends who were fishing upstream. When he saw the blue sky reflecting on the river's lazy surface, the memory of the blue eyes of Ethane' exploded inside him, knocking his breath away. As he visualized her streaming tears and swollen face, he felt her charm seeping back into his soul, consuming his innermost thoughts. He was happy to have this quiet time alone with her to ponder her frailties amid this unwinding drama of her parents. Just as his loins began to tremble with the memories of her sweet musk, he heard Moki yell, "Hey, Coahoma, wait up!"

Not far behind him, he spotted Moki and Fala. They were walking at a fast pace toward him, carrying their traveling bags, weapons, and fishing spears, leading Nita along the way. As they approached, Coahoma studied their auras against the cool dark shadows of the surrounding forest, not because he had to, but because he knew he could. As he gazed at the flowing streams of pastel lights, he recalled his lessons about the meaning of each color, and he was pleased by what he saw. He knew that they were healthy and free from any dark forces that might have staked a claim to them.

Then he turned his attention to Nita, who was quietly walking behind Moki and Fala, carrying a large woven bag and lugging a wadded-up fishing net. She was content listening to her brother and his closest friend babble over their recent adventures. Slowing as they approached, they pulled up beside Coahoma and promptly fell into a casual pace beside him, leaving Nita alone.

Moki said, "It sounds as if the whole village is waiting for us," as he looked toward the bend. "Fala and I are packed. Neither of us brought much . . . didn't think it was necessary. Father is going to check on us every day before daybreak, and Nita is going to come with him. If we don't need anything, then they are going to cross the river and begin clearing the land for the upcoming planting festival. Father is anxious to plant his new maize seeds."

When Moki mentioned the seeds, Coahoma recalled the trappers who visited their village during the muggy days of summer. He visualized the strange ways that they spoke and were dressed. At first, he was afraid of them. He kept his bow and arrows with him during the day and slept with his knife and spear during the night. He didn't trust these men who had strange tattooed black stripes across their faces, wore quills through their noses and large plugs in their earlobes. These men are evil, he thought, but with time, he realized that he was wrong. "I should have known by the color of their auras that they were good men," Coahoma scowled. *I have much to learn about people who live in faraway places*, he decided.

Moki asked, "Coahoma, do you remember the man who wore those strange claws?"

Coahoma nodded as he recalled this stranger.

Moki said, "I was surprised when Father traded his new blade and holster for a handful of seeds. How does Father know that these seeds will even grow?" Then Moki looked in the direction of his father's field and continued, "It was odd how that man explained to Father how to plant these maize seeds, but Father seemed to understand everything that he said. We will see. If anyone can grow it, Father will."

Coahoma said, "Ah, you are always talking about plants. I think that your father will be serving this maize to us during our harvest ceremony." Coahoma adjusted his traveling pack on his shoulder. He glanced in the direction of the voices and said, "I am getting mighty hungry. How about you?"

"Me too," Moki replied.

Coahoma replied, "Mother says that it is because I am growing. She wanted me to eat with her, but I told her that Nita was bringing food for us." He turned and looked at Nita who was walking beside Fala. "What did you bring for us to eat?" he asked. As he looked at her, he noticed that a soft pink glow was radiating around her. *She is in love. Who is she in love with?*

Nita's face lit up as she observed Coahoma looking at her. Seeing his rugged face smiling back, she cooed, "I brought us some hickory smoked venison, mashed tubers, frog legs, and some dried rattlesnake meat. I hope you will like it. Father spent many hours tending the smoking pit. Oh, and I bought some pecan and honey cakes."

As she talked, Coahoma watched the way she moved her lips and heard the softness of her voice. He saw her excitement as she talked about the food that she brought to share with them. Then he noticed her simple leather fringed dress and her bone necklace that hugged the warm delicate skin around her neck. When he saw her tilt her head and pull the edges of her lips into a gentle smile, he knew that she was flirting with him. *I can't believe that this is Moki's sister. She must be the prettiest girl in our tribe*, he thought as he fell back, wanting learn more about her feelings for him.

"Nita, can I help you carry your sack?" Coahoma asked.

"No, I am fine. We don't have much further to travel," Nita responded, flushing a bit. She was pleased that he was offering to relieve her load. Living in an isolated land, surrounded by wild animals and dangerous swamps, she knew that everyone had to work hard to survive; and she wanted Coahoma to see that she was a strong and capable woman. She had fallen in love with him many winters ago, but he was always too busy running with his friends and learning the ways of a shaman to notice her. Now that he was walking beside her, she hoped that he would learn the truth.

"Nita, what are you carrying?" Dakota yelled, running toward them. He rushed past Moki and Fala, scooped the sack from Nita's shoulder, and slid it over his. He asked, "Why did it take so long for you to get here? We have caught many baskets of crayfish and some carp for the old bear." Grinning at Coahoma, he asked, "Do you want me to carry them up the hill for you?"

"No, I don't need your help," Coahoma said as he fell in line behind his brother and Nita, watching his elder brother hover over her like a large buck deer, antlering his competition away. He noticed how his brother had moved so close beside her that his arm would brush against hers as she moved. Like lightning flashing across a stormy sky, Coahoma knew that Dakota was in love with Nita. *Does she love him or me?* he wondered as Ethane' crept back into his thoughts.

As the blood brothers approached the river, they saw Fala's cousin standing near the shoreline. When Etu learned that their young shaman had arrived, he yelled, "Hey, Fala, over here! Come . . ."—as he waved—"and see what we have in our nets."

As they walked down the embankment and toward their friends, Coahoma spotted Lanto and Makah tending a cooking fire a short distance away. He saw that they were enjoying their time, standing guard over the teens and young adults. When the two men saw that their sons had arrived, Coahoma knew that they were pleased by the way that they smiled and waved to them.

"Coahoma, come and eat!" Nita yelled as Dakota placed her sack on to a thick patch of green moss. Then she kneeled down and untied the cords, gently releasing the contents that were stored inside.

Sitting on a few large flat rocks, eating their food, the boys were careful not to talk about their journeys as a few of their friends surrounded them, asking, "Where did you go? Did you really see a Sasquatch? What else did you see?"

Coahoma looked at them, dropping his head, and with a large sigh, he said, "We cannot speak to you about our travels, but I can tell you about the Sasquatch. It was a girl, and she loves Moki," he said, grinning as he wrapped his arms around his bent knees and smiled.

"Hey, she did not like me! I was helping her," Moki retorted, tossing a small pebble toward Coahoma.

"She will come and steal you away in your sleep if you are not careful," Coahoma teased.

"Ah, she is too busy tending her baby to bother with me," Moki responded. "Anyway, she'll probably try to steal you away."

"Nah, but she was very pretty and a little smelly too, don't you think?" Coahoma chimed as he jumped up. "She was about this tall"—stretching his hand high over his head—"and she smiled when Fala pulled the bone from the baby's throat. I thought that she might give Fala a whopping big kiss and hug!"

"Hey, don't bring me into this. She liked Moki, not me. I was only able to yank that little bone from its throat," Fala said.

"Weren't you afraid?" Coahoma's older cousin, Akule, asked.

"Yea, a little," Fala said. "But I knew that Moki was shielding me from her, and I was more afraid that he might wake up and bite my fingers off! It had these really sharp teeth—kinda like a baby croc but bigger. And I knew that if she would attack me that she would have to run over Moki first." Smiling, he looked at Moki and teased, "Huh, Moki?"

"Who knows the ways of the Sasquatch?" Moki responded. "I would bring her home, but I don't think that she would fit in Coahoma's lodge."

He chuckled. Without hesitating, he said, "Coahoma seems to be the *ladies' man* around here."

Surprised by Moki's words, Dakota mused, "Ah, a ladies' man? He doesn't know anything about a woman." Dakota said, "Hum, I see . . . You're playing one of your strange little witchery jokes on me . . . aren't you? Coahoma isn't interested in girls. He never has been and probably never will be." Dakota walked over to his brother and asked, "Are you a ladies' man, or are you the demon slayer?"

Smiling, "Both!" Coahoma responded. "Just wait until I bring all of my women home to live with me," he said with a small chuckle. "You might have to move in with Akule and sleep beside his old grandmother. I hear that she snores so loudly that she scares all of Akule's girlfriends away, but you two can stay there and have ALL of that room all by yourself. And I'll do you a favor. I'll send over a few pretty demons too. I hear that they don't take up much room, and they LOVE snorers!"

Fala chuckled at Coahoma's silly response to Dakota's question. Then he began to laugh so hard that tears streamed down the sides of his face as he slapped his legs and as he rolled off his rock. His laughter was so infectious that the entire group of friends was laughing at their silly antics.

When the laughter died down, Lanto pressed through their group of friends, and with a flick of his wrist, he motioned for his son to come to him. Moki noticed that his father was troubled when he said, "Look, Laurel is coming toward us in that canoe. I think she is looking for you," as he stared downstream.

Falling into a single line, Coahoma, Moki, and Fala signaled to their friends to split apart, allowing them room to walk through their ranks. As they headed toward the river's edge, they saw her. She was sitting in the center of a canoe that was being paddled by Pallaton and Akando.

"Here she comes," Moki announced. "She's bringing our orders to us."

As the small canoe pulled up to the shore, Lanto and Mahkah walked out into the cold water, standing beside the canoe. They gently grasped on to Laurel's arms and lifted her ashore, signaling the large group of teens and young adults to make room for her and her guards. She walked through their passage, leading Coahoma, Moki, Fala, and her guards toward the large flat boulders that were pressed alongside the shallow ridge. When she reached a flat rock, she sat down and invited the boys to sit beside her. Then she asked Lanto and Mahkah to make the teenagers sit behind them so that she could speak without being interrupted.

"Can I stay?" Dakota asked.

"Yes, Dakota. However, you are not to discuss this meeting with anyone. We must maintain absolute silence if we are to fool Pontiac. Remember, he cannot spy on us while he is taking care of Tiponi, but when the sun moves into the Other World, and Morrigan is with her children, Pontiac will be hiding among the shadows. He will spy on us until he discovers all of our secrets."

She knew that Dakota would not betray her. He wouldn't breathe a word of her plans to anyone without her permission, and neither would the other teenagers who were watching and listening to her.

Clinching his fist over his heart, Dakota said, "I will carry your secrets with me into the Spirit World."

"Good." Then she switched her gaze to Coahoma. She said, "Coahoma, son, I hear that you have found a Great Mother's power spot somewhere near here. Can you tell me where it is?"

"Yes. It is close to the place where we found the baby Sasquatch," Coahoma said as he pointed north. "Do you want me to take you to it?"

"No, we don't have time. Just tell me how to get there," Laurel said.

"Follow the path behind my lodge into the forest. Stay on the trail and follow it to the edge of the Black Swamp. Then follow the water line toward the northwest. You will come to a small rise where you will see many fresh tracks leading up to it. On a rise, you will see many large trees with wide branches and a halo of blue lights glowing at their peaks. Pallaton or Akando can take you there."

"Good," she said as she stood up. "We will leave right away."

"What do you want us to do?" Coahoma asked.

"Coahoma, I want you to follow Ethane' and Morrigan, learn all about their activities and details about the wedding of Ethane'. You are to travel during the day when Morrigan is watching her children and Pontiac is caring for Tiponi."

Turning to Moki, she said, "Moki, you are to seek the advice of the spirits that surround the village in the Land of Flint. Learn all you can from these spirits. I also want you to learn the ways of these giants."

Finally, she sought out her little crow. "Fala," she said, "you will have the most dangerous task. You will need to spy on the witch named Kenji. I also want you to study Morrigan's lodge—learn every detail about it and pass this information on to your father. He needs to know how it is made: how tall it is, what hangs on its walls, where the fire burns, everything. Do you understand?"

"Yes," Fala answered. "I can do this."

Dakota asked, "Can I help?"

"Yes, Dakota. You must go and visit with Pontiac every day when the sun reaches its midpoint over our heads. Keep him distracted so that these boys can secretly meet with me. He must not become suspicious of our plots against him. If you fail, we all fail."

Dakota was proud to have received such a pivotal role in this strategy. He was proud to join her and his brother, and his excitement flowed in his eyes and spilled into his words. He said, "Coahoma, I will protect you and your friends from Pontiac. Be safe as you travel into the Spirit World."

Sitting quietly around their elders, listening, not moving, eyes fully trained on the shaman, witnessing their interactions, their friends were captivated as they watched these proceedings unfold. They discovered their critical roles, hearing their leaders issue dangerous commands, seeing the seriousness in their eyes and spilling into their words. Their friends knew that this unannounced gathering was dedicated to them. Then a sense of unity rippled through the young teens and adults as the chief's sons rose and simultaneously conjoined arms, sanctifying the hallowed bond between brothers, signifying their commitment to each other, their friends, and to this battle. They knew that they were watching a significant piece of their history unfolding right before them, and they were *proud* to be included in this crucial event.

Laurel stood up and pulled open a satchel that she was carrying. She carefully reached into it and pulled out six feathered headbands. She said, "Coahoma, Moki, Fala, come forward."

The three blood brothers quickly stood up and walked over to her. She handed Coahoma a headband that was made with four solid black feathers. "Coahoma, wear this headband at all times. We will know it is you when we see it." Then she handed a white feathered headband to Moki. "Moki, you will wear white." She then handed a brown one to Fala. "Fala, your color is brown."

Then she stood up, looking over the gathering of boys. Seeing many that were about the same size and appearance of her young shamans, she said, "If you think that you are about the same size as Coahoma, Moki, or Fala, please come forward."

Akule, Etu, and Koi stood up and walked forward. Etu stood beside Coahoma, Akule stood beside Moki, and Koi was beside Fala. As they looked at Laurel, they saw that she was pleased with them. After she handed Akule a white feathered headband, Etu a black one, and Koi a brown one, she said, "Boys, look at your new brother. See the clothes that he wears and how he has his fixed his hair. When we call for you, you will need to dress up like him, but do not put on your matching headband until you are told to do so. If Pontiac finds out that you are a decoy, then it will be harder to trick him in the future. Do you understand?"

"Yes," the boys answered.

"Ask your mothers to give you a sack to put your headdresses into and do not lose them. Bring them in your sack when I call for you." Then she continued, "Boys, we will call you to work in the fields with Mahkah and Nita. Coahoma, Moki, and Fala, when we call you, you will come to a secret place that we have hidden on the west side of the river. Akule, Etu, and Koi, you will join us there too. We will send you into the fields to help Mahkah and Nita. You will wear clothes to match your new brother and your matching headbands. We will make the necessary arrangements for this switch. Do you understand?"

"Yes, we understand." The boys nodded.

"Good. Coahoma, Moki, Fala, I will play the drum while you travel back to the land of the Ron-Nong-Weto-Wanca. We will do this every day when the sun reaches high overhead. Dakota will bring the message for you to come to the fields. Remember to wear your new headbands when you are around Pontiac so that he will become familiar with your colors."

"We will wear them all of the time," Coahoma responded as he removed his old headband and put on his new one.

Then Moki asked, "Are we going to help Father work the ground across the river?"

"Yes. We will hide the canoes so Pontiac will not be able to cross over to see you. If he asks about the canoes, we will tell him that the hunters have them. However, we will be sending many mothers up to keep him busy. He should not be allowed to venture away from my lodge. Dakota, if Pontiac leaves the lodge for any reason, and he doesn't take Tiponi with him, I want you to send Tunghak to warn me. He always knows where to find me. Do you remember how to make him fly?"

"Yes, I remember your commands. I will do this, don't worry, I will send him," responded Dakota.

"Boys, it is time for us to go. Don't speak a word about this to anyone. Pallaton, Akando, take me to the power spot. Dakota, take the boys to my lodge when this gathering is over. May the spirits walk with you and keep you safe during your travels," she said as she turned toward the forest, watching Pallaton and Akando canter forward with their weaponry firmly by their sides. Then they led her up the embankment and toward a shortcut through the forest and to the edge of the Black Swamp.

As soon as she passed through the brush and disappeared from sight, Dakota looked at Coahoma. "It's time," he said as he looked back toward their village. "Let's go." Then he turned around and looked at their friends who were surrounding him. "Go gather the fish from our nets and join us. Let's walk with our brothers to her lodge."

CHAPTER 15

Deadly Encounters

Silently walking ahead of his peers, following Dakota and Nita as they led the way, Coahoma felt the nervousness that hung over them like a thick fog on a cold winter morning and smelled it in the air; but as they approached the old path that led up the small hill, he stifled the terror that slid over him, making each step a struggle to take as the memory of Pontiac's evil eyes filled his mind. *What will I find up there?* he wondered as he slid his fingers over his knife's smooth handle. Working to calm himself, he studied the way that his brother cocked his head and strutted from foot to foot. He saw his father's strength as he dared anyone or anything to challenge him, yet as he watched his long sturdy strides, causing Nita to run to keep up with him, *He loves her*, he thought as he watched him brush his hand against hers, diverting his attention away from his fear.

When Dakota reached the narrow path that climbed the small hill, he said, "I've come to the end of my trail, little brother," as he scanned the pine-covered hillside for signs of danger. Coahoma felt his brother's fear and felt his love for him flow into his words when he placed his hand on his shoulder and said, "May the gods be with you tonight. I will come tomorrow when the sun is directly overhead," just as Etu moved beside him and handed him his stringer that was filled with fish.

Grateful for Etu's help, Coahoma said, "Ah, the fish—the old bear will be grateful to you for his meal tonight," as he accepted them. Then he noticed how Akule shifted his eyes and tilted his head as he backed away. Coahoma knew that Etu wanted to escort them to Lagundo's lean-to, but he had his orders, and he would obey them.

Wanting to assist, Etu said, "We will be honored if you will let us help you," as he nodded toward Akule and Koi. "When the sun returns to the land, we will rise and travel to the river and fill our nets with many fish for Old Lagundo."

"Ah, this will lift a great burden from us," Coahoma said as he glanced over at his brother. When he saw the tension that rippled through his jaw, he knew that his brother was worried about his safety. *Perhaps now he knows that I'm not a coward*, Coahoma thought as he asked, "Where will you tie them?"

"We will tie your fish to the river bank—near the willow. I will mark this spot with my spear that has red feathers on it," Etu said as Akule and Koi nodded in agreement.

Wanting to get settled before nightfall, Fala asked, "Coahoma, the sun will be setting soon. Do you remember how Lagundo wandered down the hill and stole the meat from our smoking pits when we forgot to feed him?"

"Ah . . . You are right. We need to go," Coahoma said as he looked over at Nita. "Are you coming with your father?" he asked, but before she could answer, he noticed how Dakota slid toward her, slyly placing his muscular body in front of hers and partially shielding her from his line of sight. Immediately, Coahoma saw that his brother was uncomfortable with Nita's relationship with him.

Nita walked a few steps around Dakota. She planted her feet and swept a lock of her long black hair across the side of her shoulder. As she gathered her thoughts, she knew that this was not the right time or place to reveal her feelings to Coahoma, but she suspected that he already knew that she loved him and had loved him for a long time.

Smiling, she spoke in a firm yet soft tone. "Coahoma, I will rise when Hashtahli returns from his journey and lights the night sky and the birds sing their songs to welcome his return. I will say my morning prayers and ask him to watch over you—to give you and my brother the courage and answers that you seek. I will put wood on our fire and roast your meat and gather your belongings. Then I will come with Father and bring you these things to you until I see that you no longer need my help."

She will make a fine mate, Coahoma thought as he listened, but he knew, by the way that she moved and spoke, that she was totally unaware of the danger that lurked at the top of the hill. Feeling uneasy about her role in this game, Coahoma reached forward and grasped Nita's upper arm and spun her back toward the village. "Nita, you must stay close to your father when you come to the lodge," Coahoma said, wondering why her future was blocked from him as he looked into her eyes.

Trying to appear at ease, Coahoma took a small step backward and said, "Good, we will see you in the morning," as the memory of Pontiac's angry eyes returned. "We will be grateful for the food that you bring to share with us." When Dakota stepped forward and grasped Nita's arm, seeing his brother assume his domination over her, Coahoma said, "We must go . . ."

As Coahoma, Moki, and Fala walked up toward the lodge, they stopped partway up and watched their friends as they returned to their homes. They felt a brisk breeze and heard the sounds of the night creatures howling in the distance. When they saw the shadow of the old woman's medicine lodge a short distance away, Moki asked, "Coahoma, did you see into my sister's future? Is something bad going to happen to her?"

"I don't know. Her future was shielded from me," Coahoma said.

"My sister has powers that she is unaware of," Moki responded as he watched his sister moving beside Dakota toward their village. "I have watched her change so much over the past four summers that I hardly know her. Yet I do know that her biggest problem is working through the affairs of her heart. I know that many braves have asked her to be their mate, but it appears that Dakota will be keeping them away," he said as he watched his sister disappear. Just as he looked over at Coahoma, he said, "But the one that she truly loves . . . It seems that he loves another."

Coahoma heard the sadness in Moki's words, but when he mentioned love, his mind filled with his visions of Ethane'. He was torn by his attraction to the daughter of his enemy, but his duty to his family and friends was unwavering. As he watched the smoke drifting from the village below, a small voice in the wind reminded him that it was time to move on. Without saying a word, Coahoma nodded and began his trek toward the frightening lodge.

As the boys neared the top of the hill, seeing a long narrow clearing stretching out before them, they quickly spotted smoke rising from inside Laurel's lodge. They knew that Pontiac and Tiponi were inside, waiting for them. On the opposite side of the clearing, they saw Lagundo walking toward them, heading toward his old lean-to that they had built for him many winters ago.

"Hurry, let's take this fish to his lean-to before he gets there," whispered Fala as he quickened his pace, heading toward the back of the lodge.

They scampered around the corner and over to the old bear's shelter. They quickly removed the fish from their stringers and threw them into a large wooden trough. Once the bear was fed, they knew that it was time to go inside and face Pontiac. They knew that the success of this mission depended on their ability to fool Pontiac and Morrigan, but they knew that this wasn't going to be easy.

Feeling slightly insecure about entering Laurel's lodge and facing Pontiac, Coahoma asked, "Are you ready to go in?"

"Ah, I think so. We must not linger out here any longer, or Pontiac will become suspicious," Fala responded. "We know what we must do. I hope that the Great Spirit stays with us tonight."

As the boys rounded the lodge, Coahoma reached forward and grasped her old wooden door, drawing in a breath; he pulled the door open and smelled the comforting odor of goose roasting over a cedar fire as they entered.

Sitting on the ground with a blanket wrapped around him with Tiponi by his side, Pontiac greeted the boys. "Ah . . . Look, Tiponi, the three little boys have decided to join us. Where have you been?" Pontiac asked.

As the boys' eyes adjusted to the dim interior, hearing the familiar crackling sounds of the fire and smelling the scent of the herbal blends that Laurel stored on her drying racks, feeling the dirt floor on the souls of their feet, hearts beating, stomachs in knots, they lowered themselves into an altered state. As they drifted down, blocking their thoughts and emotions, they prepared to greet the witches that were seated in front of the flickering flames.

As they walked toward them, Coahoma asked, "Where should we make our beds?"

"Make your beds? Why should I want you here? You are nothing but children. Why don't you go back to your lodges and tell your fathers that I do not want you here. You are fools in my way!" Pontiac growled as he stood up, dropping his blanket; moving forward, he stood, towering over the boys like a grizzly sizing up his prey so he can make a hasty kill.

As Coahoma studied Pontiac, he saw a blackness radiating from within, recognizing that a stranger was standing before them. They knew

SHERRY COTTLE GRAHAM

that their old friend, their beloved mentor, was now a cold blood-thirsty killer and an imminent danger to them. Coahoma knew that he needed to find a weakness in his logic and that he must do this quickly, or they will soon be breathing their last breaths on this precious Mother Earth.

As Coahoma, Moki, and Fala silently stood before Pontiac, they stilled their basic instinct to turn and run. Knowing that this was a test of their manhood, they stood their ground. Breathing in and out and stilling their fears, they studied Pontiac's temperament. *What is his weakness?* they thought.

At the same time, Moki discretely slid toward Pontiac's pack that was lying on the dirt floor near the door. With his left foot, he reached back and made contact with it. As he suspected, he saw a vivid picture of a giant red-bearded white man. *Lugh, it is Lugh*, he thought. He saw a massive man dressed in strange-looking clothes, wearing a wide-arching rack of deer antlers on top of his head and an odd copper band around his throat. He was rudely belching and complaining as a few tiny people were carting baskets of food to him as he sat propped up on his heavy bench, appearing ungracious and ungrateful to those who were serving him, banging his fists on the table, demanding, "Hurry, I am hungry!"

At this same instance, a small voice whispered in his ear a secret: "Vanity—vanity is his weakness . . ."

Stepping forward, moving to the front of his two friends, drawing in a slow breath, Moki said, "Pontiac, we are here to serve you. We are to do your chores for you, haul your water, and feed the bear. If you want us to leave, we will be happy to do so. However, Chief Ituha will send us to serve Alawa, and Laurel will return home to take care for her bear, while you can do her chores and haul her water."

Coahoma and Fala could see that Moki's words had pierced directly through Pontiac's wicked heart, hitting a cord so hard that rang through him, much like casting a heavy stone into a glistening pool of water, sending its ripples cascading outward in all directions across its watery plain. His weakness was exposed, and now he was theirs. They had won their first battle, and now they would secretly move on to discover their next barrier.

"Yes," said Coahoma. "Many days, when I come, I have to travel many times to her water hole to bring water for her bear and to our old teacher. She has many who come for her medicines, and she always brews her healing teas for them." Looking down, kicking his toe against the clay-packed floor, knocking a few crumbles of bark toward the surrounding stones, he continued, "Then the women come and stay all day, just sitting quietly beside the fire, sewing patches of leather, making their blankets—you remember, like the blanket they made for you?"

Yes, he remembered, and he wasn't going to have a bunch of old women hanging around his lodge. This would interfere with his time that he wanted to spend with Morrigan and lose what little time that she could come to be with him.

He looked at the boys and said, "This is a large lodge," as he swept his right arm around in a full semicircle, looking around the darkening room. "Why don't you sleep over there," he added, pointing to a vacant area in the corner near her central wall. "There is enough room for all three of you to sleep there."

"Where is Tiponi's bed?" asked Fala.

"She will sleep on Laurel's bed," he said as he pointed toward the other side of the rustic wall that separated the lodge into two main sections. "I will sleep on this side," he added, pointing over to the other side of the room directly across the boys. "Then I can keep my eye on you while you are walking in the land of dreams. I do not want to wake up and discover that your beds are empty. I will NOT hunt for you in the middle of the forest and under the canopy of the night sky—like your fathers and grandfathers do."

"Don't worry about us. We have learned our lesson, didn't we, Moki?" Fala asked as he looked over at his friend. Then he looked back at Pontiac, stretching a serious expression over his face. He added, "We will be happy to serve you while Laurel is away. Hum, I am not sure if you know this, but we have been ordered to work in the fields with my father and sister."

"This is woman's work," Pontiac responded. "Why would you do woman's work? And why are you wearing those strange feathers?"

"Coahoma's father ordered us to clean it and to wear these feathers," Fala responded.

"Yea, so my father can see that we are working in the field. We must work in the fields all summer to learn obedience," Coahoma explained, hoping that Pontiac wouldn't see through their excuses and find the truth. It wasn't like them to lie. Telling the truth was as natural to them as it is for the tides to follow the path of the moon.

Smiling, sensing the boys squirm over his questions, Pontiac began taunting, "Coahoma, Fala, Moki, you are like little girls. Why shouldn't you clean the fields? You even have girly names, don't you?"

Seeing what he was trying to do, trying to invoke a fight, Coahoma responded, "Why, yes, we do. Someday when the time is right, we will change them if it suits us . . ."

"Yea, if we don't grow breasts," Fala laughed. "If we do, then we'll braid our hair, put on dresses, and grind the seeds for our breads," he scoffed.

"Go, put your things down and join us. Look at all of this food," Pontiac said as he turned and swept his right arm toward the baskets of cracked nuts, dried meats, and fresh bulbs that were stacked near the hearth. Women from our village have been bringing food for us to share after they learned about Tiponi from the great council."

Trying to keep Pontiac from becoming suspicious, walking over to the fire, inspecting the baskets of food that were placed on top of a small wooden rack and the goose that was roasting over the hot flames, Moki said as he bent over to smell the aroma of the cooking meat, "The gods must be pleased with us. Look at the food that he has provided." Turning his head, he looked over at Coahoma and Fala who were standing in the corner in their sleeping area. He asked, "Are you as hungry as I am? We should bless the Mighty Spirit for this food and eat before we do our chores." Then he turned toward Pontiac, looking through the eyes of a shaman, hoping to find a trace of his old friend still resonating in the soul; he discovered a translucent image of a ruthless red-bearded killer's face staring back.

Moki quickly realized that Lugh's control over Pontiac's life was growing stronger, and with time, there wouldn't be any hope of removing this evil one's spirit from him, causing him to be trapped in between two worlds with no hope of escape if they didn't hurry. Blocking his newfound knowledge from the vile witch who was standing before him, breathing quietly, stilling the anger that was surging in his body from the tips of his high-arching cheekbones to the backs of his brawny calves, Moki slowly turned away, staring at Tiponi as he drew in a breath and somberly asked Pontiac, "What do you want us to do?"

Liking this situation, feeling a renewed sense of strength surging through his veins, knowing that the boys would obey all of his commands, he wanted to see them suffer, better yet, he would keep them busy—testing them, barking orders, denying them sleep—then watching their gut reactions as he broke them. He looked forward to discovering their weaknesses, their fears, and their private demons.

Looking at Moki, he said, "You will need to bring water to Tiponi, tend to the old bear, stack wood for the nightly fire, keep it alive through the night, and when you finished eating, clean up the lodge and hum . . . make your beds." Pointing his outstretched right arm toward the small wood pile, "Stack the wood over there," he commanded. "After you finish all of these things, you can do as you wish, but leave Tiponi and me alone!"

Uncomfortable with this living arrangement yet anxious, wanting to prove to their elders that they were truly wise and gifted shamans, capable of conducting this covert plan, cloaking their anxieties, they quietly walked over and sat down next to the fire and prepared to eat. Sitting between Tiponi and the small wooden rack, Fala reached over and picked up five small clay bowls. Then he quietly and gently passed these bowls to his right, allowing Coahoma and Moki to fill them with fresh slices of roasted meat, grilled lily tubers, and a small scoop of pecans. When the bowls were ready to serve, Moki turned and quietly passed one over to Pontiac, who was sitting across the fire from them, and then he turned and politely handed one to Tiponi.

It was a long standing custom among their people that the highest-ranking male would call upon the Mighty Spirits and thank them for providing the gifts that they were about to receive. Since Coahoma was the son of their chief, glancing over at him, his friends sent him a signal to lead them in prayer. Dropping their gaze, looking deep into the amber flames, they waited to hear the words that he would speak from his heart.

Knowing that it was his duty to say these words, raising his arms and looking inward into that magical spot that freely flows into the mind's eye, he drew in a cleansing breath and began to chant in a low melodic tone, "We invite the spirits who walk on this Great Mother Earth . . . and those who watch down upon us from the Great Father Sky to come . . . join with us in this humble lodge . . . so that we can extend our gratitude to you for providing the SUN AND RAIN that nourishes our lands and grows our food for ALL of our brothers to eat. Know that, as we look out upon the flowing rivers and flower-covered hilltops, we see your beauty that you paint over our landscapes and the blue skies above. We hear your powerful words whispering to us upon the winds. Now we want to extend our gratitude to this fine-feathered brother and these lovely plants . . . for giving up their earthly bodies so that we can enjoy the strength that they will provide. We are grateful for their ultimate sacrifice, and we hope that their journey back into the World of Spirits was a peaceful one."

As the boys sat quietly, eating their food, they were surprised when Pontiac became agitated with his cross-legged position on the ground. As he began squirming in place, he finally threw off his blanket, placed his bowl of food on top of a rock, saying with distain, "How can I eat like this? Only children eat like this! I will be right back!" He turned and disappeared out of the door. As Tiponi and the boys watched the door slam, it wasn't long before he returned, dragging in a large block of wood.

He pulled the large wooden block over to his spot near the fire, moved it into position, picked up his small blanket and covered the log. Then he turned around and sat down on it. Reaching over, he scooped up his bowl and began to talk. "Ah, this is better. No man should sit on the ground. Look, I can stretch out my legs. Ah, this is great. I should have done this a long time ago. "

"Go get me one, too," Tiponi added. "Will you go get me a wooden seat? It is hard to sit on this blanket," she complained.

Fala looked over to see the face of Tiponi was changing. He quickly spied that her eyes were a strange blue color, and her normally downturned mouth was twisting strangely upward, exposing the gaps of missing baby teeth.

"I'll go get you one. Stay here," Fala said as he jumped up. He knew that something was happening, and he could see that Tiponi was quickly changing into someone he didn't recognize.

"We'll help," Coahoma added as jumped up with Moki in fast pursuit behind him. "We'll be right back," he added as the three boys fled through the rickety door.

They quickly headed toward the pile of logs, pointing toward valid candidates that would make a good prop for Tiponi. Fearing to say many words, Coahoma whispered, "She is changing. Keep an eye on her."

"Yes," Moki responded. "We need to do our chores so we can get to sleep. Maybe we should sleep with the bear?"

"No, we must sleep inside, or they will know that we are afraid," Coahoma responded.

Wanting to return, they quickly selected a suitable stump. Picking it up, they hauled it back into the lodge and placed it into position near the fire for Tiponi. Once they covered it with her small blanket, she sat down and admired her new seat.

"Ah, this is nice. This will be my seat from now on. Fala, you and your friends will not sit here. This is mine, do you hear?" she asked her cousin in a degrading and impetuous tone.

"Ah, this is good," Pontiac said as he stuffed mouthfuls of food into his mouth. "I love the smell of this goose," he continued as continued to chew his food with an open mouth. Laughing, he reached for his long-bladed knife. Then he pulled the roasted bird toward him and carved a large chunk of meat from its breast. As he leaned forward, he released a loud burp. Belching on the food was the last gross insult that the boys would endure.

Stunned by these new outbursts of rude words and ill-mannered belching, Coahoma walked over to his spot, leaned over, picked up his bowl and said, "Come, let's get our food and eat outside. We can finish this later after we do our chores."

"I agree," said Moki. "I want to check on Lagundo before it gets too dark to see him.

The boys headed through the door, carrying their bowls of food with them. "Over here," Coahoma whispered as he headed around the corner, moving toward the lean-to. "Let's go check on Lagundo. Maybe he needs water."

Fala asked, "Coahoma, what are we going to do? Now I can only see Lugh and Morrigan. I hardly recognize Pontiac and Tiponi. Do you?"

"I don't know," replied Coahoma. "I only know that they are different. Now we know why—at least we are beginning to see. I think much more will be revealed," he said as he kneeled down to inspect the sleeping bear's feathers. "Tomorrow, let's add more feathers to Lagundo. This will give us more to do so we can stay away from Pontiac and Tiponi. They are dangerous. I can see it in their eyes, can't you?"

"Yes," answered Fala. "I do not recognize Tiponi. Her mother would not permit such vulgar behavior from her. She would not be permitted to eat if she would act like that in her lodge."

Looking toward the lodge, Moki said, "Let's get our chores done and let's go to bed."

SHERRY COTTLE GRAHAM

Stepping forward, Coahoma demanded the attention of his two friends. Once he had their attention, he whispered, "We will sleep in rounds tonight. We will need to watch Pontiac. I do not trust him, and I think it will be foolish to turn a blind eye to him."

"Yea, you are right," Fala responded. "Who is going to take the first watch?"

"Fala, you take the first watch. Moki, you go next, then me," Coahoma explained. "Don't fall asleep until you wake one of us up."

"Good idea," Moki responded. "Come on, let's do these chores and get to bed before anything else happens."

With a plan in place, the boys grabbed a couple of water pouches that were hanging on Lagundo's lean-to and headed to the small creek that trickled down the hill behind Lagundo's shelter. Once they had filled it, they returned to the lean-to, filled a large clay crock, and headed toward the hefty pile of logs. Once they had replenished the firewood in the lodge as Pontiac had ordered, they cleaned up their eating area, made their beds, and prepared to retire for the night.

Sitting on the hard ground on a few spare blankets that Laurel always kept in her sleeping area, they carefully spread another blanket over their beds to cover themselves. The warmer days of spring were upon them, but the nights were still cold, and they required a fire and a few blankets to keep the chill off while they slept. Sitting back on his ankles with his feet folded underneath him, Coahoma asked, "Pontiac, do you need anything?"

Watching the boys as they wiggled under their blankets, pulling the edges of their soft fur blankets gently up around their necks, settling back and becoming comfortable with their beds, they looked forward to entering their magical world of dreams. Pontiac was disgusted with the boys. Contorting his strange bluish brown eyes, appearing to mutate into an angry beast, he warned, "No, little girls. Go to sleep now and don't bother us! I will give you one warning: DO NOT LEAVE THIS LODGE or you may not live to see another sunrise!"

"We will not leave this lodge. Pontiac, do not worry about the fire. We will take care of it for you," Coahoma said. Spotting an eerie translucent image streaming around his old friend, Coahoma knew that this battle was going to be difficult to win and maybe impossible.

As the boys quietly lay on their earthen beds, they were quickly swallowed up in the darkness of the night as Pontiac and Tiponi sat near the flickering lights of the fire. As the boys secretly watched them, it appeared that Pontiac and Tiponi had forgotten about them as they listened in to their private but loud conversations and studied their interactions.

At one point, Lugh seemed to appear in the room. Looking at Tiponi, he solemnly asked, "Tell me about Ethane'. Is she still going to marry the king's son?"

As strange as this conversation seemed, it was getting darker and more sinister as Tiponi answered in a strange woman's voice, one that they remember hearing during their journey into the land of the white giants. "Yes, she will marry him, but she will do this because it is her duty. I do not think that she loves him. I think that he only wants her because of her connections to Isis."

Pontiac said, "I know Sangann's heart. He is an evil man. He longs for power and land. The king must be careful, or he may not live to a ripe old age."

"My husband, what are we going to do? You are trapped in this savage, while your body lies in our lodge, dull and lifeless, waiting for you to return to it," Tiponi said as she looked into Pontiac's eyes. "The children and I . . . We need for you to come home."

"My duty here is not complete. I will find this power spot that the king seeks. When I find it, I will find a way to return, but it is time for you to go back to our lodge and sleep. The children will be getting up in a little while. You will need your rest to keep the sickness away."

Then Pontiac stood up. Reaching down, he clasped Tiponi's small hand and gently pulled her up onto her feet. Pointing toward the back room, he said, "You can sleep in there. I will stay out here and keep an eye on the boys and on the old bear. I do not trust that old bear. He might break through that old door at any time and try to kill us." Looking over at the door, he continued, "Why, any fool who would keep a dangerous bear around a village that is filled with women and children is a lunatic. We would never permit a crazy arrangement like this to happen in our village. This old bear would be hanging on my wall, and the woman would never have had a right to speak to me about it."

"Do you think that you will find this power spot?" Tiponi asked. "Do you not feel the power that is coming from this land that we are standing on? The energy coming from it is very strong. I can feel it."

SHERRY COTTLE GRAHAM

Dumbfounded, Pontiac stepped back, dropping his head backward, thrusting both arms up into the air, pointing his fingers toward the sky. Then all of the sudden, the translucent image of a giant bearded man lit up the central portion of the room. "Yes, you are right. This is it. No wonder the old woman built her lodge here. She is using this power to make herself stronger. Do not say anything to anyone. I will find a way to rid myself from this pathetic body, but until we are sure, I will remain here."

Pretending to be asleep, the boys were absorbing every word that these two were speaking. They were relieved to see Tiponi disappear into the darkness of the back room, and Pontiac moved to the opposite corner of the room. They watched as he picked up a long spear and placed it within an arm's reach from his bed. Then he dropped down on to his knees, pulling his covers back. He lay down, and in a relatively short amount of time, he drifted off into a deep sleep.

As the boys had planned, Fala was the first to rise and tend to the fire. He kept guard for a few hours before waking Moki to take his turn. Then shortly before the sun's light danced in the morning sky, Coahoma served his turn. As Coahoma lay there, listening to the sounds of his friends and the evil ones who were sleeping near him, he was relieved to hear the birds welcoming the sun back into their world. They had survived their night alone, and he was ready to cross the river and proceed to the next phase of their journey.

"Wake up," Coahoma said as he nudged Fala and Moki. "The sun has returned, and I hear Dakota. He's coming to greet us with Nita and Moki's father. I can hear their voices. It's time for us to go work in the fields," he said as he straightened the feather headband. "Hurry, let's go before Pontiac wakes."

The three quietly stood up and headed for the old door. With the blink of an eye, they fled through the door to greet Dakota on the other side. Coahoma was the first to pass through, and when he saw his brother, he placed his hand over his lips to signal Dakota and Nita to be quiet. He walked over to his brother, leaning over; he whispered into his ear, "Be very careful. He is not whom he seems to be. Neither is Tiponi. They are dangerous."

Then Moki walked over to Nita. Reaching out, he snatched a sack that was filled with food for them. As he took the sack, he reached over and grasped her upper arm with his right hand and gave it a quick squeeze. Then with his eyes, he gave her such a solemn stare that she knew that it was a warning to get prepared as he pressed a vision of his nighttime discoveries over for her to see. Instantly, she understood and realized the danger that would soon be greeting them.

Then Moki turned toward his father, and with the right flick of his head, he signaled his father that they must go. As the boys headed down the path, just before they rounded the curve and disappeared from sight, they paused to look back at the lodge. As they anticipated, they saw the old door swing open and watched as Dakota and Nita disappeared inside. A strange sickening feeling knotted up in the center of Coahoma's stomach as he knew that Nita and his brother were now embracing a dark and evil couple. "May the gods be with you," he murmured as he turned back toward the bend. Motioning his head to the left, he signaled Mahkah to continue. "Let's get to the fields. We have much to do, and time is not on our side," he whispered to his friends as they broke into a full throttle run, making their way directly toward the canoes that were waiting for them.

CHAPTER 16

Odor of Death

When the boys reached the river, they joined Pallaton and Akando, who were standing in knee-deep water, steadying their hollowed-out wooden canoes, waiting for them to wade into the river and hop aboard. As Coahoma reached the first canoe, he pitched the sack that he was carrying into the craft. Bending forward, grabbing its hull with both hands, he leaped up into the canoe and quickly settled into its front seat. Then Fala, who was following close behind, hit the sidewall with both hands and seemingly sprung into the vessel, landing precisely into its center where he quickly settled his kneed-bent legs on to its smooth wooden bottom. When Pallaton saw that the boys were in place, digging his feet firmly into the murky bottom, pressing his full weight against the backside, they felt a firm jolt as Pallaton freed the canoe from the muddy shoreline. He skillfully leaped into its rear seat and began to paddle it across the river.

Once the canoes reached the opposite side, the party of men and boys leaped out into the shallow stone-laced riverbed and pulled the heavy crafts ashore. Immediately, Mahkah walked to the edge of the weed-infested flat land that stretched out before them. As they looked around, inspecting this familiar crescent-shaped clearing, seeing the stumps of the many trees that once thrived there, the boys quickly realized that it would take many days for them to prepare this land for their women.

Coahoma was the first to speak. Seeing a collection of tools that were carefully stacked against a wide-arching pine with a small fire burning nearby, eager to get started, he asked Mahkah, "What do you want us to do?"

Leading them toward the mound of flint and rock-based tools, he responded, "Boy, come over here, do as you are told, and don't ask questions. The spirits are listening, and time is on our side. Do you understand?"

Coahoma knew that a cunning plan was now in progress, and he would abide by every order that was given to him.

Mahkah walked over to the tree and picked up a long spear that was propped up against it. Turning, he carefully handed it to Coahoma. Then he turned toward a large log that was lying on the ground next to the old tree that had a thick rope tied to each end.

Pointing toward the ropes, he said, "Fala, you take this one," and pointing to the other side, "Moki, you take that one. Boys, you will pull this log around the edge of this clearing and crush the tall grass that grows beside it. It will take many trips for you to scrape them away."

A grim expression swept across Mahkah's face as he turned toward Coahoma, cocking his head squarely above his shoulders. He said, "Coahoma, you are now a man, and we are giving you the responsibility to protect Moki and Fala. You will take this spear and walk in front of them while they clear this path. You will use your weapon to drive the snakes away that are hiding in the brush. Walk with a heavy foot and rustle the grasses with the top of your spear to warn these serpents of your approach. You will find them lying in their nests, and they are cold so they will not want to move. When you hear a spit and a low-pitched rattle, stop. Don't move! Look carefully for the largest one and use the head of your spear to prod him toward the forest. Then you must wait until the others flee with their brother. Do NOT move until you are certain that your path is safe. Remember, they are more afraid of you, but if you get bitten, your spirit will leave us before the moon returns to light our night sky. Do you understand?"

"Yes, Mahkah. I will walk like I am dancing with a heavy foot and stomp on the noisy grass. Do not worry, I am not afraid." Looking up at Mahkah, Coahoma asked, "Are we ready?"

"Yes, you may go. When you are finished, we will set the field on fire and burn the dry grass and thorn bushes," Mahkah responded as he gazed at the thicket of wild plants.

First testing its weight, determining the force needed to move this heavy item, realizing that they would be able to maneuver this rustic scraper around the landscape, securing their thick hemp straps around

SHERRY COTTLE GRAHAM

their lean muscular bellies, taking a deep breath, keeping their bodies in sync, Moki and Fala dragged the log through the overgrowth. Just as they got started, Moki glanced across the river seeing a man standing on the other side, wearing a long flowing feathered headdress, holding his favorite white feathered lance.

Moki said, "Coahoma, your father is watching us," as he nodded toward him.

"Yes, I see him," Coahoma responded, lifting his spear high into the air, signaling his father that they were working.

He watched his father strut across the land, acting as if nothing were wrong. As he continued to lead his friends around the field, he noticed that Pallaton and Akando were missing, but he continued to watch for snakes without questioning their whereabouts, listening to the rustling sounds of crushing grass behind him. As he led the way, he heard the sounds of heavy rocks and large sticks that Mahkah was pitching into the timberline. As Mahkah followed them, he gazed across the river, watching the sky for Dakota's signal.

Then he saw it, piercing through the tree line at the top of the hill, a flaming arrow arched across the blue sky, alerting Mahkah that it was time to proceed with their next plan.

Mahkah walked slightly ahead of Coahoma. As he bent over to pick up a rock, he said, "Boys, do not look back. Do you see that large wood pile up ahead? Pallaton and Akando are there waiting for you on the other side. When we reach it, drop to your knees, keep your heads down, and crawl into the forest."

Their hearts skipped a beat as they eagerly prepared for the upcoming swap. As the boys pulled the log to the sweet spot that connected them to the secret path, they dropped to the ground and began to crawl, passing their decoys—Akule, Etu, and Koi—as they fled into the forest. Soon, Etu stood up, holding Coahoma's spear as Akule and Koi wrapped the ropes around their midsections and moved forward, dragging the log behind them. The swap was made in a matter of moments, and now they were traveling to a secret hideaway that was hidden nearby.

"Come, this way," Pallaton whispered as he headed into the forest, following a familiar trail into its protective shadows that the boys had followed many times during their lives. Coahoma watched Pallaton as he proudly raced along the path, jogging with grace and agility, lean and strong. He was truly a master at reading the subtle signs of the forest.

Behind them, protecting the rear, the ruggedly handsome and brawny Akando ensured that he was safely delivered to his medicine woman.

Hearing the harmonic songs echoing through the peaks of the dense canopy, smelling the fresh scent of pine needles and the musk of rotting timber lingering upon the breeze, feeling the stinging sensation of salt dripping down over their brows and into their eyes as they ran, they were content knowing that this narrow pathway, as insignificant as it seemed, was actually guiding them directly toward their old medicine woman.

It wasn't long before he spotted it. Hidden behind a cluster of wax myrtles was their secret hut. It flanked a tiny brook that meandered so delightfully through the trees and disappeared into the wilderness. Pallaton led him around the side of this crudely built exterior. Coahoma was pleased to see how it blended into the surroundings foliage, making it nearly impossible to see. He noticed how they had covered it with a thin layer of evergreen leaves, strips of bark, and mud to form a protective shield for them. As they moved around the side, he glanced up at a small stream of wispy white smoke that was rising through a vent hole and disappearing into the arching branches above him.

When Pallaton reached the entrance, he leaned over and lifted the flap. He motioned to Coahoma to enter. Coahoma studied Pallaton's fearless expression as he walked past him. Seeing his father's beloved warrior standing guard over him, he knew that this superbly built man would forfeit his life to save his. Yet he knew, by the sad reflection in his eyes, that he was helpless to protect him from the dangers that he would encounter.

As he moved toward the dark and dank hut, Coahoma smelled the fresh scent of recently timbered saplings and the enticing fragrance of smoldering wood saturating the air. He bent down and looked inside to see who was waiting inside. When his eyes adjusted to the dimly lit interior, he was immediately comforted by the familiar pop and crackling sounds emanating from the hot embers. As he looked around, he recognized the delicate shape of his old shaman's back wrapped in her blanket. She was sitting quietly on the ground beside his father waiting for them. He also recognized Fala's father, Lanto, was sitting near the fire. As he moved closer to her, he saw two drummers tucked behind her with their drums. As he struggled to gain control of his emotions, flushing with humbleness and pride, he recognized the importance of this mission.

Sucking in a long cleansing breath and slowly releasing it, calming his body after his long run, Coahoma knew that this rapidly built hideaway was now his personal portal, enabling him to slide effortlessly between the two worlds. Looking around, seeing the tied and bent saplings, hearing the comforting sounds of the central fire, anxious to get started, he knew that they were going to be spending most of the day in this bark and mud dome-shaped hut, smelling the stale scent of the drying mud, listening to the sounds of the rhythmic drummers as they prepared to jettison back into the Land of Giants.

As the boys shuffled toward the light, a baritone voice penetrated throughout the room, slicing through the silence, commanding, "Coahoma, come here and sit down. Moki . . . Fala, sit over there on the other side of Coahoma." Raising his left arm, pointing toward a vacant spot to his left, Chief Ituha was anxious to get settled and determine if the boys understood the challenges that this quest would thrust upon them.

Seeing his father's broad and powerful features, wearing his mystical fur and feathered headdress, sitting upright and facing him, Coahoma obediently slid over and sat down on the earthen floor beside him. Coahoma was happy when Moki settled down beside him. Then he watched as Fala walked around the fire and sat down beside his father.

When they were in their places, sitting cross-legged on the ground, starring impatiently into the hypnotic orange flames, Coahoma was anxious to begin. Feeling his father's dominance beside him, he knew that there would be little conversation before Laurel would guide them down into a deep trance. Using her rattles and the accompanying drummers, she was ready to send them hastily on their way.

Tilting his head up to his right, looking directly at his father, Coahoma asked, "Father, I recognized your decoy walking on the other side of the river. Do you think Pontiac will know it wasn't you?"

Smiling, Chief Ituha looked across the fire at Lanto. He said, "Ah, yes, the illusion of whom we are. Son, remember the lesson that you have learned today, that a man who sees life through his eyes is a FOOL!"

Fala said, "But Pontiac is a powerful medicine man. If I can see a decoy, then how is it that Pontiac can't see it?"

"Son, Pontiac is trapped between two worlds. His memories are fading, making it easy for us to trick him. However, I fear he is losing his ability to know right from wrong as he loses his battle against his demons. The change has already started, and he is shifting into something we fear. Every day, he slides further into a world of unnatural voices and shadows. Once he plunges into this dark abyss, witches will haunt him, no matter where he goes or where he hides. SOON, HE WILL NOT REMEMBER US OR OUR WAYS! LISTEN TO ME, COAHOMA, AND UNDERSTAND. I have given orders to Dakota to watch over him while you are away. If your brother sees that there is no hope, Pontiac will be put under the knife. Then we will carry his LIFELESS body deep into the swamp and BURN his bones. When we light his fire, we will RUN and HOPE that he does not follow us back to our lodges. We will gather our belongings and abandon this land because I WILL NOT LET A CRAZED DEMON HAUNT OUR PEOPLE! But until I get the word that all hope is lost, we will continue to conjure up these illusions to give you the time that you need to learn the secrets that we need to break the spells on him and Tiponi."

"Father, do not worry. We are not afraid. We will learn their secrets, and we will use this against them."

Leaning back, closing their eyes, the boys relaxed. Breathing in long deep breaths, exhaling in slow cleansing breaths, moving their state of awareness down, calming their minds, they were prepared to hear the chief's deep yet, charismatic voice to initiate their journey into the World of Spirits. Reciting his most powerful prayer, Chief Ituha called his gods to protect them.

As Coahoma shifted his balance back and forth, straightening his back, centering his head over his shoulders, he began to think about Silver, remembering her lovely long blond waves of hair, her hauntingly beautiful blue eyes, and her frosty white skin. Leaning to his right, he realized that his father had returned and was sitting back down in the vacant spot next to him.

As he tilted to his right, bumping against his father's side, a horrifying image of his father ricocheted through his mind's eye, instantly replacing his whimsical visions of the mysterious blue-eyed blonde with a shocking image of his father standing in the middle of a misty moonlit forest, arms up, hands outstretched, feet planted, sucking in an instinctive breath as he fearlessly braced against the impact of a deranged yellow-eyed timber wolf. He watched as the massive weight of the beast rammed his father to the ground, hearing the wolf's deep-throated snarls ripple through his mind as he felt the sensation of warm sticky ooze dripping from his skin. He instinctively knew that the wolf's petrifying teeth were ripping large chunks of flesh from his father's body. Unable to yield his knife, Coahoma recognized the familiar pungent odor of death spiraling around him.

Reaching down, shaking her rattles next to his right ear, working desperately to disrupt the spell, "Coahoma, come back to us," Laurel firmly repeated as she recognized that the young shaman was torturously deadlocked into a horrible vision. "Coahoma, it's a dream. Wake up!"

Hearing the sound of rattles and a voice whispering in his ear disrupting his vision, Coahoma began to shake off the clutches of his vision, returning to the light. Opening his eyes, seeing Lanto across him, he discovered that Laurel was kneeling beside him, firmly shaking her rattles and calling out to him to return.

Remembering the visions of his father, wanting to warn him, he turned to his right, only to discover that his father was no longer sitting beside him. Hearing his father's voice behind him, he turned to see that Moki was frantically prancing around and yelling, "Watch out . . . wolf!" Then he realized that his father and Fala were trying to disrupt his friend's vision.

Seeing the terrified expressions on the two boys' faces, Laurel saw the effect that this particular vision had on them. Knowing the full potential of their psychic powers, she wasn't certain whether they were truly prepared to deal with the dark forces. Wondering if she should proceed, sensing Coahoma's anxiety, she reached out, grasping his upper arms with her withered hands, trying to comfort him. In a calm voice, she said, "Coahoma, you are safe. Son, what did you see? Can you tell us?"

"Wolf! It was a huge mad wolf. Everything was black, and I saw him flying through the air. Father, I saw him crush you to the ground. His teeth . . . I could see his teeth and his strange glowing yellow eyes. Father, I could smell your blood on his breath!"

Chief Ituha turned and walked over to stand beside Coahoma. Seeing his son's panic-streaked face, he said, "I'm here, Coahoma. I'm all right. Look, son, look around. A wolf cannot get in here."

"No, Father, not here. You were in the forest. It was night, and this huge timber wolf was attacking you."

"Ah, Coahoma, I am okay. Son, calm down and listen to me. I am not afraid of this wolf. I am not afraid to die. You know this. It seems you have peered into the future and have seen my death, but it is not going to happen today. Believe me, son." Lowering his head, looking Coahoma directly in the eye, silently searching for a sign of his son's mental well-being, a serious expression splashed over his face as he spoke. "Hum . . . Son, you must now make a decision. Do you want me to stop this?"

With a tone of defiance, wanting to continue, Coahoma said, "No! I am fine. I do not want to stop. I am not afraid."

Backing away from Coahoma, Laurel walked over to tend to Moki who was also calming down. Seeing his wide eyes and sweat dripping down from his brow, she asked, "Moki, son, how are you? Come, sit down."

Moki saw that the chief was safe. Realizing that he was picking up Coahoma's vision, he began to relax. After taking a few long calming breaths, seeing that his chief was truly unharmed, seeing that he was still safely tucked inside the hut, he choked, "It was a wolf! A mad wolf! He came out of the blackness . . . Then he was on top of you . . . I could only watch."

"Come over and sit down," Laurel demanded as she took Moki by the arm and led him back over to his spot beside the fire. "Sit here, Moki. We are all safe here. Pallaton and Akando are outside guarding us." As she was saying this, she looked over and spotted Pallaton and Akando. They had pulled the flap back and were looking inside watching them.

Cautiously, Laurel inspected the auras of the men and boys. She saw that they were recovering from the shock that Coahoma had caused by his terrifying vision. Weighing her options, thinking about the situation for a few moments, she turned toward the chief; and in an ominous tone, she warned the group, "We must continue." She looked at Coahoma and noticed that he was calming down. She said, "Coahoma, you must learn to control your visions, or they will devour you." Laurel commanded, "Ituha, do not let anyone sit near Coahoma. Do not allow anyone to touch him, or it may trigger another vision." Once she was certain that she was making the correct decision, she asked, "Are you ready to travel?"

Coahoma said, "Yes, I am ready."

As he answered, Chief Ituha stood up and walked over beside the drummers. In his usual fashion, he threw his head back, raising both of his hands up toward the sky; he prayed to his gods. "Thank you, our gods from the Father Sky, the sun, the moon, the gods from the four winds, and the gods from our Great Mother Earth. I thank you for watching over us on this fine day. This humble man wants to thank you and the spirits of the forest who provide life and protect us during times of need.

I am calling upon you again to watch over my sons as they travel into your world. Bring them safely back to us so they too can grow into wise old men."

"Coahoma, Moki, Fala, come over here," she said as she motioned for them to sit in a semicircle and face her. They had traveled with her on many occasions, and they knew her routine like cubs. They knew her probably better than they knew their own mothers. They knew that this old woman shriveled with time yet gifted with her knowledge of the Spirit World and the laws of their Great Mother. Nothing was ever left up to chance, and today would be no different.

As they looked over at her, she greeted their stares with a complex set of mixed emotions: one feeling a deep love and understanding of these young boys, and the other a reluctance to send them on this dangerous mission. Taking a few moments to gather her words, her deeply wrinkled face seemed to grow slightly paler as she spoke. "Listen to me and understand, we are sending you on a long journey. You will travel back to Lugh's village, and if the gods are good, you will return to us before the sun sets. If you fail to return, you are on your own, and Pontiac will be put under the knife before the moon passes over our lodges."

"You do not need to worry," replied Coahoma, trying to reassure the group that they were going to be all right. "We will return before the sun casts its long shadow over our land."

"You are brave—I see your hearts are strong. Your stories will be told at our ceremonial fires for all of our people to hear. They will listen to your stories, and they will repeat them to their children. Your tales will grow into legends, and your children and your children's children will grow up knowing the great seeds that they came from."

Then she bent her legs backward. Pulling out a small bundle of custom-blended jimson, hemp, and tobacco from her medicine pouch, she continued, "Here, this is for you. It will help you move between worlds and to stay longer with the spirits. When you get there, remember your duties. Stay together. Stay on your path, and you will be safe. "

When she had the boys' full attention, Fala asked, "Will we see any black shadows . . . the ones that you have warned us about?"

"Fala, witches are everywhere. They are always lurking in the shadows and waiting to attach themselves to the weak and fearful," she said as she stretched forward, placing her hands into the fire pit and propped her small bundle of aromatic herbs on to a smoldering ember. "They are angry spirits that prey on the innocent, and it is difficult to make them leave once they find their prey." Laurel stretched forward, leaning over the fire. Sucking in a large breath, she blew on a small bundle of incense. She was pleased by the pillar of white smoke. She leaned back, and her face grew strangely sad as she continued, "I cannot go with you or tell you if a witch will find you, but I can tell you, you will see and hear things that will frighten even the bravest of warriors. Just remember to be watchful for those who can see you. Many cannot, but their witches can see you, and if they do, they will come after you. They will follow you back to this place. Do not concern yourselves with this matter. We will be waiting for them." Then she leaned forward. Cupping the wisp of smoke, she breathed it in as she ladled it down over her body. "Coahoma, Moki, Fala, it is time. Prepare yourselves as you have been trained. Remember to travel with your heart and forget about your eyes. Your heart knows the truth, so listen to it. Listen to the rhythms of the drum. Travel far and travel fast, but remember to return when you hear the three drum beats. When you cross over, ask the gods to SLOW DOWN TIME and use this GIFT OF TIME to your advantage."

Then she turned toward the drummers; she signaled for them to begin. She stood up as the boys spaced themselves equally distant apart around the perimeter of the fire. Leaning forward, spooning handfuls of the intoxicating smoke down over their bodies, inhaling long breaths of her aromatic blend, the boys were ready to begin their journey. Shutting their eyes, breathing in, breathing out, feeling their bodies drifting down, they were soon moving through their enchanted forest, walking beside their babbling brook, heading toward their sacred cave as they slid deeper and deeper into their altered consciousness. Listening to the familiar beat of the drums beating a steady beat—boom, boom, boom—they heard her rattles shaking as she called upon her gods and Ohanzee.

"This old woman is calling to the gods of the sun; the gods of the moon; the gods of the north, south, east, and west; the gods of the forests; and of this Great Mother Earth. I am calling on you to join me. Come—enter this small lodge that we have prepared. Please come and protect our sons as we send them into your world. Grandfather, please come—join us and guide our sons on their journey."

Then she began to shake her rattles louder and faster. Hearing the beads and the drums echoing in their heads, repeating her song, the boys began moving downward into their trance. Soon, they could only hear the drumming and the beats as their sounds began to resonate in their minds. Soon, the boys found themselves speeding through their private caves, racing through their damp dark shafts, listening to the chiming sounds of water echoing from their chambers. As they pressed forward, they saw the brilliant white light of their exit lying a short distance ahead.

Coahoma was the first to plunge through and enter into the breathtaking World of Spirits. Landing on all fours in a luminous patch of emerald green grass, he was exuberant to be back in his feline body, young and sleek, agile, full of power, and ready to meet any danger head on. Feeling his tail twitching behind him, he slowly raised his head, looking around, seeing the brilliant array of colors erupting around him, hearing the symphonic songs of the forest. He heard them inviting him. "Come—listen to our secrets," they were calling.

Then he turned to his right, seeing a shape of a deer standing beside him. He said, "Moki, we are here. Where is Fala?"

"I'm up here," Fala said as he flew down and landed in front of his two friends. "I am still a crow," he began to complain. "I was hoping to be an eagle or at least a hawk by now!"

"Fala, we don't have time for this right now. Be patient," Coahoma responded, trying to comfort him.

Then Fala cocked his head up. Remembering the visions that his friends had experienced just a short time earlier, he asked, "Coahoma . . . Moki, are you all right?"

Coahoma said, "Yes, Fala. We are better now."

Then the boys heard an eagle screaming in the sky as it lofted its right wing and began to soar out of the sky and coming to rest on a tree limb that was directly above them.

Looking up, the boys inspected their new animal guide as it called out to them, "Boys, I am Ohanzee. I am here to guide you into the Land of Giants. Are you prepared to make this journey?"

Moki and Fala knew that Coahoma would assume the leadership as Coahoma was always the first to respond. "Yes, we are, but before we go, we need to slow down time. Can you do this for us?"

Ohanzee looked down at the small group of young shamans and appeared to smile as he spoke. "Ah, time. The illusion of time is an easy request for me to offer you. Once we start, you will find that time will slowly pass by. I hope that it will give you the advantage that you need to save my friend, Pontiac. I miss his company. He comes here often, and he enjoys our conversations about the secrets of life. He has learned much, but I have more to teach him."

As Coahoma spoke with the eagle, he heard the voices of the forest drifting upon the wind, singing together, bringing a message in the form of a melody. Cocking his head, twisting his ears toward the sounds, he listened to their song. "We are your friends, listen to us, we know the land of giants that live in the north. They are a race of misfits, a race to distrust. Do not let their blue eyes fool you. They are cruel and a violent bunch. They are a giant race of people who thrive on war and lust. If they catch you, they will crush your bones into dust, but beware of a magician called Morrigan, for she is desperate to avenge the death of her husband. She will call upon her gods, Isis, Bridget, and Zeus. They will join with her and guide her—they never fail."

When the trees had finished their warning, Ohanzee looked back down upon the boys and asked, "Are you ready?"

Coahoma saw Moki's and Fala's nods of approval; he knew that it was time. The time had come for them to return to the land of the Ron-Nong-Weto-Wanca.

"Yes, let's go," Coahoma said to the eagle.

Ohanzee spread his powerful wings and swooped down, elegantly landing in front of them. Shifting back into the image of an old man, looking over at the boys, he said, "Boys, shift back into your human forms."

Seeing this mysterious and wise old man before them, they recognized that he was going to relay a secret to them. Anxious to hear what he was going to say, the boys obediently switched back into their human forms and stood ready to hear his words.

"Ah, this is better," he said. "Come, walk with me and listen to my words before we begin." Taking the lead with the boys closely flanking his sides, he said, "I must teach you the ways of the World of Spirits so that you will understand the power that this world yields to those who know how to control it. Once you learn these secrets, you will rise far above your kinsmen who only know the rules of their physical world.

"What is it that we need to learn? We don't have time for long lessons! We are in a hurry," Coahoma complained.

"Ah, the illusion of time . . . Son, listen to me and understand my words. Time does not exist in this world. Time is of your world, measured by man's rules, but here, these boundaries do not exist," he said as he

SHERRY COTTLE GRAHAM

looked up, raising his right arm, making a long swoop through the air, indicating everything that was around him. "You have asked me to slow down time. From this day onward, you and your friends will be able to control time by yourself," he said as he gazed at the boys. "To do this, open your mind, link your thoughts to the spirits of this world, and demand this gift. They can speed it up or slow it down. This is for you to decide, but remember, always be grateful to your guides and use your powers wisely! What can be given can just as easily be taken away."

"We will remember and honor your words," Coahoma said. "Is it about time to go? We have things we must get done, or my father will be disappointed in us."

"Ah, your next lesson . . . the illusion of space," Ohanzee responded, smiling at the boys, preparing to divulge another secret. "My granddaughter has asked me to guide you back into the land of these giant white men. I will keep my promise, but I will also teach you the secret of space," he said as he closed his eyes and disappeared.

Looking around, seeing that the old man was gone, knowing that this had to be a trick, Coahoma asked, "Do you see him? He has to be here somewhere!"

"I am back here. Behind you," Ohanzee said.

As the boys turned around, spotting him, he said, "See how easy it is to move. Like the blink of an eye, I can be anywhere." Then he shut his eyes and disappeared again. "Over here," he whispered.

"How are you doing this?" Moki asked.

"Boys, here, space is no different from time. It is another illusion of your world. Its rules do not apply here. To move from one place to another, just close your eyes and hold a picture of this place in your mind, and when you open your eyes, you will be there." Then he stretched up, looking at the boys with a satisfied grin on his face. Knowing that their lessons were over, he asked, "Are you ready to travel?"

"Yes." Coahoma nodded, signaling him that he was anxious to get started on this journey. Then he turned around, seeing Moki and Fala standing behind him. Being a son of the chief, always ready to assume leadership, he continued, "Remember the chisel-pointed log barrier into their village—in the corner near the dead man? Let's meet there."

"Yes, I remember this place," said Fala.

"Me too," said Moki. "Donehogawa will be near the gate."

"Now that you have selected this place, close your eyes, concentrate, see it in your minds, and remember my words. When you hear the drum beating its three beats . . . close your eyes and think of this place," Ohanzee instructed. Then he watched as the boys closed their eyes, seeing their faces grow still, intently focusing solely on their target; soon, he watched as they blinked out of sight.

CHAPTER 17

Mutating

Ethane'

*She is a teenage Allewegi who is betrothed to Prince
Sangann. She is the daughter of Lugh and Morrigan and
sister to Gaim, Dahey, Tomas, Bradan, and Conan.*

Coahoma was speeding through this dark and mysterious void,
returning to the Land of Flint. He visualized this terrifying barricade so
vividly that he could reach out and touch it. He recalled the howling
winds whispering, "Danger—do not enter or you will die!"

Coahoma reveled at the simple yet awe-inspiring skill that this lesson
was teaching him. As his spirit jettisoned across the land, he wondered,

Who am I that I would be given such powerful knowledge? Eyes closed, friends by his side, Coahoma struggled to stop his fears from creeping into his thoughts. He wondered, *What will I find inside this witch-infested land? If I can blink across vast distances, then what can their witches do? Do they know that we are coming? Maybe they are here, standing beside me, and I can't see them. Ah, stop it! Be brave! Trust the old woman. She will not send me to my death, not now!*

Stilling his fears, Coahoma heard Ohanzee's voice inside his head. He said, "Son, you can open your eyes now and familiarize yourself with this land. Stay in the shadows and out of sight. Remember the gods who watch over these giants are powerful and do not welcome intruders. They are merciless . . . different from us—DO NOT challenge them or you WILL LOSE."

He heard Moki whisper, "Coahoma, I'm over here."

Moki watched Coahoma and Fala fall in line behind him as they crept beside this great barrier. As they moved, they recalled Ohanzee's warning, "Stay out of sight—or you will lose!" Moki whispered, "Think of a place, then fly across our Great Mother as if we are gods." Then he turned to Coahoma. "Coahoma, we are changing into gods? Will our people begin to hold us responsible for their prayers?"

"Ah, you are too skinny to be a god." Fala chuckled. "Who would want a skinny god with big feet and a dirty face?"

Disregarding Fala's witty response, Moki continued to express his concerns. "Coahoma, are we changing into gods? Do you think that we will go and live with our sun god or moon god?" Moki asked as he peered through a crevice, trying to glimpse a golden-haired giant as he waited for Coahoma's answer.

Then Fala started in again. Pretending that he had risen into a supreme status, donning a serious expression and a voice of authority, he teased, "I am now the god of the clouds. Moki, you are the god of the dirt, and, Coahoma, you can be our god of love. The swirly pink lights . . . They betray you, my friend. She must be more beautiful than a baby fawn on a spring morning."

"Ah, that sounds terrific. Love god! I like it. Don't you, Moki?" replied Coahoma, smiling as a vision of Ethane' flashed through him. "God of love—love god . . . sounds great . . . I like it!"

"Stop it! I am NOT the GOD OF DIRT," Moki complained as he swung around, peering around the outskirts of the compound, craning his neck as he looked in every direction for Donehogawa. Moki said, "Donehogawa is nearby. I can feel him."

"Ah, don't worry about him. He will find us. Ah, your title . . . We will pick a suitable one for you," Coahoma said as he inspected the southern timberline, watching a small whirlwind of snow drift gently by, riding on a gust of wind as it twirled across the heavy blanket of trampled snow.

As he gazed across the wintry land, drawing in a breath as he thought about their situation, he responded, "Moki, I don't know what is happening to us, but I do know," Coahoma sputtered, "our people will not believe our stories. They will say we are crazy . . . or . . . we are dreaming." Pausing for an instant, thinking of his trip through the mysterious void, he continued, "Let's promise not to speak of this journey to anyone—except Laurel and our fathers. Do you agree?"

The three young shamans grasped each other's forearms. They were blood brothers, now and forever, bonded in life as well as death. Yes, they agreed to honor this promise.

Standing on the outskirts of this shocking village; smelling the smoke from their campfires as it drifted through the cracks; hearing loud garbled voices; children playing, thumping, tromping, clanking noises, and squalling babies, they knew that this village was thriving; and they were eager to sneak in to spy on it.

Deciding to inspect the exterior grounds of this electrifying place first, Coahoma saw a path that leads into the forest. He noticed that it was heading directly toward a flock of nervous blue jays that were squalling "intruders" to their woodland friends. Heightening his senses, he began to look around, memorizing the sights, the sounds, the smells, making mental notes of everything surrounding him down to the tiniest detail. He even memorized the motions of the branches as they swayed against the westward winds.

As Coahoma studied this cold dormant terrain, stunned by its forbidding appearance, he visualized his homeland of bright blue skies, moss, and green as he compared it to this bizarre forlorn world devoid of color. He was astonished to see that the dark silhouettes of its rippling forest were the only things that separated the layer of white that carpeted the land from the layer of white that blanketed the sky.

"Giants," Coahoma whispered, "over there," pointing westward toward two men who were standing beneath a large oak. They toted heavy copper axes with long thick wooden handles, leaning forward; they were resuming their work, chopping down this old tree. As Coahoma kneeled beside the wall, studying every detail of their astonishing appearance, he muttered, "Those men are taller than Old Lagundo. The gods were right to warn us they can snap us in two like twigs."

Coahoma continued to watch his enemy, looking for any signs of weakness; however, no matter how he tried, using his sight, his heart, he could see that they were outmatched by their sheer monstrous height, muscular build, and intelligence. *What are their weaknesses? We must find a way to defeat them, or we will not have a choice but to kill Pontiac and abandon Tiponi. I must listen with my heart. Maybe it will find something . . . anything.* Coahoma fretted as he opened his chakras, allowing him to see the spirits of the men who were standing before him.

"Moki, can you find any weaknesses?" he asked under his breath.

"No! They are invincible," Moki said, craning his neck, trying to find the simplest flaw in these exotic men.

"Fala, do you?"

Looking somewhat flustered, Fala seethed, "Not yet . . . but I will!"

Wanting to get a closer look at these strangers, speeding forward, stopping just short of the far corner, Coahoma and his friends studied the strange blue-eyed men with beetling brows, rounded heads, large lantern-shaped jaws covered with thick manes of rumpled hair, red and golden, flowing down across their pale tattooed faces, draping across their shoulders, and loosely gathered at their ends with bindings of sinew. Then he noticed that they had large rounded noses, muscular necks surrounded with strange metallic chokers, and lean bulging shoulder muscles, chests, thighs, and backs. Obviously, these were strong and intelligent men. They were wearing tight leather trousers with heavy high-topped fleece-lined boots, long-sleeved red and brown checked woven coats, wolf skin vests, knives strapped to their sides, and mysterious cone-shaped fleece-lined metallic headdress.

Coahoma tried to determine if these giants were men or beasts. He was awestruck by the sheer size of these manlike creatures who were working contently together, chopping through the hardened layers with their shiny axes. Face to face, they were rotating their mighty axes from one to the other, emitting deep-bellied grunts with each strike. It wasn't long before they heard the familiar thunderous crack reverberate through the woodlands, announcing to the world that it had just lost its battle

SHERRY COTTLE GRAHAM

against these sharp tools. Then they watched as the massive weight of this ancient tree began to move, leaning toward the right, squalling as it ripped away from its majestic trunk, crying out its last song as it toppled over on to the cold hard ground.

"Look," Fala warned, pointing toward the northwestern edge of the woods.

Turning to see what he had found, hearing the sound of heavy footsteps stomping through the brush, excitement rippled through the boys as they watched another man nearly twice their size exit the forest, pulling a wooden sled loaded with large chunks of beautiful multicolored flint behind him. Following him were two more tattooed giants carrying large flint spears, wearing similar cone-shaped shiny headgear with horns, adorned with strange-looking shiny neck and wrist bands. Just as the leader pulled his sled over the shallow dip, five four-legged beasts of considerable size raced past the men and ran into the clearing.

As these straggly tan—and gray-haired canines raced by, barking and yipping, Donehogawa asked, "Ah, you have returned. Did you come to find my skull?"

Hearing the familiar voice, Coahoma wasn't surprised that Donehogawa was standing behind him.

"What took you so long to get here?" asked Moki, looking slightly annoyed by his arrival. "We are here to save our people. If we have time, we will help you, but not now!" Looking back toward the beasts, he asked, "What are those animals?"

"They are called hounds," said Donehogawa. "If an Alli shouts 'KILL,' those hounds will knock you down and rip out your throat!"

"Hounds—they look like wolves," Fala said as he watched these graceful hounds race past. They darted across the snow-covered meadow, heading directly toward a red-bearded giant.

"No, they are an enemy to the wolf! They hunt in packs, and if they catch a wolf, they will tear him apart. They are always on the prowl, playing with the children, and guarding this vile place."

"Where are they going?" Moki asked as he watched the hounds run toward the western timberline.

"They belong to that red-bearded Alli called Balor. Over there," he said, pointing at a red-bearded man standing beside the fallen tree. "Every morning, they rise with the sun and go into the forest with Balor to hunt."

Coahoma turned toward Donehogawa, nodding toward the giant men. He asked, "What can you tell us about them?"

Consumed with anger, eyes narrowing, breathing in as he nodded toward the two towering men, trying to control his rage, "Crazy, vile, blood-thirsty beasts, we call them," he said, trying to speak through his mutilated mouth so that they would see his revulsion for these merciless beings. "The tall ones are bred to fight—headhunters. They live by no rules—man's or god's. They kill for the thrill of killing: our people, their own kind, animals—doesn't matter. They offer blood sacrifices to Belenus, their sun god, with the blood of our brothers on their sacred mounds. Look about you," he said as he waved his unbroken arm around, gesturing toward the half frozen and mutilated corpses that were staked high above the ground for all to see. "See our brothers. Hear their cries. We curse these demons and the ground that they walk on!"

Sickened by what he heard, wanting to know more, Moki asked, "Where is their homeland?"

"Legend says that they came to our nation many winters ago when our grandfathers' fathers were children. They came to this land after they lost their homeland to their enemy. They sailed here on ships from far away. They filled their long boats with people and brought their violent and murderous ways to our land. Now they grow stronger with each passing moon. They are like the bees. They protect their queen. They scare us from our land, and in time, we will become nothing more than a memory," Donehogawa said.

Turning his attention back toward the approaching yellow-bearded giant, who was pulling the heavy sled, Fala said as he nodded toward the stack of flint, "My father could make many beautiful blades with that flint."

"The Allewegi control the flint. See our mutilated bodies posted around their pits! They say STAY OUT! They believe who controls the flint rules the land. Their leader is named Creighton. He believes that his sons will, in time, rule because he controls it, but King Gann is the high chief. He lives in the east along the banks of the mighty Ohi:Yo' and rules over this land."

Interested in what Donehogawa was saying, Coahoma asked, "Will King Gann fight Creighton for control of the flint?"

"No. He is afraid of King Gann," Donehogawa said. "I heard that King Gann's village is armed with many of these giant warriors, and one called Cu Chulainn. They say that Cu Chulainn is taller than two of our people standing atop each other. He wears garments made with copper, carries long iron spears, metal knives, and wears a copper headdress over his long yellow-bearded face that is shaped like a grizzly with legs that move when he walks. Some say that his eyes shoot flames at his enemy, maybe he is a god, but I know that he brings terror into the hearts of his enemy just by the sight of him."

"What else can you tell us that we need to know?" Coahoma asked.

Donehogawa said, "Ah, another strange custom of these Allewegi, they build these large earthen mounds on power spots and fill them with the bodies of their dead leaders. These giant men have many strange ways. They call upon their dead and their gods to protect them in battle. These men dig copper from a mine to the north near the Great Lakes. They use rafts to carry these rocks over to our rivers and to their villages. Each village has a man who is called a black smith. These blacksmiths make weapons from this ore."

"Tell us more about the Allewegi," Fala said. He listened to Donehogawa's stories as he peeked around the corner of the fortress. He watched the giant man pulling a sled that was loaded with flint across the snow. "Can they see us?" he asked.

"Those warriors, blood suckers, huh, they are no threat to us. Watch . . . ," said Donehogawa as he slid backward and raced directly into the path of the oncoming sled. As the giant approached, Donehogawa raised his broken arm and screamed, "Stop! Give me my skull! Murders!" Then he stood still as the giant plunged directly through him, dragging his sled behind him.

Coahoma was relieved to learn that the Allewegi warriors couldn't see him. Letting his guard down, Coahoma watched three small bearded men carrying axes walk toward Balor. He realized that they were the same race as the giants. They wore similar clothes, and they had the same yellow beards and white skin. However, these men were much smaller than the giant warriors. Coahoma estimated the men to be slightly taller than him.

As Moki watched these men, he spotted a strange dark shadow moving out of the forest. It headed straight toward the front gate. "Witch," Moki blurted as he slid backward, moving toward the barricade, signaling Coahoma and Fala to follow him. "Get down!" he whispered. He looked over at Coahoma and said, "Shh, he's headed this way."

"This way," said Coahoma, turning toward the wall, moving quickly to the other side. "No, not now, not yet . . . We need more time!" Coahoma seethed as he crossed through the barrier. Then he turned, gazing around the interior grounds. Heart beating, frantically looking for a hiding place, he was surprised to see a menagerie of strangely dressed people of varying sizes, ranging from five to ten feet tall, working in small groups around their rounded lodges, chopping wood, stoking cooking fires, and hauling water.

As Coahoma glanced around the compound, he spotted a group of tall women that were chatting beside a hot cooking fire. *Who are these people who have such tall women?* he wondered. *Those women are nearly seven feet tall.* Distracted for a few moments, he looked at the odd way that they were dressed. He noticed that they were wearing long woven skirts, puffy long-sleeved blouses, and heavy hooded capes. Remembering the danger that they were in, he glanced in the opposite direction. He spotted a different race of people. These people stood nearly five feet tall. They were fair-skinned. They wore a single black braid down the center of their backs. The men had large copper earplugs, and they were dressed in suede.

Then he saw it, a long thatch-covered shelter a short distance away from them. He saw the carcasses of white-tailed deer, moose, and elk. They were hanging upside down from support beams. Right beside this slaughter house was an odd-looking branch-covered, smoke-filled, rock-and-wicker constructed hut. "This way . . . Follow me," Coahoma commanded, pointing toward the odd-looking shed."

When the boys entered the hut, they spun around and peered through its gaping holes, looking for any signs of the approaching shadow. Splitting apart, each of the boys moved to a different location of the smoke-filled shack. They wondered if they had been detected by anyone. Determined to proceed, Coahoma said, "Morrigan's lodge isn't far from here. Let's prepare to move before the shadows find our silver cords and find us."

"Do you think that that shadow will find us?" Fala asked. He was worried about the shadow, but now he was distracted by the sight of these bizarre people who were milling about.

Looking over at Coahoma, Moki responded, "It was Kenji. I know it was him. I could see his silver cord as he returned to his body. He lives in that smaller shelter that is shaped like a beehive. I hope that he didn't see us and come after us with his demon blade!"

"He's not going to find us," insisted Coahoma, "but we need to go before he does."

As the boys prepared to leave this dimly lit smoke-filled hut, they noticed how the rays of light streamed through the cracks. Then they saw the bodies of animals, such as deer, pheasant, turkey, and a few large fish that were hanging on metal hooks from the overhead beams.

But there was a shape that was difficult for Coahoma to recognize. As he gazed through the smoke, he realized that he was looking at the head of a dead man. It was draped over the smoking fire. Sickened by his discovery, Coahoma said, "Look over there," as he pointed toward the hideous sight. "It's the head of a dead man," Coahoma whispered. "Let's get out of here!"

Coahoma led his blood brothers out of the hut and moved inside the shadows of the chiseled barricade. It wasn't long before they were standing near a massive log-and-rock constructed lodge that was on the southwestern edge of the encampment. "Look, it's her home," Coahoma said. "I remember those carcasses that she has staked around it."

As Coahoma approached its backside, remembering the tall beautiful blue-eyed blonde, recalling her scent, the softness of her skin, her charisma, her sensitivity, he wondered, *Does she eat people? Is she a cannibal?* Shaking his head, trying to understand what he had just seen, searching for an answer, his inner voice began to wonder, *No, she doesn't eat people. It can't be. No one eats people. I don't even know if that head belonged to a man or a woman, but I don't care! No one cuts the head off a man and smokes it for pleasure, except for these Allewegi.*

Moki slid over beside Coahoma. He said, "Coahoma, we must go inside before the drums call to us." Then he looked over at Fala and asked, "Are you ready to go inside?"

Fala was already studying the methods used to create this gigantic lodge. He was busy counting the steps of its perimeter, noting the breadth of the logs, the color and shape of the stonework, the thickness of the mud, the thatching, and the layers of rock and bark that were used to construct such a stout lodge. "Go on," he said, nodding. "I need more time. Go, do what you need to do."

"Good," replied Coahoma. "Keep your eyes open! And warn me if you see anything!"

Stopping in midsentence, turning around, Coahoma looked at Moki as he nodded toward the outside wall, signaling that it was time to enter this nasty witch's lair. Then without saying a word, the boys pressed against the exterior wall and disappeared inside, leaving Fala behind.

As Coahoma's eyes adjusted to the dim light, smelling the foul-smelling odor of these inhabitants, heart racing, hearing the voices of women inside, he was eager to see the tall blue-eyed blonde again and listen to her innermost secrets. He wasn't sure what it was, or why he couldn't release the power she held over him, maybe it was witchcraft, the work of the demons; but he didn't care. Daring and curious, he was determined to learn more about this beautiful girl and her customs.

Realizing that Ethane' and Morrigan were in the front room, Coahoma and Moki crept into the shadows of their dimly lit lodge. Once they were settled into their hiding spots, they prepared to listen to their conversation. When Moki glanced over at Coahoma, he noticed that the lights surrounding him were glowing in a bright pinkish hue as he watched them.

When Ethane' headed toward the door, Moki studied her ankle-length brown hooded cape and the beautifully adorned clay container that she was toting. He knew that she was leaving to draw water from the local river and that Coahoma was preparing to follow her. He heard her say, "Mother, I'll be okay. Don't worry about me," as she exited her lodge.

A sense of helplessness washed over Moki as he knew that Coahoma's heart was tied to hers. When she left, he wondered, *Is Coahoma going to follow her?* When he saw the lights sparkling inside Coahoma's eyes and the deliberate flick of his head, he knew that Coahoma was asking permission to follow her. *What is this curse that she has cast over him?* he wondered as he flinched his finger, releasing him to go. As Coahoma slid out of sight, Moki thought, *Ah, my friend, you are going to learn a harsh lesson from this one. I hope his love doesn't cost you your life—or ours.*

SHERRY COTTLE GRAHAM

CHAPTER 18

The Witch's Lair

Coahoma
*Coahoma, the young Choctaw Shaman, is spying
on Ethane' as she walks toward the river.*

Coahoma felt guilty for leaving his friends behind as he followed Ethane' into her courtyard. As he looked out over the hazy white sky, he pleaded, "Ohanzee, please keep my brothers safe until I return." He watched Ethane' tug her clay pot up to her breast. *Ah, why does she have to leave now and make me desert my friends in this vile place? But I have no choice. I must follow her. Ah, just look at her. She is so different—unlike any girls that I know*, he thought as he scampered into the shadows, making sure to stay out of sight. *Look how beautifully her honeycombed hair wraps around her cone-shaped head. Her eyes, they are so blue like our Father Sky, and the fullness of her scarlet lips against the rose tones of her cheeks. No one would dare say anything about her misshapen teeth or her flattened forehead; they make her complete. She is beautiful—maybe the most beautiful thing that I have ever seen.*

Captivated by her radiance, realizing that his manhood was alive, growing inside him as a flood of vibrant feelings clouded his mind, heart tightening, eyes twinkling, struggling to breathe, he knew that he was bewitched by this amazing creature. He knew it was wrong, but he couldn't block his feeling for her. *I will follow her to the end of our Great Mother if I have to. I will learn her ways, no matter what happens. I will not let her out of my sight, but what if something happens to Moki and Fala? What if someone sees them or if Kenji comes? Father will be angry with my decision to leave.* He fretted. *Don't worry, keep going, everything will be all right. I must follow her!*

As Coahoma slithered along, keeping in the shadows, following closely behind Ethane', looking around, seeing a bizarre blend of two different races of people living together in this dangerous and terrifying community, he noticed that there were many tall, white, blue-eyed, and wild blond-haired people as opposed to others that were short, yellow-skinned, black, slanted eyes, and clean shaven. *One day, I will know who these strangers are*, he thought as he dodged around the outskirts of their smoky and musty-smelling lodges.

No one must see me, he thought, keeping his distance as he watched Ethane' who was quietly strolling through her village. Releasing his fears, relaxing as he followed this strange girl, he noticed the way she moved, her long graceful gait, the way she held her head, the whiteness of her interlocking fingers as they pressed against her ornate orange-colored clay pot, and the lean curvature of her body as she moved. *What is it about her? Why do I need to be near her? Why am I tied to her by some strange magic—but why?* he wondered as he followed her along the frozen mud-trodden path, feeling blood surging through his veins as he watched her. Struggling with his feelings, he heard a small voice on the wind. It warned, "Watch her. The power to save Pontiac lies with her."

Then as Ethane' walked around the side of a large thatch-covered gathering shelter and entered the central point of her village, Coahoma spotted a strange arrangement of three barren poles rising from the top of a cone-shaped earthen mound. *What is that?* he thought as he inspected this baffling formation. *It must be important to her people somehow*, he pondered as he studied its odd design. Gathering up his nerve, he began to move into the light, leaving the safety of the shadows behind him when he heard the squall of a hawk, warning, "Go back! Stay in the shadows! Stay away from the Nahullo's land!"

Recalling Donehogawa's story about the Nahullo, he retreated back into the shadows. He saw the hawk swooping down, soaring in front of him, blocking his path to the elevated poles, screaming this message: "Misery and death come to those who walk on it! Stay away! Go home, you don't belong here!"

Stunned by the hawk's warning, Coahoma took a long calming breath. Calming his mind, looking over at Ethane', he heard a man's voice calling out, "Ethane', girl, come here." Shifting his eyes toward the source of the sound, Coahoma discovered a young man, barely older than Ethane', lean, long-faced, dressed in long flowing clothes belted at the waist, wearing a strange ornate rack of manmade copper antlers on top of his cone-shaped shaved face, signaling with his outstretched arm for her to join him.

Coahoma was angry as he watched Ethane' walk across the courtyard, moving toward a beehive-shaped stone lodge. *Who is he? What does he want with her? Isn't that Kenji's lodge?* Coahoma wondered as he fought back his feelings. Coahoma hid in the shadows as he watched the tints of violet and green that surrounded this antlered boy's aura. *He likes her. What kind of evil magic is he conjuring up inside this place? What demon is hiding in that Nahullo's lodge?* Breathing in, *Will I find them ripping the hearts from a brother or casting black magic over a sister?* Taking a long breath in, Coahoma watched them from his hiding spot, noticing this strange blond-headed boy as he hobbled aside, allowing Ethane' to slip past him. Ethane' placed her clay pot on the ground beside his doorway and disappeared inside. The young Nahullo lifted off his sacred headdress, tucked it securely beside his right hip, and hobbled inside.

Amazed at what he had just witnessed, *That Nahullo has a weak leg*, he thought. *He is crippled. Ah, a weakness!* Coahoma was confused by this confrontation. He didn't know whether to return to Morrigan's or to spy on Ethane'. Pausing a moment, he watched two mallards waddle past him. They were heading toward some unknown destination. In the distance, he heard the familiar songs of a gaggle of geese. As his anger with himself grew, he glanced at the noisy residents as they went about doing their daily chores. Scooting to the backside of the stone lodge, he made up his mind. He decided, *I'm going in. I must know what she is doing in there.* In the matter of moments, shifting into a panther, Coahoma pressed his face against the stone wall and disappeared inside.

"How is Papa?" Coahoma heard Ethane' ask as his eyes adjusted to the dimly lit room.

Standing beside their sleeping father, he answered, "No better, Ethane'. We cannot breathe his life spirit back into him. We fear he will not live past the upcoming full moon," the young yellow-bearded Nahullo said as he placed his powerful headdress on a wooden rack beside the entrance. He waddled over and stood beside Ethane' who was standing at the foot of his bed. Looking at his gray-tinted skin, hollowed eyes, seeing the energy drain from his body, she knew that her brother was right. He was dying.

"Gaim, Mother will not allow it! She travels in the Spirit World to a distant location, to that place where he is living. She will break this curse. Papa will return to us. I know he will."

"Kenji too has found this place. Tell her what you know," Gaim said, turning toward Kenji who was sitting beside the central fire hearth, obviously in another place, softly chanting words to his gods in a mystical language that Coahoma failed to understand. He was dressed in magnificently woven garments, a handsome green and brown patterned tunic that was adorned with a handsome talisman made with the bleached bones and claws of a mighty grizzly, tight fitting soft leather suede trousers, high-topped fur-lined leather boots, and covered in a fabulously flowing bald eagle's costume that started on top of his head with the head of the bird as its wings draped comfortably down over his small face and fell alongside his miniature arms, strapped to his hands, forming an intricately feathered winged cloak that accentuated his large copper earplugs. The spirit of the eagle soared through him: strong, flying high, exceeding all boundaries, traveling far, wise and ruthless; he was the eagle. "Kenji, tell Ethane' what you know!"

Coahoma backed against the far wall, keeping in the shadows of the long rack of meticulously organized wooden masks that were built beside the rear wall where he carefully entered this mystical dwelling. As he listened to the three talking in the background, he looked over to see what Kenji was storing in his hut. *Hum, what's on his racks? What kind of witchcraft does he keep?* Creeping toward the shelves, *Go look! Something must be on them. I can sense it . . . something powerful. I must learn what magic he will use against us . . . something here . . . must see his magic . . .* Glancing at the wooden shelves, he shifted his eyes toward Kenji. *Just look at him*, Coahoma thought. *He's a tiny shrunken man, isn't he? Look how short the gods made his arms and legs—about half the size of me, and look how he suffers with his disproportionate head and goiter-swollen neck. Hum, his black eyes are slanted, different from all others that I've seen, and look how black his large hands are, but he has a clean-shaven face, and his eagle costume is amazing. He must be a powerful and dangerous man, but how old is this tiny witch?* Coahoma wondered. *He looks like a child, can't be very old, lives by himself. And look—his energy lights this room up like an old man.*

Gathering his nerve, moving closer to the racks, stretching his head up and over the lower rack, looking at the meticulously organized shelves, Coahoma recognized many familiar items: many beautifully decorated and polished rattles, drums, and pottery. Then there were a few ornately designed smoking pipes in the forms of bears, eagles, and birds; a variety of symmetrically rounded, polished, and finely decorated pottery; folded and stacked cloth and leather garments, blankets, rugs, giant tobacco leaves; large stash of copper earplugs, and odd seashell jewelry. *Must be a powerful witch to receive so many nice things from his people*, he thought as he examined his belongings.

Rising on to his back legs, slowly, stealthily, wanting to see what was on the upper shelf, using his shamanic ability to blend into his surroundings, looking around, Coahoma saw a magnificent collection of skillfully flint-knapped cutters, knives, hatchets, awls, and flint tips that were carefully laid out before him. Then he noticed a stack of severed eagle talons, deer hoofs, bear claws, hollow turtle shells; and then he spotted an unusual bone-colored bowl-shaped object resting on a soft patch of mink. *What is it?* Seeing its size and smooth rounded shape, its color, then it hit him. *It's a skull!* Focusing directly on his discovery, *It's human! They made a bowl from someone's skull! Who would do such a thing?* Breathing in, sickened by what he had just found, withdrawing back into the recesses of the darkness, thinking for a moment, wondering, *Who does this belong too?* Then the answer hit him like a bolt of lightning flashing from the overhead sky, striking directly in the center of his heart. Stunned, he realized, *Donehogawa! That is Donehogawa's skull! They made*

Donehogawa's skull into a ceremonial bowl! Oh, how will I ever be able to tell him this?

Calming his horror, he wondered, *Are their gods crazy? How can they support such vile acts on our Great Mother's children? What curse will these gods place on these white sorcerers?* As these questions flooded through his mind, he noticed that Kenji was backing up toward him.

"Tell her. She needs to know the truth," Gaim commanded.

"It's true. I know who holds your father's spirit, "Kenji said as he looked at Ethane'. Then he looked over at the giant red-bearded shaman who was sleeping on a large bed that was lifted off the ground. "Your father's spirit has been swallowed up by a medicine man that lives near the edge of a powerful swamp." Then Kenji looked at the flickering fire. "Last night, I moved into the Spirit World and followed your mother to this distant place far to the south to a place near the Great Sea where she slept with your father inside a child named Tiponi. He lives on top of a small hill in the land of swamps with a people who call themselves Choctaw. His spirit is trapped inside a man they call Pontiac. His spirit burns hot in this man's veins. Your father's spirit fights to leave and return to you, but if he doesn't return soon"—looking over at the sleeping giant—"his spirit will be lost."

Unhappy with this information, a scowl ripped across the face of Ethane', eyes narrowing, flushing in brilliant hues of crimson. "Papa is trapped in one of those filthy swamp savages! Ridiculous! Do you expect me to believe this lie? He is a powerful priest—blessed by our gods," she spat. "He is protected by the Great Cernunnos and his brother, the mighty all-seeing wolf! I think that you are being deceived by a demon!" Ethane' yelled as she whipped around to see her brother.

Kenji looked at her. "Ethane', I am sorry for your misfortune, but Gaim is telling the truth. Your father's spirit is trapped inside another man. I have been to his camp, and I have seen him."

"Then what are your plans? Can you save him?" Turning to look at her brother face to face, searching for the truth, choking tears of confusion and anger back, fighting against the rage that was festering inside her, she asked, "Why has Mum kept this from me? Does she not trust me? Do you not trust me?"

Crossing his arms, preparing to deal with this sweltering confrontation, knowing his sister's quick wit and hot temper, understanding her talents, her prominent position in their clan, trying to

SHERRY COTTLE GRAHAM

remain calm, gathering his words, Gaim countered, "Mother is shielding you from the truth. What can you do? You are only a silly girl. You are not a warrior or a priest. You must leave this to us, and you must trust us. We are not going to sit back and let a tribe of savages harm our father. Anyway, Prince Sangann has asked for your hand in marriage, and he waits for your decision. He wants to marry you at our upcoming feast day when we celebrate the summer solstice with Belenus watching over you."

"No, I won't agree to it! Not now," she huffed. "Not until Papa is better!" Then she turned toward Kenji. "Kenji, you know as well as I that all he wants is my dowry and unlimited rights to our flint. Tell Gaim that Sangann doesn't love me. I can see it in his eyes. He wants to marry me so that my dowry will elevate his position with the king! I won't have it!"

He couldn't believe what he heard as he listened to her ranting, knowing the crush that she has had on Balor for many years; Gaim was annoyed with his sister's selfish reaction. She wasn't helping him or their mother by talking this way. "Ethane', girl, are you daft? Think about it! When King Gann dies, Sangann will become king, and you will become our queen. Your children—they will become our supreme rulers over this immense land, live in the richest kingdoms, and command the destiny of our giant elite warriors. There is so much power in this land—all for your taking. That is not all. It will secure a spot for all of us—we will become advisors to the king and sit with his high council."

"Nay! Don't lay this blarney on me! You are only thinking of yourself! How can I commit myself to a man that I hardly know? How can I leave my home—my family?" Turning toward Gaim, her face was filled with bewilderment as tears began to well up and spill down the sides of her cheeks as her words continued to flow. "I love it here—you know this. I have you, Mother, my friends." Then she turned away, moving to her father's side, dropping to her knees, stretching her left arm up and over his chest, silently thinking of her love for Balor, not wanting to lose him but understanding the privileges that her union with Sangann would bring to her and her family. She wanted to think about this marriage. She had just come of age. This was so sudden. Not wanting to make a decision, speaking barely above a whisper but loud enough for all to hear, looking down at her sleeping father, she said, "Pa, I will agree to marry Sangann when and only when you are able to ride down the beautiful Muskingum River with me and take me back to the grand village of Killarney. I love it there. I want to walk back through the Corridor of Fire with you by my side as the Kumi-Daiko drummers announce our arrival to our gods. I want to marry the prince on the sweet grass beside our grandpa's mound as Belenus blesses our union."

Coahoma noticed that Kenji was moving toward him. *Should I slide outside?* he wondered. *Does Kenji know that I am here? Should I run? No! Fight if I must, but stay put,* he decided. When Kenji reached the rack, he picked up the skull with both hands. He held it into the air, walking toward Ethane'; he held it out for her to inspect its elegant finish. He said, "Ethane', it's finished. Your ceremonial bowl is ready for you to drink from at your wedding. It will bring you power and blessings from the gods as our future queen."

Gaim hobbled a single step forward, turning to look at his sister's expression, seeing the familiar flash of determination rip through her cold blue eyes, the way she cocked her mouth and tilted her head; he knew that his efforts were hopeless. The stubbornness that he had grown to recognize and accept was evident; she would get her way. He saw that she had made her decision, reckless and immature, thinking only of herself. "You speak the words of a fool, but arguing with you is like arguing with a rock. What happens if we cannot save Pa? You owe it to yourself and your children to think about marrying Sangann whether Pa lives or dies. Look at what he can give you . . . tall sons, wealth, land, protection. Who can better protect you in this hostile land against these natives who grow angrier with us with each passing moon? He can offer you a future, but I am not going to argue with you about whom you should or should not marry. Go marry a farmer or a blacksmith—a slave—I DON'T CARE. But remember my words—hindsight is always the best sight."

Gathering herself, Ethane' pushed herself back on to her feet, refusing to discuss this any further; she walked over to her brother. Then she pressed her right hand into a pocket that was carefully stitched into the lining of her magnificently woven cape and pulled out a wolf's spatula. "Look, I found Papa's wolf's teeth. Do you think his spirit will come back to get it? He loved it so."

Gaim reached out and carefully took it from her. Then he held it up into the air, rotating it in his hand, inspecting it from all angles. "This is Papa's favorite piece. He never goes anywhere without it." Looking over at his father, he said, "Kenji, put the skull back and get Papa's wolf cape. Ethane', come over here—help me sit him upright. Come on . . . get on the other side, grab his arm and pull."

Coahoma watched the three split apart—brother and sister on one side, Kenji on the other side—reaching down, grabbing his arms. They hoisted Lugh into a sitting position. When Lugh's bottom jaw dropped down, Coahoma noticed that Lugh's front teeth were missing. As Gaim and Kenji held on to Lugh, Ethane' gathered a wolf robe and draped it over her father. She adjusted it so that it fit comfortably on top of Lugh's head, and she allowed its body to fall by his sides. Then Gaim carefully placed a wolf spatula into his mouth and pushed his bottom jaw up to secure the teeth into place. Then Kenji reached down and picked up two rattles, hurried over to a wooden rack beside the door, pulling a small bundle of rolled aromatic leaves and another bundle of tied holly leaves. Turning, he placed the bundle into the fire and set it ablaze. Gaim blew out the flames, and the herbs began to smolder, releasing a sweet-smelling aroma into the stone hut. Returning to the giant's side, Gaim sponged the holly over Lugh's chest with a fan of eagle feathers as he chanted, calling to Belenus to join them. He asked the gods to return the spirit of his dying friend.

As Coahoma watched on, seeing many similarities with their chants and costumes, he knew that their words were different, but oddly enough, their beliefs were about the same. He wondered, *Why don't these witches ask Hashtahli for help?* Coahoma watched as these three hovered over this great priest, working until exhausted. Seeing no difference in their father's disposition, they gave up.

"His spirit can't escape that madman," Gaim said. "It's trapped inside that savage's head, but it won't be for much longer . . ."

"Why? What are you saying?" Ethane' asked.

"Our brothers are on their way to his homeland as we speak."

"What? When did they leave?"

"When Pa fell sick, they were here. Ma told them what was happening. You were with Kerri, gathering water for Ma, when they grabbed their traveling bags, weapons, and food. They left the fort in a hurry, heading directly south, running toward the river where they will assemble a small army to join their fight with the Choctaw. Dahey will find this man, and he will return Pa's soul to us."

"How will they recognize him?"

"They won't know. They will ambush this village under the light of the moon. They will kill and behead all of their men and carry their heads back here to us. It will be up to us to decide which one houses Pa's spirit. When we find it, we can return it to him."

"Where are they now?"

They are in the shipyards at Enniscorthy and preparing to sail down to the Ohi:Yo' River to meet up with a small army of their friends. They are boarding one of Kings Gann's vessels, and they will not stop until they reach the Choctaw village in about four, maybe five, days."

"How many Choctaw warriors will they have to fight against?"

"It's a small village, not more than a couple of hundred men and boys not strong enough to fight against our warriors. Ethane', think about it. How can they possibly prepare for an ambush against our giant mercenaries wearing their copper armor and swinging their mighty axes? Their people will more than likely run and hide in their swamps when they see their painted faces charging toward them like a herd of giant moose. No mercy. No one will be spared. Just think of it, a few less red men and more land for your growing empire!"

Confused, Ethane' asked, "What about their women and children?"

"What about them?" Gaim said.

"Will Dahey spare them?" Ethane' asked.

"Nah, he will strike down everything that is in his way. If they run, Dahey will not chase them into a swamp. They will live—for a few days anyway—then be eaten by a pack of wolves or bitten by snakes," Gaim responded in a tone of indifference to the destiny of this tribe.

Stunned by what he heard, Coahoma wondered, *How can this be?* Coahoma remained silent, absorbing the details of this conversation. His mind spun as he gritted his teeth. He hissed, "Heartless men . . . slaughter women and children . . . butcher my family . . . Ah, we will see who gets butchered." Pressing his belly against the sooty floor, trying to contain his escalating hatred of these evil ones, he wondered, *How can their gods support such savagery? Kill women and children . . . vile, nasty barbarians.* Flicking his tail against the wall, Coahoma's anger and hatred for these loathsome men snarled across his whiskered faced. He seethed, "Know this you stinking giants . . . We will see who surprises whom when you reach our village!"

Coahoma wanted to see Ethane' one last time before he retreated back to his friends. Realizing that his time was about up, looking over the rim of the wooden storage rack, seeing her swollen face, her mesmerizing blue eyes, the way her mouth arched as her teeth pushed against her lips, seeing her aura lighting the room in tones of aqua, he couldn't stay angry with her. *She's just trying to save her father*, he thought. *Like her brother said—she's just a silly girl. She has no power over us.*

Then he heard her say, "I must go. Mother is waiting for me. Gaim, I will prepare some food for you and Kenji. I will bring it to you before its time for your prayers."

As she turned, Gaim asked, "Can you bring me my heavy blanket—the one with the brown and green checks? The bones in my bum leg seem to ache all of the time now. It's much worse at night when the villa cools down. I hope that if I drink my white willow tea and wrap my legs in my blanket that I can sleep a wee bit longer tonight."

"Aye, of course, I'll bring it."

Then she flipped her hood over her head and headed for the doorway as Coahoma pressed against the exterior wall, leaving the confines of this small stone lodge in unison. He was determined more than ever to follow her as he watched her body shift from side to side as she strolled through the front gate and on to a narrow pathway that was covered with a thick layer of crushed shells. Hearing the sound of her feet as she walked through it, he noticed how the chips of mother-of-pearl sparkled in the afternoon sunlight as he followed Ethane' to the river.

What secrets will you reveal to me next, beautiful girl? he thought as he tried to separate his feelings for her against his instincts that loving her would ultimately end in tragedy. *Impossible, I must not fall in love with you, Ethane'—not now, not during this life time*, he thought. Needing to maintain control, sensing that his desire to be near her was overpowering his ability to say no, *I must stop this . . . Don't look at her—her eyes or her aura! What is the matter with me? She loves Balor. She might be a queen of these people someday. Laurel was right to send us here, but this place is filled with so much pain.*

When Ethane' reached the river, Coahoma watched her dip her pot into its frigid water as she listened to the delightful sounds of honking geese a short distance away. Spring was her favorite time of the year as the migrating geese were returning from their winter nesting grounds, and soon, the banks will be littered with hundreds of incredible-tasting eggs. Eager to see this flock of swimming birds, she placed her urn down and abandoned it as she followed a narrow path into the woods. Relaxing her guard, she was oblivious to the eyes that were hidden in the shadows watching her.

Coahoma was at peace as he watched her walk upstream to investigate these honking fowl. As he studied the way that her golden hair fluttered in the breeze, he heard someone call his name. When he turned to see who it was, he saw Moki, Fala, and Donehogawa moving toward him.

When he saw the pitiful ghost, Coahoma's heart skipped a beat. Wondering how he would take the news of his discovery, he looked at the ground as he gathered his words. He said, "Donehogawa, I have something to tell you."

"What? Did you find my skull?" Donehogawa asked.

"Yes, it is in Kenji's lodge. It is on top of a rack near the back wall."

Coahoma saw sadness in Donehogawa's eyes as he drifted backward. Moving toward the village, he whispered, "Goodbye, my friends. May the gods be with you," as he disappeared from sight.

Moki was the first to speak. "Coahoma, our time is up. Are you ready to leave this place?"

"Yes," Coahoma said. "I must warn Father about these giant warriors who are on their way to slaughter us!" As he looked over at Ethane', Coahoma spotted a slight movement in the brush line beside her. Recognizing the headdress of an Ojibwa warrior, he instantly knew that she was in danger.

No, this can't be happening! Coahoma thought. Not wanting to see her beauty extinguished by a bloody gash to the backside of her head. He raced forward, screaming, "Ethane', run!" as the Ojibwa brave drew back his weapon.

CHAPTER 19

The Wakie Wisag

The pipestone pipe that an Allewegi carved into the image of Kenji.

"No, not now!" Coahoma yelled as he heard his father's voice calling to him from across the void.

"Coahoma . . . come back . . . ," he called.

Realizing that his journey was over, becoming emotional—anger, confusion, love, hatred—all of these powerful emotions swept through him. Then the nasty tentacles of self-doubt spread through him like a fever. His heart ached for Ethane'. It stung with regrets, leaving him questioning the overall success of his mission. *I've failed everyone*, he thought. *Tiponi, Pontiac, Father, the old woman, Ethane', my friends . . .*

I call myself a healer, but I am not! I did not even see the danger that was standing right beside her. Now she journeys to the other side alone, scared, and it is my fault. Her, my people—I've failed them all. I will never become a shaman if I can't protect the ones that I love!

Seeing the familiar moss-laden cedar trees and the smell of saltwater in the air, he knew that his journey had ended. As he whipped through the familiar white ribbed tunnel and silently settled back into his body, memories flashed through his mind. Vivid ones of giant bearded men adorned with metallic horned headgear, hideous visions of human decapitations, skulls made into ceremonial bowls, a dying shaman with the mouth of a wolf, and a tall mystical Nahullo with his powerful set of copper antlers and strange withered leg as well as the terrifying and powerful tiny witch spun through his mind. Then the nagging feeling of helplessness shivered through him as he watched the attacker of Ethane' creep up behind her.

Anger clouded his thoughts as it intensified in him. He felt his muscles tighten, eyes narrowing, temperature rising, cheeks tingling; he felt as if he were a mother bear preparing to slaughter her enemy to protect her cubs. He knew that he must quickly relay his story to his elders as his silver cord masterfully finished its chore by settling his spirit back into his sleeping body. *What am I going to tell my father? The giant warriors are coming to ambush us! How many days away? Ah, but we must run—hide in the swamps. They must not find us! But what about Ethane'? Will Father think that I disobeyed his orders when I chose to follow her? Will he cast me out because I failed to find the clues needed to break the spells?*

As he blinked his eyes open, seeing the crude earthen walls, smelling the smoldering intoxicating hemp, and to his dismay, he was home, sitting in front of the fire. *No! I must go back*, his inner voice screamed, trying to recover his ability to move, to talk, thinking, *Giants are coming—Ethane' is dead. Father is going to be angry!* Forcing himself to relax, inhaling, he filled his lungs with a deep cleansing breath. Moving his fingers, toes, breathing out, feeling life returning to his body, he returned to his physical world and his people. *Ah, I feel ground*, he thought as he began to rock from side to side, forcing himself to wake up. *Oh, I can feel the fire on my cheeks, and, yes, there it is—the sweet smell of her spiritual blend, so intoxicating so calming.* Turning his attention to his gods, he silently prayed, *God of the sun, the skies, the rain, please help me! Help me save my people and Ethane'! I love her—no matter what my father might think*, he thought. *My heart belongs to her!* As Coahoma opened his eyes, he recognized the images of his elders who were watching him, waiting patiently for his return.

As Coahoma shook away the numbing effects of his journey, he replayed the horrifying memories of the merciless attack of Ethane'. Bitterness ripped through him as he whispered, "Father, I must go back!" Pushing himself to his feet, he pleaded, "Ethane' needs me. I saw an Ojibwa warrior attack her . . . I believe that she is crossing over into the World of Spirits. I want to be there to walk with her as she makes this crossing."

"Coahoma, son, come sit beside me," Ituha commanded as he held his arm out, signaling for him to come. Seeing his son's downturned eyes, the way he hung his head, the cloak of pain that saturated his young heart, sympathizing with his sense of loss, knowing the pain that is associated with the passing of a loved one, he gently whispered, "Son, hear my words—you cannot change the things that have happened no more than you can change the path of the sun, the moon, or the rising tide. You must accept that you cannot help his girl. Her fate now rests with her gods and her people."

Wanting to assist, Ituha kneeled down beside his son. He placed his arm around Coahoma's shoulders. Ituha felt Coahoma's energy meld with his. All of a sudden, before he was able to say another word, he felt Coahoma's rage rushed though him. The chief started to tremble, blood racing, muscles taut, trying to make sense of his son's attachment to this strange girl. Calming himself, he said, "Son, you must think of Tiponi and Pontiac now. Our time grows short to save them."

As he turned to inspect the condition of the other two boys, he noticed that Laurel was quietly moving toward Moki. He watched as she bent down and began to whisper directly in his ear, shaking her rattles, chanting, "Moki, come to us. We are here . . . Follow Ohanzee . . . He will bring you home. Moki, follow the sounds of my voice."

Then Moki began to stir. Rolling his shoulders, his head, breathing in, opening his eyes, he hoped that the message that he carried would comfort Coahoma. He twisted forward, searching for the lights in his friend's eyes before he spoke. When he saw that Coahoma was watching him, he said, "Coahoma, Ethane" is alive. A warrior hit her—not hard. She fell, but she was still breathing. When she was lying on the ground, I saw her aura. She is alive."

Leaning forward, Coahoma asked, "What did you see?" watching his friend's large brown eyes staring back. Remembering the legends about the bloody wars between the Ojibwa and the Ron-Nong-Weto-Wanca, Coahoma continued, "The Ojibwa hate the fair-haired people. Why didn't he kill her?"

Before the chief could interrupt, Fala joined the conversation, bringing more news to his friend. "She lives . . . Coahoma, Ethane' is alive. Just think about it, she will bring honor to those warriors for bringing home the daughter of a giant golden-haired leader, and she will become their slave."

"How do you know this?" Coahoma asked, stretching forward to question Fala who was sitting across the fire from him.

"I watched another Ojibwa paddle his canoe to the shore. He got out and helped lift her into it, and then they turned and paddled the canoe back up the stream with her in it."

"Did you see anything else?"

"Ohanzee came for me. Then the next thing that I saw were the flames of this fire," Fala said.

This was good news for Coahoma. Breathing became somewhat easier as realized that she was still alive. "She is wise and strong. Maybe she will be able to escape," Coahoma uttered, hoping against hope that she would be able to break free and return to her village.

Then Fala hung his head as he picked up a small burning stick and gently rubbed it against a round rock that was in front of him. He said, "Coahoma, there were others . . ."

"What? How many?" Coahoma asked as he stood up, looking at Fala. He wanted to know everything that Fala had seen. As he prepared to hear Fala's words, he watched a small stream of wispy smoke drifting toward his Father Sky. He felt a knot swelling in the base of his stomach when he heard the tenor tones of Fala's voice.

Fala said, "There were at least three canoes and about six warriors. Their faces were streaked with war paint. She will not be able to get away from this many men. If she runs, they WILL CATCH HER and KILL HER!"

"Did any of her people see them take her?" he asked, hoping that Balor had been secretly watching her from the distance.

Fala said, "No . . . no one saw them."

SHERRY COTTLE GRAHAM

There was much to do before the darkness settled over their land. Chief Ituha knew that he must sever his son's attraction to this girl. It was time to move on, but he understood his son's passion for her, but he also knew that he would never abandon his people's safety for this fair-haired stranger. As he stood in the center of the hut, making a decision to continue with their plan, he turned toward Lanto and nodded, granting him permission to leave.

Understanding the chief's signal, Lanto reached out and tapped Fala on the shoulder. "Come," he said as he nodded toward the door, signaling that it was time to leave.

As Fala pressed through the doorway, leaving to an unknown destination deep in the forest, the wise old chief called out to his guards, "Akando, stay with them. Meet us back at the high council's lodge before Awock begins to sing his nightly songs." Then as he turned toward Laurel, he raised his right arm, swinging it slightly toward the warm inviting fire, indicating to her that he was passing control to her. He was backing out of the conversation, passing the rights to her to question his son and Moki about their journey into the land of the giant witches. As he watched them gathering around the fire, settling their emotions, leaving the memories of Ethane' behind them, he silently prayed to his gods that she found the secrets that she needed to chase these vile witches from Pontiac and Tiponi.

Laurel looked over at the boys who were directly across the fire from her. "Coahoma, tell me what you saw," she commanded.

As Coahoma settled down, pressing the unwelcome memories of his beautiful blue-eyed girl away from his mind, recalling the visions that were locked inside, his heart skipped a beat as a chill shivered down his spine when he recalled the conversation that he had overheard. "The Ron-Nong-Weto-Wancas are coming. They are coming to slaughter us! They are a few days away and plan to attack us at night and behead us in our sleep," he cursed. Pulling away from his father, he began to pace, and then he stopped and quietly stared into the flames, gathering his words as he began to relay his terrifying message. "They are paddling down the Misi-ziibi on ships that are filled with giant warriors, armed with spear slingers, who are as tall as two of our warriors, one standing on top of the other. They will be wearing tunics that are made from hammered copper and thick leather, horned headdresses, carrying axes, long blades, and large rounded wooden shields. We don't have much time. We must gather everyone, burn our village, and run! They will be upon us like wolves on baby rabbits when the moon is full."

Laurel and Ituha were worried. This wasn't going to give them much time to execute a plan. Wanting to gather as much information as possible about the boys' trip, she demanded, "Coahoma, go sit beside Moki. Coahoma, I want you to start from the beginning. Tell us everything that you saw and heard from the time that you arrived in their village."

Coahoma was the first to speak, sharing his intimate knowledge of a terrifying young man of a slender, gentler, artistic race called the "Wakie Wisag" who lives in harmony with the tall statuesque Alli. He is called, "Kenji," Coahoma said. "He is deformed, short, strange legs and arms, but he is powerful. We must be cautious of this one. His magic is different—dangerous. It is said that when he sleeps, a large grandmother spider comes to him in his dreams and teaches him how to build these large earthworks that track the path of the moon and sun. Father, Kenji comes into our village during the night while we are asleep. He follows Morrigan. And he knows who we are!"

Seemingly not concerned about Kenji's visits, the chief signaled for them to continue. The boys talked about the frozen white lands of the fair-haired Allewegi, antlered Nahullo, shape-shifters, witches, and elite giant warriors as their elders sat, stunned by their experiences. When the chief thought that he had heard it all, the boys began to alternate one after the other, telling their stories. One memory or word sparked the next story. They spun tales of kings and queens, wars, stockades, headhunters, gods, precious metals, spinning wheels, hand-spun clothing, tattooing, mirrors, sacred pipes, earthen mounds, and hounds. As their leaders listened in awe about a fort called Lugudunon, they learned that the Allewegi built this fort to guard their flint. They learned about Donehogawa and the sacrifices that the Alli made to Belenus.

Sitting quietly and absorbing every word that the boys told about the giants and their yellow-skinned companions, Laurel and the chief realized that their situation was much worse than they had anticipated. Not only did they have to banish these two spirits, but now their entire village was in danger of being slaughtered by these giant men. Shocked by the news, they allowed their sons to continue with their tales, stopping only to ask questions.

At the same time far to the north, after two torturous days and nights, exposed to the frigid western winds, cold and hungry, resting only to warm their hands and feet, determined to save their father, the brothers of Ethane' persevered, jogging along their solid clay-based road that was finished with a top coat of crushed mussel shell and stone mortar.

This road was a massive undertaking, stretching nearly two hundred feet wide and running perfectly straight for fifty miles, representing years of sweat and toil to King Sangann who used this engineering marvel to bind his spiritual community of Cork to Enniscorthy. It became a symbol among the Aylwen of his ingenuity and determination to maintain his domination in this red men's world. With his supremacy over his elite warriors, he used brute force to sustain control over his expanding territory.

As the three elite brothers left this road and walked toward Enniscorthy's dock, they were relieved to leave their jogging trip behind them. The brothers looked for a boat that could transport them down the Siothai River to a town called Belfast. King Gann's always kept a few of his larger ships docked in a thriving community called Belfast that was located on the Ohi:Yo' River.

"Aye, Bradan, great to see you lads again," a voice yelled out behind the brothers as a villager trotted toward them along a heavily traveled road that crossed through Enniscorthy. Many of their relatives, friends, and acquaintances lived here.

Bradan was relieved to see a friend standing a short distance ahead. As he ran forward to greet him, he asked, "Did you get my message?"

"Aye! She arrived as pretty as can be . . . about two days ago. She is in a cage inside your boat. Take her with you . . . never can tell when you might need for her to bring me another message. Hey, you lads interested in some food before you set sail? Long trip, you know, this time of the year and all—cold winds seem to blow all the time. Good thing for that warming spell—melted the ice, so you don't have to hoof it all the way down to Belfast."

"No, we must go," Dahey insisted, looking at his younger brothers. Seeing the dark circles underscoring their large swollen greenish blue eyes and blazing cheeks, blond locks hanging in clumps, smelling of sweat, filthy fur coats, copper helmets chapping against their faces, mustaches straggling over their mouths, charred hands carrying long jagged spears, wearing sheaths concealing long iron swords and blades of flint, budging backpacks filled with custom-made armor, hauling their rounded wooden shields and muddy boots, he knew that they were ready for battle. Dahey saw the stress of this blistery run scribbled across their faces; however, he knew that they would be able to rest once they boarded their craft and headed downstream.

Once Dahey reached the long wooden vessel, seeing its familiar smooth upward curved bow and stern and its sturdy sculptured frame, he felt a sense of relief. He knew this river well, having traveled it many times in the past. He knew that they would need many torches to navigate through its shallow swells during the blackness of the night if they were to reach the southern village of Belfast by sunrise.

The boys carefully placed their packs into the bottom of the boat as a young girl ran forward and handed Tomas a large package containing roasted venison and flat breads from her mother's kitchen. "May the luck of Mercury be with you," she said. Eyes gleaming, seeing the tall elite brothers, handsome and brave, she was attracted to all three. "I hope you like it," she waved as the brothers jumped aboard. Pushing the craft out into the cold deep water and with a swoop, they had the paddles in their hands, pulling the water to correct their direction; they were on their way. Soon, they glided around a small bend and disappeared into the forest.

"Tomas, man, don't just sit there. I don't know about you, but I'm famished. Open the package and give me some of that food. I can smell it all the way back here," Bradan commanded as he drove his paddle deep into the water, working steadily to keep it in sync with Dahey who was minding the front.

After the brothers ate, they decided to allow one to sleep while the other two paddled, giving each a chance to rest. Keeping their swords and spears close, never letting their guard down, knowing that danger lurks in many different forms around them, such as hostiles, monster bull moose and elk, coyotes, and timber wolves could attack them at any moment.

As the sun set, darkness fell through the forest, bringing with it a whirlwind of bone-chilling screams as the animals claimed their territories. They heard the owls hooting, coyotes chatting, wolves howling, "Stay away," and the occasional high-pitched screams of wild cats, announcing that they were nearby.

"It is getting dark, better light a torch," Dahey called back to Bradan who was paddling at the opposite end. "Let Tomas sleep a little longer. We will wake him when we reach the shallows up ahead. We will need his help to get through them."

"Dahey, do you think that we will be able to save Father?" Bradan asked as he hoisted the torch and settled it down beside him. He reached into his bag and pulled out two small flint rocks. With a hard whack, he struck them together, creating a small spark that he directed into a tiny stack of dried cattail fibers that he placed on a small stone slab in front of him. Then he bent forward and carefully blew on the ember until a small flame shot up. He quickly grabbed the torch and held it over the flame and set it on fire. He held the hissing torch out over the water. He was relieved as it pressed the eerie darkness away, allowing them to see the river as it pulled them along, twisting and turning, carrying them closer to their destination.

"Aye, I wouldn't make this journey if I didn't believe that we could," Dahey said.

"Pa just looks so sick . . . It worries me, but if you and Ma think that we can save him, then I will not question either of you," Bradan said.

"Look, there's the moon. At least, Mercury can see us," Dahey responded as he watched its reflection shimmer across the water, helping guide their boat along the wavering banks. "I hope Mercury stays with us. We will need his help to find this swamp bastard. I want to be the one who brings him down."

As Bradan lifted the torch, keeping it angled toward the front of the boat as he lifted his paddle and pressed its end carefully down into the water, "I can touch the bottom here . . . think we are getting close to that muddy section . . . We need to be careful. I don't want to get hung up, not in this cold," Bradan said.

"Tomas, wake up!" Dahey yelled as he reached back and shook Tomas's shoulder. "Grab an oar, bro. We need your help."

For the next few miles, the brothers worked together, sinking their paddles deep into the black water, feeling, searching for the bottom, and skillfully maneuvering this craft through this shallow section of their route. Pleased that Cerridwen was with them, Dahey said, "Cerridwen is with us tonight. I can feel her presence. She will fill the sky with her light by the time we reach the Choctaw village."

"I will ask Mars to lead us into battle," Tomas added. "Maybe we should ask all of our gods to be with us when we attack this village. Ma will be happy with us when we return with our ship filled with their bloody heads and she finds Father's spirit inside one of them."

"Dumb savages," Bradan bolstered. "They have no idea that they will be feeling the sting of our long knives across their throats before this moon fades away." Then he looked up at the sky, seeing the trillions of brilliant stars casting down their lights upon them, tired but proud to be alive as he watched the beautiful swirling lights of the aurora borealis shimmering across the diamond-studded sky.

The river narrowed, and the young warriors had to wrench the craft through a small frozen artery. They kept the craft moving through a thin blanket of ice. Before long, the river widened, and its floor dropped off; they were freely moving again. They knew that Belfast was straight ahead. Just as they looked up and saw the Great Bear overhead and saw the faint glimmer of sunrise, they knew that Belfast was a short distance ahead.

"Do you think that Prince Sangann will join us?" Bradan asked as he kept his rhythm with Tomas.

"Power and land are all that man speaks about," Dahey spat. "He will be there because he wants to marry Ethane' and manipulate us into helping him expand his empire. I can hear him now . . . Fight for me . . . I will give you land beyond your wildest dreams."

"Aye, but don't let him hear you say that, or he might sacrifice you to Cernunnos," Tomas responded, appearing concerned about his brother's words.

"I see it this way. Pa found this land, and he sent word to us that it is powerful. If Pa found it, then it belongs to us. We will lay claim to it—not Sangann! Are you with me?" Dahey asked.

"Ethane' is our sister. I will do anything to see that she is happy and protected in this savage country. I will honor her decision, but it is our right to expand our land. If you think that you want to claim this swampland in the name of our father, then so be it. But don't be a fool and mention this before we get there, or the prince will place a hefty bounty on our heads," Tomas said.

As they rowed around the final bend, they heard the songs of robins that had returned to their summer nesting grounds singing their beautiful melodies, filling the forests with their sublime message: "Wake up, sleeping world. The sun is returning. Get up. A new day is beginning." Then they smelled the heavy yet pleasant odor of meat roasting over morning fires, voices of men chatting in the distance, chopping wood, and laughter. Just as they neared the outskirts of Belfast, they paddled around the southeastern bend and entered the calm current of the

SHERRY COTTLE GRAHAM

Ohi:Yo'. Allowing the current to carry them downstream, heading westward as their eyes adjusted to the intensifying light, they saw the distinct outline of a large battleship that was docked near the shoreline, waiting for them to arrive.

"Aye, over there!" a man yelled as he ran to meet the brothers. "How are you lads? Throw me your tow rope, and I'll pull you ashore."

Once their vessel was secured to the wooden dock, the boys quickly departed the smaller craft and greeted the small group of men who were talking of women and war. Displaying their iron and flint weaponry, they were excited to be heading back into battle. They were delighted that these three eight-foot brothers had arrived, and now they could board and prepare to hoist their sails and embark on their journey toward the swamps.

"Hey, you over there! Grab the lads' bags and take them aboard," the brothers heard someone yell. "Go, get some food. We have plenty roasting on the fire. Lads, drop your things. I will see that your things get aboard," a smaller man said. Obviously a local merchant, he noticed the physical toll that this journey had taken on them. He asked, "How long have you been traveling?"

"This is our third sunrise," Dahey responded. Motioning his brothers, he said, "Let's get aboard. Tomas, get us some food. We can eat once we get these men on board and the sails hoisted. Then we can eat and maybe get a little rest once we are on our way." Then he looked around, searching for someone. Not seeing Sangann, he asked the merchant, "Where is Prince Sangann?"

"He left yesterday mornin' with Cu Chulainn. I'd say that they have a full day's advantage on you. He has a scout who knows where those mangy Choctaw's live, and he wants to scout them out before you get there. Aye, but don't be surprised if you have to march in a ways to reach 'em. So you fellers had better get aboard and get some rest. By the looks of it, you need it. Don't worry. These men will get you down there all right."

As Dahey watched the merchant move toward the warriors who were boarding the fourteen-oared birlinn, he listened to his heavy footsteps against the crushed stone and shell pavement as he walked. Then with the slightest flick of his wrist and crook of his neck, he signaled to his sleep-deprived brothers, "Come on, let's get aboard this ol' gal. Pa's waiting . . ."

As Dahey moved alongside the *Iron Lady*, smelling her fish and decaying scents, it reminded him of the previous trips that he had taken on her. Seeing new lands, new adventures in spreading their growing empires, conquering the ill-prepared natives, he didn't foresee that this journey would be any different.

When Dahey and his twin brothers arrived on deck, they spotted who quickly moved to welcome them aboard.

"Aye, Dahey, glad to see you again," Murdock said as he reached out and grasped Dahey's hand as he studied Dahey's pale lips and the dark circles that lined his eyes. Murdock was an expert sailor. He knew these rivers well, and he welcomed every opportunity to navigate his *Iron Lady* and his team of rowers downstream and toward the sea; and today, he was eager to hoist her sails and deliver his precious cargo of thirty elite warriors to his prince. "Lads, go over to me quarters and get some rest. We'll get this ol' girl a movin' as soon as I get my men aboard and the sails hoisted." Without hesitating, he raised his arm into the air and yelled, "Man the oars! Hey, you scallywags, prepare to drop the ropes, man the sails, get ready to push off—watch for me signal." Then he walked toward the rear of the ship, barking orders to his crew as he prepared to launch his craft.

Dahey listened to the loud calamity as the men shouted orders, and then he felt the ship waver and begin to rock. As the oarsmen yelled, "Left oars reverse on signal! Now heave! Together again, heave! Right forward, ready—heave!" Then with the synchronized tugging on their long paddles, masterfully echoing each other's efforts, pulling the ship into the center of the river, adjusting its course, the captain turned toward the main mast, yelling, "Raise her sails! Get 'em up, boys!"

Dahey felt the wondrous strength of the *Iron Lady* as her two sails blew apart, filling them with the crisp wind. When he felt the craft surge forward and pick up speed, he was relieved to be on the next leg of his journey with his brothers as he watched the birlinn move with the gentle current. Standing on the port side, watching the snow-covered shoreline, listening to the chorus of birds that filled the skies with their menagerie of melodies, a warrior dressed in copper armor approached him. "This is for you," he said as he handed him a basket of roasted venison, a bladder of fresh water, and three blankets. "Captain said that you can sleep in his quarters," he said as he nodded toward a leather-canopied shelter.

SHERRY COTTLE GRAHAM

"Aye, I'm famished, but I am too tired to eat. How about you bros? Let's get some rest, and we can eat later," Dahey said.

"Aye, I thought I was goin' to freeze the other night. The wind howlin' so loud that it was hard for me to rest," Bradan said as he stretched over the ship's sidewall. When he saw Belenus fanning his brilliant streams of luminescent light across the morning sky, it gave him a renewed sense that everything would be all right. "Look," Bradan said. "Belenus is promising to protect us," as he pointed to toward the sun.

"In the eye of our god . . . ," Bradan sang as his brothers joined in, singing their childhood prayer to their glorious god, who they knew was sanctifying this venture. "The eye of the god of glory, the eye of the king of hosts, the eye of the king of life, shinning upon us through time and tide, shinning upon us gently and without stint, glory be to thee, ol' splendid sun. Glory to thee ol' sun, face of the god of life," they sang. Feeling empowered by his magnificence, they walked over to the captain's tent that was near the central bow of this craft and disappeared inside.

Back in the Choctaws' land, hidden deep inside the moss-covered swamps, Laurel called Pallaton who was standing outside her secret lodge, standing guard over her. As the mighty warrior looked inside to receive his instructions, she said, "Pallaton, go find Lanto." Then she pulled a small bundle of jimson and tobacco from her pouch, saying as she handed it to him, "Give this to him and tell him to make a bee mask for Tiponi and lace it with these herbs. She must wear it when we dance under the light of the moon and celebrate this little bee."

"Is this all you need?" he asked as he tucked the objects into his pouch.

"Ah, yes . . . wait, one more thing," she said as she reached into her medicine pouch and pulled out a few black stones. She felt their smooth cool surface and the power that they held as she handed them to Pallaton. She said, "Tell Lanto that he must bind these stones to the top of her mask. Then go to the village and tell our people that we will dance in honor of our *sweet bees* tomorrow night. Tell them to prepare food, put on their best costumes, and make new masks for the children to wear while they dance in honor of our little friends. I will have Dakota light the fires to signal the time for it to start. Now go."

Then she looked over at Moki and Coahoma as she stood up. She said, "You boys were brave, and we are very proud of you. We have much to do before the giant Alli arrive! Now go, run into the swamps, and collect as many hives as you can find. Place them into these sacks," she said as she handed them a few large leather bags and long pieces of leather cording. "And bring them back to me. I will stay here until you return."

Coahoma asked, "Do you want us to do anything else for you?" as he draped his sacks over his arm and tucked the cords into his belt.

"Yes. Find the snake handlers and tell them to gather as many of their friends as they can find. Tell them to bring them here to me. I will take care of the rest. Now go!" Laurel said as she waved her withered hand toward the doorway.

SHERRY COTTLE GRAHAM

CHAPTER 20

Rise of the Werewolf

Pontiac and Lugh's Supernatural Shift
As their souls merge, Lugh's dominating force shifts Pontiac into a werewolf.

As the darkness settled over her village, Laurel felt the presence of her pet owl as she strolled along the narrow dusty path that ended on the opposite side of the river overlooking her village. Staying in the shadows of the surrounding scrubby forest, she waited for the long shadows to disappear before stepping into the clearing. As she looked around, she smelled the fumes of burnt grass and spotted the hot embers, sparkling against the ground. She saw the whimsical puffs of white smoke, drifting up from the blackened land, and heard Tunghak's piercing shriek as he flew into a nearby tree. Dropping into an altered state, she listened to the delightful stories of the trees as they whispered, "Your sons worked so hard to make you proud. Never stopping, never complaining. They pulled that log around, mashing the grass. Then they were so gentle, carefully chasing the snakes into the woods, guiding, prodding, never harming, and always mindful of following your orders. These little boys were kind and brave. They reminded us why it is always a delight to watch them grow."

Then as the eerie plum haze of dusk plunged down over her homeland, it warned her of the exact moment that Hashtahli had left her world and transcended into the Other World. As she felt the tranquil cloak of night, her heart froze as she saw her people working beside the lights of their campfires on the tasks that she had assigned to them. Proud and determined, not afraid to die, she was awestruck by their respect and love for her. As a brisk southerly breeze brushed against her face, she fought to control her fears of these oncoming cruel giants. She fought back her tears as she recalled the words of her childhood chief, banishing her from her home. She was alone once again inside the forest, cast out and forced to survive on her own with her small cub. A stream of tears flowed down the sides of her withered cheeks; however, this time, this agony would be felt by her entire tribe if she didn't find a way to save them from this prophesied slaughter. To her, life was always a game of anticipation and reactions to the unexpected, the ability to adjust, fight, run, hide—whatever it took; her goal was always the same—to survive.

As she slipped across the smoldering and ash-covered field, watching her village on the other side of the shimmering river, she was grateful to them as she gazed at diamond-studded sky. Seeing the majestic Big Bear and the smaller one coming to life, she waited for Hashi Ninak Anya to appear. When she saw her climb into the night sky, Laurel prayed to her, asking her for her guidance and protection for the long days ahead. Live or die, she knew that her people would not challenge her orders, no matter how reckless or insensitive that they may seem. *I am the One Who Walks with the Bear*, she thought as she stood on the river's edge. *I promise, I will use my black magic to cast these giants from our land if it is the last thing that I do on this Great Mother.*

Unable to return to the comfort of her lodge, she disappeared into the blackened cloak of the western forest, carrying her favorite spear as Awock followed her. This forest was no stranger to her. She knew it well as she moved toward her secret project. Hidden deep inside its massive canopy,

SHERRY COTTLE GRAHAM

she knew that her men would work through the night and into the next day to finish their task. She knew that they would work without food or rest, breaking only to pray for protection for their loved ones.

Across the river, her three students were headed toward her lodge, wearing their new headbands, toting walleye, catfish, plump bluegills, and largemouth bass. As Coahoma hoisted his fish into the air, he said, "Old Lagundo is going to sleep well tonight if he eats all of these." Then he looked over at Moki and Fala who were walking beside him, looking for any signs that might expose their fear of these incoming warriors. Finding none, he knew that they were comfortable with playing out their roles of deception as their leaders worked on their strategies to save them.

"It's getting late. Let's run," Fala said as they approached the worn trail that curved up the hill to the lodge where they knew that Pontiac would be waiting for them.

Breathing in a long deep breath as he glanced over at the horizon, "Look, here she comes," whispered Moki. "Tomorrow, Hashi Ninak Anya will be complete, and we will do our little dance under her light."

The boys stopped to watch their luminescent mother rising out of the Other World. As she arched over the treetops, they knew that she was coming to greet them. After a few moments, Fala dropped his head and said, "We need to go. Lagundo will be waiting for his food."

As they neared the old lodge, seeing the smoke rising through the thatched roof, Coahoma knew that Pontiac was inside waiting for them. "We must feed the old bear before we greet Pontiac and Tiponi," he said. "Then we will go inside and see what waits for us."

"Do you think that he sees us?" Fala asked.

"Yes, I think he does. He has been spying on us since we crossed the river and gathered the fish," Moki replied. "So has Tiponi."

"Be quiet. Don't speak," Coahoma commanded as he rounded the rear of the lodge, seeing Lagundo sitting beside his lean-to, waiting patiently for food. As he approached the side of the aging bear's shelter, he tossed their catch into the old trough, saying, "Lagundo, here are many good fish for you to eat, my friend. Eat well tonight as we will be dancing with the bees under the light of the full moon tomorrow night, but you must stay here, my friend, and stay out of sight."

Fala stepped forward, placing his hand on Lagundo's head and stroked his thick fur. As he stood there, bonding with his old friend, Fala looked directly in his eyes as he added, "See, we have not forgotten you. Eat . . .

Fill your belly! Sleep well tonight. We will see you when Hashtahli returns."

Coahoma took the lead, moving silently around her lodge, he gazed at the amulets that she had added around her lodge as he walked past them. Coahoma stopped and her hill, looking toward his village that stretched out below. He watched the streams of white smoke rising over the jagged tree line and knew that his mother was a short distance way. *I will visit my mother tomorrow. The time of no return is quickly approaching. I must trust that Dakota and Father will keep her safe*, he thought as he reached and pulled the door open.

"Ahh, it's you again. Go away! Leave us!" Pontiac cursed as the boys entered the lodge.

Coahoma was shocked to see Pontiac perched on his log near the fire with Tiponi seated next to him. He was smoking a long wooden pipe that was filled with tobacco. He had ripped the braids from his hair, painted blue stripes across his face, and tore large holes in his clothing. His eyes narrowed. Frowning, he cursed them with words that made Coahoma's blood curdle as they spewed from his mouth.

"Aye," Tiponi spat. "Are you deaf? Go away. We don't want you here!"

As Coahoma's eyes adjusted to the darkness, he spotted Dakota huddled in the far corner of the room. As he caught his brother's eye, noticing that he was alive, but he appeared shaken by what was transpiring around him. Dakota gently cast off his blanket and walked toward his younger brother. When he reached the group, he gently grasped his brother's right arm, saying, "Coahoma, come with me. Let's go to Father's lodge for the night."

"Aye, go, little girls—run—hide behind your mama's skirts and STOP meddling in our business. Now go, run home to your mama like good little lads!" Pontiac seethed. "What is that terrible smell? Smells like the stench of blood . . . must be yours . . . stinks, don't it, Tiponi? AND when you go, take that cursed old bear with you! Stupid savages . . . feeding a haggard worthless bear. His head should be hanging on the end of my spear. Crazy . . . foolishness . . . never seen the likes of it," he bellowed. Rising up, he raised his right arm, pointed directly toward the door. He commanded, "LEAVE—NOW!"

Not certain how to respond, Fala slid backward, pressing his back against the woven branch door frame. He wasn't going to argue with a mad man, seeing his rage, his insanity. He knew that their plans to save

SHERRY COTTLE GRAHAM

them were worthless if they left, but before he could push the door open and exit, he realized that something was blocking him. Then a large hand gripped his right shoulder and firmly pushed him aside, locking him against the wall. Unable to move, he watched as Ituha came face to face with these two horrifying witches.

"Ah, do we have a problem here?" Chief Ituha asked as he folded his arms in front of him, addressing the crazed man that stood before him in his fearless and rigid tone, demanding authority.

"Aye, I no longer require the assistance of these scoundrels," Pontiac spat. "When you leave, take these bastards with you. We want to be left in peace!"

Chief Ituha saw that Pontiac and Tiponi had slipped into madness. Taking his time, he evaluated the situation with these two demon-possessed kinsmen, not wanting to put them under the knife; he knew that a small band of warriors were stationed outside, waiting for his decision. Seeing the horrific changes in Pontiac's appearance—no longer recognizable to him, seeing the signs of a raging demon growing in strength and power, he realized that this prized shaman had lost control of his spirit and was now possessed by some unknown mad man; and he was quickly growing into an uncontrollable beast. He realized that his best option was to order his men to drag these two deep into the forest where this problem would be resolved with the quick slice of a blade, but his alliance to the gifted healer kept him at bay.

Fala spotted an eerie shadow, moving through the room. Wanting to alert his companions, he reached out and grabbed Moki's wrist, sending him a warning through his touch. Moki was aware of the invisible intruder that had joined them. Grasping the severity of this situation, Moki reached forward and touched Coahoma's left hand, and Coahoma knew as well.

"Father," Coahoma said as he stepped forward, taking his father by his arm. "We need to speak to you . . . over here . . . Dakota, join us." Moving aside, Coahoma looked up at his father, locking eyes and with the squeeze of his hand and a riveting glance. He seized control of the room. "Father, we want to address our friend. Please remain perfectly still and trust us. We will handle this! You too, Dakota," he whispered.

The blood brothers turned around, forming a human barrier between the two ghastly humans and the two highest-ranking people in their tribe.

Standing tall, backs straight and heads held high, they drifted down and quickly moved into the World of Spirits.

Dakota was the first to feel the hairs on the back of his neck and arms rise. Just as he turned toward his father, he watched the color drain from his skin, changing into an odd grayish white cast as vapors from his warm breath began to ooze from his nostrils and mouth, forming clouds around his head. Sensing an entity was among them, his stomach began to churn. He looked over at Coahoma as he tried to make sense of this situation. Deciding if he should run for help, Dakota held his position. Seeing his brother and his two friends standing in front of him, locked into some strange statuesque position, he knew that they were in the Spirit World, confronting these terrorizing witches that were invisible to him.

Coahoma was the first to cross over and waited for Moki and Fala to join him. As they emerged, sliding quickly behind their stilled bodies, they hid in the shadows behind his father so Lugh or Morrigan wouldn't see them. Remaining completely still, they watched the room, waiting for the shadow to reveal itself. It wasn't long before they saw Kenji moving across the room. As he approached Lugh and Morrigan, they noticed that these two had completely forgotten about them as they waited to speak with Kenji.

Remaining still, they listened to the exchange between this powerful little man and the two vile witches that possessed their two friends. Kenji drifted up to Lugh and said, "Lugh, all is not lost, my friend. Your sons are coming for you. They are on the king's warships, and they are approaching the mouth of the river that leads to this village. They plan to reach you by tomorrow night as the full moon crosses over this land. Ol' Wolf, be still tonight and give them a chance to find you and to bring you back home. Our warriors have been instructed to look for a man who is painted in blue."

Then he turned toward Tiponi, seeing the image of Morrigan looking back. Not wanting to send Lugh into a rage, he said, "Morrigan, you must return home with me. We need your council with an urgent matter."

"What is it that brings you here? Why do you seek my council? Can you not take care of it yourself?" Morrigan hissed.

"No, my lady. Trust me—only you can deal with it, or I wouldn't be asking. You can return tomorrow night when your sons arrive. You can watch the bloodbath and lead your sons to this lodge if you so desire," Kenji said.

Then Tiponi looked over at the chief and his sons who were pressed into the darkness of the far wall. She crooked her neck toward them, asking, "What about those fools? Do they know of our plans?"

Seeing their familiar forms, he emitted a deep throaty giggle as he retorted, "What . . . those ignorant savages? What is to fear from them? Ha . . . Look at them. They are no match for your mighty Cu Chulainn. He will mash them into the ground—like ants. Come, we must leave this place," Kenji said.

Coahoma knew that this attitude of superiority was ultimately going to be their undoing. *What foolishness*, he thought. *They know nothing of our powers . . . or relationship with our Mighty Mother or our gods. We will soon see who the fools are!*

As they watched the three, they were relieved when Morrigan announced, "Husband, I must leave. I will return tomorrow night when Cerridwen rises over the far horizon. We will be together again very soon—I promise." Then she backed out of Tiponi and the two shadows blinked out of sight.

Once the boys realized that Morrigan was leaving, they quietly slipped back into their bodies as Tiponi began to whimper, "I'm tired. Can I go to sleep?"

Pontiac reached down and picked up the child as he carried her toward the back room toward her bed. He appeared to forget about the men who were watching him from across the room. As they waited, he sat her down and watched her as she scampered under her covers. Tiponi said, "Good night, Pontiac," and closed her eyes.

Remembering his unwelcome guests, Pontiac gathered his composure as he returned to the gathering area. "Go away . . . all of you! I am tired. I do not need your boys to protect me from what—that old bear. Huh, what good are they anyway? They are gone all day, doing what—burning grass. Ah, send them back to their mothers. Now scat!"

As Pontiac turned away, he wondered how Chief Ituha would react to his demands. He was pleasantly surprised when the chief and his boys exited the lodge, leaving him in peace. Wondering if they were actually abandoning him, he walked over to the door and watched them disappear over the hill. As he walked back to the fire, speaking out loud so only he could hear, he gloated, "Never seen the likes of it. Dumb savages! Can't they see that I am changing, becoming stronger with each returning moon? Soon, I will walk the earth on four legs and return to my pack!

I will be invincible . . . Nothing in this mortal world can hurt me. Then when my sons get here, I will join their fight—we will annihilate this village. I will rip their leaders' throats out and claim this land as mine." Lugh reached his arms toward this ceiling, breathing in, flexing his broad shoulder muscles. "Ah, feels good. Strong, invincible, look at me. My dream will soon be complete," he snorted. Then he pulled his sleeves back and stretched out his arms, seeing the thick matted dark hair. He raised his hands to his yellowing eyes, slowly twisting them as he inspected the claws that were forming at their tips. Then an ominous smile formed across his face as he growled, "I will run with my pack tomorrow." Then he cocked his head back and released a blood-curdling howl, sending a shrilling message to all who could hear. He was dangerous, beyond saving.

"Coahoma, boys, follow me," Ituha said as they galloped across the clearing, heading toward his council's lodge. As they entered, he asked, "Son, what did you see?"

Organizing his thoughts, Coahoma knew that time was not on their side. "Father, we saw Kenji. He came to get Morrigan. He grabbed her and took her away with him. I think that he wants her to look for Ethane'."

Chief Ituha asked, "What about Pontiac? He is a mad! What do you know about him?"

Coahoma said, "Father, Lugh has taken over Pontiac's body, and now he is changing into his totem, but he is crazy."

Chief Ituha replied, "I know. I looked into the eyes of a man and saw a wolf looking back. His scream terrorized me. It even made the hairs on the back of my neck rise. He is no not a man, but some kind of dangerous beast. Son, I should go back and kill him right now and stop this madness."

"No, we need him to entice Morrigan to us. Our hope of saving them lies with her. We MUST retain our control over both of them for a while longer," Coahoma said.

Making his decision, Ituha turned around and looked at Pallaton who was standing near the entrance. "Pallaton, pick three of our strongest warriors to help you guard Pontiac. Do not let him see you. If he steps outside her lodge, kill him. If Tiponi comes out, carry her far into the swamp and leave her there. Her fate will be determined by the gods. Now

SHERRY COTTLE GRAHAM

go." Then he turned back around to confront Coahoma. "I am not going to allow that mad man harm any of our women or children, not tonight!"

Coahoma knew that his father was right, but there were more urgent issues that he had to discuss. "Father," Coahoma said, trying to articulate his warning. Finding no easy way to begin, sucking in a deep breath, pressing his apprehension deep into his heart, linking eyes with his father, he said, "Cu Chulainn, a giant and fearless warrior, is leading a band of his mightiest warriors down the great rivers to our village. They are planning to massacre our people and steal our land. They will be here by tomorrow night. They plan to behead us and carry our heads back to their village so that they can find Lugh's spirit. Then they will turn our skulls into bowls and drink from them during their festival that honors their god, Belenus."

The chief saw that this message had a devastating impact on Coahoma. He was their chief, and he wasn't going to run away like a child. Trying to gain his son's confidence, he gently replied, "I know, son. The wind gods betrayed their secret plans to our old shaman when she read those old bones. This is why we sent you into their village to spy upon them. We needed to know more about their ways so that we could prepare to defend ourselves against them."

Coahoma choked, "But, Father . . . We cannot fight them. They are born killers . . . headhunters."

"Coahoma, you must leave the fighting to Dakota and I," Chief Ituha said. Looking solemnly at his son, he continued, "We have a plan. We know what their warriors can do, and we will tell you what you are to do. Until then, you and your friends stay with the old woman. Stay with her, no matter what you hear or see. Now go and take your friends with you. You must prepare your bee costumes because you will lead our people into this false celebration, and the three of you will become sweet honey bees with powerful stingers and feast on bowls of our sweet nectar."

Coahoma asked, "Father, what are you going to do?"

Looking toward Laurel's lodge, he raised his right arm. Pointing toward the northeast, Ituha said, "Dakota and I will be hiding in the shadows on the far side of her lodge. We will stand guard over Pontiac tonight. His mutation is shocking to me—to everyone. The way he flexes his muscles, the way he shifts in weight, the way he twists his head; even a child can see that he is different. He is a monster. His yellow eyes see through us, smelling the scent of our blood through our skin. Son, we too can sense the danger that festers inside him. My only regret maybe is allowing Laurel to convince me into letting him live through the night." Trying to remain strong, the chief dropped this head and choked slightly. He continued, "I will pray to our gods that they will watch over and protect us as we prepare for the battle." Then he turned toward Dakota. Looking upon his eldest son, he sent him a slight signal with the quick jerk of his head, indicating that it was time to depart. As the two headed toward the door, the chief turned back toward his son. Seeing the strain of this situation splashed across his face, wanting to comfort his youngest son, he said, "Coahoma, stay here. Laurel will come soon to inform you about her plans. Listen well, and remember, it is an honor to die for those that you love. I am not afraid to fight to die. Son, don't worry about me. I am an old man. Save Tiponi. We will save the rest!" Then he turned and disappeared into the darkness with Dakota.

Coahoma knew that it was going to be a long night—different from all the rest. It wasn't going to be spent meandering beside his lodge's flickering fires, listening to the laughter of his brother as he talked about his hunt or smelling his mother's favorite food roasting over the flames, the smell of his father's favorite pipe as he sat quietly on his blanket in front of their fireplace or the soothing sounds of his people comforting their crying babies, chopping wood, singing their glorious songs to the spirits of the forest as they asked for guidance and protection for their loved ones through the night. Tonight, he knew their songs would be filled with fear and anxiety; they would be praying for life to be able to live another precious day with their families.

The boys walked over to the low smoldering fire that was burning in the center of the high council's lodge. Seeing that it was quickly fading, Moki strolled over toward the entrance and quickly returned with an armload of dried logs. As he positioned them over the flames, he picked up a wooden poker and chipped at the ash-covered wood, releasing a hidden flame that was delighted to get out. The boys watched as it burst up into the air, flashing its bright vibrant orange light throughout the lodge, and bringing with it the hope that they will be victorious against their demonic and horrifying enemy that were quickly approaching them from all sides. The darkness that was once their friend, now an enemy, is filled with lurking monsters and hidden demons, each vying for the opportunity to pluck their god's essence from their souls.

"Do you think that we will defeat the giant warriors?" Fala asked.

SHERRY COTTLE GRAHAM

"Of course, we will. Their feeling of superiority will betray them," Coahoma responded.

"What of Pontiac? What do you see in his future?" Fala asked.

A grim expression flashed over Moki's face as he prepared to respond to Fala's question concerning Pontiac's fate, but before he could begin, the door to their rustic thatch-covered hut opened, and Laurel stepped inside with Nita following closely behind her. They toted two large bags filled with supplies to be able to make the three young shamans their handsome bee costumes.

Nina walked over toward the fire and opened a sack as she smiled at Coahoma. He watched as her eyes flickered when she looked at him, seemingly ignoring everything else that was surrounding her. "Look what we brought to you," she said as she carefully dumped a large stack of beautiful black and yellow feathers on to the ground with pieces of fur, snakeskin, long flexible strands of grape vines, beautiful cords of twisted black fur, and balls of sinew. "We are going to make you into a handsome bee, and look—this can be your stinger," she said as she pulled three long carefully wrapped gray plumes from her bag.

Laurel saw that the boys were in good hands. She knew that they would create impressive costumes for her celebration. She was smiling at the youngsters as she prepared to leave the high council's lodge. She had one more vital thing to do before she returned to her men who were working on a secret project for her in the distance. As she opened the door to leave, she was met by Akule, Etu, and Koi. They were running through the darkness toward the doorway, coming to help their heroes to assemble their outfits.

As Laurel disappeared into the night, she was proud of her children as they came together to work on this tedious yet essential project of tediously binding hundreds of small feathers into clusters and tying these clusters into mats to form three handsome costumes for the boys. She anticipated their inspiring abilities to bring these costumes into life. As she moved up the hill toward her home, keeping inside the trees that surrounded her path, she felt her heart swelling as she anticipated her overdue reunion with Lagundo who she knew was quietly grieving for her in his own way.

He knew that she was coming. Smelling her odor from across the clearing, he rose from his sleeping position to acknowledge her presence as she approached his lean-to. He pushed his massive body up and anxiously trotted over to welcome his mistress back home, forcing her to stop and soothe his needs, to feel her touch and smell her scent upon his body. As she bent down and lightly rubbed the backsides of his ears, pressing her face against his, smelling his breath on hers, wanting to protect this unyielding and unconditional love of her life, she twisted forward and sweetly whispered into this ear, "Come, baby. It's time to go."

SHERRY COTTLE GRAHAM

CHAPTER 21

Dark Side of the Moon

The *Dragon Lady*
This is the Allewegi ship that carries Prince Sangann
and Cu Chulainn to the Choctaw village.

Casting his warm illuminescent rays down upon his elite warriors, pushing the white haze aside, opening a whimsical window into the blue sparkling heavens, warming the southwestern breeze, Belenus saturated the souls of these giant men with sweet promises of a swift victory over the Choctaw. As he slid his chariot of fire directly above the *Iron Lady's* leather sails, Dahey joined his twin brothers at the ship's starboard rail. As the three leaned against it, listening to the synchronized and basal groans of their oarsmen and the rhythmic splashing of their exotic oars, feeling the pressure of the ships powerful onward thrusts and the foul odor of sweat, the three stood spellbound as they gazed out over the ever-changing landscape, noticing the richness of its virgin soils and the incredible abundance of wild life that it supported.

"Look," Bradan said as he anxiously pointed toward a western hillside as the double-masked ship sailed around an eastward bend of the mighty Misi-ziibi River. "Will ya look at all those of buffalo! Aye, have you ever seen anything so pretty in all your life?" As the warriors scrambled to see this massive herd, Bradan continued as he pulled his knife from its sheath, "Dahey, we need to do some huntin' and get a few hides before we go back home. Just look at 'em. We can sure use a few more spears and knives. Will ya just look at this?" holding it out so Dahey could see. "Old—worn-out blade. Dull—can't even slice through a stage's belly with this old thing."

Running his hand down along its rusty and dulling blade, he continued, "Dahey, we could sell them to that merchant that we met in Belfast. Pa sure can use another axe or maybe another hoe." Then as he looked over at his twin brother, he added, "Aye, Tomas. Maybe we could buy Ethane' a pretty little necklace for her wedding. What d' ya think?" Then he swung back around toward Dahey, studying his elder brother's reaction to his request, continuing to belabor his idea, voicing the feelings of all aboard. "Do you think that Sangann would join us on a hunt? Just look at them," he pleaded as he stretched his right arm forward, sweeping it from his left to his right. Waiting for his brother's answer, Bradan quickly turned his full attention to the massive herd, numbering in the millions that stretched across the rolling hillside, covering the land as far as his eye could see, turning it into a thick carpet of rust and brown. "Listen, it seems that they are calling to us to come—hunt," Bradan whispered as he reveled at the sounds of the herd's noisy bellows and grunts.

Wanting to hunt as badly as Bradan, Dahey promised, "I will ask the prince. Will ya just look at the size of those bulls? Their hides will certainly fetch a hefty bounty for the king. He could use some of them to pay his workers who are building his new roads."

"Roads, who cares about them?" Bradan scoffed. "Look at this spear thrower," he said as he reached over his left shoulder, pulling a small leather pouch that lay behind his back, and extracted his old wooden spear thrower. "Look at this old beat-up thing. It's old. How can I fight with this old worn-out thing?" he complained as he rubbed his hand across its splintered and withered frame. "It still works. I can still pitch a spear just fine with it, but I want to get a new one. One hide would make a good trade for new one, don't you think?"

"Aye, me too," Tomas echoed. Not wanting to be outdone by his twin, he was certainly going to quibble over the same belongings.

"Aye, I will talk to the men and the prince. I am sure that Sangann will not deny us a little pleasure at the end of this journey," Dahey said, convincing himself and his brothers that the promise of a hunt was clearly growing brighter.

The river twisted back toward the east, leaving the herd behind them. Dahey looked over at his brothers, a younger reflection of himself, born during his second spring, maturing into tall, lean, and talented war machines. They were proud and content with their nobility, standing nearly seven and a half feet tall and still growing, a product of perfect breeding that was signified by their boarded heads and harboring gifts of extraordinary intuition. Then he quietly studied their slanted and crossed green eyes, flattened foreheads, protruding birows of upper teeth, long braided golden locks, six fingers and hidden six toes, proudly flashing their distinguished sets of tribal tattoos, quick witted and strong; they looked the same yet so different, but the four long jagged purplish wildcat scars that ran across Bradan's left arm were the marks that distinguished him from his twin.

As Dahey stood in the presence of his sun god, pride rippled through his eyes and down his chest, realizing that his brothers would equal, if not surpass, his eight-foot stature by the following winter solstice if not before. Then his thoughts drifted over to his eldest brother, Gaim—different, weaker, following a spiritual path. Dahey exposed his meandering thoughts as he softly cooed, "I wish Gaim could be here to experience this with us."

"Aye," Tomas replied. "He's so much like Pa, but even a fool can see that Pa disapproves of his weak leg and his height. Then he looked at Dahey, only two springs older, wiser, decisive and proud, but quick to anger. He continued, "I am glad that you decided to become a warrior and not follow the spiritual path like Ma and Pa pushed on to you. It made it easier for Bradan and me to break away and become warriors—like you. Now look at us. We are heading into our first battle . . . to save Pa. Ma will be so proud of us, won't she? What about you, Bradan? Would you rather be a priest or a warrior?"

"Me? Aye, no way I'd want to be a priest. I'd rather take a spear than to pull my teeth out and to sit cross-legged all day, burning incense and trying to mutate into some werewolf or weredeer," Bradan joked. "Dahey, do you think that Gaim will ever be able to hunt with us? It seems to me that he is getting weaker and suffers more pain with each passing winter. Sometimes I hear him crying in the wee hours of the night, hopin' that we won't hear, but Ma hears, and so does Pa."

"It's up to the gods. He prays daily to Belenus and the Great Cernunnos to heal him, but I think his best chance lies with us," Dahey responded, appearing inspired, hopeful with Gaim's destiny as he looked at his other two siblings. Then as he gazed into their eyes, seeing youthful determination, inexperience, raw ambition looking back; realizing that they were potentially too young to be following these wild mercenaries into battle; barely welcoming their sixteenth spring, Dahey added, "I hope we can find this man who houses Father's spirit. Gaim's best chance lies with Pa and Kenji—to cast off his pain." Then he turned away, masking his anxiety, gazing at the sliding landscape, rejecting thoughts of doubt as he began to worry about his little brother's upcoming safety.

"Look! Seagulls . . . over there," Tomas said, pointing toward the southern sky.

They could feel the tensions continue to grow: escalating tempers, discussions of how to sever a man's head, swift ways to drop an enemy, allowing the force to flow through one's limbs, the best way to hold a shield, how to swing a sword, survival tactics, dreams of amassing many heads, and gods were all vital and relevant topics to these wild men.

Then as the temperature continued to grow warmer and the vegetation turned into waves of moss and evergreen, they sensed that they were getting closer to their destination. The sun began its downward swing, drifting past large-antlered bull moose, elk, white-tailed deer. Abundance everywhere, the brothers were amazed with this land's seemingly unlimited provisions of food. They were also privileged to watch many large packs of well-fed coyotes and timber wolves that were yapping and running near the banks, as well as hundreds of shiny brown-furred mink, dedicated and hardworking flat-tailed beaver, and countless nests of little otters swimming and playing in the water—all oblivious to their presence. Then as this mighty river twisted westward, remaining in its deep belly, the brothers marveled at the massive flocks of noisy water fowl: swans, ducks, herons, and geese that covered vast sections of the river, honking and quacking, screaming warnings out to their mates as they surged bye.

Occasionally, Dahey could sense the tensions rising among the thirty armed and dangerous warriors as they drifted past a new village, wishing that they could pull ashore, vocalizing wild aspirations of drawing their sharp iron swords and rush against these remote tribes. They visualized the right to claim this land in the name of their father and their father's father, erect their earthen effigies, and christen this new kingdom with a name earned by their blood, sweat, and tears of this uncontested victory.

Looking down the throat of this old river, Dahey had been this far south only once during his seventeen summers. Now like then, he could feel his excitement grow as he watched the banks come alive with its countless groves of massive live oaks filled with layers of grayish moss that drifted down from the low-lying branches until it gently touched the surface of this smooth flowing river. Breathing in, he could smell the faint scent of cedar along with the musty stench of swampland and the pleasant odor of fish from the nearing salty sea, saturating the surrounding territory with its subtle effervescence.

As he listened to the deep-throated bullfrogs and high-pitched buzzing and rhythmic chirps of this countryside's insects, the perpetual splashing oars, Dahey spotted a cluster of nesting eagles. Bending forward, bracing himself against the sturdy oaken rail, he watched as a bald eagle lifted from its perch and with a few strong downward thrusts of its powerful wingspan; he was delighted to see that the bird was soon flying against the blue sky. Dahey stood there, studying his totem, an omen, listening to his high-pitched squeals. He knew that it was signaling him that his journey was about to end.

As they moved past a grove of wax myrtles, a man standing watch near the bow shouted, "Captain! *Dragon Lady* . . . straight ahead. Signal the men . . . slow ahead!"

Dahey and his brothers quickly headed over to the port side to see two familiar large leather sails being hoisted into the air. Then they watched as their ship fell in behind the *Dragon Lady*, pausing for a few moments as it lifted its anchor, and soon, they turned into the mouth of a western flowing river, and the oarsmen began to scream adjustments to right their vessels, just as the southwestern winds took a dramatic southern twist, causing them to adjust the position of their sails before resuming orders to gain speed as they curved south and entered the last leg of their trip. He knew that they would dock along an eastern bank of the Atchafalaya River, granting them time to disembark, gather their armory, and organize themselves into ranks. Then they would begin their silent march down the river to surprise this unsuspecting and remote Choctaw village before the first light of dawn.

As the ship came to an abrupt halt, inspecting the surrounding forest, thickets of gnarled vegetation, and shimmering stump-infested bogs, Dahey watched as this weary captain approached. Looking tired and hungry, he uttered, "Gather your warriors and go ashore. We will wait here for your return." Then he turned toward the stern. It was time to rest.

Then these giant mercenaries disembarked these two sleek Keltic war crafts after traversing more than five hundred fathoms inside the bellies of these two mighty rivers, lugging ashore heavy packs stuffed with meticulous handcrafted plates of armor and a variety of lethal weapons. Leaving their heavy winter gear on board, wearing their lighter tunics and knee-high shorts, the men assembled in a small clearing beside the river.

As Bradan walked over to greet Tomas, he spotted Dahey who was speaking with the prince. Wanting to hear what these two were discussing, Bradan tapped Tomas on the arm, saying, "Hurry, let's find out what the prince has planned for us."

As the five men gathered together, they walked a short way up the narrow dirt path to distance themselves away from the dangerous clamoring men. As they turned around, it was the first time that Dahey had seen the instantly recognizable Cu Chulainn who was quickly approaching them with his monstrous strides. Not knowing what to expect from this gigantic man, nearly four heads taller than him, he waited in awe.

As he approached the eight-foot brothers who were standing eye to eye beside the prince and towering over his smaller elbow-sized scout, they were amazed at the pure size of this approaching lean, rippling, powerfully built ally whom Dahey realized could easily bring down a fully grown bull moose with his bare hands. Then they studied the exquisite symmetrical blue tattoos that were meticulously embroidered across his forehead and over the upper fleshy sections of his cheeks and spaced vertically down along both sides of his neck. Then coiling around his budging upper arms was a venomous snake, facing forward, fangs presented, preparing to strike if anyone should choose to come close enough to touch it. The brothers realized that many of his tattoos linked them to him and him to their great-grandfathers. These brave men abandoned their warring lifestyles in the old world, preferring to migrate their families in sizeable flocks into this new world. Slowly and methodically, they wove their Keltic dominance into the Ohi:Yo' River Valley.

As Cu Chulainn moved, Dahey noticed that the ground beneath him vibrated with his shifting weight. Large rounded head; strong lantern-shaped jaws; a perfectly slanted forehead, signifying his ties to a royal bloodline; mouth covered by a long braided blond mustache that was joined below to his beard and tied into uniform sections under his chin; wild long hair pulled back and gathered behind him; bare upper legs; thick high-topped leather boots; wearing a suit of exquisitely adorned leather and copper armor covered his young torso; golden armbands that matched his golden torque, symbolizing his immense value to the king, he was ready to fight.

When he opened his mouth, the brothers noticed that he was young, approximately the same age as Dahey, and then they spotted his massive birows of teeth, same as theirs, as well as his six-fingered hands. In his deep-throated voice, "I am Cu Chulainn, great-great-grandson of Lug, king of Ulster, son of Ferghus of the fair-haired Aylwen," he boasted as he stomped the butt of his iron spear into the ground beside him. Pulling his long iron blade from his sheath, running his fingers along its mighty length, taking in a long breath through his nose, looking down at the shorter men, looking around, seeing the mushy and algae-covered ponds that bordered the interior floors of the surrounding land, he scoffed, "This had better be the right way into this village, or I'll be hanging your scout's head on a pole beside my front door."

"Look," the prince said as he pointed toward the southeast. "You can see the smoke from their campfires rising over there. Don't worry—you will be properly rewarded for your time. Father will pay you well for your services to us," Sangann reassured the giant warrior as he stretched his fancy spiked helmet over his head, allowing the nose guard to slide down across his nose. Then he turned toward his scout. Glancing back at the brothers, he commanded, "Men, get ready to march. We are heading in," as he inspected the shadows that were falling across the vile eerie land as the sun began to drift downward toward the western horizon. Holding his spear high up into the air, he yelled so all of his men could hear as he slammed its iron tip deep into the ground. "I seize this land in the name of my father, the king of Dublin. May our gods bless this land and for those souls who live here. They are now and forever bound by the laws of their new king—King Gann."

The men fell in line with the prince, the brothers watched as Cu Chulainn allowed everyone to pass in front of him, and then he lifted his hulking bear-shaped copper helmet complete with dangling legs and allowed it to fall comfortably down over his massive head, covering his protruding eyebrows and exposing his large blue eyes, cheeks, and bulging teeth-filled mouth. As he began to walk, the three brothers fell into step, watching the bear's legs swivel back and forth on his helmet as he stomped forward. After he was comfortably past the brothers, heading inland, Dahey noticed that the southern winds were growing stronger as he turned. Noticeably agitated by the prince's comments, he whispered to his two younger brothers, "Steal our land will he! Pa is going to be mighty pissed all right—when he learns what the prince has done!"

As the sun continued to race across the afternoon sky, Laurel walked into a small clearing deep inside the woods, standing beside her newly constructed secret lodge. Changing into the form of a raven as she crossed into her rainbow and harmony World of Spirits, she was soon flying over her massive tree and bog-covered wilderness, listening to the songs of the spirits as they cried, "Laurel, dangerous men are moving toward your village! Laurel, take your people and run—hide! They are carrying spears and knives. Look, death is traveling with them!"

Perching high upon a nearby outstretched tree limb, seeing this army stomping forward in a quiet methodical line, sneaking up their worn riverside trail that would eventually dump them directly into the clutches of her village, she was amazed to see so many tall brawny men and boys gathered into a single unit that were equipped with so many horrifying weapons of destruction. "Come on, giant babies," she whispered. *We are waiting for you. Soon, you will learn a new respect for us*, she mused. Then she turned and, soon, was entering the lodge where her young shamans were waiting for her.

Coahoma, being the leader that he loved to be, was waiting in the World of Spirits for her. When she drifted up to him, he marveled at her beauty, no longer an old woman, but an extraordinary Shawnee princess, dressed in her white fringed and beaded buckskin dress, wearing her bone

SHERRY COTTLE GRAHAM

and shell necklace, feathers in her long free-flowing black hair that was pulled tight by her exquisitely beaded headband. When she looked at him, giving him the signal to start, he acknowledged, "I know, the trees told me—they are coming. The rain god will be here after Hashi Ninak Anya begins her downward decent."

"Everything is in place. The spirits are with us, young shaman. Go and let Fala start the fires. His task is complete, and it is perfect," she responded.

As the long shadows began to slice across the Choctaw village, Coahoma stepped back into the physical world and signaled to his friends that the crossroads of their lives had arrived—no longer boys from this point forward. It was time for them to dance and whip their warriors into formation and prepare themselves for the long night ahead.

Wanting to be near him, to touch him, longing to hear the words that she knew that he would never say, Nita reached softly around Coahoma, pressing her face gently against his midsection as she gathered the straps of his long flowing black tail feathers into her hands. Leaning backward, she finished strapping up the final pieces of his delicate black and yellow furred and feathered costume. She stood up. She glanced over at her younger brother and his best friend, his blood brother, Fala. She was blushing with pride at them and their splendid costumes that she and her friends had created. Then she choked slightly as her eyes seemed to glaze with happiness, revealing her feelings of pure unconditional love and trust for these three as her heart screamed, *May our gods be with you . . .* , inside her chest. She knew her brother's secrets, and they were safe with her. She would smile and act as if nothing were the matter tonight as she danced with the children around their ceremonial fire under the rising light of the full moon, keeping in step with the rhythmic beats of their gifted drummers.

Then Dakota abruptly entered the lodge, wide-eyed. Fear and excitement flickered through his eyes as he looked at his brother. Seeing Nita, he quickly moved close to her. Standing slightly between her and Coahoma, he said, "It's time." Then he turned to gaze over at Moki and Fala. He added, "Fala, Laurel has asked you to light the fires tonight."

"Yes, we know," Fala responded as he headed toward the door. "Come on, little bees—let's go dance."

Coahoma waited for everyone to leave this old trusted stick-walled and dirt-floored lodge. Turning toward his elder brother, he said, "Dakota . . . take care of her."

"Don't worry, little brother," Dakota responded. "We will see you on the dark side of the moon." Then he looked at his little brother, seeing the signs of pain scribbled across his face. Dakota reached out, pulling his brother close. He hung on to him, saying "Goodbye" wasn't easy, holding him for a few moments as he whispered, "The long knives will soon learn to respect us tonight, and it is because of you. I am proud to call you my brother." Pushing away, cocking his head, he whispered, "Listen . . . They are here. Pallaton and Akando are escorting Pontiac and Tiponi to our ceremonial fire."

Hearing Pontiac's curses, screaming profanities from the other side of their ceremonial grounds, "Sounds like someone is unhappy," Dakota said, slapping his right hand around Coahoma's left shoulder. "I'll get Fala's torch." Dakota walked up to a large stack of torches that his father kept stored in his lodge. Picking one up, walking over to the central fire pit, Dakota tilted the end over and jammed its head down into the flames. Once it was on fire, burning, crackling and popping, singing its song to the world that it lives, ready to scorch a hand, light up a room, move the cloak of darkness backward, or set their ceremonial wood on fire, Dakota and Coahoma exited the high council's lodge with it glowing above their heads. "Here you go—we are honored to have you light our fire . . . You deserve it," Dakota said to Fala as he passed the hissing torch over to the young bee.

As the boys looked over at their ceremonial grounds, seeing their people amassing around the large stack of dried logs and branches, men, women, children—everyone were there, including Pontiac and Tiponi. They were seated on a heavy log near the bonfire with their backs facing them as Pallaton and Akando stood nearby, keeping guard over them. It was time.

"Come, let's dance!" Fala yelled, holding the torch upright as he ran toward the gathering, leading Coahoma and Fala. He ran alongside the large wooden and thorn-covered barrier that his people had built along the entire length of their higher ground, severing access to Laurel's lodge, forming an impenetrable barrier to the land that lie behind it.

As he neared the log pile, feeling the southerly winds gusting against his feather and paint-lined face, he began to yelp, "Ah . . . eee . . . ," as

SHERRY COTTLE GRAHAM

he ran through a large opening between his people and headed toward the towering wood pile. When he reached it, he held the torch high into the air, looking upward, seeing a few rolling clouds drifting past, seeing the parting streaks of light splashing across the sky; he knew the sun was leaving their world as it fled into the Other World. As it escaped, not wanting to watch its children battle against these massive man-beasts who were closing in, he thrust the flaming torch down into the kindling and set the brush on fire. Then he began to dance around the entire circumference with Coahoma and Moki dancing beside him, singing, "Aaah, eee, aaah," stopping at equal intervals, plunging his torch into the kindling until the flames shot up, and the entire stack was ablaze. Then he let out a large hoop, drew back, tossing the torch high into the sky, signaling the drummers that it was now their turn to begin beating their loud powerful rhythms on their large wooden drums and for the parents to send in their children. It was time to dance.

As the children gathered behind the boys, they began to stomp their feet into the dirt, twisting, turning, rising, and falling, synchronizing their movements with the beats of their drummers. The singers chanted to the spirits to protect these young ones, screaming their words into the night sky. When the drummers began to call out in unison their chants to their people, they signaled that it was time to bring out their ceremonial food. They ended their dance with a large whoop and three loud bangs. The night grew quiet as the women passed out a special blend of honey and blood-laced drinks as well as a small bowl of sweetened mashed roots that were mixed with a small round of hemp that Laurel had added to calm their nerves against the traumatic events that were now unfolding.

Once the warriors had eaten their fill, Chief Ituha appeared beside Coahoma. Lifting his arms in the air, keeping true to his routine, he prayed, "I call upon the spirits of the sun, the moon who watch over us, and to the spirits of our Mother Earth and Father Waters who feed and protect us, to the mighty winds of the north, south, east, and west who stand with us and guide us, keep our children healthy and happy. Join us in this night of ceremony . . . and . . . dance with us around this ring of fire to feel the love that we have in our hearts for our people and our devotion to you." Then he began the heel-toe dance, shifting from one foot to the next, rising, falling, lifting his magnificent and powerful body with ease in perfect synch with the loud penetrating tones of the drummers as they labored to support his dance to honor his gods and his mighty totem, the grizzly.

As he circled the fire dressed in his warbonnet, he raised his hand and signaled the parents to send their children in to dance with him around the fire. A woman reached over and gathered up Little Tiponi into her arms and headed toward the stream of dancing children. Another woman passed a special brew of mashed meats, blood, and roots to Pontiac before he had a chance to complain. As he settled back on to his wooden log and began to eat this potent peyote-laced concoction, he didn't notice the presence of this strong narcotic that was secretly blended into it. Pontiac sat back, relaxing, watching the children, feeling the heat and the flicking flames shooting up in front of him. He began to lose control of his thoughts as the beat of the drums pressed him into an altered state of consciousness. Feeling his body grow numb, becoming disoriented, Lugh's spirit was slowly dislodging from Pontiac's body. Then with his father's signal, Dakota silently walked up behind him and with a quick whack with his tomahawk to the backside of his head, Pontiac collapsed on to the ground.

At the same time, Coahoma was standing near the bonfire watching the lavender sky, waiting for Morrigan. He knew she would be on her way to find Tiponi. He knew that she would be bringing news of the kidnapping of Ethane' to her husband. Coahoma watched with vigilance, knowing that this was the time that she traveled into their village. Then he saw it—the tiny specks of her silver cord floating across the barbed barrier and heading directly toward Little Tiponi who was dancing hand in hand with a young woman around the fire. When he watched Morrigan's spirit move into Tiponi's body, taking control over her young mind, seeing a swift change in the child's demeanor, Coahoma signaled Moki and Fala to begin.

The boys jumped into a ring of dancers and danced toward her, keeping in perfect step, swinging, twirling until they reached the little girl. Once they were upon her, Etu ran up to Fala's right side and passed a child's mask to him. It was a mask that Lanto had made for Tiponi that contained a custom blend of tranquilizing herbs and laced with powerful stones. As soon as Fala felt the mask touch his hand, he gently placed it over Tiponi's head and allowed it to drop down over her chubby little cheeks. Then he picked her up and danced around the outskirts of the fire until Little Tiponi fell asleep inside his arms, trapping Morrigan's spirit inside her.

Confirming that the child was asleep, seeing that the silver cord was still spinning into the darkening sky, Coahoma stopped and waited for his father's signal. Glancing at Moki who was standing beside him, he murmured as he handed the sleeping child to Nita, "It's time! We have to go!"

As the boys were swallowed by the cloak of the night, standing beside the thundering fire, maintaining his authority over the escalating chaos, sensing the impending danger, raising his arm, signaling his warriors to prepare for war, Chief Ituha shouted, "Akando . . . Pallaton, take Pontiac and go. Run!" Seeing Hashi Ninak Anya moving toward him, he yelled, "Hurry, you must deliver him to Laurel before she crests!"

Then he turned and ran toward the drummers. A massive leader, assuming immediate control over his people, yelled at the top of his lungs as he ran into the escalating winds. "Don't stop! Keep on drumming!" he screamed. As he turned, he spotted a large group of women and children that were assembling near the cluster of teepees. As he ran across the clearing toward them, he noticed that Dakota was trying to attract everyone's attention by waving his favorite lance into the air, signaling the men to bring their families over to him. He was preparing to gather their women and children and abandon their village.

Hoping that Dakota could maintain an organized exodus among this mass of bewildered kinsmen, waving his muscular right arm, signaling to his son to join him as Dakota approached, he commanded, "Dakota, go—leave now! Get the women and children away from here!"

Then he twisted his head around to watch Pallaton and Akando as they fled their village, hauling the unconscious demon-possessed Pontiac toward the woman who would ultimately determine whether he would live or die tonight. Satisfied with what he saw, Ituha said, "Dakota, gather as many of our warriors that you need and move our children on to the high grounds on the far side of the Black Swamp. Get everyone into our storm shelters and prepare for a great storm. The rain god will be here before Hashi Ninak Anya leaves our sky." He pointing toward the southern exit through his massive raspberry and thorn-spiked barricade, "There are packs of food and water waiting for you. Gather what you can. Once you leave, we will close the opening. You will not be able to return. Do you understand?"

As he searched into Dakota's eyes, looking for a clue that Dakota was prepared to accept this responsibility, seeing his reflection looking back, he knew that his son was ready. Reaching out, grasping Dakota by his upper arms, pulling him close, he whispered, "Son, may the gods be with you. Now take your mother and go!"

He wasn't finished with the duties that his old medicine woman had assigned to him. Looking around, noticing the tenderness, trembling hearts, tears, pain, he rushed over; and in a swoop, he hoisted Little Tiponi into his muscular arms and fled into the northern forest. They were on their way to a powerful spot where they were going fight these two demons that possessed this little girl and their gifted friend.

As the chief left the village, Dakota signaled the women to gather their children and line them up into a single long formation. As they assembled themselves, a few of the elderly men and younger braves continued to dance and whoop around the fire, keeping the celebration loud and joyous as they distracted the approaching enemy, allowing their women and children to flee into the southern swamps, following a few skilled warriors, carrying torches and spears, moving toward a secret location where they would be safe from the oncoming bearded headhunters.

Once they were safely out of sight, a few braves raced to the river and hoisted two nets across it—one at the southern end of their village and the other near the northern end—creating a barrier to corral many sacks of alligators that they set free inside the belly of this muddy ol' river that bordered the western edge of their village. When the gators were in place, they headed back, rejoining their celebration, anxious, determined, dancing, and chanting with their brothers around the roaring fire. As they twisted and turned, keeping in step with the beats of the drums, they were content with the knowledge that their escape route was primed and that their strategically placed gators, bees, snakes, spiders, and fire ants were ready to greet these approaching and unwelcome guests.

Far away, under the light of their Father Moon, barging through their dense and gnarled terrain, Coahoma and his friends were guided by an eerie illuminescent bluish haze that shimmered down through this ancient and venomous canopy. As if by some godly force, lighting this blacken earthen floor, the boys raced effortlessly forward to greet their gifted old medicine woman. As they neared their destination, Coahoma was the first to spot three sets of handsomely beaded and fringed buckskin clothes and their magical amulets that Laurel had prepared for them.

"There they are," Coahoma whispered as he tossed down this black and yellow feathered headdress. "Hurry! Help me get out of this bee costume. Look, the moon is approaching its crest. We have to hurry!" The boys shed their feathered costumes and suited up into their prestigious shaman outfits. Adjusting their eagle-feathered headbands and adorned their necks and chests with their spiritually blessed armor that was made with pieces of bone, teeth, and claws. Streaking lines of white across their faces, they were ready to meet their fate.

Continuing, they rounded the edge of the swamp and began to climb the small swell, seeing a line of freshly killed varmints that were dangling on stakes beside the path, warning everyone to "STAY OUT!"

It wouldn't be long now. They knew that this was the first true test of their virility, feeling the heaviness of the demands that were lying ahead. Not saying a word, their eyes and expressions said it all. They exhaled the tainted air, breathing in again. Now or never, they were going to expel these two evil witches from their friends, or they were going to die trying. And without hesitation, they jumped, crossed the powerful demon-repelling earthen mound, and charged inside.

Coahoma was the first to see the results of Fala's brilliant leadership. Shimmering against the backdrop of the evening haze, he recognized a perfect replica of Morrigan's lodge that was erected before him. As he pressed forward, following a path that lead directly toward this horrifying entrance, visions of witches, demons, silver cords, bizarre man-beasts were flowing through his mind. Gazing at the surrounding mounds of dirt that sculpted its perimeter, he walked toward the entrance. The sight of this earthen effigy rekindled his painful memories of his lost love as he glanced at the multiple paths that led outward from its center, each terminating at the mounded perimeter. He recognized that this old woman had strategically built her battlegrounds into the center of this earthen replica of his childhood's indispensable tool, the woven circle, the captor of bad energy, the "dream catcher" and that their gods were pleased with her work.

As he paused to study its circular design, devoid of its characteristic feathers, he recognized that she had meticulously outlined this mounded boundary with small chips of red cinnabar, quartz, and finished it with a thick line of salt. Then at the ends of its worn paths, deep into the ground, she drove demon-repelling wooden amulets that were wrapped with thick strands of black hair, crow feathers, and animal bones. They screamed, "Pass and die!" to the demons who would soon be trapped inside.

Coahoma felt his heart thumping a warning to him to "calm down" as he led Moki and Fala into the darkened lodge. Seeing the faint shapes of Morrigan's lodge spring to life, devoid of color, only shades of black and charcoal, he spotted Pontiac sitting on the ground as his eyes grew accustom to the dark interior. Then he noticed that his hands were securely strapped behind a post, holding him upright, while Little Tiponi lay sleeping on the large table beside him. Then his heart stilled as he sensed Laurel's presence approaching him from the far corner of the great room.

Without speaking, Moki grabbed a long cape, wrapping it around him. He turned and disappeared into the darkness as Fala went over to the central fireplace, picking up a couple of large pieces of flint. He proceeded to ignite a small fire with it. While he was concentrating on fulfilling his tasks, Coahoma stood beside Laurel, waiting for the firelight to spring forth and fill the room with its tones of warm glowing orange. Becoming impatient, praying silently for guidance and protection, he welcomed the subtle tones of dim light that Fala brought into this dangerous and witch-infested room.

Reaching down, Laurel pulled her sacred vibrating knife from its sheath and carefully severed the bindings, allowing Pontiac to fall forward on to the hard dirt floor. Then she waited as Coahoma reached forward and carefully removed Tiponi's tranquilizing mask and placed it down on the table beside her. Then he reached down, cupping the back of her small head into his hands, shifting her forward. He gently blew across her brow, confusing her, forcing her to return from her world of dreams.

Watching, waiting for the exact moment, feeling an eerie chill fill the room, seeing the image of Morrigan's spirit lifting and moving out of the sleeping child, Laurel silently kneeled down beside Pontiac, picking up a perfectly sculptured pipe that was shaped into the exact image of Kenji, Lugh's precious young shaman, and lit it with a small flame that Fala brought to her. Once its bowl glowed with the fresh aroma of burning tobacco, she twisted to her right and picked up a tiny bundle of strong-smelling herbs, holding it directly under Pontiac's nose. She waited for him to spring back to life.

Seeing the two spirits confused, dazzled by the images of their home, forgetting the strangers that were nearby, invisible, swallowed up by the supernatural shadows, they waited for the two giant witches to find each other. Then as Morrigan's spirit lifted and moved away from the dazed child, looking at her husband, she drifted forward, bringing with her the tragic news of their daughter.

Once the two spirits were reunited, this was Coahoma's signal to fill this ghostly room with the narcotic sounds of his seductive rattles and cooing chants, calling to the spirits of the surrounding forest to join them in this quest to free their people. Just as Fala swept past him and snatched the dazed child into his arms, he then fled through the front door and raced across their magical barrier, heart pounding, tugging this little girl tightly to his chest as he sprinted toward a large magnolia where he gleefully handed his little cousin over to her anxiously awaiting father.

She was free! Little Tiponi was now safe from the clutches of this evil white witch, but it wasn't time for Fala to stop. As Nashoba reached out and firmly clasped Fala's upper arm with his strong right hand, he reflected his gratitude with the return of his child. Eyes smiling, the grip of his hand said it all. "Thank you."

With a nod, Fala motioned to Nashoba to follow him. Nashoba followed Fala with Tiponi firmly tucked inside his powerful arms through the venomous terrain, moving her away from these two white witches and toward a secret hiding spot that lies on the far side of their dangerous gator-infested swamp.

CHAPTER 22

Dream Catcher

A Choctaw dream catcher with decorative feathers.

Purpose overshadowed Coahoma's thoughts of triumph as he prayed to the surrounding spirits, thanking them for saving Tiponi. As he slid back into the shadows, he heard the disembodied voices of his whispering world, chanting, "Get prepared, young shaman. Stay alert, the worst is yet to come!" He knew that these spirits were never wrong as he listened to their foreboding lyrics.

Breathing in, breathing out, assuming control, stilling his revving heart, recalling his expanding knowledge of these witches and their black magic, he wasn't surprised to hear Awock hoot, "Danger! Danger! Strangers are coming!" As he listened to the old owl's warnings, his thoughts returned momentarily to Tiponi. It didn't matter what happened to him or his comrades as a sense of victory surged through him. He knew that this little girl would never be held hostage by Morrigan—never again. However, he knew that it was going to be a long night for him and his comrades as they turned their attention to charming Lugh's spirit away from Pontiac.

Standing in the center of this dark and dank room, moving ever so slightly, sliding toward the wall, cloaking his presence into the surrounding void, invisible to the untrained eye, Coahoma welcomed this challenge of skill and wit as he felt the temperature plummet. Keeping true to their plan, they watched and waited for that sweet moment in time when they would coax Lugh's spirit from Pontiac, providing the opportunity for him to pull his friend to safety.

He was feeling invincible as he watched the vapors of his warm breath spraying out, betraying his mortal presence. Coahoma was comforted with the knowledge that both Laurel and his father were nearby. Waiting for his next signal, he watched as Morrigan's translucent silhouette and the silver specks of her lifeline betrayed her presence as she waited near Lugh, waiting for him to awaken.

It wasn't long before Pontiac began to stir, shaking his head, shifting his weight up onto his hips as Lugh's spirit began to contort his friend's face. A wavering hologram of these two men was visible as they fought for control over Pontiac's powerful body; however, it wasn't long before Lugh's victory was obvious as his scarlet-toned silhouette greeted his wife.

When Lugh sat up, he felt an odd sensation of a pipe that was pressed into the sensitive folds of his hands. As he smelled its sweet aroma, he didn't see the old medicine woman as she retreated into the shadows, leaving him alone with his wife.

He gazed at his oddly shaped pipe that was barely visible to him in the flickering orange firelight, smelling the familiar scent of smoldering tobacco as he ran his hand along the carving of "Kenji." Seeing and feeling the tiny image of his friend, he remembered as visions of his family and friends came flooding back, saturating his mind with the knowledge of who he was and what he was. "I am Lugh, the Ol' Wolf," he uttered. Seeing Morrigan standing in front of him, sensing that something was horribly wrong, he asked, "Morrigan, woman, what brings you here? What has happened?"

Reaching her rough six-fingered hands toward him, she whispered, "Lugh, Ethane' has been kidnapped. Our daughter has been taken by the Ojibwa. Lugh, come home—she needs you. I need you!"

Wrapped in a hooded cape matching Ethane's, Moki began his task of deceiving Lugh and coaxing his spirit away from Pontiac. He cried, "Papa, help me! Pa, I am over here—Papa!"

Seeing the image of his daughter standing near the front entrance, disoriented as he heard her pleas for help, Lugh sprang forward, leaving his avatar behind as he moved toward her. He was determined to save Ethane' from a fate worse than death as his wife remained by his side.

Realizing that his deception was working, Moki turned and fled into the moonlit night. As he ran past a man dressed in a shocking demon costume, hearing sounds of his hissing torch and the tone of his voice as he growled and waved his torch in front of him, he knew that Laurel's plan was working when he felt the tingling sensations fade from the back of his arms and neck.

As Moki jumped across the boundary of this supernatural effigy, he knew that *the bewitching hour* had arrived when he felt Hashi Ninak Anya's power join with the Great Mother's. He saw an impenetrable shield shoot up around Laurel's sacred circle, imprisoning Lugh and Morrigan inside.

When Morrigan reached the perimeter, seeing the trail of salt and demon repellants that encircled it, feeling the energy of Cerridwen and the odd blue haze around her, she was horrified. Racing back to Lugh, she grasped his arms with her long fingers. She choked, "Lugh, where are we?" When she looked up and saw the ominous silhouette of her villa and the eerie breeze wrestling through the unfamiliar pines and heard the euphoric distant drummers, she screamed, "Trap! Lugh, this is a trap! Run, Lugh . . . Ethane' needs you!"

Morrigan raced along the spokes of this earthen dream catcher, trying desperately to escape its woven clasp as she screamed, "Help! Isis, help me! Cerridwen . . . Brigit, save me!" But it didn't matter which way she ran around this web. She would find herself back in its supernatural center and looking at the decoy of her home.

When she realized that she was hopelessly trapped, she quickly returned to her husband's side who was watching her futile attempts to leave. Seeing her desperation, he wrapped his arms around her, comforting

SHERRY COTTLE GRAHAM

her as he said, "Morrigan, all is not lost." Nodding toward the entrance, he reassured, "You know what we must do! Our way out lies within."

"Pontiac, get up," Laurel whispered as she tugged on one arm with Coahoma on the other. "Come, we have to get you out of here before Lugh returns," she demanded as they pulled him upright.

"I am all right," he countered as he placed his left hand over the gaping wound on his skull. "What happened?" he asked.

"Later," she whispered. "We have to LEAVE . . . NOW!" she responded.

Head spinning, Pontiac stepped forward, seeing—feeling the desperation that was scribbled across Laurel and Coahoma's faces, pushing and pulling on his arms, prodding him to move faster as he listened to the muted sounds of the distant drummers that were calling to him through the void, coaxing him to run as he stumbled forward. As he regained his strength, memories of his family, his mission in life came flooding back. Pausing for a moment, searching upward with his eyes toward the heavens, he uttered, "I am Pontiac!"

Looking down, seeing his old master and his young apprentice, recalling many strange memories of a bizarre wolf man, visions, voices, people's names, Pontiac realized that his soul was now freed from the grasp of a powerful Alli. He jerked his arms away from his friends and stretched his arms above his head. Breathing in, feeling his strength return as his heart and mind cleared from the blackness that had consumed them, he searched the boundaries of this bizarre witch-infested room. He commanded, "WHERE ARE THEY?"

"OUTSIDE," whispered Coahoma. "Follow me . . . over here . . . We have secret way out," he said as he jumped forward, leading the way to a blanket that was draped across the nearby wall. "I hope that they don't find us," he whispered as he carefully pulled a corner of the blanket back and poked his head outside, not seeing any shadows; but before Coahoma could move, he felt a strong firm hand press against his right shoulder and move him aside as Pontiac resumed leadership over them.

As Pontiac bravely stepped through the passage and into the clearing, glancing up, he was relieved to see that his beloved Hashi Ninak Anya, goddess of his glorious moon, was helping them to slip through this cloak of darkness by her welcomed illuminescent light. As they crept forward, he realized the seriousness of this dilemma. He felt the powerful radiation of the earth beneath him penetrating up through his legs, and then he recognized the ominous and mystical blue energy that was encircling this outlandish lodge. As he witnessed these unusual forces, he instinctively knew that their lives were in imminent danger, especially Coahoma since he was the weakest of the three. Reaching back, he gently pulled Laurel through the small door and guided her toward the rear of the lodge. Once she was moving, he turned and latched on to Coahoma's arm. Pulling him close, he commanded, "STAY BEHIND ME!" Then he slowly inspected the sacred grounds as he spied the light of the chief's flickering torch. He instinctively knew that he needed to keep everyone hidden within the shadows of their escape route as he looked for the two spirits that were lurking nearby.

As Lugh and Morrigan raced through the interior, looking for these mortals, they were unaware that their three sons were hunkered down outside alongside the mighty Cu Chulainn. They were hidden behind a small cluster of wax myrtle. They were watching the flickering light of the chief's flaming torch as he stood near the doorway of their false home.

Dropping on to bent knees, the four warriors had broken away from their pack and had ventured down this remote path, hoping to charge through the backside of this Choctaw village when they stumbled upon this peculiar site. As they looked upon this barren land, seeing the dark silhouette of a familiar lodge, smelling the stench of freshly cut pine, devoid of trees, land scarred with large trenches of missing soil, vegetation stripped away, it was a sign that something rather significant was happening inside.

Becoming alarmed at what he was seeing, aware of the full moon, blue haze, drumming, and increasing winds, Dahey and his team began to crawl over the small rise. As their eyes adjusted to the image that was forming in front of them, Bradan was the first one to recognize the silhouette. Bradan uttered, "Tomas, would ya just look at that. Doesn't that look like our villa?"

"Aye, it does," Tomas replied. "Look . . . over there . . . Do you see three people climbin' out from the side of that villa?" Tomas said as he pointed toward Pontiac and his two companions. "I count four scoundrels. Do you see any others?"

"No, only four . . . maybe more inside. May Mercury be with us," Bradan silently responded as he felt the hair on the back of his neck raise and a shiver ripple down the backsides of his arms.

"Get down," Dahey hissed. "Be quiet," he whispered as he settled back on to his knee-bent legs. Watching, waiting, he studied this odd earthen effigy, smelling the sickening odor of cedar, seeing the flickering movements of the decaying animals that were staked around its perimeter. A tiny voice in the back of his mind screamed, "Pa is in there!"

As the four giants crouched in the distance, watching this evil fortress from their vantage spot, Laurel prepared to engage in a fight for her own life when she felt a chill sweep over her. Feeling her sacred blade vibrating against her leg, noticing that the muted sounds of the distant drummers were replaced by the loud thumping sounds of her beating heart, she knew that anger and death were upon them. She swung around and signaled Pontiac to prepare for a fight.

Laurel twisted around and saw Morrigan's ominous grin floating toward her. She heard her laugh as she cursed, "So, old woman, you think that you are stronger than me. Take the child from me, will you, you old hag. Now I will take yours—to do with as I please. But know this, that when I finish with you, you will rot forever in the Under World along with this curse that I place on you and your people. Know this you, old fool," she said as she continued her forward motion. "You and all of your apprentices will die under the light of tonight's blue moon!"

Before Morrigan attacked, Pontiac jerked Coahoma behind him. He stood his ground, facing Lugh, recognizing this deranged spirit's odd toothless grin, recalling the secret passions that were locked deep inside the recesses of this powerful sorcerer's heart. Pontiac pulled Laurel close to him, forming a human shield between these angry spirits and his young apprentice as he yelled, "COAHOMA—RUN! DON'T LOOK BACK!"

Watching from their vantage point, the four Allewegi quietly observed a young boy break away from the two older ones and race away from this replica of their home and disappear into the forest. Dahey pointed toward the spot and commanded, "Cu, go get that boy!"

Nodding, Cu Chulainn slid into the nearby shadows and crept along the tree line, hiding his massive size. With his lethal copper axe in hand, he crept toward the north, moving toward Coahoma. Dahey watched as Cu Chulainn disappeared from sight before he twisted back toward the towering thatch-covered lodge. He spotted a man sprinting northward along the outer perimeter, waving a flaming torch over his head.

"What is this foolishness?" whispered Bradan as he watched this man pitch his torch on to the ground, and like a butterfly leaving its chrysalis, he wrestled free from his strange costume. Once he tossed the last piece on to the ground, he bent over and snatched up his flaming torch and gallantly rushed back inside, blocking the path toward the boy. "Look, he is preparing to fight," Bradan whispered as he watched the brawny man pull a large blade from its sheath with his right hand as he firmly planted his feet into the ground and waited. "Dahey, do you think Pa is over there?" Bradan asked.

"Aye, I think he is there! Ma too by the looks of it! Will ya just look at that . . . disturbing . . . looks just like our home. Aye, he's got to be in there, all right? Come, let's get a closer look—before we charge 'em," Dahey whispered as he dropped on to both knees and crawled toward these strangers across the hallowed ground as his brothers followed his lead. As they slithered along, they felt rushes of adrenaline surging through their veins as they sensed their parents' presence. "This is going to be an easy kill," Dahey whispered to his brothers as he crept forward. It wasn't long before Dahey signaled to the twins to stay down as he monitored the activities of the two natives who were standing side by side near the replica of their home, looking at something that they couldn't see.

As the brothers pressed their bodies against the ground, Awock launched from a nearby perch and swooped down over them, heading into the nearby forest just as Pontiac and Laurel slid over into the World of Spirits to meet their attackers. Seeing Lugh and Morrigan in front of him, Pontiac spat, "Come get me! I am not afraid of you!" Standing his ground, he watched the blue fixated eyes of this tall bearded white man as he floated toward him.

Then Laurel cackled as she held an odd woven wood cross with streaming crow feathers, the tooth of an alligator, and a few long strands of twisted black hair in front of her. As the two spirits drifted toward them, she stretched her arms into the air as she braced for the upcoming attack. She cursed, "Witches, your words mean nothing to us!" Laughing, she continued, "You have no power over us. We laugh at your curses. Ridiculous meaningless words, they are. Look around you! Your gods have deserted you. Your daughter has been kidnapped, and your sons are out there." She signaled with the bob of her head. "Unfortunately for them, they don't know what lurks in their future or they would run from his place!"

Rage sprayed across Lugh's face as he spat, "Liar! Morrigan, don't listen to that hag. She is trying to deceive us!" Then he paused for a moment. Becoming still, he looked around, studying the placement of the moon, seeing rays of powerful energy lifting from the ground and sensing the presence of Cerridwen. Turning toward Morrigan, he said, "Morrigan, do not come after me! Do you understand, woman? I want nothin' more than to walk in this life as a wolf. I want to see what he sees, smell what he smells, and eat what he eats. Look around you, can't you feel it? The power . . . the gods . . . Tonight, I will see through the eyes of a wolf. I will travel to the north and find those men who took our daughter."

"Aye, but what about your body that Gaim is watching over?" asked Morrigan.

"Ah, that shell means nothing to me," he sneered. "Place it into a mound and don't mourn for me. Look at what I will become," he snorted as he nodded toward Pontiac. "I will run with the wolves!"

Without uttering a word, Lugh and Morrigan charged forward and viciously rammed their spirits directly into Laurel and Pontiac. They battled these weak humans for control over their bodies. Morrigan knew that this was her way out of this trap.

"Would ya look at that," Dahey said as he watched the two natives moving, twisting, distorted faces, reeling back and forth. "I've seen that before," Dahey said. "They are battling some kind of demons. My gut says that it is Ma and Pa." As he watched the struggle, he muttered, "Wish I'd learned a little more about the Spirit World. Be a good time to be able to see what is going on over there."

Coahoma was hiding behind a bush with Moki. They watched Laurel and Pontiac fight the two spirits. Coahoma felt the power in the night as he watched Pontiac losing his battle against Lugh. When Pontiac staggered and Lugh's spirit disappeared inside him, he knew, by the way that Pontiac's stance changed and how he moved his body, that Pontiac was lost. Then he watched in horror as Pontiac's body twisted and shifted into the image of a wolf. By the light of the moon, he saw this horrifying creature covered with a thick blanket of hair. A large snout protruded from the center of his face and tail. He felt the blood drain from his skin, and a shiver rippled through his spine when he saw the beast rear up, spewing saliva from his deadly canines. Then when he heard the beast release a terrifying howl, he froze as it echoed through the forest behind him. He had heard it once before, the day that Laurel had read her bones.

Sickened by what he saw, *Father*, Coahoma panicked. "He's going to attack Father," he whispered, but before he could move, Moki tackled him to the ground.

"May the gods be with us," Tomas whispered. "Is that a werewolf? Is that Pa? He talks rubbish about changing into a wolf, but never believed him though, but look! Dahey, that's Pa . . ."

Before Lugh's sons could comprehend the powerful black magic that was erupting around them, they watched as the beast ran forward, dropping on to all fours as he had neared the statuesque man. Then without hesitating, he smashed into the man who was holding a knife in one hand and torch in the other on to the ground.

As the man fought this massive beast, "Get him!" Bradan yelled as he stood up and raced toward them. "Don't let him get away. Get that beast's head!"

As the brothers surged forward on their long outstretched legs, keeping the beast firmly in their sight, hoisting their long knives from their sheaths as they ran, they watched this man struggling against it. They saw that it was mauling him with his razor-sharp canines and claws as they fought. Slowing their pace as they neared the battling duo, inspecting the demeanor of the beast and the man, they stopped when Lugh, teeth barred, blood dripping from his white canines, twisted his head to address the approaching strangers. With the grace of his gods, he recognized his sons standing before him.

"Dahey" was the last word that the beast uttered, losing his ability to speak as he moved away from the chief. He turned on all fours and faced his three sons. Standing before them, eyes yellowing, hair matting, watching, not knowing how to respond, feeling the expanding mutation consuming his body as these two powerful spirits continued to merge into one, smelling the enticing aroma of blood, realizing that it was the odor of his sons, he turned and raced northward, heading directly toward Coahoma and Moki who were hiding behind a large magnolia.

Fear of the unknown swept through the boys as they listened to the heavy footsteps and horrible-sounding grunts of this approaching demonic beast. "Coahoma, listen . . . I can hear him. He's coming for us," Moki whispered.

The wild-eyed boys primed their bows with garnet-tipped arrows that were laced with the venom of rattlesnakes. They pulled their bowstrings tight as they listened to the sounds of this beast as it approached. "He's on the other side of this tree," Coahoma whispered. "Wait until you see his eyes!" Holding his breath, Coahoma was trying to calm his nerves as he felt his mouth run dry. Heart beating so loudly that he was sure that the wolf man could hear it, he waited.

As the boys listened to his rustling steps and the synchronized rhythm of the wolf man's deep rumbling breaths, they began to slide backward, trying to extend the distance between them and this beast. When they moved one last step backward, they bumped into something odd, feeling helpless as it grabbed on to them and lifted them into the air, causing them to drop their arrows. Looking up, they saw the large bearded and tattooed face of Cu Chulainn looking back.

"Aye, got you lads," he said as he secured them by the backs of their necks. "What ya hunting?" he scoffed. Just as they looked up and saw the frightening fangs of the wolf man looking back, "Aye!" he hollered as he released the boys, allowing them to race behind his long and powerful legs and hide behind him. The boys pressed their bodies into the hard muscles of Cu Chulainn's hind legs, remaining out of sight as he ripped his sword over the top of his left shoulder, creating a slicing sound as he whipped it back and forth in front of him. They confronted this shocking creature.

Jaws open, displaying bloody jagged canines, narrowing merciless yellow eyes, head cocked downward with his hair standing up on end, snarling as he stalked forward, moving one paw cautiously in front of the other as he evaluated his prey glancing behind him, accessing the distance between him and the others, no longer remembering their faces or names—now everything was his mortal enemy. He twisted his head toward Cu Chulainn as he rose on to his two powerful hind legs, threw his head backward, and released a deafening howl. Dropping back on to all fours, he disappeared into the northern forest.

As the boys peeked around the sides of this giant's legs, they watched as Morrigan's sons ran after the wolf. As they sped by, Bradan yelled, "Cu, it's Pa! Come on—help us catch him before he gets away!"

Forgetting the boys who were crouching behind him, Cu Chulainn stomped a few steps forward. Turning northward, he fell in line with his comrades, joining their quest to capture this creature and bring back his head.

"Father!" Coahoma yelled as he picked up his bow and headed back into the earthen dream catcher. Running as fast as his legs would carry him, looking around, seeing the five giants swiftly disappearing into the venomous forest, looking up seeing a thick blanket of clouds rolling across the blackening sky, "Come on! Hurry! Father's hurt . . . He's down!" Coahoma choked as he raced back toward his injured father.

As Coahoma and Moki entered the forbidden ground, not far away, they noticed that Laurel was lying perfectly still on its hard surface. "Moki, is she dead?" asked Coahoma as he dropped down beside his father. "Go check on her. I'll tend to Father," he responded as he pulled his knife from its holster and began cutting long strips of leather from his tunic. Turning, he reached into his medicine pouch and pulled a few strips of rabbit fur from it and a few of his healing stones. As he looked down at his father's massive wounds, he was grateful that he was trained in the fine art of healing as he placed these stones over his father's heart. Carefully, trying not to hurt him, he began to chant words of healing as he tightly wrapped the long straps around his father's gaping wounds, sealing the oozing blood with the soft absorbent strips of fur. As he pulled the straps tight, sealing the wounds on his arms and hands, he knew that he would have to transport his father to Fala so he could cauterize his injuries and sew these deep lacerations that were slashed across his left cheek.

As he was completing his treatments to his father's wounds, a dozen of their men came charging into the forbidden circle. As they circled around Coahoma and his father, one man stepped forward, announcing, "The giant warriors are preparing to attack."

"So it starts," Coahoma bravely responded. Seeing the wisest man of his tribe standing before him, he commanded, "Kuruk . . . you . . . take leadership of this battle. Take two of your best men with you and get back to our village. You know Father's plan—now go!" A feeling of pride rippled through him as he watched this witty and hardworking man race toward their village. He trusted Kuruk, and he knew that their warriors were safe under his leadership. As he twisted toward his father, he said, "Chitto, pick two men and take Father to Fala. His wounds are deep, but he will live." As the men gently gathered up their chief, Coahoma felt the pressure of the increasing winds. As the two men disappeared from sight, he said, "Let's get out of here!" as he jumped up and ran across the mounded perimeter with his men beside him. Once he was safely across, he drew his bow, primed an arrow in it, and waited for Moki.

When Moki reached Laurel, seeing signs of life, he quietly settled down near her head. Leaning forward, he carefully placed his hands over

SHERRY COTTLE GRAHAM

her temples as he prepared to see what she was experiencing. Soon, he was watching her as she battled Morrigan on the other side for control of her soul. Morrigan was determined to win this fight for her freedom. Moki watched as Laurel twisted and turned as she fought in the Spirit World, remaining old and fail. She was sparring against a younger and powerful redheaded white witch. However, as her strength began to waiver, he heard a whip-poor-will singing to her, "The boys are safe. The beast is gone. You can return home." He instantly knew that this was her signal to finish this fight.

Looking up, Laurel saw Morrigan's deep green eyes and slanted forehead coming at her with outstretched hands. Morrigan screamed, "I call on the demons of the underground to come forth! Come, seize this old woman's spirit and carry it back into your Under World and seal her fate there with you—forever!"

Before Morrigan could place a stranglehold on Laurel and offer her spirit as sacrifice to the approaching demons, the old medicine woman leaned backward, smiling. She said, "Things are not always as they seem," as she shifted back to an image of a young woman. No longer a withered hag, she was a beautiful, healthy Shawnee princess. She was dressed in a white fringed and beaded dress covered in bone and shell jewelry, feathers twirled in her long soft black hair, and she was wrapped in a handsome wolf skin. *Now we will see whose spirit the demons will be dragging back into their Under World*, she mused, taking Morrigan by surprise. As Morrigan backed away, she added, "You have chosen to challenge us. Now you will be forced to watch what you have created." Then she turned ever so slightly as calmness drifted over her. "Do you see his light?" she asked. "He's coming. I can feel him," she whispered as she patted her hand over her heart.

Just as Laurel looked upward, a brilliant blue light burst forth around her. She heard the songs of a thousand spirits as they burst forth in an astonishing melodic harmony, announcing the arrival of her beloved husband—Tecumseh. Soon, his energy radiated around the two as he softly moved beside the woman that he loved.

As he stood beside her, he raised his muscular arms toward the heavens and commanded, "Spirits of the forest, come . . . assist us with this woman." As the massive hologram of ten thousand hands sprang forth, creating an impenetrable wall around Morrigan, trapping her spirit inside—now with no means of escaping; Tecumseh continued,

"Morrigan, do you remember us? Think back . . . to a time . . . long ago, back during your childhood. It was on a hot summer day when your father brought you to our village. Remember when you swam with us in the river? Do you remember this innocent time when we became blood brothers and sisters?" Tecumseh glanced over at Laurel, signaling the time of truth had come. They held out their right hands for Morrigan to see the scars that were sliced crossed their palms. Hesitantly, she pulled open her right palm, recalling the day that she had taken a blade to her hand, symbolizing her eternal allegiance with her new friends.

"No, it can't be," Morrigan sputtered. "Why are you doing this to me?"

Tecumseh responded, "You are growing too powerful to be allowed to roam the earth and prey on people as you choose." Then Tecumseh moved forward as his eyes narrowed and his mouth dropped into a scowl, "The way of spirit is love and light. The path that you are on is pain and darkness, one that must be corrected if we are to save our people. Know this . . . Every night, when the full moon rises over our land, you will see through the eyes of your husband's prey. You will feel and see their anguish as they lie dying and are forced to cross over into the World of Spirits."

"I have a baby at home. He needs me . . . ," Morrigan begged, hoping to hear those sweet words that they would set her free. "I promise, I will change my ways! "

"Not until you learn the consequences of this evil that you have selfishly unleashed. This will take time. How long, I cannot say," Tecumseh said.

"I am sorry. What can I do to change your mind?" Morrigan asked.

"Woman, you speak with a forked tongue. We hear your words saying one thing, and your heart says something different. Spirit will know when your words match your heart. Until then, you will remain in this circle and experience life through your wolf man's prey, but before I leave, let this be known—Lugh has no memories of whom he is or who you are. His ultimate goal is to find and kill a young girl that you call Ethane'. Her only chance of surviving this monster is when we join forces with your sons. Then we might be able to save her!"

Horror flashed across Morrigan's face as she stammered, "If my sons are here with our warriors, then they are preparing to kill every man, woman, and child in this village—tonight! I must stop them!" Growing

SHERRY COTTLE GRAHAM

frantic, Morrigan's eyes grew wide as she realized that the fate of her daughter lie solely on her ability to understand the way of these native people and the way of their spirits. How was she going to do this? *How many were going to enter into the World of Spirits tonight?* she wondered as she looked around, seeing a mass of transparent faces and hands encircling her. Panicking as she realized the severity of this situation, she twisted around to beg Tecumseh for mercy, but he was gone, so was Laurel. Seething, she thrashed around inside her invisible prison, but it wasn't long before she learned that she was now utterly alone and trapped inside this forbidden space.

CHAPTER 23

Night of Terror

Dahey and Coahoma
*Dahey—an elite Allewegi warrior of the mound builder clan who is
searching for his father; leads a band of warriors into the Choctaw
village to behead their people and find his father's spirit.*

Dahey was confident that he would catch his father as he chased
him through the swamp. Ignoring his instincts to stop and turn back,
he wondered, *Why didn't Pa recognize us?* as he jumped over a stump and
plunged into the eerie grass-laden water. He felt the adrenaline surging
through his veins, making him feel invincible; however, a voice in the

back of his mind nagged, *Is the price of saving your father worth sacrificing yourself and your brothers?*

Dahey was a proud member of the king's militia, and he wasn't about to let anyone call him a coward. He was strong, and he would run all night to capture this beast. Just then, as he stomped through a bed of stinging nettles, he heard Tomas's voice yell, "Dahey, slow down . . . Wait up . . . Don't leave us!" but he ignored his pleas. *How can I stop?* he wondered. *I have to keep going, or we'll lose Pa.*

Dahey was worried about the impending battle against his pa. He dreaded the idea of confronting his pa, especially his rage. He had grown up with this man, and he knew the extent of his redheaded temper. It was this essence that secured his position as a gifted spiritual leader, but over the years, he watched many wise men cower to his temperament. Dahey wasn't certain what he would greet when he caught up with him, but he knew that it was going to be bad.

From the corner of his eye, he spotted the slithering movements of snakes and alligators that crisscrossed his path. Relying solely on his survival skills, he was angry that his father would put him and his brothers into this deadly position. He didn't understand the way of the shaman nor did he truly care to understand them. Rituals, gods, animal spirits, dreams of turning into a wolf were not things that he cared to understand; but he loved his father, and nothing would stop his efforts to save him as he yelled, "Listen to my footsteps . . . Stay with me! He's up ahead. Can ya hear him?"

Just then, the land gave away as Dahey entered another small murky pool. He felt the cold water against his legs as he realized that this pursuit was over. The tiny hairs on the back of his neck began to rise as he waded upward onto the embankment. Dahey heard the growling sounds of this animal that was warning him of his presence. *So this is where you choose to fight me—but why? What is so special about his place?* he wondered.

Dahey positioned his axe in front of him, holding it with both of his hands as he waited for his brothers and Cu Chulainn to catch up. As he prepared for the assault, visions of his father flashed through his mind. He recalled the times that his pa would sit on the hard ground for long stretches at a time as his spirit ran with the wolf. As his ability to shift grew stronger, his stories became stranger, sometimes beautiful, as he described his experiences. Lugh would say, "Today, I ran with my brothers. We chased a large white-tailed buck through the forest until he grew tired. Then I joined with my brothers, and we sang our songs as we surrounded this beautiful animal. Today, they honored me by allowing me to make the kill. The wolf is wise and will only attack when he knows that he will win." Then he would cock his face into a contorted smile and warn, "Never underestimate the intelligence of a wolf!"

Cu Chulainn, Tomas, and Bradan drew their spears and axes and formed a straight line beside Dahey. Remembering his father's words as he crossed the small pond, he saw the image of this wolf man as he paced across a small knoll on the other side. Spreading apart, giving each man the space that he needed to wield his weapon, they prepared to capture this beast.

On the other side, Lugh stood his ground, growling warnings to these giant intruders. "FOOLS . . . COME and GET ME! YOU ARE NO MATCH FOR ME," he scoffed in his bizarre language. Eyes seething, flashing his razor-sharp canines, craving the taste of fresh warm blood to soothe his rage, he continued to pace as he howled, "FIGHT ME, YOU FOOLS!"

"Wait," Dahey uttered as he studied this animal's odd disposition. Recognizing his obvious invitations to fight, the men lifted their hollow-shafted copper spears and cocked their spear throwers. When Dahey was confident that they were ready, he signaled, "Go!" As they stepped in unison into the shallow pool, they felt the earthen floor give way. "Quicksand!" Dahey screamed as the four young warriors sank up to their waists inside this deadly pool.

Enticed into this trap by this witty beast, the beast was amused as these four warriors slid down into its murky depths. He knew that he had won as he howled, "GOODBYE, FOOLS! HAVE FUN IN THE UNDER WORLD!"

Dahey yelled at his brothers as he sank, "Get rid of your armor! Throw it ashore! Don't thrash or you will sink faster!"

Panic, disorientated, a feeling of gloom trickled up through them as they heaved their precious helmets, armbands, and chest plates on to the shoreline. As he pitched his last piece of armor, Tomas snorted, "Can you find anything to grab on to? I can't find anything over here!"

"No! Me either . . . can't find a dang thing over here . . . Cu, how about you?" Bradan whimpered. "Dahey, I can't find a way out—can you?"

"Listen, listen . . . Do you hear 'im? Aye, he's up there, all right? Demon beast I'd call it. Wish I could get my hands on that mangy scoundrel. I'd rip his nasty head clean off his shoulders with me bare hands," Cu Chulainn snarled. He twisted his right leg through the thick sand. Trying to feel the slippery drop off with the bottom of his foot, he began to lean sideways and tilt toward the shoreline, hoping against hope that he would find a root, vine, a log, anything that would help wrench him free from this death trap. He continued to snarl at the brothers as he struggled to break free. "Call that creature your pa, will ya? If you call him that one more time, I'll rip your tongues out. Never thought that I'd die like this—drowning like some rat in some god-forsaken demon hole!"

Moving to the edge of the pool, the werewolf watched as Cu Chulainn struggled to wrench himself free from this impending tomb. The wolf man began to pace directly in front of Cu Chulainn, displaying his hideous canines as he moved, deliberately squelching Cu Chulainn's efforts to escape.

The sound of downward strokes of flapping wings was heard as Awock swooped over the beast and disappeared into the darkness. At the same time, a loud crack and heavy footsteps of a large animal were heard stomping toward them. The four Allewegi watched as Lagundo launched up on to his rear legs, waving his lethal paws. He roared, "GET OFF MY LAND!" as drool spewed from the sides of his razor-lined jaws.

Effortlessly, the werewolf reared up on to his rear legs, unafraid of this old bear, looking for his vulnerable spot so he could cripple this nuisance. However, before he could decide on this next move, he noticed a band of flickering torches and the sound of men running toward him. *How can this be?* he wondered. *How do they know where I am?* As he turned to assess the strength of this enemy, he heard Awock hooting his location to the oncomers. Instinctively, he knew that this battle was over as he yelped, "I will fight you another day!" He ran into the dank, rhythmically croaking, and screeching swamp as Lagundo and the four Choctaw men, carrying torches and bearing weapons, chased after him.

The heads of the Allewegi were hardly visible as Coahoma and Moki peeked over the edge. Without hesitating, the boys stabbed their torches down into the ground, uncoiled their ropes, and threw one end of each rope to the drowning men and secured the opposite ends to a nearby tree. Armed with bows and arrows, they stood their ground as the four scrambled to stabilize themselves to their lifelines.

"Tomas, Bradan, can you get out?" Dahey hollered. "Cu, how about you? Can you get out of this god-blasted hell hole? I'm in too deep . . . can't break free," he groaned.

"Me too, I can sure use some help gettin' out of here," uttered Bradan. "What do they want? Are they going to pull us out, or are they playing with us?"

Coahoma stepped forward, seeing that they were safe. Realizing that it was going to be a difficult task to pull these giant men from this treacherous pool, he asked, "We are looking for the brothers of Ethane', sons of Morrigan and Lugh."

Surprised to hear his sister's name, "How do you know my sister? Is this some type of trick?" Dahey spat.

"It is important that you listen to my words and agree to our terms if you wish to live," Coahoma answered.

"You, why should we listen to you?" Tomas retorted. "You don't know us!"

Moki stepped forward, smiling. He said, "You . . . the tall one, you are Cu Chulainn, great-great-grandson of Lug, king of Ulster, son of Ferghus of the fair-haired Aylwen. The rest of you are Dahey, Bradan, and Tomas. You are the sons of Lugh and Morrigan of Lugudunon from the northern tribe of Allewegi. You have a sister named Ethane' and a brother named Gaim."

Shocked at the exact names that this young native was providing to them, proving that they did in fact know them, unnerving Tomas, he asked, "Is this some type of witchery? Did you kill our warriors and twist our names from their dying tongues?"

"No! We are here to help you," Coahoma said as he crouched down to look at the men. "We don't have much time before the storm hits. If we don't get you out before it hits, then you will lose all hope of saving your sister. Now listen to my words and listen very carefully! You must make a decision, and it must be the truth, or I will cut these ropes and let you slide into the Under World," he retorted as he pulled his knife from its holster.

"What do you want?" Dahey hissed.

"Do you know that Ethane' has been kidnapped?" Coahoma asked.

"No! Trickery . . . This is witchery," Dahey responded, becoming angry that he would speak such outrageous words.

"I speak the truth," Coahoma said as he bent down beside the edge of the pool, looking sternly at the bobbing heads, studying their expressions as he continued his attempts to convince these stubborn men of his commitment to her. He knew that this was not time to divulge his love for her as he added, "She was attacked by the Ojibwa beside your river. She was kidnapped and is now living as a slave among their people. If we let you die, then your prayers will die with her."

"How do you know this?" Dahey asked, struggling against the pressure of the heavy sand and water.

Moki stepped forward. Looking down at the four, he uttered, "We have walked with the spirits, and they have shown us your futures. Know this—if you want to save your sister and your father, then we must unite as one against this demon. Otherwise, the one who calls himself the Ol' Wolf will be lost to you, and so will your sister."

Conflicted, "What if we say NO to your trickery?" Dahey asked as he glared at Coahoma.

Coahoma responded, "Know this—your weapons are useless against your father. Heed this warning. His QUEST to walk this land as a wolf is now a curse against all of our people. He now stalks this land to feast upon the blood of his children and his children's children. Since he is half Choctaw and half Allewegi, it will require the knowledge from ALL OF OUR GODS to stop him, or he will bring misery and death wherever he roams."

Bradan looked over at Dahey. "Dahey, he speaks the truth. Tell him that we accept . . . Don't we, Tomas?"

"Aye, I agree. He speaks the truth. I can feel it. Accept his terms!" Tomas yelled back, trying to keep from swallowing a mouthful of this nasty-smelling sand.

"How about you, Chulainn?" asked Coahoma. "What is your decision?"

"Aye! I saw the evil in his eyes, and I saw that he is dangerous! I will join this hunt with you." Then he inspected the two boys that were crouching on the shoreline. He asked, "How can you pull us out of here? You are too small. You will need many men to pull us out!"

Coahoma was relieved to see that they had accepted his terms. He turned toward Moki and signaled for him to call for help.

Moki could smell her. She was close. He was hoping that she would understand his signal and come to him. For some odd reason, she loved him, and when he saved her baby, her attachment to him grew stronger. As he picked up a dead branch, he prayed that she would come and pull these strangers from this pool of death. Moki chanted a few words to

Ohanzee, asking him to guide her to him as he leaned back and slammed his pole against the base of the tree. Then he visualized her presence as he cupped his hands over his mouth and screamed for her to come.

"What is he doing?" Dahey asked.

"Looks like he's sending a message to those men to come back," Tomas replied.

It wasn't long before Dahey heard the sounds of heavy footsteps crashing through the forest. He detected an unfamiliar rancid smell radiate over the pool as two large hairy male Sasquatch and a younger female, carrying a baby on her shoulders, walked up to Moki. He was startled as he watched Moki reach out and touch the young female's arm. For some odd reason, Dahey knew that Moki was instructing them to pull these warriors from the quicksand.

"Would ya look at that," Cu Chulainn uttered in amazement. "No one is going to believe this story! Who are these boys? Would ya just look at them! They must be some kind of powerful witches!"

As the large hairy beasts labored to pull these four from the grip of this silent killer, not far to the south, Prince Sangann was sneaking into the Choctaw's trap. As he maneuvered his militia into place, feeling the gusting breeze blowing against his skin and hair, seeing the smoldering ceremonial fire and the massive wall of brush on the opposite side of the village, he was hoping that Cu Chulainn was safely on the other side, waiting for his signal to attack. However, he was confident that this long wooden corral would funnel the escaping villagers directly into his deadly clutches.

Taking the time to establish the layout of this village, he spied a few men that were sleeping under blankets near the smoldering fire. Signaling his men, he directed half of them toward the darkened lodges and for others to follow him. It wasn't long before the warriors were in place and ready to attack.

As the prince crept up to the sleeping man, he hoisted his heavy sword into the air and signaled his men to begin as he plunged it down into his chest. To his surprise, a familiar humming emerged from the gaping hole as thousands of angry bees began to shoot out from this newly formed escape route. Waving his arms to shoo them away, he shouted, "Ah, get them off me!" But it was too late as the swarm of bees rose and surrounded him. They angrily pelted his soft skin with their red-hot stingers, causing his entire body to tremble against their wrath.

SHERRY COTTLE GRAHAM

As Sangann swung around, swatting, dancing, trying to see where to hide, he began to feel a strange burning sensation on his legs. As he focused on the ground, realizing that it was crawling with insects, he realized that he was standing in a pool of tiny red fire ants. Nowhere to run, he heard the screams of his men as they fought against these angry bugs. Scampering away from the darkened lodges, running toward the prince for their next set of instructions, they witnessed a thick cloud of angry honey hornets that were organizing into massive black swarms. Sangann began to move toward the river as her heard a voice scream, "Hurry—get into the water!"

As the warriors approached the banks of this gator-infested river, Kuruk ordered the snake handlers to light the fires that ran entirely along the backside of their corral. Once it was burning, the drummers began to beat their drums as the snake handlers released their snakes. They watched them disappear on to their ceremonial grounds as they headed toward the blinded giant yellow-bearded warriors. In a matter of moments, a third assault was successfully launched.

"Stay out of the river—gators!" a voice screamed as the men rushed toward it. "Get back to the ships!" a voice yelled.

As quickly as it had begun, it was over. The prince wobbled beside a few men, trying to escape from the poisonous village. As he moved toward the path, he felt a sting on the backside of his right leg. Without asking, he knew that a snake had bitten him as his world faded away.

"Grab him!" a man yelled. "Catch him! He's falling," he said as he turned and caught the prince. Five warriors gathered together to fight for their lives as they tried to escape. Two men dropped their weapons and scooped up the prince as the other three shoveled the slithering water moccasins, rattle snakes, and copper heads away with the heads of their long weapons. "He's been snake bit!" a voice cried. Then he commanded, "Let's get him back to the ship . . . Maybe the captain can help!"

Just as the men rounded the path that ran alongside the river, the wind began to howl, and a crashing sound was moving toward them from the south. "Listen!" someone yelled.

"A storm is coming! It is going to be a bad one," another voice groaned.

As the men dragged their prince toward his ship, they came to an unexpected abrupt halt. As they huddled behind their comrades, they felt the rain pelting against their swollen faces and arms. It rinsed off the stinging ants and bees.

"Why are we stopping? What's going on?" a man yelled, but before he could utter another word, he spotted a band of armed Choctaw warriors that were looking down the barrels of venomous arrows. Blurring vision and swollen throats, barely able to walk, much less fight, the men threw down their weapons as they prepared to be slaughtered by this uncanny enemy.

Angry with themselves, their king, and their prince, "How can this be happening to us?" they questioned as they looked around. Hoping against hope, they prayed that death would come swiftly as they mentally prepared to join their forefathers in the Other World. Breathing in their last breaths, visualizing the loving faces of their mothers and lovers, they were privately saying, "Goodbye, I am sorry that I won't be coming home—not this time. I hope that Belenus will protect you. Please don't worry about me . . . I'll be watching over you!"

As the defeated men stood ready to meet their demise, they heard someone call out, "Look, it's Cu Chulainn! What is he doing here?" Hope rifled through the men as they recognized Cu Chulainn as he emerged from the shadows along with Dahey, Tomas, and Bradan.

"Throw down your weapons," Cu Chulainn instructed. Without hesitating, he yelled, "Where is Sangann?"

"Over here!" a voice yelled, and continued, "Come quickly, Sangann's hurt!"

Coahoma and Dahey ran to Sangann to investigate as Bradan, Tomas, Cu Chulainn, and Moki tagged along. When Coahoma reached the prince, he stepped forward to examine this powerful man who was draped between two men. As Coahoma looked at Sangann's face, he was startled by the damage that these bees had inflicted on him. His face was swollen beyond recognition. Coahoma whispered to Moki, "He needs help—he can't breathe."

A sense of urgency ripped through Coahoma as he reached into his medicine pouch and pulled a sacred stone from it. Then he reached down and pulled his knife from its holster and cut a small strip of buckskin from his tunic. As he was securing the stone in a small noose, he commanded, "Take off his helmet and drop him to his knees."

He felt Moki touch his arm as they moved forward to assist the prince. Coahoma sensed the men's distrust as he reached up and tied his sacred green-banded agate to Sangann's neck. Coahoma knew that he didn't have much time. He bent over and cut the bottom of Sangann's trousers off. Using his knife, he made a large X-shaped incision across the fang marks and sucked out the venom and spat it on to the ground. As he reached into his medicine pouch for his serpent root, he chanted, "Spirits of the plant, please help this man. Do your magic and pull the venom from his body," as he packed it into the wound. He wrapped a leather strap around the wound that Moki had handed to him. As he tightened it into place, he knew that he wouldn't leave Sangann's side until his gods would reveal his fate.

Coahoma stood up and looked around, seeing the miserable condition of this defeated army; he knew that it was time to herd them into their nearby shelters. Coahoma realized, perhaps with time, that these men would grow to understand that they wanted to be their friends—not their enemy. Perhaps this was an unattainable dream; but years of walking in the Spirit World, learning the ways of plants and listening to their songs, he struggled to understand why one man would bring harm to another. Yet Coahoma knew that death was a natural part of life as he turned and said, "Dahey, you and your brothers and Cu Chulainn will follow me and bring your leader with you. We are taking him to our medicine woman. She will be able to help him." Then he looked at Moki and continued, "Moki, pick a few of our strongest men and take the rest with you."

As the two groups split apart, Moki ushered one group of men toward one shelter, while Coahoma took the prestigious leaders to another. The giant warriors were guarded by a team of Choctaws as they walked through the high winds and heavy rain and flying debris to reach their shelters.

Not far away, hidden behind a cluster of live oaks were many ancient long houses. These long-arching dwellings were built long ago by their fathers' fathers to protect their people from these dangerous storms. They were built above ground on heavy stilts, covered with thick layers of wood, stamped clay, and stone. Their thatched roofs were secured with layers of hardwood poles, strong vines, and ropes that were staked in regular intervals to the ground to stabilize them against the howling winds. These visionaries built these shelters on high ground, away from creeks and streams, and inside the forest.

Coahoma was anxious to help this unconscious Allewegi as he climbed the short ladder and pulled the flap back. He signaled his medicine woman that they had arrived.

"Ah, bring them inside," she signaled said. As Coahoma stepped aside to allow the Alli to pull their prince up the ladder and through the small doorway, Mountain Laurel said, "Coahoma, put him over there—beside your father."

"How is Father?" Coahoma asked as he approached her, allowing Pallaton and Akando to monitor the Allewegi.

"Ah, he will live, but he is in a lot of pain," she said as she swabbed a small rabbit skin soaked with a solution of witch hazel over his injuries. She was ready to sew his gaping wounds together with a long porcupine quill that she had threaded with a long thin cord. "He is strong and will live to tell this story to his grandchildren," she said before leaning forward to secure her first stitch. Sensing Coahoma's empathy for these strange men and his father, she glanced over to observe his spirit. She saw many of his guardian spirits were clustering around him. Contented with her vision, she continued, "Coahoma, you are in good company. I will stay here with your father. You and Fala must tend to these men. Do what you must to save them, but get those warriors out of their wet clothes before the demons find them. You know what to do. Wrap them in those blankets that are beside my medicine rack."

As he prepared to treat the Alli, he noticed the first rays of their sun god had appeared through the entrance. It was dawn, and he was hungry and exhausted, and he knew that these men were exhausted and hungry too. He could tell by the dark rings that formed under their pale eyes. Their mouths were drawn downward and pulled tight, lips pale, and their skin was covered with blisters and scratches. *Lucky, it rained. I must thank the rain god for being so prompt. Otherwise, they would be covered in mud,* he thought. It was time to begin as he motioned to Fala to gather a few blankets for their guests.

"Kuruk, take care of these men. Make them take off their wet clothes and wrap them with these blankets," Coahoma instructed, "and get them something to eat and drink." Coahoma was confident in Karuk's ability to assist these powerful men as he signaled Pallaton, Akando, Akule, Etu, and Koi to stand guard over them. When the elite warriors were in their rightful place, Coahoma diverted his attention to the king's son.

I need my bowls, healing drum, and medicines, Coahoma thought as he rummaged through the old woman's supplies. As he gathered these items, he glanced over at the naked Alli. They had stripped down to their chamois pouches that covered their manly parts. As Coahoma inspected their nakedness, the size of their rippling muscles, the length of their legs and arms, he was awestruck by their differences. He noted the creamy whiteness of their skin and their strange six-fingered hands and six-toed feet and birows of teeth. *How can our gods make us look so different?* he wondered. *They must be the children of a powerful god. Just look how different that they are from us. But if they are so powerful, then how could they let their children walk into a simple trap?* As Coahoma dropped into a healing trance, he looked up and saw Sangann's spirit hovering directly above his body. *I can see his spirit*, he thought. *He is still with us. I must hurry if I am to save him.*

Coahoma pulled his healing mask over his face, picked up his small leather drum, and began to sing. As he beat on his drum, he was happy to hear Laurel and Fala join in. The three raised their voices, chanting in unison so that their guides could hear their prayers over the deafening winds and thundering rain. He knew that his guides had never failed to help him as he sang:

> O, Great Spirit,
> Spirits of the sun, moon, and four winds,
> I invite you to join me in this sacred place.
> O, Great Talking Spirits,
> look down on this ailing spirit.
> Tell me what you see.
> O, Kindred Spirits,
> The Great Givers and Takers of Life,
> if it is your will that he should live,
> then I invite you to join me and show me the way.
> O, Kindred Spirits,
> show me the way to heal this man.

"What should I do first?" he asked the spirits as they appeared. Coahoma was quiet as he listened to their instructions. Then he heard a gasp as he pulled his knife and began to cut through the thick armor. "I have seen a man stung by many bees before but never like this. He is so sick, so swollen, so much venom," he uttered to his guides as he tugged on the man's copper breastplate.

As he removed the last of his garments, he watched Fala pulled off his boots, exposing his ruddy six-toed feet. *What strange tattoos these men burn into their skin*, Coahoma thought as he watched Fala smudged him with the cleansing sage smoke.

"Fala, I must lay my healing stones on him before we make his medicines," Coahoma said. He reached into his medicine pouch and pulled out a few sacred stones. Fala watched as he opened his hand and displayed his precious assortment. "He needs this one," he said as he picked up a small quartz stone and placed it on to this belly. "This one will protect his liver and kidneys." Then he picked up a small piece of polished garnet and placed it over his heart. "This one will protect his heart. Turquoise, he needs this to protect his mind," he said as he picked out a small pale blue stone and laid it on to his third eye. "Now we hurry and make his medicines and get this venom out of his body," Coahoma whispered to Fala.

Working in unison, the boys retreated to the medicine rack where Coahoma selected the ingredients for his salves and teas. He asked Fala to assist. Years of training under the gifted one were paying off. The two worked side by side. Each knew exactly what the other one was thinking: the seven sacred plants that Kachina had told them about. They recalled her words, "They are chamomile, comfrey, crowfoot, dock, evening primrose, goldenseal, and burdock. Blend these sacred plants together and use them as a poultice on the body. Next, you will need to call the spirits to come to you. The body knows what it needs, and it will heal itself if it is its will."

Coahoma was thankful that Fala was there to assist. It wasn't long before Fala passed a large bowl of salve to Coahoma. As Coahoma turned to apply the salve, he said, "Go see what you can do for the others." When Coahoma glanced over at Cu Chulainn and seeing his anxious expression, he said, "Maybe we should give them something to ease their worries."

As Fala walked toward Dahey and his lounging companions, he was amused to see such large men in such a small dwelling. Visions of them crouching and crawling to their beds were replaying through his head as he approached. "They are all right. They need to sleep," he heard the spirits whispering to him. "Make them a strong sleepy tea. Use the stem of Lady's Bedstraw and brew it four times stronger than normal. Sweeten it with honey and serve it hot. Now hurry, little shaman."

Coahoma knew that Fala was brewing the tea for the group of warriors as he carefully smeared the salve over Sangann's swollen body. When he was satisfied with the coating, he covered him with a thick layer of blankets and waited for the hallucinations to begin. He signaled Fala that it was time to serve the snakeroot tea to Sangann. Working together, they reached down and pulled the man's heavy head up and allowed it to drop backward, permitting his mouth to open. When Coahoma was satisfied with the angle, he carefully lifted the medicine and poured it down his throat.

"Are you ready to sing?" he asked as he picked up his sacred drum. "It is time to drive the witches away," he added as he sat down on the hard ground and crossed his legs. For the rest of the day and into the night, Coahoma chanted his prayers, asking for protection and healing for everyone.

Shortly before sunset, Fala served Dahey, Bradan, Tomas, and Cu Chulainn a strong brew of Lady's Bedstraw tea as he was instructed to ease their discomfort and to help them sleep. Sore and exhausted, these large men fell into a deep sleep and slept through the night. The noisy flocks of chattering birds jarred them from their dreams shortly after dawn. They realized that the storm was over, and they were starved.

Dahey pushed himself up onto his side and asked Coahoma, "How is Sangann?"

"We will know soon if he has chosen to live or die," Coahoma responded. As he looked over at his teacher, he recalled her words and her insistence for perfection. Her words, "A man's life depends on your ability to listen," was ringing through his mind. "I am listening," he whispered as he picked up his rattles and began to chant. Then he paused for a moment as he looked over at Dahey and added, "We are doing our parts. I just hope that we are walking on the same path."

Coahoma was talking with his spirit guides as Dakota entered the shelter. He was the first visitor to enter their dwelling after the storm had passed. "How's Father?" he asked.

Laurel stood up. She wanted to move the chief to her lodge so he would have solitude. "Dakota, your father will live. He is in a lot of pain, and I need to take him to my medicine lodge. Can you take him to it?"

"Yes. What about these men?" Dakota asked. "What should we do with them?"

"The one they call the prince needs to stay. The others can join their friends," she responded.

She had watched the spirits hovering around these men, whispering words into their ears as they slept. She was no stranger to the ways of the spirit, and now these Alli were about to experience the power that her young shaman yielded over them. She was proud of these young disciples. They had flawlessly executed every lesson that she had taught them throughout the night. Speaking to their guides, mixing brews, chanting their songs, she knew that their lives would never be the same. Then her thoughts switched back to the naked giants. *These men are hungry. Feed them and give back their clothes. I'm tired of seeing their giant asses, and for god's sake, make them put their boots on. Their feet stink.* She smiled at Dakota as she said, "It's time to send them home."

SHERRY COTTLE GRAHAM

CHAPTER 24

Sleeping Prince

Coahoma and Moki remained in seclusion with the unconscious prince for two full days and nights, but on the morning of the third day, Coahoma began to question his ability to heal this stranger. As Moki woke him from a short nap, he knew that his confidence was dwindling as Moki whispered, "He is still asleep."

Feeling a bit disoriented, Coahoma glanced over at the sleeping giant as he sat up. He reached up and rubbed the sleep from his eyes and swept a lock of his long black hair away from the side of his face as he wondered why their medicine wasn't working. Sitting motionless for a few moments, he pondered the time when he would sit and watch Pontiac and Laurel as they worked on their patients. *Are the plants keeping their promises?* he wondered as he lowered his state of awareness to investigate.

Soon, he saw that the plants were vibrating their healing green energy and singing their sweet harmonic songs over the man. *Yes, they are keeping their promises that they made to me,* he thought. "What is wrong with this man?" Coahoma asked Moki as he moved down beside him and placed his ear over Sangann's heart. "His heart is strong—breathing relaxed. His color looks better—not as red. And the dark purple bags around his eyes are fading. Moki, what are we missing?" Coahoma asked.

"Why is Laurel making us treat this man by ourselves? Your father is getting stronger, yet she hasn't come back to help. Don't you think that this is a bit unusual for her?" Moki asked. "I have never seen anyone this sick before. Now that I think about it, I have only seen one man who was bitten by a snake, and it wasn't a bad bite. The snake didn't release much venom. But look at this man—he is so different, and he is filled with venom. Maybe our medicine isn't strong enough for him?"

Coahoma leaned forward and took a small whiff of Sangann's breath as he lightly brushed his right hand over the curly blond hair that grew over his chest. His differences never ceased to amaze him as he looked up at Moki and said, "Watch this." He pressed three fingers down on Sangann's skin and studied the streaks of white that erupted in streaks across his swollen arm and tested the tightness of his skin. "The swelling is better, and his color looks normal. Why doesn't his spirit return?" Coahoma uttered.

Moki walked over and poked the fire with a long stick as he gathered his thoughts. After a few moments, he responded, "Do you remember our lesson about the young woman who refused to wake up from a strange sickness?"

"Ah," Coahoma said as he stared at Sangann's long locks of matted blond hair that covered his face and neck. "I remember. She was happy on the other side, and she didn't want to return. She wanted to stay with her child who was in the Spirit World."

"Yes, that's the one. Do you remember how Laurel got her to return?" Moki asked.

"That's it," Coahoma said with a smile. "She gave her a reason to return."

"Then that's what we must do," Coahoma said. "I'm going to cross over and find out what is troubling him," he said as he moved over to the fire pit and lit a small bundle of sage. As he blew out the flame and watched the smoke rise from the smoldering end, he visualized his first lesson with Pontiac as he carried the smoldering herb over to Sangann and began to fan the cleansing and aromatic smoke over his body with a sacred eagle feather fan. When he was satisfied that Sangann was purified, he sponged the smoke over himself and began to chant a short prayer, asking his sun god, the spirits of the forest, and of the Four Directions to join him. When he was finished, he returned to the fire pit and placed the smoldering bundle on a large rounded rock.

"You have not been trained to do this," Moki warned. "What will you tell him if you find him?"

"I don't know, but we can't wait. His men are getting stronger, and I'm afraid that they will attack us if we don't heal this man. If need be, I will call on Ohanzee when I enter into the Spirit World and ask for him to help me," Coahoma said. "It seems that he is always watching over me when I enter into his world."

"But what if he isn't there?" Moki asked.

"I will worry about it when the time comes, but I must try," Coahoma said. "I want to earn Dahey's trust so I can learn more about their gods and their magic. The only way for me to be able to do this is by healing this man and delivering him back to his men."

Moki squatted down beside the unconscious prince and picked up his medicine mask. "His men are anxious to leave. You can see it in their eyes and hear it in their words. But they won't leave until they learn his fate," Moki said as he gently stroked the Alli's swollen wrist. He felt the tightness of his skin against his finger as he ran it across his arm. "Look how different they are," he said as he pointed to the man's five swollen fingers and his thick red thumb. "The gods made them bigger and stronger than us, but they certainly didn't make them any smarter, did they?" He looked at the green paste that covered the large man's body and said, "The plants are healing him just like they promised. The serpent root and the Sacred Seven are working. He is getting stronger. Maybe it is good that he is unconscious," Moki said. "At least, he isn't feeling the pain that the insects and snake had inflicted on him." Then he turned around and asked, "I wonder if he knows that his ships and crew were lost in the storm."

"He knows. He sees and hears everything, but he refuses to return to his body," Coahoma said as he walked over to the medicine rack and picked up his rattles. He handed the rattles over to Moki and settled down into a cross-legged position on the floor. "I am ready," he said as he drew in a breath and waited for Moki to put on his mask and to shake the rattles.

Once the rhythmic sound of the rattles filled the lodge, Coahoma observed the walls of his private tunnel as he sped by. Focusing on the brilliant dot of light at the opposite end, he was relieved when he burst through it and found himself on the other side. He assumed the form of a panther as he leaped through the air and landed on his four paws. *Maybe if I confront this man as my animal spirit, I will learn more about him*, he thought. *Perhaps he enjoys being here in the Spirit World, but he can't stay here.*

Coahoma located Prince Sangann's silver cord and followed it. It led him southward through the pristine cypress forest and deep into the beautiful, yet merciless, Atchafalaya Swamp. The silver cord ended on a grassy embankment, overlooking the skeletal remains of two large battleships. Ripped apart by the hurricane force winds and crushed against a thicket of cypress. The ships were destroyed, and their crews were gone.

Coahoma was captivated by the splendor of this deadly swamp. He looked out over a large pool of shimmering water that stretched across the low-lying ground as far as the eye could see. He noticed the blue sky and twinkling lights that were reflecting off its dark and ominous surface. He glanced at the rotting stumps and at the tall live oaks and smelled the swamp's damp and earthly scents. The swamp was dripping in layers of gray-colored moss that hung in streams from this magnificent canopy. He was mesmerized by the rainbow-tinted highlights that silhouetted the plants as he walked toward Sangann. As he approached, a movement to his right distracted his attention. When he looked to see what it was, he recognized Moki. In the form of a deer, Moki blinked his eye and nodded as he lifted up and headed toward the crippled ships. *Why is he here?* Coahoma wondered, but he knew that someone had to be guarding Sangann's body. Maybe it was Laurel or Fala. Either way, he didn't care. It was necessary to stay focused and to learn as much about this man as possible.

"Sangann, what are you doing here?" Coahoma asked as he moved close to his side.

Seeing a panther standing beside him, Sangann replied, "Do you see that ship over there? The one crushed against those trees with the head of a dragon on it?"

"Yes, I do. What about it?" Coahoma asked.

"That's my pa's new *Dragon Lady*. Would ya just look at her? It took my pa two years to build her. He was so proud of her, and the last thing I told him was that I'd take care of her and bring her home," Sangann said.

"Surely he can make another one," Coahoma said.

"Aye, but that's not the problem. Pa put me in charge of these men, and he is waiting for me to return with news of a swift victory. My first victory—ain't that a hoot! This was supposed to be a tiny little battle against a bunch of swamp bastards. I never gave it a thought that they might be waiting for us. Now would ya just look at the mess that I've made," Sangann said as he nodded toward the debris. "I was so sure of myself, and I let some old woman beat me. Now every one of my men is either sick or dead," he said as he stared at a small deer that was snooping

SHERRY COTTLE GRAHAM

around the debris. "I just don't understand a wretched thing that has happened here, and just where are my gods? Why did they abandon me?"

Ah, that's it, Coahoma thought. *He's afraid of his father. How can someone so big be so afraid of his own father? There is nothing honorable in this,* he pondered as he watched Moki's silver cord skipping around the perimeters of two crippled ships.

Coahoma heard a bald eagle screaming to them as it landed on a nearby tree limb. The bird looked directly at Sangann as it lifted its head and began to speak, "Sangann, your father is calling for you."

"Aye, my father doesn't want me. It's better that I am dead," Sangann replied.

"I am your totem, and I don't lie about such things," the eagle said. "You must gather your warriors and return home. A beast is on its way to kill your family—including your father."

"How can this be? What kind of beast is it, and why does it want to kill my family?" His face turned red, eyes seething as he added, "This is another one of your blarney tricks, isn't it?"

"No, this isn't a trick! Perhaps if you care about the safety of your family and your fortune, then you better stop feeling sorry for yourself and go home and save them," the eagle said. "This beast will hide in the shadows until his time is right. Then under the cloak of a full moon, he will attack. Your family won't have a chance to run or fight. They will die a swift and merciless death if you don't go and warn them. Now tell me, what better gift could you give to your father than to save him, his family, and his kingdom?"

Coahoma sat quietly, not moving a muscle, as he listened intently to the eagle's message. As the eagle was speaking, Coahoma wondered, *Who is this eagle?* He cocked his ears toward the bird and closely observed his movements. He wanted to hear everything that he had to say.

"I gotta go back and save them!" Sangann yelled as he jumped up. Then he looked down at his totem as he bellowed, "Tell me what I must do to kill this beast!"

The eagle twisted his head and looked over at Coahoma as he replied, "Your weapons are useless against this wolf man. He is a blend of two powerful forces. Your only hope of defeating him lies with three Choctaw medicine boys who live in the village. When you figure out who they are, then you will need to ask—not demand—for them to help you. Your greatest challenge, however, will be to convince their fathers that they will be safe with you and among your people."

What? Coahoma thought. *Is talking about me? He wants me and Moki and Fala to go with him to fight this beast? Father will never allow us to leave. Laurel is old, and Pontiac is gone. We are the only ones left to treat our people. Impossible . . .* Coahoma watched the bird as he lifted his wings, but before he flew away, he twisted his head and winked a single eye at him. Instantly, Coahoma recognized that the eagle was Fala.

As he stretched out his feathery torso and lifted his head, he looked directly at the prince. "Ethane' was kidnapped," he said. "She was injured, but she is alive. However, you must save your family and let Dahey save his. Allow the boy who calls himself 'Coahoma' to search with her brothers for her." Then the bird lifted up and disappeared from sight.

What, I can search for Ethane? Coahoma wondered as he watched Sangann lift up and race back toward his body. He was stunned by this information, and it took him a few moments to decipher its relevance in his life. *The gods are sending me to the land of the Ron-Nong-Weto-Wanca, but will Father permit it?* he wondered.

Coahoma watched Moki leap into the air and disappear from sight as he headed back to this body. Now it was time for him to return too. As he turned, he spotted a shadow approaching from behind a thicket of gnarled bushes. He recognized Laurel. She was coming to greet him. She threw up her hand and smiled as she approached.

"How is Father?" Coahoma asked.

"Your father is sleeping," she said as she looked around the swamp's lush interior. As she listened to thousands of tiny voices that were screaming their existence to their Great Mother, she said, "This is such a beautiful spot, isn't it? Coahoma, just look around you," she said as she swept her hand in a wide arching motion. "Boy, can you see the power that resides here? I want you to close your eyes and inhale a long breath and pull this energy into your body and allow it to reenergize your mind and soul." She continued to stare at the streams of energy that were vibrating everywhere as she continued. "Coahoma, it is vital for you to remember to merge with your surroundings, no matter where you are or where you may go, and to allow its energy to merge with yours. I also want you to remember to walk softly, and be aware of the dangers that lurk in the shadows. They are always there, hiding like snakes in the grass. Son, you still have much to learn, but this will be our last lesson. But be warned, you must always be prepared to battle the dark forces. If you do this, then you will be able to outwit your most cunning enemy."

Coahoma knew that she was preparing to tell him something significant, but before she did, he knew that she was trying to teach him something. But he already knew this. *Why is she making small talk?* he wondered. As he looked at her, he could tell that she looked different, but he couldn't determine what it was as she kneeled down and plucked a small stone off the ground and held it in her hand.

"Hold out your hand," she said as she clasped the stone in between her fingers.

Coahoma opened his hand and held it out, waiting to receive the stone. He watched as she held it over his hand and allowed the stone to drop through his palm and hit the ground. *Why is she doing this?* he wondered. *I need to get back to the sleeping giant,* he thought as he watched the stone disappear into the grass.

"Coahoma, listen to me. It is vital that you hear and understand what I am about to say," she said.

Coahoma looked directly at her as he searched for clues about this mysterious meeting.

"Until you can hold the stone in your hand, you will always be my apprentice," she said. "Now I want you to go to my medicine lodge and get my favorite mask. It is the one with the turquoise beads, bear teeth, and wolf claws. DO NOT allow anyone to touch this mask, or it will be rendered useless. It is a magical mask, and it is for you and you only. Hide it in a secret place and use it only when you need to speak with me," she said. "Now you must return and get ready to leave this place. We are sending you to live with the yellow-haired men," she said as she evaporated from sight.

Coahoma heard the rattles shake three long shakes, and they called out for him to return. Without thinking, the silver cord whipped him through the vortex and back into his body. When he opened his eyes, he saw Dakota, Pallaton, and Mahkah standing beside him. He watched Mahkah reach down and pull Moki to his feet. Then he heard Moki whisper, "Father, come with me." The two exited the dimly lit shelter without looking back.

Dakota reached down and pulled Coahoma to his feet. Smiling, he looked at his brother and said, "He is waking up," as he nodded toward Sangann. "Coahoma, you saved him!" In that moment, Dakota was proud that his brother had saved this powerful warrior, but perhaps he was more grateful that it would sever the doubt that these strangers had in their magic.

"Dakota, come with me," Coahoma whispered. "Pallaton, stay here and watch Sangann. If he is hungry, then give him some water and some meat to eat, and if he is strong enough, then take him to his men. He won't give you any problems," Coahoma said as he lifted the edge of the blanket and exited the shelter with his brother.

Coahoma ran as fast as his legs would carry him to the old medicine woman's sacred hut. When he arrived, he burst through the door and was startled to find his father leaning over Laurel's body.

"Coahoma, come quick! I think she's dead," his father said. "She was putting a new bandage on my shoulder when she fell to the ground."

Coahoma walked over and gently picked her up. He didn't have to check. He knew that she was gone. It all made sense now. She was telling him that she was leaving when she met him on the edge of the swamp. As he laid her down on her bed, he spotted her sacred mask. She had placed it on top of a small leather bag at the foot of her bed for him. He was sad. He would miss her and Pontiac, but most of all, he would miss his people. He knew that his father was aware that he was leaving as soon as he had entered her lodge.

It was the role of the Choctaw medicine men to prepare their dead for burial. Now that Pontiac was gone, this responsibility fell on to Coahoma and Fala. It was against their customs to display emotion, but they cried as they cleansed her and wrapped her in her favorite blanket. They chanted to their gods to guard her as they prepared for her final celebration. She had changed their lives by sharing her knowledge and her love with them, and they would never forget her influence on their lives.

Dakota picked a spot on top of her hill where she could watch over her village, her lodge, and remain near her bear. "She will like it here," he said. "She can travel between her Happy World and Our World as many times as she wants."

Coahoma and Fala carried Laurel's body and laid it in the shade under her favorite magnolia tree as the men finished the construction of her burial tower. Old Lagundo walked over and lay down beside her and rested his large head on top of her body. The boys knew that the old bear's heart was broken as he panted and moaned with each breath. He didn't move as they lifted her body away from his and hoisted her into the air and positioned her on to her bed.

The people of the Choctaw Nation gathered together to chant and to bid her farewell. They invited the white warriors to join them as they grieved the loss of their gifted medicine woman. As they stood together, united with these large warriors, the boys saw that their friend, Old Lagundo, was dying as he lay under her platform. They knew that the old bear was following her.

Chief Ituha sent Pallaton to usher everyone to a special celebration that he had planned. When everyone gathered beside the bonfire that was built beside the river, he stood up and raised his hands to silence everyone. He said, "I want to announce that we are now friends with the Alli. We are honored to be able to work with them and to share our traditions and our knowledge with each other." His face was sad as he announced the happy news. He was holding a stream of tears back as he continued, "We are proud to send three of our boys to live with them and to study the ways of these great people." Then he turned toward Coahoma and continued, "When the white ships arrive to carry these white warriors back to their homes, my son, Coahoma, and his two friends will travel with them. They are going to fight the beast that was unleashed from our land the other night. Tonight, we will eat and dance in their honor," he said as a single tear overflowed and streaked down the side of his cheek. "Moki and Dahey, come forward and prepare to send your message to bring your ships," he said.

Dahey stepped forward as a light murmur erupted among the people. They watched as Moki carried a small crate forward and placed it on the ground beside Dahey. They knew that Moki had traveled many miles with his father to retrieve this valuable crate from the wreckage for Dahey. Everyone watched as Moki pulled the crate open and lifted a dove from it. He held the bird as Dahey tied a small leather signal to its leg. When the strap containing a single red bead was secure, Dahey took the bird and gently tossed it into the air. The giants and Choctaws watched the bird fly in circles around their village. It determined its direction and flew northward. Once the bird was out of sight, Chief Ituha signaled to the drummers to start the celebration.

While the villagers and their guests were enjoying each other's company, Laurel and Tecumseh were standing on her platform and watching them. She was young again. She was alive and vibrant as she felt his loving arms around her. She was satisfied that her people were safe for the time being. She looked at Tecumseh, and without having to say a word, they flew over to check on Morrigan who was still trapped inside her mystical dream catcher. As they approached the outer perimeter, Morrigan greeted them.

"Let me out of here," Morrigan hissed. "I want to go home."

"When the time is right, we will release you," Laurel said, "but for now, you will remain with us."

Morrigan prepared to argue with her. When she opened her mouth, Laurel and Tecumseh were gone. She screamed, "Come back! Let me go home!" but it fell on deaf ears.

Tecumseh and Laurel were home. As he led her across the grassy meadow toward their home beside the waterfall, they heard a squalling noise behind them. When they turned to see what it was, they spotted Baby Lagundo racing through the grass to greet them.

SHERRY COTTLE GRAHAM

BIBLIOGRAPHY

"Advanced Celtic Shamanism [Paperback]." *Advanced Celtic Shamanism: D.J. Conway: 9781580910736: Amazon.com: Books.* N.p., n.d. Web. Apr. 02, 2013.

"Ancient Adena—Image Results." *Ancient Adena—Image Results.* N.p., n.d. Web. 02 Apr. 2013.

Baldwin, John D., A.M. *Ancient America, in Notes on American Archaeology.* New York: Harper & Brothers, Franklin Square, 1871. Print.

"Celtic Names Glossary." *Celtic Library RSS.* N.p., n.d. Web. 02 Apr. 2013.

"Choctaw Mythology." *Wikipedia.* Wikimedia Foundation, 04 Feb. 2013. Web. 02 Apr. 2013.

"Choctaw Tales [Paperback]." *Choctaw Tales: Tom Mould, Chief Phillip Martin: 9781578066834: Amazon.com: Books.* N.p., n.d. Web. 31 Mar. 2013.

Cowan, Eliot. *Plant Spirit Medicine.* Newberg, Or.: Swan·Raven, 1995. Print.

"Fomorians." *Wikipedia.* Wikimedia Foundation, 04 Feb. 2013. Web. 02 Apr. 2013.

Gardner, Joseph L. *Mysteries of the Ancient Americas: The New World Before Columbus.* New York: Reader's Digest Association, 1986. Print.

Garrett, J. T. *The Cherokee Herbal: Native Plant Medicine from the Four Directions.* Rochester, VT: Bear &, 2003. Print.

"Giants of Ohio, Mound Builders, Race of Giants Found in Ohio, Burlington UFO in Burlington Wisconsin." *Giants of Ohio, Mound Builders, Race of Giants Found in Ohio, Burlington UFO in*

Burlington Wisconsin. N.p., n.d. Web. 01 Apr. 2013. <http://www.
burlingtonnews.net/ohiogiants.html>.

Harner, Michael J. *The Way of the Shaman*. San Francisco: Harper &
Row, 1990. Print.

Jones, Prudence, and Nigel Pennick. *A History of Pagan Europe*. London:
Routledge, 1995. Print.

Joseph, Frank. *Advanced Civilizations of Prehistoric America: The Lost
Kingdoms of the Adena, Hopewell, Mississippians, and Anasazi*.
Rochester, VT: Bear, 2010. Print.

Joseph, Frank, and Zecharia Sitchin. *Discovering the Mysteries of Ancient
America: Lost History and Legends, Unearthed and Explored*. Franklin
Lakes, NJ: New Page, 2006. Print.

King, John Robert. *The Celtic Druids' Year: Seasonal Cycles of the Ancient
Celts*. London: Blandford, 1994. Print.

Kowalchik, Claire, William H. Hylton, and Anna Carr. *Rodale's Illustrated
Encyclopedia of Herbs*. Emmaus, PA: Rodale, 1987. Print.

Lyon, William S. *Encyclopedia of Native American Healing*. Santa Barbara,
Calif: ABC-CLIO, 1996. Print.

Mella, Dorothee L. *Stone Power*. New York, NY: Warner, 1986. Print.

"Native American Indian Baby Names, Girl, Boy, Meanings." *Native
American Indian Baby Names, Girl, Boy, Meanings*. N.p., n.d. Web.
01 Apr. 2013. <http://www.cutebabynames.org/nativeamerican-baby-
names.aspx?originID=47>.

"Native American Survival Skills [Paperback]." *Native American Survival
Skills: W. Ben Hunt: 9781602397651: Amazon.com: Books*. N.p., n.d.
Web. 31 Mar. 2013.

Nerburn, Kent. *Wisdom of the Native Americans*. Novato, CA: New World
Library, 1999. Print.

O'Donohue, John. *Anam Cara: A Book of Celtic Wisdom*. New York: Cliff
Street, 1997. Print.

Person, Carla, and Hillary Johnson. *The Calico Shaman: True Tales of
Animal Communication*. Veneta, Or.: Coccora, 2005. Print.

Roza, Greg. *The Adena, Hopewell, and Fort Ancient of Ohio*. New York:
PowerKids, 2005. Print.

Simmons, Robert, Naisha Ahsian, and Hazel Raven. *The Book of Stones:
Who They Are & What They Teach*. East Montpelier, VT: Heaven and
Earth Pub., 2007. Print.

Wallach, Joel D., and Ma Lan. *Let's Play Herbal Doctor: An American Home Herbal.* Bonita, CA: Wellness Publications, 2001. 439-40. Print.

"Who Were the Talligewi." *Talligewi Lodge 62—.* N.p., n.d. Web. 04 Apr. 2013.

*   *   *

www.EasyBib.Com—Online resource for generating this bibliography
www.StepMaps.Com—Online resource for generating the maps.

CPSIA information can be obtained at www.ICGtesting.com
Printed in the USA
LVOW100556100713

342096LV00003B/8/P